Serena Stoll

Sealed with a Kiss

Aelius Year 1

YA Version

Disclaimer

Ebook ISBN: 978-1-7383163-9-7
Paperback ISBN: 978-1-7383163-8-0

First Paperback Edition: 2024

Edited By: Amanda
Cover Art By: Serena Stoll

Printed By: Amazon

Dedication

To Amanda - for getting me back into reading

Prologue

Once, long ago, the legends told to children were very real. Magic flowed freely, and creatures of nightmares and ruin roamed the earth. Those capable of wielding elemental magic fought tirelessly to protect the world from Demonic Creatures in various shapes and forms.

For centuries, humans battled against darkness, until finally, there was one who was blessed with the power of Spirit. With this new form of Magic, this one man was able to purge the evil like never before. His powers levelled the battlefield and mankind was finally triumphant. For his work, he was appointed the First Emperor of the Realms. The ability of Spirit passed down through the bloodline; the power of the Empire remaining in the hands of his ancestors.

Centuries have passed since the gates were put in place to seal the realms off from our world. Average humans, (otherwise known as Middlings), have been allowed to live in peace, with tales of magic being nothing more than legend. Magic has since been hidden from the Middlings; glamoured away from prying eyes. Mages and their Guardians have continued to protect the Realms; terminating any Demonic Creatures that may have remained in hiding.

Rumours and whispers have been heard, however. Some say that there have been cracks and gaps in the Gates. Some say that Mages and their Guardians have been dying at an alarming rate. The public has been assured all is well, but one has to wonder...

Chapter 1

Emily crumpled the latest letter in her fist before incinerating it. She scowled at the glowing pile of ash on the dirt floor of their tent. She knew exactly who had sent them and why. She knew there would be a limit to how long she could ignore their sender, but she prayed that she could find a solution before the time came.

She whipped her head around as she heard the flap of her tent open. Her daughter, a near perfect copy of her, stepped in. She was dressed in a simple pair of khakis and a fitted blue t-shirt. She wore lace up ankle boots that were sturdy and practical on the Artefact sites they lived at. Her golden blonde hair had been braided back to keep out of her face while she worked. She gave her mother a look of confusion as she pushed up the delicate pair of glasses that rested on her sloped nose. "Everything okay, mum?"

Emily plastered a fake smile on her face as she kicked at the pile of ashes. "Everything's fine, love." She lied. "I just was going over this one translation and...I dunno, hun. I think we should move on."

Aurora frowned at her mother in disbelief and crossed her arms at her chest. "What do you mean, move on?" She demanded. "We just broke through the second wall of defence. You know as well as I that we should be able to get through the next set of barriers in a week or so."

Emily stood to her feet and sighed. "I know, but I just don't think it's worth the work for this one. We can let the Tanners take over and head to the next one."

Aurora studied her mother. They had always worked site to site, but had never once left a dig site before the Artefact had been recovered. "What's wrong?" She asked.

"Nothing's wrong, Rore." Her mother insisted as she touched the side of her face.

Aurora stepped back from her touch. She knew she was lying. "We have never *once* left early. Not during the mud slide in Peru, not during the typhoon in the Philippines... Not once have we abandoned a site before we recover the Artefact. So again, mum, *what is wrong?*"

Emily debated with herself for a moment. She could be honest. She could tell her daughter everything. She looked at her daughter, just nineteen with a full life before her. "We just need to go."

Aurora's face set into determination. "I want to go to the Academy then."

"*Absolutely* not." She hissed.

"If we're not bothering to finish extractions anymore, I don't see the point in me staying. I want to be *normal*. I want to be a Mage."

Neither had ever spoken to each other this way before. This was not the relationship they had. They had discussions and dialogues, not demands and decrees. She swallowed the sick feeling in her stomach at what this had become. She had hoped that Aurora wouldn't have cared or noticed. She had hoped her daughter had been just that little bit too young and unobservant in this moment. She loved her brilliance, but in this moment... "It's not up for discussion." She finally stated as she headed for the tent flap. "I'll go talk to the Tanners now. We leave tomorrow."

***

Nothing had started the way she had hoped for. Aurora stood before the endless castle that was home to all of the aspiring Mages and Guardians of the Empire. The Royal Academy of Magic had been her dream since before she could remember. Those worthy of training spent their early years at the Academy to become the protectors of the realms.

The map in her hands, an enchanted Artefact, had been included in her summons letter. Part of her still didn't believe that she was finally here. The entire Academy was a series of buildings, connected through tunnels and pathways. There were a few buildings that stood independently near the grand entrance gates, but it all worked together to form one grand castle.

She studied the map before her. The building before her formed a U like shape. The West wing was the Primary campus, the East wing was the Secondary campus, and straight ahead in the centre, was the Collegiate campus. The parchment's illustrations made it all seem so simple and small, but looking up, Aurora found herself in awe of the entire grounds.

Aurora hurried along, doing her best to avoid gawking at her surroundings. Her mother had told her countless stories about her time here many years ago. Aurora had dreamed what it would be like to walk these halls herself. Guilt washed over her in waves; guilt of their fight; guilt of finally living the dream she wanted; guilt of...

She took a deep breath and braced a hand along the centuries old staircase railing. The stone was smooth and cold against her fingers as she climbed the stairs. She turned left after the entry stairs and walked down the long hall. Her eyes scanned the gold plaques that labelled each door. Several administration offices lined the walls, but the main office, the Dean's office awaited her at the end. Outside the door, an assistant, an older woman with pure silver hair, sat at an ornate mahogany desk. She peered up at Aurora from her work, only to squint her eyes in discernment. It was clear that Aurora was an outsider, simply from her attire. The Empire, hidden from the Middling Realm, had its own particular fashions and designs. Everything in the Empire was colour coded to define one's role. The style of clothing itself was beautiful and refined; closest in Middling definition as Victorian or Edwardian. Aurora, however, stood before the older woman in a simple black pencil skirt, white fitted blouse and black flats. She had a small cross body bag, containing a few personal effects. She knew her choice would have been perfectly appropriate back in the Middling Realm, but here she knew it would be sorely out of place, save for her glasses. The glasses, and a necklace she had tucked under her blouse, were the only accessories she had that did not stand out against Empirical fashion.

"May I help you?" The assistant finally asked. Her face had the hint of a sneer, clearly unimpressed by the young woman who stood before her. The woman wore a modest women's suit of deep purple. Here, purple indicated one was either a scholar or in administrative work.

"Yes please, ma'am." Aurora replied with a slight bow of her head. She reached inside her bag and presented her summons letter. An off white parchment with ornate scrawl detailed her appointment at the academy. "I have an appointment with Dean Reyes at sixteen hundred hours."

The assistant took the letter, pulling out a pair of reading glasses to examine. She took her time reviewing the letter, somehow convinced that it could possibly be counterfeit. Aurora fought the urge of an exasperated sigh. She peered over the woman's shoulder and saw that there was note of her appointment written on her schedule. Her name written clear as day on the day's calendar, but for some reason, she was to be scrutinised.

"You may go through." The woman finally responded dryly, placing the paper on her desk rather than handing it back to Aurora herself.

"Thank you," Aurora replied, pocketing her letter back into her bag. She turned to the door ahead, thick, heavy and ornate. Aurora grabbed the handle to the door, quickly finding she would need to use both to heft it open. With a grunt of effort, the door opened, revealing the collegiate Dean seated behind a grand wooden desk. She peered up briefly over her thick black glasses, and returned to the mounds of paperwork before her. A quill, enchanted with air magic, worked in the background as it wrote whatever the Dean needed. Aurora stepped quietly to the desk. She hesitated for a moment before she took her seat.

The Dean looked up from her work and truly studied the young woman before her. The Dean's stare had a heavy weight to it, and turned Aurora's stomach in knots. The Dean, a petite woman in her late forties, gave a mischievous grin after what felt like an eternity. Her dark grey hair was styled into an asymmetrical bob, framing her delicate jaw nicely. Her purple suit jacket was hung over the back of her chair and showed off a white frilled sleeveless blouse.

"What brings you here so late, Aurora?" She finally demanded after a lengthy silence.

Aurora found herself glancing at the simple watch on her wrist. She had been a few minutes early to the meeting despite her worry of running late. The Dean noticed the look of confusion, and continued. "Students begin their journey at the Academy as early as five years old. We have never had a student start in the Collegiate level before."

"I...I am aware that it is out of the norm." Aurora stammered. "I had always wanted to apply, but my mother preferred to handle my education herself."

The Dean stared back a moment, before waving her right hand in the air. She beckoned a file from a cabinet several feet away. The file zipped into hand like a magnet. She set it down before her and leisurely flipped through the pages. "I am aware of your mother, Aurora. Emily was one of the Academy's most promising Mages back in my day." She paused as she studied the folders' contents. Aurora resisted the urge to lean forward to read the details. "We do not accept late term students for several reasons." The Dean resumed, snapping the folder shut. "Most importantly being that our standards are extremely high. The Royal Academy of Magic is only for training the elite of Mages and Guardians for protection of the realms. Students who do not meet our standards fall to the other Academies. We have had students fall out of our standards, but never rise to them. We cannot afford to accept below a certain level of magic if we want to continue our standard of protection."

Aurora fidgeted with her hands in her lap, trying to keep her nerves from reading on her face.

"It seems, however," the Dean continued, "that an exception has finally been made." She tapped a finger on the folder, "I have yet to see results such as these, and would have not believed them if your examinations hadn't been conducted by one of our most trusted professors."

Aurora released a breath she had been holding. "I promise I will work hard. I *very* much want to be here." Aurora was fully aware that none of this would be easy. The coursework alone would be an exciting challenge. Settling in with her peers here would be a whole other endeavour.

The Dean gave her a small smile in response. "I have no doubt of that." She replied, ushering the folder back to its home in the cabinet. "I simply wish that Emily would have allowed us to get our hands on you sooner."

The glint in the Dean's eye and her tone sent a chill down Aurora's spine. She let out a nervous chuckle in response, not quite sure she was comfortable with the Dean's comment.

"No matter," the Dean continued with a dismissive wave of her hand. "We will get you settled in before you know it. Your things will be in your dorm room by now. Pass me your map." She demanded with a beaconing hand.

Aurora passed her map Artefact back to the Dean. With a simple wave of her hand over the parchment, a faint light glowed. "There," she responded handing it back across the desk. "You'll have your updated details to your dorm. Here is your key." She slid a heavy iron key across the desk.

Aurora slid the weighted key into her bag and rose to her feet. "Thank you very much, Dean Reyes. I promise to upkeep the Academy's standards."

Aurora felt a wave of relief wash over her as the heavy door shut behind her. She let out a sigh and took a moment before bothering to check the map. She could feel the eyes of the Dean's assistant on her, but paid her no mind. She knew she would have to get used to it sooner or later.

Aurora checked her map and saw a new meeting point. She started down the hall, thankful it was empty. She knew that tomorrow the other students would start to arrive, and with it likely a lot of questions. It was hard to determine if she was more excited or nervous for it. For so many years, it had only been her and her mother. She had met plenty of other people her age, but very few from the Empire. Most of her encounters had been with Middlings. Aurora had found it interesting to learn about the different countries and regions of the Middling realm; no two seemed quite the same. She wondered just how varied the Empire itself would be.

As Aurora turned a corner, she found herself face to face with her first peer. She quickly stopped herself, holding her breath. Before her stood a tall young man, very clearly a Guardian. Guardians were built completely different from Mages - their Magic coursed through their bodies instead of presenting as Elemental Magic. They were faster, stronger, and even known to wield special abilities in some bloodlines. They were almost always the tallest in the room, and known for their super human physical abilities.

The Guardian stood before her, a glower in his amber brown eyes as he studied her. He raised a dark eyebrow, unsure if it was due to surprise or simple intrigue.

"Excuse me," Aurora finally mustered to say. The hall itself was tighter then many of the others. He stood in the middle, his wide shoulders not allowing for much room to pass by without invading her personal space.

The Guardian seemed to debate moving aside for her. The expression on his face seemed to read that he believed her to be in the wrong. He begrudgingly stepped aside to allow her to pass. Aurora continued on her way down her path. She swore she heard a low voice mutter something about "Middlings".

It wasn't long until Aurora reached the women's dorms. She walked through a large doorway which led to an expansive common room. A circular fireplace lay in the centre of the room. Several arm chairs and couches littered the room. Across from the entrance, a dozen or windows scaled the wall. Thick midnight blue curtains were drawn back by gold silk ties to allow the sunlight to flood the area. The room itself looked like it could easily host over a hundred students. Aurora walked further into the room spotting a massive kitchen. Several industrial sized refrigerators and ovens could be seen opposite a lengthy island. A few tables with bench seating were beside the kitchen, presumably an eating area. She smiled to herself, thankful that she was able to take this all in without the distraction of others. She looked forward to discovering more throughout her day.

She continued further into the dorms, a wide hallway leading to the bedrooms. She checked her map, leading her to room 121. She fished out the heavy key from her bag and turned the lock. All the advancements and specialities of magic, and some things were still so traditional.

With a click her door opened to a beautiful large room. Aurora let out a small gasp at the sight. Three large windows, similar to those in the common room, lined the wall to the right. Two large beds were located in the room, a roommate clearly to be expected. Behind the beds was a custom book shelf which formed around the beds. To her left, across from the beds, were a pair of arm chairs and a small side table. She turned, spotting a moderate fireplace along the wall. Currently, the fireplace was empty, but it looked like it would be quite welcoming in the chill of winter. Aurora stepped in further, allowing the door behind her to close. She heard the door lock click automatically behind her.

Further to the left of the arm chairs were two doors. The first she opened lead to a full washroom with shower. Everything looked to be stocked with soaps and towels. She turned to the next door, noting a walk in closet. The closet had already been filled with neatly lined uniforms with shoes and boots lined nicely on a shelf over the clothing rack. Aurora walked in deeper, running her fingers over the clothing. First were the lighter fall uniforms, leading to the heavier winter wear. There were three of each season it appeared, allowing for ease of wash. She looked up to see if anything would determine which was hers, a name plate overhead indicating Aurora's attire was to the left. She turned to the right, seeing if she could determine her roommate. Amaris Cirillo read the gold name plate. She looked down at the uniforms lining Amaris' side and noted several copies of what looked to be an athletic uniform.

A smile formed on Aurora's face as she left the closet. Female Guardians were quite rare. Guardians, more often than not, tended to be male, whereas most Mages were female. Researchers had pursued if there was a precise reason why, but there was no definite answer. Some theorised it boiled down to physical abilities, but others reasoned that the magic itself decided. Whatever the reason, Aurora was excited to get to room with a Guardian and learn more.

Aurora stood in front of the pair of beds. Her small suitcase stood at the foot of the bed. It contained the few Middling outfits she had and some personal items. She slid the suitcase under the bed to put it out of the way. She would take care of it later. She sat on the edge of the bed with a sigh and kicked off her shoes. She turned and laid back. She stared up at the plain white ceiling. Her hand began to fiddle with a yellow gold necklace around her neck. "I miss you, mum." She muttered to herself, tears welling up in her eyes.

Chapter 2

Aurora woke with start as the daylight broke on her face. She hadn't realised that she had fallen asleep, her glasses fallen off beside her on the bed. She picked them up and checked for smudges before she wrapped the beaded strands over her ears. Her watch read it was nearly eight in the morning. She slid out of bed and reached for her toothbrush from her suitcase. She felt a staleness in her mouth that she needed to be rid of.

Aurora started her morning with a quick brush of her teeth and a shower. She stepped out of the shower refreshed and wrapped one of the soft towels around her body. She brushed out her wet hair and quickly plaited it. She headed back into the dorm room, lifting her suitcase onto her bed. Inside, she had the few personal possessions she had. She pulled out a pair of dark blue jeans and a light weight lavender sweater. She headed back to the washroom to hang her towel and froze at the sound of her door opening.

Aurora waited a breath before stepping out of the door. Before her stood a tall young woman, most likely near six feet tall. Her chin length hair was thick, dark and curly. Her skin looked as if it radiated the sun's warmth, making her olive green eyes pop in contrast. She wore a white blouse with a pair of high waisted, fitted breaches. The sleeves had been unbuttoned and rolled up to her elbows. Her long black boots had a slight heel, but looked easy to move in. It took her a moment to notice Aurora observing her, but once she did, the young woman burst into a bright smile. She dropped the bags slung over her arms to the floor and swiftly closed the distance between the pair.

"You're a Middling!" She gaped. "I mean," she shook her head. "you can't be, you're just dressed like one." Her face fell into a look of slight embarrassment. "Sorry,"

Aurora stared back at, who she presumed was her room mate, with widened eyes. "I'm Aurora." She finally explained with reservation.

The young woman broke into an assured smile. "I'm Amaris, but I go by Mari." She explained, setting her bags down on the floor and extended a hand.

Aurora paused a moment and shook her hand. Her hand radiated warmth and strength.

"I need to work on the whole thinking before I speak thing." Mari continued, picking her bags back up and set them down near her bed. "I didn't mean to imply there was anything wrong with Middlings or their clothes. I just have never seen them *here* in the Empire."

Aurora sat on the edge of her bed as Mari started to unpack. She pulled at the edge of her sweater absentmindedly. "I didn't think about clothes." She admitted. "I grew up around Middlings, so I honestly don't have anything."

Mari stopped a moment and scanned Aurora. "I'm taller, but I'm sure I have a thing or two that can fit." She remarked. "If you want, that is."

Aurora turned to Mari. "Really?" She stared back in surprise. She had no reason to be so kind to a total stranger.

"Why not?" She responded with a shrug. "We're about to live together. I can lend you a few things."

Aurora let a small smile cross her lips. "Thank you."

Mari opened one of her bags, riffled through the clothing inside, and tossed a few pieces across the bed to Aurora. "If you want, I can give you a bit of a tour around the campus. I'm presuming you aren't familiar with it yet?"

Aurora slung the borrowed clothes over her arm. "That would be great, actually. I was a little nervous about exploring on my own."

"You got it." Mari replied.

"Would you mind if I get changed into this first, though?" Aurora asked.

"Not at all!" She assured. "You take your time. I'll just put the rest of this away and we'll get going."

Aurora thanked Mari and headed to the closet. Mari had given her what looked like three pieces that she could mix and match. All three were the same shade of navy blue that their school uniform was. Colour coding was very important in Empirical fashion. Any shade of blue indicated that you were a student in the Empire. Navy blue, specifically, indicated that you were a student in the Royal Academy of Magic. Mari had given her a long pleated skirt, a vest, and a pair of fitted, high waisted pants. She grabbed one of the white blouses that went with her school uniform to go with the skirt and vest. She grabbed a pair of ankle laced boots overhead to complete the outfit.

"I'm so glad it fits." Mari remarked once she stepped out. "Ready to go?"

Aurora nodded, and the pair headed out. With a click, the door locked behind them. Mari assured Aurora that she had her key, as they headed down the hall.

"The kitchen here is for anything we want to make ourselves, and isn't restricted to the Dining Hall hours. The fridges and pantries are always stocked with essentials, but you're always welcome to bring something back from town if you need something special." Mari explained as they walked past.

Mari lead her away from the common room. "The Dining Hall will still have breakfast running until 9. We can grab a bite if you're hungry."

"Yes please." Aurora responded, her stomach growled in agreement.

Mari turned down the halls until they reached a grand Dining Hall near the centre of the building. Rows of long tables with bench seating was available for the students to eat at. Along the wall opposite of the large doors was a buffet of food. Aurora followed Mari, grabbing a plate and cutlery to load up with breakfast. She poured herself a cup of tea with milk, and followed Mari to a spot closer to the wall. Mari continued to explain some basics of the area as they ate and sipped. Aurora let her eyes wander over the several other students in the hall, all wearing the same navy blue and hints of white. She wondered how busy the hall would be at peak hours.

"Right," Mari declared, setting her cutlery down on her empty plate. "Do you want the interior, or the grounds first?"

Aurora thought for a moment before deciding, "Let's cover the interior first. We can head outside as it gets busier."

"Great," Mari responded as she stood to her feet. They dropped their dirtied plates off to a spot near a side door and continued on.

"This entire area is for Collegiate students only. I'm sure you've seen the overall map, but each school level is broken off into a separate area." Mari led Aurora into the grand foyer. "First level is all dorms, common rooms, and what not. We have one of the libraries and the Dean's office here," Mari explained pointing at the doors. "And across the hall are the private tutor rooms." Aurora studied each as they walked on past.

Mari led Aurora up a long staircase. "Up here on the second floor, we have a variety of classrooms. Typically, the Guardian specified classes are to the West, and the Mage specific classes are to the East." Aurora's eyes widened at the sheer size and number of doors.

The pair climbed another staircase, leading up to the third and final floor. "Up here," Mari continued, "is the lecture hall classes. These rooms are generally set up to hold both sides and need to be a lot larger."

"How many people are in our class?" Aurora asked as they walked past the doors.

"Thirty." Mari replied simply.

Aurora's eyebrows shot up with surprise. The castle seemed far too grand to house a mere thirty students per class.

"There are fifteen Guardians, and fifteen Mages. They make sure to keep it even."

Aurora felt a small knot of guilt form in her stomach. "How is that possible if I'm just joining now?"

Mari shrugged. "I heard one of the Mages failed out at year end last year. I thought it was just a rumour until I saw you. Looks like you applying balanced everything out."

Aurora let out a small sigh. She hadn't replaced someone. She didn't want to be here at the expense of someone else being removed.

By then, Mari had led Aurora back to the main floor. She turned to Aurora with a hint of mischief in her smile. "Are you ready to see the grounds?"

"Lead the way," She replied, pushing her gold rimmed glasses back up the bridge of her nose.

Mari grabbed her by the hand and quickened her pace, eager to show off her favourite part of the Academy. "The main building is where the dorms and practical classes are held. Out here," she indicated with her arms spread wide, "is where the fun happens."

Mari lead Aurora to the rear of the school. In the furthest north east corner was the Collegiate Guardian training area. "We have two main areas for training. One is the obstacle arena. It is never the same day to day. Over there," she pointed towards the south, "is our sparring arena."

Aurora followed Mari's direction and noticed a pair of male Guardians sparring already. The taller of the pair matched Mari's colouring, with loose curls pulled back into a low ponytail. Some strands, slick with sweat, had already fallen near his eyes, but they did not seem to bother him. His thick muscular build looked like it would be difficult to move and evade easily, but he was far more agile than he seemed. The second partner was a leaner build, but was no means weak. He looked to be slightly shorter than the first, and was fair in his colouring. His gold blond hair was slicked back to be kept out of his dark blue eyes. He was quick and adept at evading the first Guardian's attacks. The pair, though very different, seemed to be evenly matched.

"Aelius!" Mari cried out with a wave over her head. The first Guardian stopped and turned at the sound of his name. His sparring partner noticed the distraction and took full advantage. He landed a blow to his sparring partner, landing a crack to the jaw. Aelius staggered a moment, bringing a hand to his jaw. He let out a deep laugh and clapped a large hand on his friend's shoulder. They both laughed and hopped down from the sparring arena to meet the girls.

"Aurora," Mari began, "this is my brother Aelius. Technically older, but not by much."

Aelius gave a small smile and bow of his head, his arms crossed beneath his chest. He did not seem to share his sister's talkative nature.

"And this here is Edwyn." Mari continued. Aurora turned her attention to Edwyn.

"Aurora, she said?" He asked with a hint of disbelief.

Her brow creased in confusion for a moment, "Yes?" she responded. "Aurora Thomas."

Edwyn seemed to study her for a time. He seemed to register his serious expression and relaxed his face into a friendly smile. He inched closer to her. "Are you a Mage, then?" Aurora felt her pulse quicken as he inched closer. "Why such a late start at the Academy? I've never heard of anyone starting so late."

"Yes, I'm training as a Mage." She replied. "I was homeschooled. My mom moved around a lot for work and didn't want me sent off to boarding school."

"You must have seen a lot of the Middling realm then." Edwyn continued. He spoke to her as if they were the only ones present.

Aelius notably perked up at the mention of the Middling realm. "Did you?"

Aurora blinked at the sudden enthusiasm from Aelius. She had been so drawn in by Edwyn's questions, she had nearly forgotten the others were listening in. "Did I what?"

"Did you spend a lot of time in the Middling realm?" He repeated.

"Aelius is *obsessed* with the Middling realm. He finds all their gadgets and customs *so* fascinating." Her tone had an air of teasing.

Aelius made a face at Mari and shoved her shoulder. "At least I *have* interests."

Mari glared at her brother and threw a punch at his shoulder. He didn't bother to move, knowing it wouldn't be a hurt in the first place.

Aelius turned back to Aurora. He had uncrossed his arms and left his hands relaxed on his hips. "I've always wanted to explore some of the Middling Realm. I have a few books about it, but I'm sure by now they're...outdated."

Aurora gave him a small smile. "Some of it changes a lot, but other things remain the same. Having an Allspeak ring helps a lot when traveling. Some of the slang can be really hard to pick up, though." She fiddled with a small gold ring on her right middle finger. Allspeak rings were standard issue in the Empire. They automatically translated any language being spoken, and, if necessary, gave the wearer the ability to speak the local language with ease. It eliminated the issue of mistranslations or misinterpretations. There were always certain phrases, idioms, and slang that were nearly impossible to translate, but the rings caught most of it. Her mother had always encouraged her to learn languages without the Artefact, but had gifted her very own ring by her eighth birthday.

"Did you ever spend much time in the Empirical Realm?" Edwyn cut in.

She turned back to Edwyn. "Not...really." She admitted hesitantly. "I was mostly at Artefact sites."

"Well," He began. "If you're ever unsure about anything, I'd be more than happy to help you out. I'd be happy to tour you around if you like." Edwyn offered with a smile. She could easily see how a girl might be drawn into his easy air.

"You guys can follow us if you want." Mari offered with a sigh. "I showed her through the Collegiate building, but we just started touring the grounds." A slight squint of her eyes almost dared Edwyn to try and take Aurora from her.

"There's nothing wrong with going together." Aelius declared, ever the peacemaker it seemed.

Aurora thanked them for their offer, letting them lead the way. Mari and Edwyn took turns spouting off information about different parts of the castle grounds. As they walked, she noticed that the entire campus was squared off by a man made lake.

"We use the lake for training," Edwyn explained. "But no one is able to enter or leave using the water. The main gate is the only way in or out."

She studied the landscape. She lowered her glasses to the tip of her nose for just a moment. It was then that she could see the shimmer of a Magic barrier. A barrier like that would definitely prevent anyone from entering or leaving. She slid her glasses back up to where they should be and turned back to the group.

Edwyn stared at her, his mouth slightly agape. "Your glasses..." He started, unsure how to finish his sentence. Aurora stepped closer to Mari to avoid whatever he had planned on asking. She slowed their pace ever so slightly to allow for more physical distance between the other Guardians. Mari turned to Aurora with a look of confusion. "You alright?" She asked in a hushed tone.

Aurora paused for a moment to find the proper words. "Edwyn asks a lot of questions." She observed. "I don't know if that's weird or not. Is it?"

Mari shrugged. "He's a shameless flirt with most of the girls. You're new. Maybe he likes you, maybe you throw him off. Who knows?" She added with a laugh.

Aurora made a non committal sound in response. She kept her arms linked with Mari for the rest of the tour. There was a sense of familiarity and comfort with Mari. It felt oddly natural to be her friend.

"I think I might be ready to head back to the dorm, if that's okay?" She admitted quietly.

"Of course." She responded. She turned back to Edwyn and Aelius, shouting out "We're heading back! I'll see you guys later."

Edwyn and Aelius gave a slight wave and let the pair head back inside. Aurora gave a slight nod of her head and a small wave in response, and turned back to the Collegiate building with Mari.

Mari and Aurora walked back in silence for a time. "Did you want a cider or anything?" Mari finally asked. "The shot of whiskey is optional." She added with a slight grin.

Aurora noted a slight chill in the air. "That sounds great, actually." She replied with a hint of relief.

Mari insisted that Aurora relax in one of the chairs by the fire as they returned to the common room. It felt awkward to let someone take care of her, but she listened and settled herself into one of the cozy chairs. She watched the fire as it crackled soothingly. Aurora let out a small sigh as she watched the flames flicker and dance.

"And who is *this*?"

Aurora snapped out of her little daydream. She looked up to see a small gathering of like aged female students before her. "Excuse me?" She responded in confusion.

The source of the question was a stunningly beautiful young woman. Clearly the leader of the group, she was slender and tall with creamy pale skin. Her hair, nearly white in colour, flowed in delicate curls down to her waist. She wore a beautiful corseted navy gown. Her tiny waist seemed to be impossibly cinched in contrast to the pleated skirts that reached the floor. It was her piercing ice blue eyes, however, that stood out the most. They studied

Aurora with a fierce intensity, even though her pink lips read a soft smirk. "I just asked who you were." She responded in a mocking tone. She let out a small laugh and the others followed suit.

"Oh..." Aurora awkwardly responded. She had no idea if she should stand or remain seated. They gave off such an odd aura. "I'm Aurora. I'm a first year Mage." She explained.

"Reeaaaally?" The young woman replied with feigned interest. "Did you hear about a new student?" She asked, as she turned to the young women behind her.

The others murmured that they hadn't heard anything of the sort. One whispered about someone named Helena failing last year, but no one had confirmed anything about a new student.

The ring leader turned back to Aurora. "Well, *Aurora,*" She began, "I'm sure there is going to be *so* much catching up you need to do. I've never heard of anyone entering the Academy like this. If you need any advice on how you should be conducting yourself, you can always reach out." She added with a smirk.

Aurora had no doubt the young woman in front of her was completely disingenuous. She had no intention of making any enemies, however, so she gave the young woman a small smile. "Thank you, uhh..." She stammered. She realised she had no idea what to call her.

"Astraea." She introduced herself with an arched brow. "Astraea Solis."

Aurora felt her stomach drop. She immediately shot to her feet. "Your Majesty." She responded with a panicked bow.

The group of women burst into a cackle. Astraea's tinkled above the rest. "Oh, sweetheart," She mockingly assured. "Don't worry about all that. At the academy I'm just a student like everyone else. But thank you."

Aurora laughed nervously with the others. They gave a small wave and left towards the dorm room hallway. Aurora's ears burned red as she could hear them giggle to themselves at her expense.

Mari returned with a pair of steaming hot mugs of cider as the gaggle of young women left. She rolled her eyes as she passed them and returned her attention back to Aurora. Aurora had remained frozen on her feet, her cheeks and ears were still hot with embarrassment.

"What was all that?" Mari asked as she offered a mug.

Aurora grabbed the mug with both hands and glared down at the amber liquid. The smell of whiskey mixed with the warm spices singed her nose. She took a sip, the hot liquid warming her from the inside.

"I met the *Princess*." She said with a groan.

"Oh shiiiit." Mari responded as she slunk into a neighbouring chair. Aurora followed suit and continued to sip on her drink. It helped.

"I had no idea who she was until she said her name, and then I embarrassed myself with bowing, and they cackled." She confessed in an awkward ramble.

Mari sighed. "It's best that you don't pay her any mind." She explained. "She didn't always used to be like that. She actually was pretty fun when we were kids." Mari paused and scanned the area for eavesdroppers. She leaned in a little to Aurora. "Honestly, I felt she changed once Prince Hesper was born. Not sure why, but we all noticed." Mari sat back, resuming her original volume. "If I were you, I'd just do my best to avoid her."

"Good to know..." Aurora responded. She offered her mug of cider in a cheers, and the room mates downed another sip.

Chapter 3

The first day of classes had finally arrived. Mari had woken at the crack of dawn, much to Aurora's dismay. She peered out from under her soft duvet to glare at her energetic room mate.

"Sorry!" Mari whispered apologetically. She was already dressed in her training gear. Mari wore a loose white blouse with a small corset vest over top. Her pair of high waisted shorts looked to give plenty of room for dexterity. She wore a pair of knee length socks and boots that reached half way up her shins. A pair of delicate black leather gloves matched her belts and leg halter.

Aurora grumbled that it was okay in response and buried herself back under her duvet. She knew she had another hour before she would need to get ready to eat and then head to class. After her run in with Astraea, she was not feeling entirely confident of dealing with her new peers.

An hour later, her watch chimed with an alarm. She sighed and whipped the blanket off. She had not been able to really fall back asleep, but there was no sense in avoiding things. She slipped out of bed and got herself into her new uniform. Her white blouse had bishop sleeves that billowed out and tapered at the wrist. She slipped on the white petticoat skirt and tightened it at her waist. Her main dress layered overtop. A small tie reached just past her breasts. She buttoned the few buttons at her chest, and fastened the black belt that cinched in her waist. From there, the dress split and flared with three gold chains connecting three pairs of gold buttons. Her skirts flared out around her and fell at her knees. She fastened the buttons of her knee length boots to complete the look. She smiled at her reflection in the mirror; she finally looked the part.

Aurora grabbed her brown leather book bag and slung it over her shoulder. Her textbooks and a blank notebook were inside, as well as her room key. She headed out for the morning and headed to the Dining Hall for breakfast. Aurora felt a bundle of nerves in her stomach as she started on her way. She noticed a few stares and whispers, but was thankful that it wasn't over the top.

She quickly found her way to the Dining Hall and tucked into a light breakfast. She sipped at her tea and appreciated how it soothed her nerves. She spotted Mari running off with a piece of toast in her mouth, no doubt headed back to their dorm to change into her standard uniform.

Aurora put her plate off to the side and headed up the stairs to her first class. First up for the day was Pact Formation 101. Aurora quickly stepped to the side as other students raced up the stairs. She steadied her footing and grabbed the railing for support. They were long gone before she could consider shouting after them. She continued to the third floor where Mari had shown her all the lecture halls. Pact Formation would be one of the few cross over classes with both Mages and Guardians attending. She reached the third floor, and tried to remember which direction the class was. She reached into her book bag with her class schedule information written down. Pact Formation was scheduled at 9:30 in room 320. She glanced up and checked the room numbers scrawled on the doors. She headed down the west end, following the ascending numbers. She heard footsteps running behind her and tensed. She turned to see another group of Guardians trying to beat one another to class. She recognised Edwyn in the group, but several others were new faces. She stopped in place to avoid being a moving target, but one of the young men still managed to clip her as he rushed past. She winced at the pain in her shoulder as she teetered off balance. A firm hand grabbed her by the elbow to steady her.

"Sorry about that," One of the Guardians stated. He stood several inches over her, but not nearly as towering as some of the other Guardians. His thick dark hair was slicked back and close cut underneath. His warm brown eyes studied her a moment. He released his hold of her once he realised she had steadied herself. "On your way to Pact 101?" He asked with a smile.

"Idiots…" She muttered to herself as she dusted off her skirts.

"I'm sorry?" The young man asked in surprise.

Aurora looked up at him, her hands on her hips. "If you're all going to run around like idiots, you should at least have the ability to avoid running *into* people. I thought Guardians were supposed to be athletic..." She scoffed and turned to continue on to class.

After a pause, Aurora heard a laugh break out behind her. The Guardian quickly caught up with her. "You're not wrong." He answered. "He *is* an idiot. And he shouldn't have knocked into you. I'll give him shit for that."

Aurora let out a small laugh.

"Can I walk you to class?" He offered out an arm as if to literally escort her.

Aurora arched a brow at him. She didn't accept his arm, but also didn't stop her pace.

"Cael Torres." He responded with a slight bow of his head. "Not that you asked, of course. I'm presuming you are the replacement Mage?"

She studied him a moment. He was observant. It seemed as if there had been several rumours swirling about, but Cael was direct. "It would seem that way." She responded indirectly.

"You're not going to tell me your name, are you?" He surmised.

She looked over to him, a smirk on her lips. "Now where would the fun in that be?" They had reached the doors of the lecture hall with perfect timing. She pushed open the door and headed in. She could hear him chuckle behind her as she tried to figure out where to sit.

"I'll see you later, mystery Mage." He replied, awfully close to her ear. She felt a chill go down her spine as she felt his breath on her skin. She refused to let his effect on her show on her face.

Aurora scanned the room. The door had opened to the floor level of the lecture hall. To the left wall was a large chalkboard and a pair of desks raised up on a platform. To the right was a series of desks in rows. The aisles fanned out in width as they escalated, counting 12 in total. A staircase ran through the middle and along each wall to allow for ease of entry and exit. The room looked sorely empty, however Aurora knew that most of the students had already arrived.

Mari was seated in one of the middle rows on the furthest end. She waved a hand over head to call Aurora over. Aurora smiled in thanks and made her way over to join her. Mari scooted herself down the bench seating, allowing Aurora to comfortably join them. She turned to a young man behind her. He leaned forward on his desk, his dark almond shaped eyes locked on Mari. "Aurora, this is Dae." She explained as she swatted a hand on his shoulder.

Dae finally turned to Aurora, a polite smile on his face. "Mari was telling me all about you."

"All good things, I hope." Aurora replied as she settled her leather book bag on her right.

"Maaaaaybe." Mari teased in response. "Dae is a Mage as well." She explained. "I've known him since...oh god we were toddlers weren't we?" She asked as she turned to check with Dae.

Dae nodded with a small chuckle. "Our mothers were close friends when they were at the Academy. They figured it would be nice for their children to carry on the tradition."

Aurora smiled. She could feel the close bond they had immediately. "That *is* nice." She replied. It must have been nice to have life long friendships.

"What about you?" Dae pressed. "Is there any family or friends here for you?"

Aurora swallowed. "No." She replied simply. She turned to her bag to pull out her notebook and text as a distraction. The change in tone was palpable, but thankfully at that moment, both professors entered the classroom.

Pact Formation 101 was lead by a pair of teachers in their forties; a Mage and Guardian. The female professor, quite obviously a Mage, was tall, but lithe. Her chocolate brown hair was swept up into a simple bun, with not a single strand out of place. She wore a high waisted a-line skirt with the cropped, form fitting jacket in deep purple. Her ankle boots had a small heel that clacked as she crossed the floor. The male teacher, most definitely a Guardian, followed closely behind. He wore the same deep purple in a form fitting pair of slacks and vest. His white dress shirt was rolled up to his elbows and revealed a strong pair of forearms. His dark hair had flecks of grey at the temples, as well has his close trimmed beard.

"Welcome everyone." The Mage professor started. "I am Professor Stein,"

"As am I." The Guardian chimed in. His voice was a low rumble. He gave a small smile to his wife on his left.

"We will be your Professors for Pact Formation for the next three years." The Mage Stein continued. "The Pact formed between a Mage and Guardian is one of the most sacred bonds that can be formed. It is a truly unique experience that must be experienced to be understood."

"Mages and Guardians each have different needs with the Pact." The Guardian Stein added. "It is a symbiotic relationship that benefits one another in protection, strength, and shared power. The pact is a permanent bond that can only be broken through death, and that itself is excruciating."

The class broke out into a tense murmur. The severity of Pact bonds were a widely known matter in the Empire, but the suffrage of a broken bond was a bit of a taboo subject.

"You will experience a temporary, partial pact during your Collegiate years." Mage Stein resumed. "When Pacts were originally started, they were formed without preparation. Over the past several decades, it was decided that it would be beneficial to attempt trial Pacts. This allows Mages and Guardians to understand the severity of what they are embarking upon, as well as test if the partner they have chosen is a worthy life long partner."

"Not all of you will be lucky. Some of you will choose poorly. Some of you will choose on infatuation or lust." Guardian Stein added. A small rumble of laughter emanated from the class. "This is why we practice. We advise you choose as wisely as possible, but this is a practice pact for a reason."

"You will be expected to select a pact partner by next week. This will be your partner for the remainder of the year. Your pact will last both semesters, and will be broken at the end of the school year." Mage Stein explained.

"You will be graded on your strength of bond, ability to access the bond, ability to manipulate the bond, and more. You will be tested emotionally and physically by this." Guardian Stein stole a quick glance at his wife, a flash of a smile crossed his face. "Boundaries can become blurry when bonded with someone. It is important to discuss things and understand that this bond will effect everyone in a new and different way."

"You will be expected to take this seriously." Mage Stein added with a grave tone. "This is not an excuse to date someone. You are preparing yourself for your future career."

"With that said," Guardian Stein added, "Let us open our texts to chapter one."

***

The moment class was dismissed, the entire group was in a buzz. The energy was a wild mixture of excitement and nerves at the prospect of selecting a pact partner so quickly. Aurora headed out of class in a slight daze. It wasn't until Mari jumped up behind her and clapped an arm around her neck that she snapped back into reality. "Great first class, right?" Mari asked.

Aurora gave a small laugh. "Right." She responded.

Mari gave her a sidelong glance. "What's wrong? That was a great lecture. Back in secondary we had this one professor that would drone on in the most *monotonous* mumble."

"No no the lecture was great." Aurora admitted. "It's just that I didn't think that we would be selecting a pact partner so *soon*. I stupidly thought that first semester would be all history and theory or something."

"Ahhh," Mari responded, removing her arm from Aurora's neck. "Yeah that would be...a lot. I guess I take for granted that most of us have a good idea of who we're going to choose."

"Oh you mean Dae?" Aurora asked with a teasing tone to her voice.

Mari flushed bright red and refused to meet Aurora's eye. "Why do you have to say it like that?"

"It looks like that there is something more than friendship is all. I just met you and I can see it."

"I don't know what you're talking about..."

"Well," Aurora paused as she thought out loud. "They have to partner me with someone. I guess that's why they make sure it's equal numbers of Mages to Guardians."

"Right," Mari confirmed. "Worst case you just take whoever is left at the end."

"Great..." Aurora groaned. "Not awkward at all."

Chapter 4

The pair parted ways as Aurora headed downstairs for Defence Magic 101. She shook off the nerves from Pact Formation. Magic she knew. This is where she would excel and show her strengths. The Dean herself had even confirmed that her test scores were unlike anything they had ever seen. Aurora walked into class with a fresh feeling of confidence. Just like the lecture hall, the classroom seemed far too large for the number of students it housed. Solid wood desks were lined neatly before a large desk in front of a blackboard that took up the entire wall.

Students had already started to seat themselves. Aurora spotted Dae towards the middle of the desks and he gave her a little wave. She returned his wave and gave him a small smile as she headed to a seat beside him. "I'm glad to know another Mage now." She admitted as she took her seat.

"Mari only introduce you to other Guardians?" He asked with a slight chuckle.

"Yeah I got to meet Aelius and Edwyn while she was showing me the grounds." She explained as she set up her books.

"How did *that* go?" He asked with genuine intrigue.

"It went well. They were both polite. Aelius is definitely Mari's social opposite."

Dae laughed. "Yeah, he's a good guy, but Mari is *definitely* the more extroverted one. He's just..selective about who he opens up to."

The class hushed as their professor stepped in the classroom. She was an older woman in her sixties with marbled silver hair. Her face was stern, but she also had an air of knowledge and wisdom to her. She stepped behind her desk and studied the students for a moment.

"I am Professor Rossi," She announced. "I will be handling your education in Defence Magic this year. You will be expected to demonstrate your abilities in Defensive Magic over this term. I will be testing you in particular forms of magic, but also your ability to think on your feet and respond in the moment. By the end of this term, you will be expected to demonstrate a personalised defence technique."

Aurora noticed that Professor Rossi used Air Magic to write bulletin points of her expectations on the board behind her. "Students will be expected to work extensively in one element this term. Unlike previous years, you will be allowed to specialise in the element of your choosing."

Aurora's brow furrowed in confusion. Professor Rossi took note of it. "Is there a problem, Miss...?"

Aurora was taken aback at the sudden address. "Aurora Thomas, Professor Rossi."

"Ah," She paused. "Is there a problem, *Miss Thomas?*"

"There is no problem, Professor Rossi." Aurora insisted as she shook her head.

"Then keep your faces to yourself." She sneered.

A collective snicker could be heard through the class. Aurora clamped her jaw shut to avoid it gaping open in shock.

"As I was saying," Professor Rossi continued. "You will be expected to present a single element this year. As I call your name, you will announce your selection."

Aurora turned to Dae with a worried look on her face. "You work in single elements?" She whispered as she leaned in.

Dae looked at her with confusion. "You *don't?*" He whispered back. "That's third level magic, second year if you're *really* good."

"Miss Thomas," Professor Rossi projected across the room. Aurora sat up and snapped back towards the front of class. "Pray tell what is so fascinating that you feel the need to chatter away with Mr Choi?"

Aurora gulped. "I was asking Mr Choi about the use of elemental magic in class. I asked if single elemental use was the norm at the Academy."

Professor Rossi's eyes squinted in discernment. "It certainly is in *my* classroom, Miss Thomas."

"Excuse me, Professor Rossi?" A lyrical voice rang out. Astraea had called out innocently and risen a delicate hand in the air. "I think poor Miss Thomas here simply isn't used to how things are run here at the Academy. It seems that she has been homeschooled instead of being part of a formal education." Aurora stared in disbelief at the back handed defence Astraea had to offer. "I am sure she just needs some time to adjust and get used to how things are done properly."

Professor Rossi's thorny demeanour melted the moment Astraea started her explanation. She nodded in agreement. "You are lucky, Miss Thomas, that Ms Solis here has such insight and compassion. You would be wise to adjust yourself to how we conduct ourselves here. I will not abide back talk or a lack of manners."

"Yes, Professor Rossi." Aurora managed out meekly.

"On that note," She continued. "What element will you choose for this term?"

"I will present Earth magic." Aurora informed quietly.

"Very well." Professor Rossi noted in a small book in front of her. "Mr Choi?"

"I will present Water magic, Professor Rossi." Dae responded.

"Alright." She replied as she made note of his decision.

***

Aurora trudged out of class with her stomach in knots. Dae cautiously approached her from behind. "You okay?" He asked after a moment of hesitation.

"Yeah..." Aurora managed dryly. "It's just...an adjustment." She explained.

She tensed as she heard a distinctive giggle. Astraea sauntered out of class behind them, her laugh ringing out into the hall. "Oh, Aurora. I am *so* sorry that class was so difficult for you." She stated sympathetically. She feigned a look of concern. "I'm sure you'll get the hang of things in no time."

She headed off down the hall with her collection of friends. A couple of them turned back to stare at Aurora. A fresh round of giggles burst out. Aurora rolled her eyes and sighed. "I'll get used to it." She elaborated as she turned back to Dae. "It will just be weird doing things separately after being so used to wielding hybrid magic."

Dae fell in beside Aurora as they headed down to the Dining Hall. "You'll have to show me how you do that." He replied with a sense of awe in his voice. "Here they are so strict on wielding magic separately. They want it to be perfect before complicating the weaves I guess."

"I can see that." Aurora admitted. "It just always felt more natural to weave things together depending on what I needed to do. It didn't make sense for things to be isolated for the sake of practice."

"I guess that's the benefit of homeschooling and self learning." Dae replied. "You have more room for creativity and exploration that way."

Aurora smiled to herself. She had a renewed sense of appreciation for her mother's teaching methods. It wasn't long before they reached the Dining Hall for lunch. The hall was busy with students at this hour. By the time they finally sat down to their meals, Mari had appeared from the grounds. She rushed over to the pair with a bright smile on her face. "Hey!' She exclaimed as she took a seat beside Dae. "Glad to see you two getting on."

"Thanks for introducing us." Aurora responded. "It helped having someone I could talk to in class. I'm pretty sure I completely screwed up with the professor already."

"Oh man you should have seen it, Mar." Dae gushed as he swallowed a bite. "Rossi was something else. I am pretty sure she put Aurora on a list of some sort."

Aurora felt her stomach drop. "Really?"

Mari sighed and smacked Dae on the shoulder. "Why would you say that in front of her? Like she isn't worried enough about it."

"Sorry," Dae apologised sheepishly. "I'm sure it will be alright." He added. "I'm sure once she sees how you work and what you do that she will forget all about today."

"Hopefully..." She trailed off.

Mari went on to gush about her second period and how great it was to get back into training. Aurora excused herself after a while. She needed a moment to herself before her next class. The pair waved her off and happily went back to catching up.

Aurora found herself wandering the halls lost in thought. Dae was likely right that she needed to take the time to prove herself. It was foreign to her to need to prove her worth. Aurora realised that she had wandered near her next class. Aurora inched towards the open door and peered inside. A quick scan revealed the class was empty. She stepped inside, thankful for the peace and quiet. The classroom was a similar design as her previous with solid wood desks lined opposite of a large professor's desk. The main difference in this classroom was the several cased Artefacts which lined the walls. Special cabinets had been designed with glass walls to show off various magically made items.

Aurora smiled to herself. Just being in the classroom surrounded by the items gave her a wash of nostalgia. Her mother had spent her entire life researching and searching for ancient Artefacts. She stepped closer to one of the cases.

It had been several weeks at this dig site. Aurora, at just twelve years old, knew that her mother had been increasingly frustrated with the lack of progress. Emily was bent over a series of parchments scrawled in an ancient text that littered the table. She set a simple sandwich in front of her mother, insistent that she eat something.

"I'll get to it in a minute..." She dismissed without looking up from her work.

"You said that twenty minutes ago, mum." Aurora pressed. She pushed the plate on top of the papers. "Eat."

*Emily sighed and finally looked up at her daughter. Her eyes were weary from lack of sleep. She grabbed the sandwich and took a bite. "I feel like we are **this** close." She explained with a mouth full and held her thumb and forefinger just millimetres apart. "I just need to figure out this last bit." She explained, as she tapped a section of papers.*

Aurora grabbed the parchment in question. She studied the contents a moment before she handed it back to her mother. "One second." She stated as she turned to a tower of old texts. She scanned the spines and selected a century's old book near the bottom of the pile. She gingerly opened the book and flipped the pages to the section she had in mind. Emily watched her daughter with utter fascination. "Here," Aurora said as she passed the book. She pointed to a specific paragraph. "This has the same phrasing. I think the translation you have been working with is off."

"I was working off of Alister's method." Emily explained as she set her meal aside. "You don't think it's right?"

Aurora shook her head. "You yourself told me that no method is definite when it comes to translation. I think they may have written this in a local dialect instead of the widely used language." She pointed back to the book she had selected. "This one is in the dialect. Here you see the same phrase you're having trouble with. I think tunnel was mistranslated as chamber. You told me that the tunnels have a series of intricate designs in the walls. Is it possible that they hid the Artefact in a hidden wall in the tunnel?"

Emily's mouth dropped open in surprise. Once the realisation had set in, she burst into a bright smile and grabbed her daughter in a tight hug. "Who made you so bloody brilliant?" She exclaimed as she kissed her on the cheek.

Aurora's fingers were warm against the cool glass of the case. She never thought she would see one of her mother's discoveries here at the Academy. The Artefact was the intricate golden cylinder they had found on that dig site. It was delicately carved with ancient scripts. She felt her eyes start to well with tears at the memories. She sniffed and wiped the tears from her eyes.

"May I help you?" A woman's voice sounded from behind.

Aurora whipped around to see a woman in her early forties standing before her. She was shorter than Aurora in stature, but had an energy about her that made her seem much taller. Her porcelain skin was a stark contrast to her sleek black hair and dark almond eyes.

"I'm sorry," Aurora began. "I was just recalling something."

The professor before her studied her for a moment. "You have no reason to touch the cases." The professor stated sternly. She turned away from Aurora and took her place at her desk.

Aurora felt her stomach sink as she found herself a seat. She had managed to make a poor impression in two of her classes already. She blinked back the sting of tears and focused on getting out her books. It wasn't long before more students trickled into the class. Dae quickly spotted her and took a seat beside her. He glanced at her with a look of concern for a moment, but decided against asking at the moment.

"I am Professor Jung." The professor announced to the class. The room immediately hushed. "I will be conducting all classes dedicated to Artefacts, ancient and modern. This class, specifically, will cover Ancient Artefacts. It is important for us to first understand our past before we can comprehend our current tools."

Aurora breathed a small sigh of relief. She had some experience with modern Artefacts, but due to her mother's work, her expertise really was in the historical items.

"Can anyone tell me what any of the items on display are capable of?" Professor Jung asked as she indicated a hand to the display cases to the right.

Aurora paused a moment to see if any other students would offer any knowledge. The class murmured, but not a single hand was raised. With an air of hesitation, Aurora raised a hand to answer.

"Yes?" Professor Jung asked as she pointed to Aurora.

"The golden cylinder is a recording system." She answered. "It was developed to record audio and store in the device. When the symbols on the outer shell are input correctly, the device opens and gives the user access."

Professor Jung was impossible to read. Her face remained neutral and cool. "Correct." She finally replied.

"And what of this one?" She pointed to the Artefact to the cylinder's left.

Aurora stood slightly in her seat to get a better glance. After a moment she explained, "I believe those are an early pair of distance spectacles. They were worn by early Guardians to enhance their visual abilities to see up to 3 kilometres away." She paused for a moment. "I would have to take a closer look to see if it has night vision capabilities though."

Professor Jung remained silent for a moment. She pulled open a drawer from her personal desk. She approached Aurora's desk and revealed a necklace pendant in her hand. "What about this one?"

Aurora felt her pulse quicken. The pendant in Professor Jung's hand looked awfully similar to the one she currently wore around her neck. She absentmindedly brought a hand to her chest where her own necklace remained hidden under her blouse. "I'm not sure," She admitted.

"Hmm," Professor Jung replied as she furled her hand closed. She returned to her desk and shut the Artefact in the drawer with a snap.

"It seems as if we have at least one student who knows their material this year." Professor Jung announced. We will cover Artefacts such as these and more. We will discuss their abilities, their origins, as well as how they relate to Artefacts of present day. We will begin with chapter one."

***

Once class had released, Aurora found herself surrounded by curious peers. "Where did you learn all that?" Dae asked.

"My mother was an Artefact archeologist. She specialised in finding and researching ancient Artefacts." Aurora explained simply.

"That must of have been so exciting!" A young woman to her right exclaimed. She was a bubbly young woman with thick dark curls and soft brown eyes. "You must have been so many different places."

"We did travel around a lot." She admitted. They had never stayed in one location more than a year. There had been times they had only been on site for a few months at a time. Her mother had never been one to put down roots. "We should get over to History." She stated with a glance at her watch.

"Oh, you're right," the animated Mage realised as she gathered her books as well. She extended a hand. "I'm Leila, by the way."

Aurora shook her hand with a smile. "Aurora."

Leila joined Aurora and Dae on their walk to History. They climbed up the third floor for one of the lecture halls. A few Mages and Guardians had gotten there already. Astraea had arrived ahead of most. She noticed Aurora enter and gave her the quickest hint of a glare. She stood beside a tall Guardian, a hand on his back as if she owned him.

"Let's grab a seat." Leila suggested as she pointed to the rows. By the time they had selected an area to sit, Mari had entered the class. It looked as if her previous class had been rough. Mari's hair was dishevelled and her uniform was covered in flecks of mud. She scanned the room and found them quickly. She broke into a bright smile and ran over.

"Good sparring?" Dae asked her with a laugh.

Mari returned the laugh and ran a hand through her hair. "Felt good to scrap with someone other than Aelius."

The rest of the students took their seats as their professor walked into the lecture hall. He was the youngest of the professors that Aurora had seen, seeming to only be a few years older than them. He wore a pair of thick rimmed gold glasses that framed his long face well. He brushed his sandy blond hair from his eyes as he organised his texts and papers at his desk. He cleared his throat, "Welcome to Empirical History 101." He began. "I am Professor Andersen, and I will be covering the introduction of our great Empire's history."

Just like Professor Rossi, Professor Andersen wrote bullet points behind him on his chalk board. "We will delve into the formation of the Empire, its structure, and how its great gifts have supported our efforts to protect the realms. We must understand our history in order to thrive in the present. What we learn here will be instrumental in your studies of Demonic Creatures, and will be essential to you all in the field."

Chapter 5

Class broke for the day, and there was a collective energy shift. The students, Mages and Guardians alike, were clearly tired, but also excited for the first day to be at a close. Some students left class immediately, whereas others lingered in conversation. Aurora herself had tuned out to her newfound friends chatting away and was absorbed in thought. It was unfortunately obvious just how much she was lacking in Empirical history after Professor Andersen's lecture today. She knew she would have a lot of catching up to do.

"Aurora?" She finally heard. Aurora turned to Mari as she registered her name.

"Sorry?"

"We were just asking if you wanted to come with us for coffee?"

Aurora watched as Professor Andersen packed up his materials. "Another time?" She asked. "I need to speak with Professor Andersen."

Her friends said their farewells, and Aurora gathered her books. She hurried down the aisles to catch the professor before he headed out for the evening. "Excuse me, professor." She called out.

He looked up with a look of slight surprise. "Yes?"

"I was wondering if you might be able to recommend any textbooks, aside from our course book, on Empirical history."

Professor Andersen brightened at the question. "I'd be delighted!" He beamed. He spent the next several minutes listing off several texts and their significance. Aurora nearly regretted her choice in asking, but also knew that she needed to make sure she didn't fall behind. She had already made a poor impression in two of her classes. She did not need to add a third. "Oh! That is likely enough." He concluded as he realised he had been on a several minute monologue.

Aurora thanked him for his time and headed straight for the library. She had noted a total of ten different texts. She doubted she would have time for them all any time soon, but it never hurt to get started on a couple.

Aurora reached the first floor where Mari had pointed out the library. She entered the grand doors and was immediately met with a sense of pure tranquility. She breathed a sigh of relief. Books had always been a sanctuary for her. There was nothing like the smell of an book. She absorbed it all. The high ceilings of the library allowed for staggeringly tall bookshelves. The rows and rows of shelves seemed endless. Aurora smiled to herself, eager to explore it all.

She approached the librarian's desk and quickly received guidance on where to begin. She held the note the librarian scrawled for her tight and started down the aisles. The history section wasn't far from the doors, a mere several rows deep. She scanned the shelves and found her first two texts quickly. The third, she realised, was just a few centimetres out of reach. She stretched to her tip toes to try and reach, but still fell short.

A hand reached over on her right to grab the book. She held her breath and scaled back at the sudden invasion of personal space. She turned towards the culprit. It was the Guardian from her first day that seemed to be claimed by Astraea. He stared down at her with an unreadable expression on his face. "Here," He stated simply as he handed her the text.

He dropped the text into her extended arms. "Thank you." She mustered, unsure of what tone to take with him.

"You might need this one too." He offered another text to her. She checked the title on the cover and noted that it was one of the others on her list from Professor Andersen. As she grabbed it from him she heard a voice call out.

"Victor!"

Aurora felt her entire body tense, and noticed the Guardian in front of her do the same. A grimace crossed his face for a brief moment before he sighed. Astraea called out the name again. The Guardian nodded to Aurora before leaving the aisle. She watched him head out towards the library entrance. Astraea waited for the Guardian with hands planted firmly on her hips. She beamed up at him as he obeyed her call. She peered around his broad shoulders as she fixed his tie. She glared as her eyes met Aurora's.

Aurora receded back into the aisle, safe from Astraea's sneers. Clearly, she would do best to avoid Victor in future. She had no need to get mixed up in whatever claim Astraea had on him. She waited a moment before heading to the check out desk, not wanting to run into the pair again. She checked out her texts and made her way back to her room to drop off her books.

When she got to her room, she noticed Mari waiting patiently on the edge of her bed. She shot to her feet, elated that Aurora had finally gotten back. She was bouncing with excitement over something. Aurora let the door shut behind her and lock with a click.

"Aurora!" She exclaimed, excited to be able to share her good news. "Dae asked me to be his partner!"

Aurora placed her history books down on the nearby chair. "You look really happy about that." Aurora observed with a smile.

"I am." Mari admitted with a flush of her cheeks. "I was really hoping he would ask, but didn't want to presume he would."

"Does he know you like him?" Aurora pried.

Mari seemed to debate her answer for a moment. "I'm not sure." She finally admitted. "We've known each other forever. I haven't wanted to push anything and lose his friendship."

Aurora wasn't sure what words would be best. She could push her to make a move, but she didn't know either one well enough. Instead she grabbed her new friend's hand and gave her a small smile. "I'm sure you will both figure it out."

Mari gave her a smile and squeezed her hand in return. "Now we just need to figure you out!" She retorted.

***

The following days passed with more and more ease. It wasn't long before Aurora found herself in a comfortable groove. She created a decent schedule, and even started discovering the best routes from class to class. Before she realised, a week had passed.

Aurora's stomach was a bundle of nerves. This morning she would be pact bonded with a classmate. She had been so focused on her studies and correcting her impression on her professors, that she had completely neglected finding a partner. She knew in the back of her mind that she could easily take whoever was leftover at the end of class, but she also didn't want to be someone's last option. She had met a few of the Guardians thanks to Mari, but hadn't had the opportunity to get to speak to any of them beyond basic introductions.

She chewed her bottom lip as she finalised getting ready that morning. She knew most of her classmates were buzzing with excitement for the day. Mari had definitely been one of them, and had even skipped her early morning training. She lingered while Aurora finished pinning up her hair. "I can't *wait* to get to class." She admitted with glee. "You ready to go get a bite before we head up?"

Aurora nodded, although she knew that she would only be able to stomach a tea. They made their way to the Dining Hall for a quick breakfast. Many of the students were in a rush that morning, and had formed a cluster around the lecture hall door. Aurora stood on her toes to see why the students had formed a crowd. Normally the doors were left open, but today they seemed to be locked. Finally, after what felt like ages, the doors opened. The Guardian Stein welcomed the students in with an open arm, as they poured in.

Aurora heard an audible gasp from one of the first students in. She leaned forward to see what had sparked the reaction. The platform on which the professors had been giving their lectures had been painted ornately in a series of symbols. Aurora could not seem to take her eyes off of it, even as she climbed the stairs to her seat. As she climbed, she could see the design even better. The symbols worked together to form a massive circle that took up most of the floor. She recognised several of the patterns from her work and research with her mother.

"As you can see," Guardian Stein began, "today is trial Pact Formation day."

"This circle is where you will form your trial pact for the year. A similar circle will be drawn to break your pact at the end of the year." Mage Stein elaborated. "Each pair will step into the centre of the circle. Professor Stein and I will activate the circle, and you will seal the pact."

"We will call you up by Mage. You will come down as we call your name."

"Today may be an overwhelming day for many of you. All other classes are suspended for the day in order to become better adjusted to your new bond."

The class was alive with murmurs, whispers, and the occasional giggle. Aurora felt a reassuring hand on her shoulder. She turned to Mari and gave her a small smile.

"Dae Choi." The Mage Stein called out.

Dae stood to his feet and stole a glance at Mari before he announced, "Amaris Cirillo." Mari stood up with a slight flush in her cheeks. The pair headed down the stairs and got themselves settled into the centre of the pact circle. Each professor Stein stood behind their respective student. Within a moment, the pact circle began to glow. A couple of gasps could be heard at the sight.

"The circle is active. You are good to seal the pact." Mage Stein explained.

Dae nervously stepped closer to Mari. The pair were matched in height and came eye to eye. Mari stood frozen in place; her hands fidgeted nervously in front of her. In the moment, Dae decided to be bold. He brought a hand to her cheek and kissed her softly. The glow of the pact circle brightened at that moment before finally turning off. Dae stepped back and gave Mari an embarrassed smile. Mari, however, positively beamed at him.

A round of applause rang out for the pair. They returned to their seats, and Professor Stein called out the next name. "Elena Turner."

One of Astraea's followers stood up, and Killian called out his name in response. The pair headed down to the circle for their turn. They sealed their pact with a kiss on the cheek, and resumed their seats. Aurora scanned the room. She knew very well that the professors could call her name any moment. She couldn't very well say that she knew any of the Guardians well enough to rope into being her partner for the year.

"Aurora Thomas." Professor Stein called out.

Aurora felt her pulse race. She slowly stood to her feet as she tried to figure out the best way to pass her turn. As she hesitated to find the words she heard a voice call out behind her...

Chapter 6

His voice had cut through the class clearly. "Aelius Cirillo." He stood up a few rows behind her, an unreadable expression on her face.

She turned to Mari and gave her a questioning look. She looked just as confused as she was, shrugging in response. "I mean...you could do worse."

She looked back up at him as he started down towards her. He paused as he reached her row, extending a hand to her. She gave him a small smile and accepted it, her hand feeling tiny in comparison to his. He let her go as soon as she was down safely and walked a step behind her. She wondered if Mari had put him up to this. She had barely spoken to him, yet here was was volunteering to be bonded to her for the school year. From what she had heard, Aelius was top of his class and eyed as *the* Guardian to recruit upon graduation. Why would he risk his grades and training on an unknown like her?

She reached the platform and took a deep breath. Worrying and wondering would do her no good at the moment. She needed to focus on the present and ask questions afterwards. She climbed the steps of the platform and walked towards Mage Stein, settling herself on her spot on the pact circle. Her eyes trailed along the sigils that had been meticulously painted on the floor. She knew the rough meaning of most, but some were beyond her. *I share my power. I share my strength. I bind myself to you.* Her heart quickened as she turned to Aelius before her. It suddenly felt very real.

The Steins activated the circle, the floor suddenly radiating a bright white light. She audibly gasped as she felt the rush of power that flooded her veins. The power that coursed through her was wild and erratic, making her feel as if she was on fire. Aelius stepped closer to her and brought a hand to her chin. As he stood before her, she really noticed just how much taller than her he was. She closed her eyes for the seal bond as he leaned in. He pulled her chin to him, only to leave his kiss on her forehead. A small part of her felt a shred of confusion and disappointment, almost certain that he had intended to kiss her on the lips. Perhaps it was for the better that he hadn't. The instant his lips touched her skin, the power snapped into place and settled. Instead of a raging wake, it flowed as a steady river. The flow itself pulled across from her: Aelius.

A light clap rang through the class at another pact formed. She turned to see her classmates applauding politely. Her eyes lingered on Leila, however. Angry tears stung her eyes as she clapped rather unhappily. She bit her lip as she stepped down from the platform. She had a fair wager who was meant to bond with Aelius instead of her. He trailed closely behind her as she climbed the steps back up to her seat. She sat herself back down beside Mari and leaned in. "Did I just make a mess of things with Leila?" She whispered.

Mari made a non committal sound in response. "Hard to say. It's not like he told me who he was planning on bonding with."

She turned to check Aelius back in his seat. She could feel the pulse of his power behind her. His face was calm and stoic, but the sheer heat of raw power that radiated from him was a little overwhelming. How he could appear so calm when this is what he felt like was beyond her.

Class continued until the last pair sealed their bond. A total of fifteen bonds took just under two hours to perform. Guardian Stein rushed to his wife's side as she staggered slightly from the exertion. She assured him she was fine, but just a little spent. The professors used a special Artefact filled with deposited Spirit, but it still took a lot of magic to fuel the pact formations. It was no wonder she was exhausted. She thanked both professors before leaving class. Mage Stein gave her a small smile and a nod in response before they headed out on their way. Guardian Stein cradled his wife's arm and fussed over her as they walked out slowly.

As she watched her professors leave, she realised that she had her own bond to be concerned with. She closed her eyes in focus and could feel him nearby. It was surreal to be able to feel someone through an intangible source. She knew that with training she would be able to feel his physical state as well as the emotional. In the short time she had come to know him, Aelius had seemed quite serious. She wondered if being bonded to him would reveal more beneath the surface.

She followed the flow of classmates heading out into the main hall, wondering what exactly she was supposed to do with the rest of her day. Other classes had been canceled in order to focus on getting used to having a bond in place. It stood to reason that it would make sense to spend the time with her brand new Guardian.

As if the sheer consideration of it was enough to summon him, Aelius stepped out of the lecture hall door. She gave her new Guardian a small smile as he approached her. "Thank you." She said simply.

A small smile flashed across his face. "You're welcome."

Mari approached them from behind and she slung an arm over her shoulder. "You guys should go have some fun and explore the grounds." She started, her eyes darting to Dae beside her. "In fact, a few hours might be a good idea."

"Mari!" Dae exclaimed, his face completely crimson.

"Gross..." Aelius muttered barely audible. Her own body felt like it shuddered at the comment.

Aurora brought a hand to her mouth to stop herself laughing out loud. She appreciated the warning. Walking in on her roommate was definitely something she wanted to avoid. "I'll make sure I'm scarce." She hooked her arm in the crook of Aelius' elbow, not bothering to wait for his response. "Let's go. I'm sure we can find something to do."

Aelius responded with a slight sigh and lead the way. She could hear Mari laugh in response and tease Dae about the embarrassment. "You bonded me, and *just* confessed how you feel about me..." She put distance between them to avoid hearing something intimate. Mari would undoubtedly fill her in later.

As she left the lecture hall behind, she realised just how long Aelius' legs were. He stormed off down the hall to put distance between himself and his sister, but his stride was much larger than her own. She quickened her pace to keep up, not having the heart to ask him to slow down. It took him a moment, but he clued in to her speed and slowed his pace. They walked leisurely through the hall in silence. She took in the details around her from paintings, hangings, and even some graduating class photos. She turned to check the other side and caught Aelius looking down at her. He paused a moment, "Is there anything you haven't seen yet?" He asked. "Anything you have been meaning to, I mean."

She mulled it over. "I know that there is the town nearby, but haven't been yet. Mari mentioned going sometime soon to check things out. I've seen most of the campus, but I'm sure there's still a lot I don't know. We don't really have to do anything though. I'm honestly just happy being in the library or something." She knew she was rambling, feeling rather awkward and afraid to say the wrong thing. It was odd having to take someone else's wants and needs into so much consideration.

"It's up to you." He responded calmly. "Part of us doing well is strengthening the bond. We do that by building a connection and getting to know one another."

She recalled the theory they had gone over in class last week. Researchers stated that the strongest bonds were forged by strong emotional connections. Pacts were formed under a range of relationships spanning from friends, to family, to lovers. All data pointed to the strongest pacts were formed with those who were strongly emotionally bonded. "We might be at a bit of a disadvantage with that." She half muttered to herself. She swore she saw him nod slightly at the comment. Guardian hearing was quite sensitive she recalled. "I have an idea..."

She guided Aelius towards the common room. It was fairly quiet due to classes being in session, but there were a couple of other students scattered through the room. She scanned a bookcase along one of the walls, hoping to find what she needed. She could feel Aelius watching her while she searched, wondering what she could possibly be looking for.

"Aha!" She exclaimed, grabbing a packet of cards. She turned to him with a smile. "Let's grab a table."

He chose a table by the window, pulling a chair out for her. She paused a moment, taken aback by the simple gesture. She took the seat and slid herself in as he seated himself across from her. She slid the cards out of their box and clacked them against the table to ensure they were flush. "You play Go Fish?" She asked.

He arched a brow at her, considering the card name, before it clicked. "Oh! You mean Hunt or Steal."

She cocked her head to the side slightly at the correction. "I'm sorry?"

He let out a soft chuckle as he gently took the cards from her hand and started to shuffle. "We grew up calling it Hunt or Steal, but I heard that Middlings call it Go Fish. Not sure what the game has to do with fishing, but it's more or less the same thing."

She listened and watched as his hands made quick work of shuffling and dealing. Once they each had their cards, he set the remainder in between them. She picked up her cards, carefully fanning them in front of her. "Hunt or Steal it is then." She replied with a slight laugh. "You make a pair, you get to ask a question. Sound good?"

He eyed her a moment before giving her a small smile. "Sounds good. After you." He replied as he scooped up his cards.

She checked her hand, setting aside a pair of twos. She looked at her remaining cards, and peered up at Aelius. His face was unreadable, but being bonded to him would perhaps give away some hints. "Do you have any queens?" She asked.

He met her gaze and gave a shake of his head. "Go hunt."

She picked up a card, revealing a Jack. Nothing for her to do. It was his turn. He set down two pairs of cards on the table and looked back at his hand. "Do you have any Jacks?"

She tsked as she slipped her new card out and handed it across the table. He set the pair down, now able to ask the first question. He pondered a moment before deciding. "Do you have any siblings?"

She eased a little, thankful that he had chosen to start with something simple and innocent. There had been a brief concern of him asking something vulnerable or difficult off the bat, but he hadn't. "I'm afraid not. I'm an only child." She admitted.

He gave a nod in response, before taking his next turn. "Do you have any tens?"

She shook her head. "Go hunting." She paused a moment for him to collect his new card. "Do you have any Kings?"

He arched a brow at her as he slid out a card and passed it across the table. She smiled in triumph and set the pair down. It was her turn to ask. "What is your favourite pass time?"

He sighed as he pondered the question. She felt a muddled mixture of emotions through the bond, not quite able to place what they were. She wondered how long it would take to discern them better. "Cooking." He finally stated.

She was surprised. Part of her expected him to declare training or something sports based on his ranking in the Academy. Everyone went on about how he was the top Guardian and how often he was seen practicing. "What do you like to cook?" She asked.

He set his cards down and gave her a hint of a smirk. "A question a pair, I thought." He commented. He was right.

She leaned back in her chair, tucking her cards close to her chest. "I see how it is." She responded with a teasing tone. "Do you have any fours?"

He shook his head. "Go hunting."

She grabbed another card, placing it with her others. He picked his cards back up. "Any sixes?" He sighed as he pulled a six out of his hand and passed it to her. She placed the pair down in front of her. "What's the best book you've ever read?"

He set his cards down and leaned back in his chair. He mulled the question over, his arms crossed at his chest. "I'm not much of a reader, to be honest." He confessed. She felt a twinge of something that felt like embarrassment through the bond. His face seemed unbothered, but the bond said otherwise. "There is a book about Guardian kinesiology and movement mechanics that I have read a few times over, though."

She fought the urge to smile at his reaction. He seemed ever so slightly on edge, as if him not being a reader would make her think poorly of him. "Everyone has different interests. There's no wrong answer, you know."

He relaxed ever so slightly in his seat, and she felt the twinge of embarrassment ebb away. She turned back to her cards, losing another round and having to pick up.

They bantered questions back and forth, getting to know one another little by little. It wasn't long before they had were down to the last pair. "Why did you pair with me?" She asked. She had been debating whether or not she would ask it, but she figured she would rather regret what she did over what she didn't.

He sat back, mulling over the words to use. As she stared into his eyes, she noticed the flecks of gold mixed in with the olive green. "You're good to Amaris, and I had heard how you weave your Magic. Anyone good enough to get into the Academy this late, has to be someone special." He explained.

The mix of emotions that swirled through the bond seemed to be honest. She had to appreciate that her relationship and treatment of Mari was the first point he made. The siblings could not seem more different. It was sweet that he held her in such high regard. "Fair enough." She finally replied. "I hope I don't disappoint." She added with a small smirk.

Chapter 7

Early on Mari had declared that she wanted to spar with her. Mari found it fascinating that she could dual weave naturally and was dying to see it first hand. The idea of training with Aurora and seeing what she was capable had become a top goal of hers. Aurora had finally agreed, knowing that physical training would be a good idea if she truly was to become a Mage. She couldn't rely on her magic alone to protect her.

The early morning air was crisp on her cheeks as she followed Mari out to the training arena. She had put on her breeches that morning, knowing that Mari wasn't likely to go easy on her. The campus was beautiful in the early morning dawn. Birds sang out from the trees and a few squirrels darted around foraging for the upcoming winter. Several Guardians ran past in a group, conducting their own morning training session. They gave Mari a wave as they passed, picking up the pace as they hit a bend in the path.

They continued towards the back corner of the campus grounds. Mari had brought her there on her first day: the Guardian's training arena. The sparring arena was empty, reserved for them at this hour. A Guardian she didn't know, likely a second year, worked through an obstacle course. She winced as she saw him fall from a height of twenty or so feet. He hopped to his feet, checking around to see if there were any witnesses before getting back to it.

She followed Mari up onto the arena, feeling quite exposed in that moment. "Now, we should really figure out where you are starting out. Show me what you've got." She stated, beckoning her over.

She stared at her awkwardly a moment. Did she really want her to just come at her and attack? She took a deep breath and decided to go for it. She started at her in a jog, throwing out a punch with her right fist. Mari took a simple step back, dodging her swing with ease. Aurora realised she had missed all too late, her body falling over with momentum. Mari grabbed her at the wrist and spun her around, pinning her arm behind her back. She winced in pain for a moment, before she was released.

"Well..." Mari stated.

"I never claimed to have any sort of skills with fighting." She stated, laughing at herself ever so slightly. "Magic makes sense. But this..."

"Ahhh, I'll teach you. Half of it is correct form." Mari dismissed. "Besides, you find a way to combine physical combat and magic, and you'll be terrifying."

She laughed, knowing that there was a touch of teasing in her tone, but she knew that Mari also had a point. Mari ran through several drills with her, seeing where her skills were. Her dexterity and flexibility were pretty good, but her stamina and strength needed work. After a half hour of drill after drill, she was knackered. It was then that she felt him approach. She felt him through the bond first, but the sound of his boots crunching through the dry grass announced him a moment afterwards. She turned over her shoulder, seeing him prepped in his training uniform. He rolled his sleeves up to the elbow, the chill of the early morning air not having the same effect on him as it did her.

"What are we up to?" He asked, trying to hide the curiosity in his eyes. She was sat on the ground, recuperating after a particularly exhausting drill.

Mari passed her a bottle of water. "We're running through some drills to see what Ari needs to work on."

"Oh?" He asked, arching a brow at her.

"She's going to make me terrifying." Aurora chimed in, taking a sip of the cool water.

Aelius snorted, surprised that she had made him laugh. "And how are we possibly going to do that?" He asked, trying to suppress a laugh.

"We train her. Strengthen her up and teach her how to fight. Couple that with her magic, and she'll be the best Mage the Academy has seen in a century."

"We?" He remarked, staring at her, not his sister.

"Unless you have something better to do." She shrugged, hiding the smirk on her face behind a sip of water.

He broke out into a laugh, low and hearty. "Oh, Aurora I don't think you quite know what you've gotten yourself into."

***

She knew her entire body was going to ache. Fiercely. The Cirillo twins were something else. She knew that Aelius had been ranked the top of his class, and it was certainly for a reason. They had her running drill after drill, technique after technique, until she had been ready to drop. Her limits must have read through the bond, because it was Aelius who finally insisted they stop for the day.

She let the pair continue on their way, knowing that her level of training was nothing compared to what they would normally do. She felt drenched in sweat, despite the chill in the air. A shower and breakfast was exactly what she needed, in that order.

She stepped through the doors, catching sight of a few others starting their morning. Liam and Eli, a pair of Mages from her year stood off the side. Eli was a flood of tears, inconsolable as he ranted off to his partner. "It's torture, Liam!" He cried, trying to turn away from him.

"I know it's not ideal—"

"You have *no* idea!" Eli snapped, turning back to him. "There is nothing redeemable about that woman."

Liam grabbed him into a hug, leaning his chin on top of his head, despite Eli's protests. He settled after a moment, wrapping his arms around his waist. "It'll be okay, babe. It's just for the year. We tough it out for the year, and if you *still* can't make it work, we'll switch, okay?"

Eli leaned back, looking up at him. "You promise?" He sniffed, tears in his eyes.

Liam leaned in, planting a gentle kiss on his forehead. "I promise. Lily and I discussed it and—"

"You discussed it with *her* before you talked to me about it?" He demanded, pushing back against his chest. "I'm your boyfriend. Not *her*."

"Baby, it's not like that." Liam protested, trying to pull Eli back into them. To regain the semblance of peace they had had just a moment ago. "Mackenzie is having a hard time too. Lily brought it up and we just ended up talking about it. We both want what's best for everyone."

Eli glowered at him, arms crossed at his chest. "Why don't you two just figure it all out for us then and let us children know what you decide. You're clearly better at making decisions for us..." He spat, storming off outside.

Aurora stepped aside, frozen in the door frame at walking in on the lover's spat. It mustn't have been easy for them having to bond with other people. In a simple world, one would have been born a Guardian to pair with. She looked off to the side, trying to make it less obvious that she had just overhead everything.

She turned back, finally feeling as if she were okay to proceed to the common room. She came face to face with a dejected Liam, his head hung low.

"Hey, Liam..." She greeted feeling every ounce of awkwardness.

He looked up, letting out a loaded sigh. "Hey Aurora." He replied with a small wave. "You heard everything, huh?"

"Well..." She started, unsure what the proper answer would be. "Yeah, sorry." She answered, ultimately deciding it was better to be honest.

He gave her a forced side smile. "Yeah, well it's hard to miss something like that when you have it out in public. Sorry to involve you." He apologised.

She sighed as her shoulders sunk ever so slightly. "Liam, I don't imagine it's an easy thing to navigate. It sounds like it's really hard on Eli. I'm sorry."

"Yeah we were hoping that things would be...well easier. Lily and I get on great, but Mackenzie and him are...well like oil and water. I...I have no idea how we're going to last the year." He admitted, running a hand through his hair.

"Have you talked to the Steins at all?" She asked cautiously. He wasn't asking for an answer, but she felt bad not at least trying to help.

Liam's brow raised, a thought he hadn't considered. "No...that's not a bad idea actually." He stated, almost as if thinking out loud. "They might be able to suggest something."

"I hope they can." She added, taking a step forward. "I'm sure they have hours open today. I'll catch you later? I'm just on my way to..."

"Of course, of course." Liam said in a rush. He started on his way after Eli. "Got to go catch him." He explained, breaking into a jog towards the grounds where Eli had gone.

She started back towards her room, hoping that they could figure it out between the four of them. She was suddenly all the more thankful for the easy nature of Aelius. There was Leila's upset to handle, but it wasn't as if she had gotten in the way of an actual relationship. She wondered if she would be able to talk things out with her soon. She felt like they had really been on their way to building a friendship before all of the bonding business. Maybe Edwyn would be able to put a word in for her.

As she rounded the corner into the common room, she found Dae making himself a tea. He perked up as he registered her, giving her a wave. "Morning!" He called out, making his way over to one of the tables. "How was training?" She joined him at the table and audibly groaned in place of words. He chuckled, taking a sip of his tea. "Yeah that sounds about right."

"They're going to kill me. They decided that they are going to train me. *Together.* I think Mari alone is enough. But the pair of them? Very well might be the death of me." She ranted.

"Ah they mean well." Dae assured her. "Take it as a compliment. They only train the people they like. It's...like an expression of love in their family."

"Didn't think of it that way." She commented, giving her legs a stretch. "Maybe they can like me just a little less." She added with a chuckle.

"Hey, speaking of training," He added. "Does your offer for dual weaving still apply?"

"Of course!" She stated, perking up at the comment. "Any time you want."

"I'm sorry, did I hear that correctly?" A voice called out beside them. Aurora turned to her left, seeing a pair of second years seated together on the other end of the long table. The one who spoke was the taller of the two, her dark hair swept up in a simple bun, bangs hanging over her rounded eyes.

"Maybe?" Aurora asked, not sure what the second year was referencing.

"You're first years." She stated disapprovingly. "You have *no* business messing around with dual weaving. Do you have any idea what you're putting yourself at risk for?"

Her friend opened her mouth to speak, but stopped herself. She timidly put a hand on her hand. "Georgia, it's okay, you don't need to—"

"Of *course* I need to!" She snapped. She turned back to Aurora, pointing a finger at her. "It is completely reckless to be experimenting with magic you can't possibly understand. You don't even *think* of touching magic like that until you're third years."

Aurora sat up in her seat, lifting her chin ever so slightly. This was beyond an older student being concerned for naive juniors. This was pure judgement and arrogance. "I would suggest you listen to your friend, Georgia. My friend and I were having a conversation. We were minding our own business. We did not invite your opinion on the matter."

Georgia's mouth dropped open at Aurora's words. She knew that there was an unspoken hierarchy within the Academy - a 'listen to your elders' mentality of sorts. Different years tended to keep to their own, so it didn't come up much, but for Aurora to retort like that could have been seen as a massive insult. She rose to her feet, storming over to Aurora's side. "What did you just say to me?" She seethed.

Aurora turned her body, her face remaining cool and unaffected. She did her best to mimic Aelius in that moment. "We were minding our own business. We did *not* invite your opinion on the matter." She repeated icily.

Georgia leaned into her, her hand resting on the table, her face inches from hers. "It becomes my business when stupid first years are messing around with magic they don't understand. Do you have any idea how many students are burning themselves out these days?" She demanded. "Every Mage that burns themselves out makes it harder on the ones that *do* make it."

Aurora stared up at her defiantly. "What makes you think I don't know what I'm doing?" She asked cooly. "You don't know me. You have no idea who I am or what I can do. What makes you think that you know any better than I do?"

Georgia stood back, her arms crossed beneath her chest. "Show me then." She stated. "If you're *so* confident in your abilities, show me *right now* what you claim to be so versed in."

She shot Dae a quick look, checking that he was alright before standing to her feet. "Let's head outside then." She answered.

By the time they stepped outside, a small group had gathered to watch. Even more stood inside, wanting to observe from the warmth of indoors.

"What do you want to see?" She asked simply, Georgia standing opposite of her.

The second year faltered a moment, suddenly unsure of what she should request. She glanced at her friend that had been with her, who gave a simple shrug. She sighed, collecting herself, as she turned back to Aurora. "Whatever is fine." She answered in a dismissive tone.

Aurora fought the urge to roll her eyes as she held a palm open. She conjured a small ball of fire in her hand. "You start with some fire," She explained, starting off simple enough. "and you add in weaves of air." She continued, starting to feed the fire. It grew in intensity, the colour changing from a brilliant red into a white hot blue. She moved her hands, guiding the flame into a thin tunnel of fire. Georgia jumped, trying her best to make herself smaller and cling to her friend.

Aurora fought the chuckle that tried to escape at the second years' reactions. "You're alright." She assured them, guiding the trail of fire further from them. The air magic she used fuelled the fire in intensity, but also gave her a better control of its direction. She raised her hands up, spinning the fire into loops and patterns. It was mostly for show, but she could have easily turned it into something nefarious had she wanted to.

After a minute of demonstration, she closed her fists, extinguishing the flames. She turned back to Georgia, a sour look on her face. "Would you like another example?" She asked.

Georgia simply huffed and stomped off with her friend back inside. It was then that she noticed Mari and Aelius on their return from their training. He arched a brow at her, wondering about the crowd that had gathered. "Was all that you?" He asked, a note of impression in his voice.

She rubbed the back of her neck, not expecting him to see her little demonstration. "Well..."

"That was *so* cool, Ari!" Mari chimed in. "You *have* to show Dae how to do that."

She laughed. "Thanks, Mar. A second year was trying to lecture me on not knowing what I was doing. She wanted proof."

Aelius made a discerning sound as he looked at her. "Just be careful. Best not to piss off the upper years." He cautioned.

Chapter 8

It wasn't long before the weekend was upon them. Mari had been insistent on taking her into Vilcas to help her shop for a very much over due Imperial wardrobe. She needed her own set of clothes aside from her uniforms, and

Mari apparently had an in with the best seamstress in town. She put on the set that Mari had lent her on her first day. She was thankful to borrow from her, but it would be far better to have something of her own. She had some currency in both Middling and Empirical funds, but she would have to keep an eye on her spending. It would be an expensive day, but it was a necessary one. She wanted to feel like she belonged instead of borrowing to fit in.

A quick rap on the door sounded as Dae arrived to pick them up. As soon as Mari had mentioned their plans, the boys had been keen on the idea of joining them. They would break away for their own errands, but the walk down and some lunch would be together. He broke out into a bright smile as he saw Mari. She leaned in, giving him a kiss. "Morning."

He wrapped his hand in hers as they left towards the main hall. Aurora followed a few steps behind, not wanting to invade their little bubble. It was wonderful to see them both so happy, but she couldn't help but feel like a third wheel half of the time.

As they reached the main hall, she could see Aelius and Edwyn waiting by the door. Both wore breeches similar to their uniforms and brown laced boots. Edwyn chose a medium weight jacket, silver buttons lining the lapel. Aelius, in contrast, had a simple navy cloak that draped over his broad shoulders. The fall chill was enough to warrant a few extra layers, especially when they would be outside so much. She grabbed her own cloak closed, realising just how similar hers was to Aelius'. She wondered if it was a side effect of the pact bond, or mere coincidence.

"Is Leila not coming?" Mari asked, checking around to find any hint of her. Edwyn had stepped up and bonded with her a few rounds after Aelius had volunteered to be her Guardian. They seemed well suited all considering, but it had been clear who her heart had been set on.

He sighed, shoving his hands in his jacket pocket. "She said she might meet up with us later. She's out with the girls. She's still a little, well…"

"Let's go." Aelius grumbled, not wanting to discuss the matter.

Mari shook her head and headed out, Dae in beside her. Aurora ended up following, Edwyn joining closely at her side. They descended the stairs and out the doors, a brisk breeze greeting them.

"How are you finding the Academy so far, Aurora?" Edwyn asked as they walked through the grounds.

"I feel like I'm starting to settle in." She admitted. "I really like my classes, and things are fairly challenging in a good way. It's just…"

He tilted his head, unsure if she was going to complete her thought. "What?"

She chewed her bottom lip, unsure of how to put it politely. "I knew the course work would be hard. It's a good level of difficult. I like a challenge. It's…well it's the personal navigating that's the biggest challenge." She confessed.

He listened, processing her words as they walked. "Leila?" He asked, understanding a big part of what she was getting at.

"Well, that's part of it, yeah." She admitted. "But not all of it. I don't…fit."

He nodded slightly. "You walked into a group that has been together since childhood. It's a…weird tight knit group here at the Academy. It's not like other schools."

"I'm definitely coming to understand that more and more." She acknowledged.

It wasn't long before they passed through the Academy's main gate. She had passed through before when she first arrived, but it was still fascinating to her. Portals and gates were still fairly new experience for her. Her mother had kept to Middling means of travel during their adventures, relying on vehicles or going on foot. Light shimmered around them as they walked through the giant arch that protected the grounds. There was supposed to be no sensation to the gate itself, but she still felt a chill go down her spine as she walked through.

As she walked through, she could see the small town below. The Academy stood about a fifteen minute walk north of the town. A slight hill gave them a perfect view of the collection of buildings and streets below. Mari slowed to be able to explain the details to her better. "There are several districts depending on where you want to go." She explained, pointing to different areas of town as they went. "Over there is the textile district. We'll head there first to look at some of the seamstresses. Over there is the food district where we can get some lunch later. There are some great pubs if we want. Oh and over there is where they have some of the book shops. I asked around and got advice on the best shop to take you to after we're done."

She loved listening to the way Mari spoke sometimes. She was so animated and passionate, even about the most simple things. She had such a warmth to her that simply made her feel at ease. "Thanks, Mar." She appreciated, linking her arm in the crook of her elbow.

Mari chuckled and leaned her head against Aurora's. Part of her felt a little guilty stealing her away from Dae, but he didn't seem to mind.

The worn path from Vilcas to the Academy eventually turned into cobblestone roads. Townsfolk and students lined the streets, each going about their own business for the morning. It was easy to see who was a local over a student from the Academy. The navy blues of the Academy were a stark contrast against the hues of cream to brown that the locals wore. Occasionally, a child in pale blue could be seen running about, a student from one of the base schools.

She took it all in, trying not to openly gawk. She let herself be guided and pulled by Mari as she took in the various styles of buildings. Several smaller shops with some apartment homes over top were seen as they first entered the town. Most of the homes tended to be on the edge of town, with more and more shops gathered as they would go further in.

"We're going to leave you to it, Mar." Dae explained as he leaned in for a quick kiss goodbye. "We'll meet you at the Sun and Scribe at one?"

"Sounds great." She replied as she leaned in for a second kiss.

The others gave them a wave before heading off in the other direction. She felt a little bad to divide the group, but appreciated it just being Mari to join her for shopping. She wasn't quite sure how comfortable she would have been trying on and purchasing things with such a large group.

"Now," Mari began. "I'm going to take you to my favourite shop. My mom has known her for years and she always has the best selection. She'll make something custom for you if you need as well."

She let herself be pulled along, listening to details that Mari rang out as they toured the town. It was if she had her own personal tour guide as they twisted and turned down the streets. She stopped a moment, a crash sounding out from behind them. It was sudden, but the sounds of a scuffle nearby rang out in a side street. Just as she registered one, a second clashed out from another street over. She turned to give Mari a look of confusion, only for her to shrug. It was then that she saw Aelius round the corner, an unhappy look on his face.

"What're you doing here?" Mari asked, a hint of annoyance in her tone.

He glared behind her, making sure to close the distance between them. "Two creeps have been following you for several blocks now. They were looking to corner the pair of you the next street over. Are you *that* oblivious, Amaris?" He asked her in disbelief.

Mari squinted her eyes at him, hating it whenever he used her full name. "You worry too much."

Aelius closed his eyes a moment and took a deep breath. "And you worry too little."

"I guess you're following us then?" She asked as she started back on her way to the shop.

Aurora glanced over at him, feeling the agitation through the bond. It was possible that he was being over protective, but if what he said was true, then he had saved them from trouble. She had every faith that Mari would have been able to handle a couple of cowards, but for him to look out for them was also reassuring.

It wasn't long before they arrived at a well sized shop with several mannequins in the window. A figure with a beautiful high waisted skirt in dark brown caught her eye. The skirt flowed beautifully from the small waist and flared at the bottom. It felt elegant and refined, if not a little mature for what she needed. Another on the side wore a pair of high waisted billowing dress pants in navy. An intricately embroidered vest was paired with it, making it look all the more feminine in its design. Mari opened the door, a bell ringing out overhead to announce their arrival.

A beautiful woman in her forties came out from the back at the sound of the bell. She wore a design similar to those in the window, looking refined and elegant as she approached the shop counter. "Miss Cirillo!" She exclaimed, clasping her hands together.

"Hey Bella." Mari greeted cheerily. "My friend here is looking for a few options in navy. Would you be able to help her out?"

"Anything for you and your mother." She responded fondly as she stepped out from behind the desk.

Aelius stood by the door, his arms crossed at his chest, looking rather out of place in the shop as Mari started flipping through options hanging on a rack along the wall.

Bella stepped closer, examining Aurora as she circled her. "I'll pull a few options. Go wait for me in the dressing room, dear." She explained as she pointed toward a curtained area in the back.

She followed her orders, taking off her cloak as she stepped in the dressing room. After a few minutes, Bella returned with several options. "I pulled a few simple pieces for you, and a few that your boyfriend will enjoy as well." She commented with a twinkle in her eye.

Aurora opened her mouth to protest, but she was gone before she could object. She could hear Mari snicker from outside. She just hoped that Aelius hadn't heard it as well.

She eyed what the owner had brought her. She undressed and put on one of the first selections. She started with a simple white blouse with wide sleeves and a billowing skirt in navy. She fastened the button at her waist before overlaying the under bust corset. "You ready?" She heard Mari call out.

She peaked out from behind the curtain, opening it ever so slightly for Mari to see. "Twirl." Mari encouraged. She obliged, feeling awkward as she spun. "I like it. What do you think, Aelius?" She called out over her shoulder.

Aelius leaned over from his spot by the door and gave a small nod. "Looks good."

She felt her cheeks flush with slight embarrassment as she headed back into the change room. She tried on a few more options, other simple every day outfits, before turning to a more formal dress. She stood back, looking at it on the hanger. She wondered where she would possibly need something so nice, but she knew that if she didn't at least try it on, that she would get an earful from Mari.

She peaked her head out of the curtain, holding up the dress at her chest.

"Oooo is that the dress?" Mari perked up, approaching the dressing room.

She nodded. "I need a hand with the back." She confessed, turning around.

Mari was quick and gentle with the buttons. There were several at the top behind her neck, and more down at the small of her back. Once she was done up, she stepped out. It was a trumpet flare dress in navy blue, so dark it was nearly black. A bolero of delicate lace covered her collarbone and trailed down to her wrists. The dress itself was a sweetheart neckline, the bodice almost perfectly fitted through the torso. She looked at herself in the mirror, suddenly feeling much more mature.

The shop keeper came in with a set of pins. She motioned for Aurora to turn so she could see how it fit. The back of the dress left most of her back exposed, being quite racy for Empirical designs.

A flush of heat hit her all of sudden. She looked around, wondering what the source of it was, when she noticed the look on Aelius' face. His eyes met hers in that moment, his mouth ever so slightly agape. He cleared his throat and averted his gaze once he realised she had caught him.

"She's pretty right?" Mari teased, seeing the look on her brother's face.

She would have rushed into the changing room if it weren't for the dozen pins the shop owner had placed.

He stole a glance at her, a slight tint of red at the top of his ears. "She is." He finally admitted.

After several changes and trials, she finally walked away with several options in the academy navy. A few of the items she chose would need altering, but the shop owner assured her that they could be sent up to the Academy for her.

A smile spread across her face as she cradled the bag over her arm. She wouldn't have to borrow clothing anymore to feel like she belonged. What she wore hadn't really mattered growing up, but here it did. The fashion itself wasn't the major aspect for her, but the ability to fit in. She had had enough of standing out. Blending in was just fine with her.

"Better?" Mari asked as stepped back out onto the street.

"Yeah." She responded with a smile.

"Good." Mari said with a nod. She checked her watch before deciding their next stop. "Looks like we're due to meet the guys. Let's head over to the pub."

She followed Mari, but before she could take a second step, Aelius lifted the bag off of her arm. "But—"

"What kind of Guardian lets his Mage carry things?" He interrupted.

Mari snorted in laughter at the unexpected comment. "God you sound like dad."

"Go play in a Harpy's den." He grumbled at her.

Aurora's brow rose at the comment. She forgot some of the Empirical insults. Every once and a while she would hear one and it would make her do a double take. Maybe Dae was right after all. Maybe Aelius *was* becoming more comfortable with her if he was cursing out Mari in front of her.

The smells that swirled through the air told her that they had neared the food district. Aromas from fresh baked bread to freshly fried chips hit her. The pub would certainly be nearby, various signs displaying names overhead. Her eyes scanned them, keeping an eye out for the Sun and the Scribe.

She finally spotted it, nestled in between a couple of other busy looking spots. Mari lit up into a smile, seeing Dae and Edwyn just ahead of them. She quickened her pace, eager to be reunited. Aelius remained in step with her, not rushing her in the slightest. She knew it must have felt slow to him with his gait, but she appreciated it.

Aelius reached into his pocket, pulling out a small pouch. He handed it over to her, dropping it into her open palm. Aurora stared at it a moment, wondering what he was possibly giving her. It was light enough that it wasn't coins or anything, but there was definitely something inside.

"Miss Thomas?" She heard from behind, distracting her from the offering.

Aurora turned to see Professor Jung, a small bag of books slung over her shoulder.

"Professor Jung." She greeted with a smile, tucking the pouch into her bag. Aelius gave her small nod of his head. He wasn't one of Jung's students, but he knew of her from campus.

"May I borrow you for a moment?" Professor Jung asked, giving Aelius a fleeting glance. "I don't mean to interrupt."

Aurora shook her head. "We were just on our way to lunch. How may I help you?"

Aelius took the hint and continued towards the pub, giving her a moment of privacy. She gave him a small nod in thanks.

"I was wondering how you feel about your current workload at the Academy." Jung asked.

She tilted her head to the side slightly. "I think it's fair at the moment. It's not too much or too little. Why do you ask?"

"I have been speaking with Dean Reyes about possibly bringing in a tutor who specialises in Artefacts. I find that my secondary students are having a particularly difficult time grasping some of the concepts this year. The position has been approved, and I was wondering if it would interest you at all?"

"Me?" She asked in surprise. "Are you sure?"

"We both know that you are the top of your class." She elaborated with a knowing look. "Your background gives a better understanding of the history and development of many Artefacts. The Secondary level classes are mostly theory and history. They don't go into the full functions or mechanisms that the Collegiate level classes do. You are the only one of my students that I have zero doubts would be able to handle things. The job is yours if you're interested."

She had never considered tutoring as an option. If she were making her own money, she wouldn't have to worry or budget her spending quite so much. "Yes please."

Chapter 9

Her face was bright as she stepped into the pub. It was cozy and welcoming, just as Mari had described it. Several tables and booths filled most of the space, a large bar directly across from the doors. Off to the right was an empty stage and dance floor for special entertainment nights.

Mari flagged her down with a wave towards the back. Many of the tables were already filled with a mix of locals and students, drink and food a plenty. As she made her way over to their table, Aelius stood up and pulled out a chair for her. She thanked him, taking the seat beside him. She unfastened her cloak and laid it over the back of the chair.

"Good news then?" Aelius asked her once she had settled herself.

She turned to him, wondering how much he felt through the bond from her. "Professor Jung asked if I would be interested in taking a tutoring position for the secondary students." She explained.

"That's amazing!" Mari exclaimed.

"She's easily the top of our class." Dae added, taking a sip of his pint. "I can see why she asked."

She tucked a strand of hair behind her ear as she tried to suppress a smile at the compliments. "I'm sure it will keep me busy, but it should be fun."

Mari let out a laugh. "We need to get you out more, Ari. Your idea of fun seems a little skewed."

Aelius leaned forward, his forearms resting on the table. "Studying is training. Nothing wrong with training." He argued.

"Alright, alright." Mari dismissed as she leaned back in her chair. She reached into the side of her jacket, pulling out a palm sized copper Artefact. She sat back up, sliding the Artefact across the table. "You want to let your mom know? I'm sure she'd want to know." Mari offered her.

Aurora stared down at the Artefact on the table, a communicator used for audio and visual calls similar to cell phones used by Middlings. Her stomach dropped as she looked back up at her friend's eyes. "I...uh..." She stammered, unsure if she could say it. Not here. Not now. She had been avoiding the topic, but she knew there was only so much redirecting and avoiding she could do before it became outright lying. She didn't want to lie to her, but she also didn't know how to come out with it.

Aelius leaned in, placing a hand on hers. She looked up at him, the look in his eyes telling her he could feel the turmoil inside her. She pulled her hand away, heading for the door.

She let out a sigh and tilted her head to the sky as she stopped just outside the doors. She rubbed the sides of her arms, realising she had left her cloak behind. She was running from her problems like a coward. A shivering coward. Aurora heard the door open beside her, Mari and Aelius following her. She looked up at her Guardian, a slightly sad look to his eyes as he passed her her cloak wordlessly. She took it and gave him a small smile of thanks, wrapping it over her shoulders.

"I'm sorry." Mari confessed. "I didn't mean to overstep. If I said something—"

"No." She cut in with a shake of her head. "I've just been avoiding being honest, Mari. You've done nothing wrong."

Mari knitted her brows in confusion, placing a hand on her upper arm. "Is everything okay?"

She looked up between the pair. Both looked down on her with concern and care. "I should have told you sooner, but it was hard." She took a deep breath. She knew she had to say it out loud. "My mom passed earlier this year."

Mari brought a hand to her mouth to hide her gasp. She felt a sharp pain through the bond. She instinctively looked up to Aelius a moment, his face unreadable despite the emotion that shot through.

"I'm so sorry." Mari responded with pain in her voice. "Are you okay? What happened?"

Aurora looked down at the ground, uncertain if she could look at either of them while she spoke. She could feel concern swirl in with the pain through the bond. Her hands fiddled under her cloak as Aurora tried to find the words. "Thing is I don't even fully know. We fought. Mum told me that we were leaving a site, and I told her that I wanted to... to come here and be a Mage. She got angry. She told me that she was going to talk to the other researchers and we would be gone by morning. I was upset and went to bed early. I thought she was out late making arrangements..." She felt her voice catch. She took a deep breath to stave off the tears that threatened to form.

"When I woke up the next morning, I saw that she wasn't there. She had never come back." Hot tears started to roll down her face and her words trembled. She felt Aelius pull her into a hug, bringing her in tight and close. She grabbed a hold of his cloak, her hands clenching the fabric tight as if it might ground her. Her knees felt as if they might give way any moment, and Aelius was the only thing keeping her upright.

"Someone attacked her while she was out. They said they have no idea who it was, but it looked like someone surprised her and robbed her. She didn't even have a chance to fight back. She died thinking I...I was angry with her. Th...that I didn't want to be around her anymore."

Aurora felt his hold on her tighten as her voice wavered. She buried her face into his chest unable to stop the tears from spilling out. Aelius held the back of her head, as her shoulders shook, his other hand on the small of her back. She hated this. She hated showing emotions like this. For being anything other than smiling or strong. Aelius was the last person she wanted to do this in front of. He needed the best, the strongest Mage. Not someone who fell to pieces.

Aurora tried to slow her breathing in attempt to calm down. She stepped back, wiping the tears from her eyes with the back of her hand. She still couldn't bear to look Aelius in the eye. "I'm sorry." She apologised, her cheeks blotchy and red.

Mari placed a hand on her shoulder. "Why are you apologising, Ari? If I had had any idea..." She paused, unable to find the right words. "I'm sorry if you felt like I pushed you into sharing that. I can't even imagine..."

Aurora shook her head, finally able to look up at Mari. "You didn't. You were being a good friend."

Mari brought her into a tight hug, making Aurora laugh as she wrapped her arms around her.

"A drink would be good about now." Aurora admitted.

Mari released her, slinging her arm around her shoulder instead. "Let's take care of that then."

Dae and Edwyn greeted them as they returned, politely ignoring her red rimmed eyes. The pair acted as if nothing had even happened, picking the conversation up where it had left off. "So when do you start?" Dae asked.

Aurora gave him a smile of thanks, grateful to not need to rehash it. She took a sip from the cider Mari had gotten her. "Professor Jung will send me over the details, but as soon as I like, really. I get to take on as many students as I want and create the schedule. I'm really looking forward to it."

Little by little she would get better. The hurt would start to ebb away and be less obvious. It would never leave her, but friends like Mari and Aelius made it seem like it was doable.

***

Before they realised it, the sun had started to set, turning the sky a beautiful shade of pink. She staggered ever so slightly as she stood to her feet, recalling just how many pints of cider she had had. Each one had helped numb the feelings that still felt so raw.

Without thinking, Aelius reached out, steadying her by her arm. She looked up at him, her cheeks a similar shade to the sky outside from booze and slight embarrassment. "Sorry." She said as she straightened herself.

"It's okay." He said, just loud enough for her to hear as he picked up her cloak. He set it gently around her shoulders, leaving it up to her to clasp shut. She felt her pulse quicken a beat with how close he was. She paused a moment before giving her head a slight shake. He was simply being nice. He was being a good friend and a good Guardian. He was protective by nature, nothing more.

She closed her eyes and took a deep breath of the crisp air as they stepped out of the pub. It was perfect against her cheeks, cooling her ever so slightly. Aelius waited by her side, giving her a small smile as he watched her.

They fell in with the others, Edwyn and Dae breaking out into song ahead of her. Mari shook her head and groaned as they failed to hit a high note. "The pair of them..." She laughed to herself.

She smiled, listening to them belt out song after song. Most seemed to be training chants the Guardians would sing out while they ran drills. Mari joined in every so often, but left a majority of the off key renditions to Dae and Edwyn.

She glanced up at Aelius, noticing he remained silent. "Not much of a singer?" She asked.

"Ahh, they're having fun. I'll join in if it's something good." He explained.

"Something good, hmm?" She asked, thinking out loud to herself. "And what would that be?"

"I guess we'll just have to wait and see." He replied with a smirk.

She started to hum a tune out loud, a song she remembered from childhood. She felt his eyes on her after a time, peering up at him. "What?" She chuckled to herself.

"Can't say I know that one." He explained with a small smile.

"No?" She asked, the effect of the alcohol swirling through her head. "I thought it was a pretty common one."

He chuckled, finding her rather amusing. "Well how's it go?"

She looked up at him, fighting a smirk. "I'm not going to just sing it."

"And why not?" He seemed to rather enjoy egging her on.

She glanced ahead, seeing that they had put some distance between themselves and the others. If she was going to embarrass herself, it would at least only be with him. "Come away with me, and you all will see a world beyond what you have known..." She stopped, catching the expression on his face. "What?" She asked.

"Must be a Middling song." He commented. "Don't know it."

She shrugged. "I just remember it from when I was little." She couldn't remember exactly where she had heard it before, it was simply one of those things that was wedged somewhere deep within her memories. She had slight wobble in her step as they switched from the cobblestone streets to the worn path, her arms spreading out as she did her best to regain her balance.

"Let's get you back in one piece." He stated, reaching out for her.

She looped her arm into the crook of his elbow, leaning her head against the side of his arm. "Thanks..." She mumbled, enjoying the warmth he radiated as they headed back home.

Chapter 10

Aurora rubbed the sleep from her eyes as she heard her watch chime away. She groaned as her hand fumbled around for her glasses. Professor Rossi had instructed the class would be meeting early that morning in the South building. She was excited to see the specialised facility, but could have done without such an early wake up.

She made her way to the closet and examined her collection of uniforms. She knew that she would be fully capable of training in her preferred dress uniform, but the breeches wouldn't be a bad idea. After an internal debate, she pulled out the breeches and vest. She turned in the mirror after she got herself dressed. She still preferred the dress, but this would definitely provide better range of movement while training.

She slung her book bag over her shoulder and headed down to the Dining Hall for a quick bite. She had made sure to wake with plenty time. She knew that the South building was a good fifteen to twenty minute walk from the collegiate campus, and did not want to add to her reputation by being late. After gulping down some food and coffee, she headed out to the grounds. The fresh morning air hit her lungs and woke her fully. She debated with herself if there was enough time to double back for a jacket, but knew that there wasn't. She cursed to herself as her teeth chattered. She quickened her pace and hoped that the faster she moved, the warmer her body would become. She sighed with relief as she reached the South training centre and hurried through the doors. She blew on her hands to warm them up and rubbed her arms. She heard a few chuckles from her classmates, but discarded it.

Instead, she took the time to really admire the facility. She had read about training facilities like this one, but had never seen one in person. The training facilities at the Academy were enclosed arenas used to train Mages. The centre of the facility currently looked like a simple compacted dirt ground. Beneath them, however, were a series of complicated mechanisms that would change the arena as needed. The entire facility was set up to adapt and change to whatever the professor chose. Along the walls were rows of bleachers to watch and observe the trainees techniques. She couldn't wait to test it out.

It was only a few moments later that she saw Dae and Leila enter. Leila cast her a glance, letting out a sigh as she pushed past. She found Joanna and Tica further in the arena, far from Aurora.

"She doesn't have to storm off like that." Aurora sighed.

"Ahh, she'll cool off." Dae assured her. "She's stubborn, but she'll get over it eventually."

Aurora opened her mouth to object, but shut it the moment she saw Professor Rossi step out. She emerged from a door opposite of them. She wore a fitted pant suit in purple and braided her silver hair back in a pair of French braids. It was clear from the look on her face that an intense class was about to start.

"Today you will be showing me your baseline." Professor Rossi announced from the middle of the arena. "I will not be grading you on a specific target. I will be grading you based on how much improvement I see from you."

Aurora was surprised. She had expected Rossi to be a very target oriented professor.

"I will call on you one by one. Your skills in your chosen element will be tested. Should you need to stop the simulation for whatever reason, you must immediately let me know. You may do this by either calling out 'stop' or by waving one hand above your head. At that time the simulation will be stopped and you will be removed from the arena. Any questions?"

The class was silent and a few heads shook no. It seemed that the rules were fairly standard from their years in previous training facilities. Aurora eagerly took a seat with her peers to watch the first of her classmates be evaluated. A few classmates were called ahead of her before Rossi called out her name. A smile spread across her face as she jumped to her feet. She practically raced down the aisle to the arena floor. She positioned herself in the centre of the arena floor and turned to face professor Rossi. She gave a thumbs up signal just as her predecessors had. With a nod, the professor clicked a button on a hand held device.

With the click, the entire arena shifted. She braced herself as the ground quaked and gave way. She raced away from the centre as the cavity began to rapidly fill with water. Within moments, the arena was transformed into a lake scene with a rocky terrain surrounding. Aurora scanned the area to take in her surroundings. She had noticed that each student had received a different location with each evaluation so far. She wondered what lay in store. As she took the scene in, a sound cried from above. The shriek that rang out from the skies could only mean one thing: harpies. There were varying Middling accounts of what a harpy was. Mages and Guardians knew them as vicious creatures with the face and torso of a haggard woman and body of an eagle. No matter how frequently they fed, they were always raging with hunger. The talons on their feet and human hands were razor sharp and easily capable of slicing ones bowels open for their evening meal.

As Aurora studied it from below, the harpy let out a second screech. It dove down, razor sharp talons outstretched for the kill. Its face was ablaze with hunger as stringy hair flung in the wind. Aurora took a breath and reminded herself that she was only permitted Earth magic. It would take focus to obey only one element at a time, but she could do it. She rose her arms up above her head, and with it grew several trees. By the time the harpy came crashing upon her, it was met with a small forest of maples. The harpy squawked in disdain as it corrected course. Aurora watched from below as a few disturbed leaves fell around her. The harpy took to the sky again to recalculate its attack.

A second, third, and final fourth cry caught her attention. The arena had conjured more, undoubtedly at the command of her professor. She pulled up additional trees to grow a forest. As she moved along the wall, more and more maples sprung up to give her cover. Every so often, she would glance up to check the gaggle of harpies. She counted five total, but knew that more may join. She knew a little about harpies, but not enough to bet on their attack formations. The only thing she was certain on was their tendency to attack in groups. The more time she allowed them to gather, the worse it would be. She decided to test things. She crouched down and touched the ground. She formed several fist sized rocks from the earth. Normally she would use air magic to shoot them off as she formed them, but she knew she had to rely only on earth right now. She didn't have much strength, but she was able to toss the first rock several feet and caught the attention of one of the smaller harpies. It honed in on the movement and dropped to the ground with a shriek. It landed to the ground and whipped its head around as it searched for its target.

Being this close gave her full view of the creature. Its bright yellow eyes had slit pupils like a cat. It turned its head in a frenzy trying to find the source of movement. The harpy tucked its wings in as it stepped cautiously down the rocky formations. It moved in a mixture of steps and hops as it moved from rock to rock, ever closer to Aurora's forest line. She held her breath as it hopped closer. It tilted its head in inhuman angles as it tried to determine where the human smell came from. She knew that here on the ground she had the advantage. The harpy squinted its eyes in concentration as it approached the tree line. "That's it..." She muttered to herself.

Once under the hidden view of the forest canopy, Aurora struck. She quickly called up a tomb of earth. The harpy barely had a moment to cry out before it was encased in the thick walls. As soon as the edges of earth formed a closed box, she retracted it. With a stomach churning mixture of crunch and squish, one harpy was down.

Aurora heard a few cheers from the spectators and smiled to herself. It felt odd to only channel one element at a time, but she seemed to be getting the hang of it. She peered back up at the skies to see if the others had noticed their companion had met its end. The skies grew thick with clouds and the harpies took to cover. She creased her brow in concern. Professor Rossi seemed intent on making sure she didn't have an easy go of things. She receded back into her forest coverage while she reformed her plan.

She checked her watch for the time. She knew that if she took too long to dispose of the harpies, it would also effect her grade. It would be best to get it over with quickly, opposed to waiting them out. She took a deep breath and let out a long exhale. Best to get on with it, as her mother would always say.

She kept her eyes on the sky as she stepped out of her forest coverage. She could hear them shriek and call to each other despite their cloud coverage. She stood out in the open, raised her hands above her head, and cleared away her trees. One by one, the trees crashed to the ground with deafening cracks and bangs. The movement and sound was too much for the creatures to ignore. The clouds swirled and trailed after each harpy as it fell from the sky. Each one stretched out its talons at her, hungry for her flesh. Her pulse quickened despite knowing her plan would work. The look in their eyes was enough to make even a seasoned Mage doubt.

She waited. Despite her growing nerves, she waited for the right moment. Ever closer they fell, out for her blood. She counted down to herself, "...five, four, three, two..."

As she reached one, she released clenched fists. As she did so, the earth opened into a small hole, just large enough for her to drop down. She heard one, then two hit the ground with a bone crunching splat. That was three down, with two left. She heard two shrieks of agony off in the distance. She cautiously raised the ground beneath her to be able to take in her surroundings. Two harpies circled the skies above her.

Aurora briefly turned her attention over to Professor Rossi. She scribbled away in her notes, only taking a moment's pause to click the hand held device again. With that click, the sky above her darkened. The temperature dropped, winds picked up, and a rumble could be heard. The lake before her started to churn, with waves reaching ever closer to her boots. Lightning started to dance between the clouds, but would undoubtedly touch the ground before long. She knew that it wouldn't be long before they were forced from the skies to attack.

The lightning struck from cloud to cloud, forcing the harpies from their cover. They turned towards their target. She braced herself, half crouched as she touched one hand to the terrain. As they dropped, so did the rain. Fat, cold drops of rain started to pelt down from the black clouds. She had to hand it to Rossi: she certainly wanted to make things difficult. Her glasses quickly became a hinderance as pelts of water came thundering down. She kept her eyes on her attackers, however. The same trick wouldn't work, but she had another in store. She a second hand to the ground as they dropped ever closer. They had to be just close enough to...

Within a heartbeat, she called forth two thin spires of earth. The first impaled itself square in the heart with a squelch of dark blood. The second, the larger of the two, stopped just short of Aurora. She had nearly missed, but had thankfully managed to hit it through the throat. She brought a hand to her cheek, slick with blood. It had been close, but one of those talons had gotten her. She smiled in triumph as both sputtered out of existence.

She recalled her audience as a cheer broke out from the seats. She looked up to see Dae cheer out for her. The others slowly started to clap as she stood up and the terrain reset itself. She had done well. None of the others had been tested to that degree. She glanced up at Professor Rossi to see what sort of impression she had made. Her face gave nothing away, much to her dismay. She wondered what she would have to do to impress her.

"That was *awesome!*" Dae exclaimed as she regained her seat.

She felt her heart swell with pride. She had always had her mother's love and support, but this was different. She had never had peers to impress. "Thanks," She responded with a smile. "I just hope that was enough to change Rossi's opinion."

Chapter 11

It was her first tutoring session that night. She had gone over her lesson plan half a dozen times already, but she still felt unsettled. There had always been a part of her who thought being a teacher would suit her, but now that she had the opportunity, she felt suddenly unprepared. She shook her head, knowing it was all ridiculous. Professor Jung had asked her for a reason. She wouldn't have trusted her with it if she had even a thread of doubt. A glance at her watch told her she had twenty minutes before her session began.

She headed out into the main hall, passing by several other students on their way to the Dining Hall for the night. She veered to her left, heading to the east building. She had never ventured through the connecting doors. Mari had assured her that the secondary campus was much like their own, but she still had a slight concern of getting turned around. She pushed open the doors with a grunt of effort, thankful that they hadn't been locked at this hour.

She walked down the hall, admiring the works of art along the walls. Faculty portraits, and even a few old class portraits trailed along as she ventured towards the main hall.

Mari had been right. Much of the layout was the same as she made her way deeper into the secondary campus. Students walked past, some giving her some side glances and whispers along the way. Their uniforms were the same navy blue with white, but the design itself set them apart from the collegiate level. Girls walked past in pleated skirts that reached their knees. Short cropped jackets overlaid simple white blouses and navy blue bows at their collar. Some wore thick tights, whereas others chose knee length socks to go with their black shoes. The boys wore full length jackets, opposed to the shortened ones the girls wore, and pleated pants. They wore the same navy ties as the collegiate level, tucked beneath a close fitted vest.

"Right on time." Professor Jung commented, standing outside of the tutor room.

She gave her a small smile. "Are they ready?"

"They'll be in in a moment." Jung explained, as she opened the door.

Inside was a room set up like a small classroom. A large rectangular table stood in the centre, three chairs on either side, and one on either end. A chalkboard took up the wall across of the door, available for demonstrations. A small desk and chair was tucked into the left hand corner, set up for her to lay out her notes and materials.

"Three signed up for the group session today. I told them that you will offer private sessions as well, but they cost more." Jung explained.

She gave her a nod. "I prepared tonight's lesson, but I have made sure to leave room for any specifics they want to cover."

"We can go over a practice exam closer to the end of the semester." Jung explained as she checked her watch. "I'll leave you to it. They should be here any minute now."

Aurora gave her a slight wave as she headed back towards the faculty wing. She took a moment to settle herself in, slinging her book bag over the back of her chair and emptying her texts onto the desk. She reviewed her notes as the first of her students entered.

The first Mage to enter was a shy seeming young woman with long raven hair. She knocked politely on the door frame despite the door being wide open. "Excuse me." She announced timidly. "Is this the group tutoring session for Artefacts 401?"

She gave her first student a warm smile. "It is. I'm Aurora Thomas, your tutor. Please take a seat wherever you like. We're just waiting on the others."

She smiled back and grabbed a seat near the door. Next to follow was a young man, surprisingly tall for a Mage. He was a lean build with sandy brown hair that was messy in his eyes. He flashed her a wide smile, surprised to see how young his tutor was. He grabbed the back of a chair closest to the chalkboard and sat himself down. He didn't say a word, despite seeming like he had plenty of comments to make. It seemed to her as if he thought better against speaking his thoughts aloud.

Last to enter was another young woman, small in stature, with curly auburn hair. Her size made her look far younger than she was, but the look in her eyes read that she was quite fiery. "Are we all here, then?" The last young woman asked, seating herself at the chair on the end of the table.

"We are." Aurora answered, using a gentle gust of air magic to close the door behind her final student. The first young woman jumped slightly, not expecting the sound as she was unloading her book bag. "I am Aurora Thomas, a First year in the collegiate Academy. I will be reviewing lessons based off of Professor Jung's teachings, and helping in any specific problem areas you might have. Before we begin, I'd like to go around and have you introduce yourselves please."

"I'm Jessica Baker." The timid Mage stated as she fiddled with her arrangement of materials before her.

"I'm Jenson James." The male Mage introduced with a glint in his eye.

"And I'm Graciela Morales. Most people call me Grace." She explained with a shrug.

"Do you prefer Graciela or Grace?" She asked.

She gave her a look of surprise at the question. It seemed as if many didn't ask it of her. "Graciela." She finally admitted.

"Graciela it is then." She confirmed with a nod. "Do you have any questions for me before we dive in? Any specific areas you want to make sure we cover?"

Jensen raised his hand, his elbow resting on the table. "I have a question." He stated. "Why don't we know you. We're familiar with all of the Mages the year ahead of us. You're not one of them."

She could see glances between the girls confirmed they were thinking the same thing. She had expected the thought to occur to them, but she was surprised that he had been so bold to ask it outright. "I'm a transfer. I just started this year." She explained simply.

"Transfer from where?" He asked, his grin widening.

"Jensen, shut up. We're here to learn, not hit on the new girl." Graciela sighed.

Aurora pursed her lips, fighting the urge to laugh. She covered her mouth a moment while she turned to the desk with her notes. She grabbed a nearby piece of chalk, casting a weave of air magic to pick it up and start writing on the board behind her. "We'll go over the key aspects that are used when constructing Artefacts. We will cover the easiest ways to differentiate between the materials used, as well as how to determine general usages."

All three began taking notes, personal questions seemingly abandoned for the moment.

***

History class had quickly become one of Aurora's favourite subjects. Part of her had expected Ancient Artefacts to be her prime subject, but learning more about the Empire's conception and inner workings fascinated her. Her mother had always glossed over anything relating to the Empire's dealings. If it hadn't related to the Artefacts they were researching, she hadn't bothered teaching it. She had started to wonder what else she had missed out on.

Aurora stepped into class and was taken aback by the change in atmosphere. Normally, Professor Andersen kept a very simple classroom. As she entered the lecture hall she noticed the lights had been turned off, save for a glowing Artefact in the middle of the professor's desk. The Artefact illuminated the room like a Middling star projector, but far more robust. Lights danced and swirled emulating a breathtaking night sky. She had to remind herself to pay attention to where she was walking before she ended up on her face. She eventually found a seat and pulled out her books.

"As you can see, things are a little different today." Professor Andersen acknowledged as he ensured the doors were finally closed. "Some of you had commented that my class has lacked flair, so I have brought in props."

A few chuckles rolled through the class, but his point seemed to ring true. The rest of the class already seemed more engaged. She knew she was likely the outlier being so interested in the content on its own.

"Can anyone tell me about the Equinox?" Professor Andersen asked as he clicked a button on the Artefact. The lights changed from dancing stars to a captivating dawn sky.

Leila was one of the few to raise her hand. "The Spring Equinox is considered the Empire's holiest of days. It marks two occasions: first being the birth of the Empire; second being the return of light."

"Correct." Professor Andersen stated. "The Spring Equinox is a time that we use to celebrate the formation of the Empire. It was on the Equinox that the first Emperor was crowned. We celebrate the bringer of light as the earth rotates out of darkness."

As she took her notes, it started to sink in just how zealous he sounded about the Empire. It seemed like it was part of the job due to the subject matter, but she wondered how he acted around the Imperial Family. She realised that she had never seen him interact with Astraea at all. It would be interesting to see if he had her raised on a pedestal or if he treated her like a normal student.

"We have traditions that we carry out for this day. Can anyone list them for the class?"

Leila had her hand raised again, but the professor passed her over to accept the answer from Aiden. "Families gather together and celebrate together at dawn."

"Yes that is a great one. And why do we celebrate at dawn?"

The Guardian thought a moment before answering, "I think it's representative of light banishing the darkness?"

Professor Andersen nodded. "Very good. The days grow longer on the Equinox. This links with our Emperor banishing demonic creatures from the realm and his work beginning. Can anyone think of another?"

"Gifts are exchanged." One of Astraea's followers answered shyly.

"Yes, but not just any gifts are exchanged." He corrected. "Gifts are only exchanged with people you consider most dear. Unlike other holidays where we give gifts to friends or acquaintances, to give someone a gift on the Equinox says a lot more. There is a third tradition we follow. Can anyone tell me?"

To Aurora's surprise, she saw Mari shoot her hand up. "We wear white."

"Yes!" Professor Andersen exclaimed with a clap of his hands. "It is the only day we, as common folk, are allowed to wear all white. Does anyone know why?"

The class was silent. A few students turned to one another to ask, but they all seemed to be at a loss. Finally, Astraea raised her hand demurely. "It is the belief that we are one on the Equinox. It is a show of faith and unity that everyone may wear white."

Professor Andersen lit up as he listened to the princess speak. He seemed positively fan struck by her words, as if he were meeting a celebrity. "Perfectly put, your Highness." He gushed. "It is one of my favourite traditions of the season." He cleared his throat as he collected himself. "These traditions are part of what make the holiday special to us. This year is especially important being the five hundredth and fiftieth anniversary of the Empire. I know I certainly am looking forward to seeing what grand celebrations we have for this anniversary year."

Professor Andersen continued to go over the history of the first celebrations and other minor traditions that did not carry over into the modern holiday. She tried to remember the holiday with her mother. She recalled waking at dawn and watching the sun rise, never had they worn white. The more she thought about it, her mother had never owned a single article of white.

Chapter 12

As class let out, Mari called out to her. She had been so close to sneaking away into the library for the night. Aurora stepped off to the side to avoid the flow of classmates pouring out of the lecture hall doors. "A few of us are headed out to the pub tonight. You want to come?"

She had been invited out a few times now, but she had never taken her up on the offer. There always seemed to be one thing or another in the way. She scanned her mental list of studies and tasks, wondering if she could make it work.

"Aww, come on." Mari pleaded. "You promised me last time that you would come. I know for a fact that you have caught up on all of your assignments and have even been working ahead. *One* night out won't kill you."

She laughed. "Alright." She finally responded. She was right. "I have a session booked, but we can head out after."

A wide mischievous grin broke out onto Mari's face. "Perfect."

***

The sun had long since set by the time they reached the pub. Mari had made sure to send the guys ahead to grab a table for them. She was thankful that she had thought of it; the pub full and bustling with life by the time they arrived. A sea of navy and brown filled the room, an occasional pop of crimson catching her eye. She turned to Mari, a look of confusion on her face.

Catching her expression, Mari laughed. "Rescue team. Police or fire." She followed closely as they weaved and dodged through the crowd of people. "Guardians that don't quite make RAM qualifications generally end up in red. It's second best to serving."

There was still so much for her to learn about the inner workings of the Empire. Just when she thought she had it figured out, there was something else that poked a hole in her understanding.

They finally reached the table, tucked away in the back corner. The guys stood to their feet, Dae taking Mari's jacket for her. She moved to take her own cloak off, revealing her new outfit for her night out. The seamstress had sent up a drop waisted corset with gold detail work scrawled across the bodice. Mari had given her a hand in tying her in, knowing that she never would have managed on her own. Navy skirts layered underneath, leaving a slit for her left leg when she moved just so. She brushed her loose hair back, leaving it down for once.

A swell of heat hit her, causing her cheeks to flush. She blinked, confused at the sudden change in temperature, wondering if there was a fireplace nearby.

"Drinks?" Dae asked, setting Mari's jacket on a nearby chair.

"Please!" Mari answered emphatically. "My usual and…" She trailed off turning to Aurora.

"Gin and tonic, please." She answered, placing her cloak over the back of a chair. Taking a seat with the others.

"Coming right up." Dae replied, heading off to the bar, Mari deciding to follow at the last minute.

"You look fantastic." Edwyn complimented, flashing her a warm smile.

She tucked a lock of hair behind her ear. "Thanks. Mari helped pick everything out."

"She's got great taste." He complimented. "Maybe she can give me a pointer or two." He chuckled.

An uneasy feeling washed over her, so quick she thought she may have imagined it. She looked up at Aelius, meeting his eyes for a fleeting moment, his attention turned away as soon as he realised he had caught her stare. "Have you guys been here long?" She asked, turning back to Edwyn instead.

He leaned back in his chair, slinging an arm over the back. "Ahhh not too long. Just a couple in." He indicated, raising a glass before taking a sip. He looked as if he was about to say more, but the band on stage took up their instruments. A bright smile spread across his face. "Fancy a —"

"Bottoms up!" Mari declared, returning with a larger than expected gin and tonic for her. She passed it across the table, a drink of her own in hand. "Down that and then we're dancing."

She let out a laugh, obliging Mari in her orders. The moment she finished, Mari grabbed her by the hand, pulling her out onto the busy dance floor. Music rang out through the pub, stirring up plenty of locals and students to the dance floor. Mari twirled, laughter escaping her lips, her joy positively infectious. As she spun in time with Mari, she quickly found herself turn right into a Guardian's arms. She gulped, uncertain for a moment just who she had bumped into. Ivan, one of the first years from the Academy, broke out into a wide grin, bringing a hand to her waist. "Why hello there, little fox." He chuckled.

Her shoulders raised, uncertain how she felt about the way he stared down at her. She had seen him around campus before, paired with Elena from her class. He was tall and lean, his dark blond hair slicked back to keep out of his dark blue eyes. There was a glint in them, a hint of lust and flirtation as well.

"Who do we have here?" Another Guardian chimed in, clapping Ivan on the back. Damien, a thicker build of Guardian appeared on Ivan's right, a few inches shorter than his friend. His russet brown skin made his olive green eyes pop admits his thick dark curls. "Hey new girl." He greeted, realising who she was after taking an extra moment. "Almost didn't recognise you. You look *good.*"

"I think we should go for a spin, don't you?" Ivan asked, leaning in closer. Her pulse quickened as he grew closer. There was an air about him that read more wolf than man.

Before she could answer, a large hand clamped down on Ivan's left shoulder. She saw his face tense before she even registered who it was. Ivan turned around, immediately stepping back from her. "Heeeey Aelius!" He greeted nervously. "I was just asking Aurora here to a dance. You don't mind, do you?"

Aelius glowered at him, a simmering anger building through the bond. "I do." He answered simply.

"Awww come on," Damien interjected, his tone attempting to diffuse the sudden tension. "She's beautiful and all alone here. It's not like you're using her."

His glare was venomous as his attention whipped to Damien. The look in his eyes was enough to make Damien take a step back. "Never mind." He stated, his hands up defensively. "Later, newbie." He dismissed.

Ivan cast her a quick glance before following Damien off. She made sure he was out of earshot before turning her attention to Aelius, his temper at a near boiling point.

"What was *that?*" She asked, knowing that there must be more than what met the eye.

He turned to her, a grumble she couldn't quite discern escaped his lips. She squinted her eyes, arms crossed beneath her chest. Mari snuck up behind her, a warm hand on her bare shoulder. "What's with the face?" She asked Aelius, a laugh in her voice.

He scratched the back of his neck, clearly not wanting to discuss whatever it had been. Instead, Aurora turned to her. "He had a problem with Ivan asking me to dance."

Mari's face fell a little, putting pieces together. "Yeah well...makes sense."

She arched a brow at Mari, missing the details. Mari glanced at her brother, guiding Aurora away from him. "Not all of the guys are as...well intentioned as others." She elaborated in a round about way.

She looked up, noting Ivan and Damien already finding another target over by the bar. "It was a dance." She pointed out, feeling the pair of them overreacting over something so simple.

Mari made a face, unsure of her words for a moment. "Yeaaaah, but let's just say there's some history. He's looking out for you."

She looked back to Aelius, his back against the wall and arms across his chest as he surveyed the room. His temper had lessened, but there was something that simmered beneath the surface. She sighed, deciding that she would not allow him to simply sulk and brood. She marched over to him, surprise registering on his face as he saw her approach. "Come on." She ordered, grabbing him by the hand. "If I can't dance with someone else, you're joining me."

It took him a moment to gather himself, but he finally gave her a small smile and a chuckle as an answer. He allowed himself to be pulled along to join her back on the dance floor. He stood rigidly, being more of a body guard than a dance partner. She twirled in time with the music, rolling her eyes at his lack of movement. "That's not dancing." She teased, leaning into him as a song ended.

He cocked his head ever so slightly to the side. "I never claimed I would."

She gave him a slight glare, teasing in nature. "You know you're allowed to relax and have fun right?"

He softened his shoulders ever so slightly, but still didn't look at ease. "Crowds generally aren't my idea of fun." He admitted.

She turned, scanning the room. It was then that she really registered just how many people filled the room. She grabbed Aelius by the hand, pulling him back to the table. "Alright then," She began, being able to hear him a little better off in the corner. "What *is* your idea of fun?"

The pair slid into a pair of chairs at the table, his back to the wall. "Depends on the scenario." He eluded, taking a sip of his pint he had left behind.

She leaned her chin on the back of her hand, elbow on the table. "Tonight for example. Say we leave here. What would you be doing for fun instead?"

The same wave of heat that she had felt earlier washed over her. She blinked a moment, wondering what would possibly cause it. There had to be something wrong with the temperature in the corner of the room.

He let out a short laugh, sitting back in his chair. "If we were doing something fun, not here..." He thought it over. "Cards or a game back at the Academy." He finally decided.

She tilted her head to the side, surprised by his answer. "We can do that." She answered.

His brow shot up in surprise. "That's not what I was—"

"I know. But if this isn't fun, why not head back?" She genuinely offered.

He studied her a moment, his eyes seeming to search for something. "You shouldn't ruin your fun because of me. I'm fine staying back."

She tilted her head, studying him. She could feel how out of place he felt through the bond. Now that she paid attention, she could tell just how much it wasn't his idea of a good time. "A compromise then. You give me a dance. A *proper* dance. After that we head back to play."

He looked at her, trying his best not to smile at her offer. "Fine." He grumbled.

She shot him a smile, happy that he accepted her offer. She let out a soft giggle and grabbed him by the hand, pulling him to the dance floor. It was in no way graceful or pretty, but it was a step out of his comfort zone.

He eventually relaxed a little by the time the song ended. It was in no way his idea of a good time, but he had done it. He held her hand above her head, twirling her as the notes rang out. She let out a laugh, appreciative for his effort. "Thank wasn't so bad, now was it?"

"It was something." He chuckled, following her lead back to the table.

She picked up her cloak from the back of her chair, slinging it over her shoulders. "Heading out so soon?" Mari asked her, seated quite cosy with Dae.

"Yeah going to head back and play a round or two of cards I think." She explained, fiddling with the clasp of her cloak.

Mari shot a look at her brother, a brow arched suspiciously. He responded with a glare, putting a protective hand on Aurora's arm. "Alriiiight." Mari responded, taking a sip of her drink. "Have fun kids."

As Aurora and Aelius headed out, Edwyn returned to the table, slightly breathless from dancing with a local girl. "They leaving?" He asked.

Mari nodded. "She got him to dance, you know."

"You're kidding!" He exclaimed, doubling back and looking to his friend. As he looked back at the table, a glimmer of light caught his eye. He bent down, finding a delicate gold necklace on the floor. "Is this...?"

"Oh hey that looks like Ari's!" Mari remarked, seeing the jewellery in his hand. He turned it over in his hand noticing the broken clasp. "You might be able to catch her."

He started towards the door, but noticed the look Aelius gave her as he held the door open. He stopped in his tracks, slipping the necklace into his pocket. "It's alright. I'll give it to her later."

Chapter 13

The late autumn air sent a chill down her spine, but next to Aelius, it wasn't all that bad. He had start to relax around her - opening up to her a little. It was slow work, but she felt that he was finally becoming more comfortable around her. There was a sense in pride at that. She had never really had to chance to make friends with a lot of peers growing up. She was always the kid around adults. The fact that she was able to make such good friendships with Mari, Dae and even Aelius meant the world to her.

She walked, her arm brushing against his, as they made their way through the streets. The food district was the busiest at this hour, with the bustle of locals and students dying out as they headed north.

"Is it different?" He asked, looking over at her.

She turned to him, confused by what he meant. "Is what different?"

"Being here." He elaborated. "In the Empire, I mean. Is it different than being back home?"

She sighed as she pondered it. It was, absolutely it was. But every place she had lived had been had been different. "Yeah, but I wouldn't say I really had a specific home exactly. Home was where mum was, not a place. We moved so much that there wasn't anywhere to put down roots."

He listened, giving the occasional small nod of understanding. "Mari says you've been getting used to how things work here."

She nodded. "It's been a bigger culture shock than I thought it would be, if I'm being honest. I thought there would be little aspects. Little random things that I wouldn't be aware of. The longer I'm here, the more I realise that I grew up in between worlds. Like tonight even. I had no idea what it meant to wear crimson. Mari had to fill me in. And the Equinox lesson in History the other day. There's so many little things that are obvious to you guys, but I have no idea."

He let out a small sigh, a sad look in his eyes. It wasn't quite pity - more like concern. "If there's anything that you're not sure on, you can always ask me you know." He offered gently.

She looked up at him, appreciating the softness in his expression. There were so many new sides to him later. "Thanks. I'll make sure to let you know."

"What about the Middling Realm?" He asked, subconsciously taking her hand to help her over a small puddle in the street.

She took his hand, hopping over to avoid soaking her boots. "I mean, I probably have more knowledge about it than most of the students here, but I was pretty removed from it as well. Most dig sites are pretty removed from civilisation, so I wasn't going to a local school or anything. We would tour the bigger cities when we had down time. That was always fun." She commented with a bittersweet sort of smile.

"Well, I imagine you have a much better chance of being able to blend in after graduation. I don't believe most of our peers have ever visited any Middling cities."

She smiled, appreciative of his attempt of building her up. He was quite sweet when he wanted to be. "Mari mentioned you have some Middling collections." She remarked, guiding the conversation away from her misfit nature.

Aelius let out a sigh, his head hanging ever so slightly. "Amaris..." He groaned, a pang of irritation shooting through the bond.

"I'm sorry, should I—"

"No, no." He insisted, realising she likely thought that the annoyance was at her. "I'm sure she just wanted to tease me about it."

Aurora tilted her head as she watched him. "I mean... maybe." She shrugged, knowing how Mari enjoyed bugging her brother. "But I don't see anything wrong with having an interest or a hobby. She didn't mention what you collected, if you don't mind me asking."

He looked over at her, seeming to work out whether or not to divulge his interests or not. "Batteries." He finally muttered.

She creased her brow a moment, unsure if she had heard him correctly. "Batteries?"

A twinge of embarrassment filtered through. "Yes, batteries." He confirmed.

"How so?" She asked, wanting to make sure she understood what he meant.

He sighed, knowing that the only option now was to explain himself. "We don't have anything like that here. Sure we have magical reserve Artefacts, but it's not the same as needing a small power source to operate something. The fact that Middlings have these different fuel cells to power their devices is fascinating. There are disposable ones and rechargeable ones. There are massive ones for powering vehicles, and tiny ones for watches or hand held devices. Why are there so many? I understand that size comes into factor, so yes you would need something different for a different device, but there are so many varieties even when it comes to the same device. Why is there no universal issued fuel cell? And the different code names. The same battery can have so many different names, that you have to look them all up to make sure you are indeed choosing the correct one. It is so illogical, but so intriguing at the same time."

It was then that he realised he had gone on a tangent rant, and stopped himself. His cheeks and tips of his ears flushed red - barely noticeable in the dark. He cleared his throat, averting his eyes from Aurora's gaze. "Sorry." He apologised, his rigid tone back in place.

"Why are you apologising?" She asked, a slight chuckle in her voice. "I asked a question and you answered."

He looked back at her, surprised at her reaction. "I was rambling." He stated.

"So?" She shrugged. "It's something you find interesting. Why should you have to apologise for that?"

He smiled, his shoulders a little more relaxed by her statement. She realised as she watched his reaction that it was likely that others didn't quite share her sentiment. It was clear that he was passionate about it. It was wonderful to see him brighten and open up about something - even something like batteries.

"What else?" She asked, enjoying the new side of him. "She said collections plural. What else do you collect?"

***

It was nearly midnight by the time they settled back in the common room. She had learned so much about him in just one night. She had never stopped to consider something as simple as batteries and how they would be considered so odd to someone in the Empire. Why would they need a power cell when they had rigged Artefacts to work directly off of one's magical energy? She felt like she was learning so much about him as a person, but more about her peers as well.

She had learned that another one of his collections was Middling games - board games specifically. He had listed off many that she had never heard of, but there had been several that she knew of. With most of his collection back at home, they had settled on him teaching her a new card game back in the common room.

She sat across from him, cards fanned before her face. They had gone over the rules and done a practice round, but she still felt a little uncertain on some of the game play. She placed a pair down, guessing at the outcome.

He set down his cards on the table with a small sigh. "You win." He declared, leaning back in his seat.

She sat up further, looking at the cards laid out on the table. "You're letting me win." She observed, taking a sip of wine that they had opened on their return.

He stared back at her, a smirk finally creeping across his face. "Maybe..."

"Stop." She insisted, a playful tone in her voice. "You can't go easy on me if you want me to learn."

He leaned forward, swiping the cards in his hand. "You sure?"

She felt her pulse quicken at the way he bantered with her. It must have been the wine starting. "Positive."

"This is what you guys came back to do?" Mari commented, returning from Vilcas with Dae in arm.

Aurora sat up, snapping out of the little bubble she had been in. "Mari! Hey!" She greeted, unsure of why she felt so anxious all of a sudden.

"Not everyone likes a busy loud pub, Amaris." Aelius commented, fanning his new set of cards out in front of him.

A twitch of annoyance read on her face for a moment, always hating her full name. He knew it was a quick way to bug her. "Fine..." She grumbled, knowing it wasn't worth it bickering with her brother. She approached the table, leaning into Aurora for a hug. "I'll be at Dae's tonight. And you can say no to him. You don't have to play games if you don't want to."

She cocked her head to the side. "I know." She stated, uncertain why she would think otherwise. "It's fun."

Mari leaned back, hands on her hips as she burst out into a laugh. "Oh you *are* made for each other..."

Aelius' eyes widened at the comment, embarrassment flooding the bond. "God..." He groaned.

"Night, Ari!" Mari departed with a wave, Dae starting in on a lecture as they headed down the hall. Something about staying out of it and leaving poor Aelius alone.

"You're lucky you're an only child." Aelius grumbled, running a hand through his hair.

Aurora did her best to stifle a giggle as she picked up the cards he had dealt her. "Probably..."

Chapter 14

As she got ready in her breeches, nearly a week later, that it finally hit her. Her necklace, the one her mother had given her as a child, was missing. She tore back her sheets, hoping to find it somehow buried beneath her pillow or some folds of fabric. Nothing. Panic bubbled in her stomach. Her mother had made her promise to keep it on her always. She racked her brain trying to figure out just when she had lost it.

She closed her eyes and calmed her breathing. Where had she seen it last? She knew she had had it on her earlier that week for certain. The only time she ever took it off was in the shower. She went back to the bathroom and tore it apart. She scoured through the hamper of clothing, shaking each article out in hopes of it tumbling to the ground. Nothing. She lifted the edge of her blankets to peer under her bed.

It was then that Mari stepped in, a concerned look on her face. "You alright, Ari?"

She looked up from under the bed and stood to her feet. "I'll be fine." She lied. "Just thought something rolled under the bed. How was training?"

Mari slunk into one of the side chairs with a grunt. "Not bad. Just wanted to get warmed up for whatever the Steins have in store."

"Not going to lie, I am a little nervous." She admitted as she sat herself on the edge of the bed.

"Don't worry about it." She dismissed. "No one is ever fully prepared for Pact exams. The Steins change it every year. Everyone says they're the best though. They somehow always find a way to make it fun."

"Really?"

Mari leaned forward, her forearms resting on her knees. "Yeah, a third year was telling us that one year they had everyone separated and blindfolded. You had to find your way to your partner through the bond alone. Sounded pretty fun the way he told it."

"I wonder what they have in store this year." She thought out loud.

"Whatever it is, I'm ready." Mari added with confidence. "We have a few hours before we're expected over there. You ready to grab some breakfast?"

Dozens of other students littered the halls. It was easy to see who had finished their exams for the season and who had more to finish. A handful of third years headed home early for the holidays.

"Do you have any plans over the break?" Mari asked as they watched a trio of third years head towards the gate with bags slung over their shoulders.

"Honestly?" She asked as they rounded the corner into the Dining Hall. "I'm just looking forward to some peace and quiet. Mostly reading. If I'm feeling *really* ambitious, I might head into town. But really I just want to burrow in."

"Come home with me then." Mari insisted. "Holidays are hard on your own, especially after loss. My mom took it really hard her first solstice without my grandma. You shouldn't be alone."

She gave her a small smile. "Thanks, but I'm okay, Mari. Really. But if I change my mind, you'll be the first to know."

She gave her a look like she didn't entirely believe her as she scooped some eggs onto her plate. "You better."

They finished up the last of their meal, most of the remaining students starting to filter out for their morning exams.

"Aurora!" She heard call out from behind. She turned around, hearing Jensen call out for her.

She rose to her feet, a look of concern on her face. "What are you doing here, Jensen? You should be in the Secondary campus."

"I know, I know." He dismissed, taking a seat without asking. Mari gave him a surprised look, knocking back the last of her tea. "I just had to catch you before my exam."

He knew the material. He knew it. She knew it. She couldn't fault him for over thinking and second guessing, however. "Alright," She sighed. "but make it quick. I have an exam to get to too, you know."

He gave her a wide smile, happy to have convinced her. He dug out his note book from his book bag, opening it up on the table. "Alright, so..."

***

They had gone over the Artefacts material at a rapid speed, not wanting to risk missing their exams. Jensen had tried to protest, but she warned him the Jung had been known to lock the doors come start time. With that, he ran off, worried of being on the wrong side of the door. By the time Mari and Aurora managed to step into the lecture hall, they saw that the entire class buzzed with anticipation.

Both Steins entered the lecture hall, Guardian Stein carrying a burlap sack over his shoulder as his wife addressed the class. "For your exam today, you will be playing a game of hide and seek."

A few whispers broke out through the class. Guardian Stein placed the sack on the ground and took out a small Artefact. The copper device fit in his hand and had two simple buttons on it. He held it up for the class to see. "This here will be your tracker. It will tell us where you are, and how long it takes you to run through a game. You press this button here when you start to hide, and press again when you have been found. You press this button here when you start to seek, and when you have found your partner."

"This will demonstrate just how skilled you are at finding your partner through the bond, but also demonstrate your evasion skills. You will be graded on both abilities. The data collected by your Artefact will give us the information we need to grade you." Mage Stein elaborated.

Guardian Stein tossed the Artefact back into the bag. "Are there any questions?" He asked.

One of the Guardians rose his hand. "Are abilities allowed?"

"Good question, Killian." Guardian Stein smiled. "Abilities, Guardian and Mage alike, are permitted. You are expected to use any talents you possess to evade or capture."

Joanna raised her hand. "What are the boundaries? Is anywhere off limits?"

Mage Stein nodded. "The entire campus is at your disposal, save for the Primary and Secondary buildings. We do not need you disrupting their schedules. Everywhere else on campus is fair game. However, you are *not* permitted to leave the barriers. We will know if you try to leave through the gate. It will be an automatic failure."

"It is not your goal to harm your partner," Mage Stein added. "That would be incredibly foolish. Use your abilities, but also your intellect. We want to see creativity and problem solving."

"We will give you five minutes to plan a strategy. Consider your partners strengths and weaknesses. We will call you up shortly to grab an Artefact." Guardian Stein explained.

The class was immediately alive with chatter. She turned to Mari, a mix of pure excitement and delight on her face. "This is going to be *so* much fun!" She exclaimed.

"You have to admit, you guys have an unfair advantage." She pointed out.

"I'll give him a fighting chance, don't worry." She dismissed with a wave of her hand. Not every Guardian had a special ability, but Mari and Aelius both possessed a very valuable one: teleportation. The trait stemmed from their father's bloodline. Her mother had an ability as well, but Mari had never disclosed just what it was. Their father had been strict in his training of their ability. Neither one used it in every day life; it was only for training, battle, or emergencies. She imagined it must have been so difficult on their mother; raising a set of twins with the ability to teleport away at will.

She found herself in the same boat as Dae - how did you possibly win a match of hide and seek with a Guardian who can teleport? She wished they have covered bond masking this semester. Professor Stein had mentioned they would work on the ability to block their Guardian from feeling them through the bond, but it wouldn't be in practice until next semester. It would have been invaluable in sneaking up on him. She bit her lower lip, suddenly very concerned for her exam mark.

"You just need to outsmart him, Ari." Mari admitted, seeing the worry on her face.

She sighed, knowing that it would most definitely come down to tactics with him. He was smart, unfortunately. If he was oblivious, it would be so much easier.

"Time's up!" Guardian Stein bellowed. "Come on down for your trackers."

Students trickled down to the platform where the Steins passed out the tracker Artefacts. Aurora held hers in her hand. It was surprisingly light weight. She tucked hers in her pocket as she scanned the room for Aelius. He reached over from behind to grab his own tracker, surprising her at how close he was.

They stepped out of the way of the others as he placed his tracker in his pocket as well. "Would you like to hide or seek first?" He asked, tucking a strand of hair behind his ear.

She debated it a moment. She had never seen him use his ability. If she let him hide first, she could waste the whole day chasing him down, trying to figure out how he worked. If she hid first, she would at least get a glimpse of his plans. "I'll hide first." She decided.

"You got it." He agreed. "Remember, you said to stop going easy on you…"

She felt her heart flutter a little at the way he spoke to her. It almost felt as if there was a hint of flirtation in the way he spoke. She shook her head of the thought. He was simply referencing when they would play card games together. He was playing mind games with her. It was a tactic, nothing more.

"Seekers on the left, and Hiders on the right!" Mage Stein called out as the last of the trackers had been given out. "You will be given to the count of twenty as a head start. Once the Seeker has found the Hider, you switch. You will report back and hand in the trackers as soon as you finish."

"Good luck." Guardian Stein added. "Do try and make things interesting." And with that, the count down began.

Chapter 15

Guardian Stein started a steady count down. "One... two...three..." The right side of the room was off in a flash. She paused a moment as the lecture hall door became a bottle neck of students shoving and pushing their way past one another. Dae held behind her to allow her a moment to squeeze through. She gave him a nod in thanks and took off down the hall.

She found herself heading towards the stairs at full sprint. She knew that she would have a measly twenty seconds before he would start after her. He could quite easily teleport directly to her once the count was up, but she was hopeful that he would give her a fighting chance. She reached the stairs, noting that the Seekers had been released from the lecture hall from the corner of her eye. She fought the urge to pause and check for any sight of him. It would be a waste of precious seconds.

There was no time to spend running down the stairs. She leaned over the ledge of the railing, and swung herself over. She earned herself a few concerning looks as she took the quick route down three flights of stairs. As the floor quickly approached, she called up a collection of vines and vegetation to break her fall. It had been a trick she had developed as a child, giving her mother several panicked moments. She stepped easily on the first floor before breaking back into a run. She headed straight for the exterior doors, figuring that the the training field would give her more room to work with. She felt her heart pounding in her chest as she ran. She was thankful for the training she had started to do with Mari and Aelius, giving her more stamina than she had before. Her lungs didn't burn like they did before, but she was still no where near Guardian endurance or speed.

Her feet crunched in the snow as she ran towards her goal. She ran past a small snow fort that looked like it had been used for a Guardian snowball fight and laughed to herself. It looked as if Mari had gone ahead with a game without her.

She froze in place as she heard a cry out from behind her. Mari crashed into one of the snow forts, revealing Dae from the crumbled snow and ice. She straddled over top of her Mage and they both burst out into an infectious round of laughter. She leaned down and kissed him in triumph.

"Good call on the snow fort." She complemented as she broke from their embrace. "It looked just like the one we did yesterday."

He laughed in response and ran a hand through her thick curls. "Yeah, but it's *really* cold. I didn't exactly think that part through." He leaned forward and pulled her back into him. "Come warm me up..."

Aurora's cheeks flushed as she quickly realised that she was in the middle of something personal. She broke back into a run, knowing that Aelius could very well catch up to her and do the same any moment.

As if the very thought of him were enough to conjure him, he appeared mere feet in front of her. She stopped immediately, nearly skidding and slipping to the ground. She called up a wall of earth to block him, a chuckle heard from behind her defence. She grabbed onto the ground for traction and broke back into a run. Again he teleported before her, this time causing her to conjure ice around his legs. She could feel a slight wince of a the sudden cold through the bond, but knew it wasn't enough to hurt him. She turned back to her original plan: the lake.

She ran at full speed, hoping to make it in time. If only she could dive in, she could envelop herself in a pocket of air. She would be safe in the water and be able to buy herself some time. Her feet slid ever so slightly on the icy dock, but she maintained her pace as she pushed herself faster and faster. She smiled to herself, knowing that she would make it. She gave it her all, leaping in the air as she reached the end of the dock.

With a blink, he was in front of her, his arms enveloping her as they came crashing down into the icy waters. They both plunged into the subzero waters, a cry escaping her lips in shock. He held her tight, not letting her tense and drown. He pulled her with him, bringing her back to shore. She got to her feet, her teeth chattering away as she reached into her pocket for her tracker. She clicked the button, conjuring warm air around them both.

His hair flew in the air, coming undone from his hair tie as she dried them both. Snow melted beneath their feet as she engulfed them in the warm air. She refused to let either of them go into hypothermic shock.

"You couldn't have teleported us back before we went in?" She laughed, watching his shock at the instant drying effect she had.

"I thought you were going to create an air pocket." He countered as he clicked his own tracker.

"Yeah well someone surprised me." She admitted. It was her first time seeing his hair down completely. He always managed to have it pulled back, but now it hung in thick waves to his shoulders.

He gave her a smirk as he reached into his pocket for another hair tie. "The Steins did say to keep it interesting..."

She fought the urge to push him back in the lake, wondering how much time it might buy her for the next round. "Your turn to hide." She finally stated, deciding to play fair. He looked at her, a smirk on his lips as if he saw the gears that had been working in her mind. He stared at her a moment before she closed her eyes. "One...two... three..."

She felt him shift in location through the bond as she counted down. Such a difficult ability to combat against. She was thankful that she had the bond to rely on at least. If she was working blind, she knew that there would be no way she could successfully track him down.

She eventually stopped counting, focusing instead on trying to locate him. She had gotten better the more she practiced, but a moving target was so much harder to locate. She felt him teleport several times before finally settling on a location. She wondered if he was only able to travel short distances, or was doing it to make things more difficult on her. She would have to ask Mari later.

She started on her way towards him. By her estimation, he was located in the north wing. It was hard to tell which floor from where she was, but she was sure that she would be able to tell once she got inside. She made sure to keep her eyes open, seeing other students out on the grounds as well. It seemed as if heading outdoors was a common tactic.

As she entered the campus doors, a slight shimmer of the light caught her eye. It looked similar to the defensive barriers if she truly focused on it. She stepped back, wary of what it may be. She knew that several of the Guardians had special abilities, but not everyone advertised what they were. It could be a trap, a glamor, or any number of possibilities. She didn't have time to get caught into someone else's game.

She hurried along, putting the shimmer out of her mind. She needed to find Aelius soon if she wanted to maintain a positive grade. She tested the bond again, hoping to be able to get a better grasp of his location. As she closed her eyes, she could feel him above her. By her estimation, he had settled himself up on the third floor.

The stairs would take longer then she cared for. She conjured vegetation beneath her feet and lifted herself upwards, much the way she came down earlier. She made sure to not rush it, or risk the the growth being too thin.

She hopped down from her lift to the railing ledge, and then the third floor. She turned behind a moment to dissolve her work, not wanting to make extra work for the Academy staff. They would surely have enough to contend with after the exams.

She reached out again, feeling him off to her right. She followed the bond, letting her draw to him guide her. She felt his awareness snap into focus, very much aware of her. She would have to be quick with him. He was fully aware that she was on her way, but she would need some sort of way to keep him in place long enough to tag him.

She opened the door to the lecture hall he had stationed himself in. It was one of the furthest rooms, clearly unused for some time due to the state of dust. He sat leisurely in one of the front row seats, no sense of urgency on his face. She conjured vines to keep him in his seat, but it was useless. He chuckled at her, teleporting himself to the back row of seats.

She started up the seats, only for him to teleport himself down to the professor's desk. She let out a groan of frustration. She could feel his amusement through the bond. She doubted that he ever got to really play and use his ability for fun like this. It was likely something that was used as a battle tactic, not a game.

She rushed down the steps, Aelius settling himself on the edge of the desk. She stopped as she reached the bottom of the steps, seeing that he was about to teleport away again. He was having far too much fun toying with her. If that was how he wanted to play, she could play too.

A row of three large windows lined the wall to her right. She walked over, not paying him any mind as she did so. She opened one of the window locks with a loud creak. It had been some time since someone had bothered to open it. She pushed the window open, making sure it was high enough for her to hop out of. She felt a twinge of tension as he started to piece together her idea. He held himself back a moment, knowing that it was likely her plan to get him worried and close enough to grab him. She lifted herself to the window sill, crouching in place as she turned over her shoulder to look at him. She gave him a smirk before she jumped.

Chapter 16

She was glad he hadn't seen her little trick earlier. Had he seen her free fall back at the staircase, he wouldn't have rushed to her. She looked up as she fell, Aelius standing at the open window with a look of worry on his face. She waited. She knew she had a moment before she would have to catch herself if her idea didn't work. It was this or nothing. Worry and protection was the only way she could think of possibly catching him.

And she was right. With a breath before she hit the ground, Aelius teleported to her, catching her in his arms. He teleported instantly, landing them perfectly fine on the snowy grounds just a few feet away from where she would have landed. A wide grin broke out onto her face accompanied with a light chuckle.

"Why would you—" He started, realising as he saw her face what she had done. Aurora grabbed her tracker and clicked it. He let out a defeated groan as he set her to her feet, clicking his own. "Well played." He admitted.

She cocked her head to the side, rather proud of herself. "Why thank you. You're not an easy one to catch, you know."

He chuckled as he followed her back towards the lecture hall. "You told me you don't want me going easy on you, remember?" He teased.

She rolled her eyes. "In games..." She replied, reaching to push the campus door open.

"Well...this was a game." He countered, leaning forward to open the door before she could reach it. He held it for her as she walked through.

She gave him a smirk, not rewarding him with a response. It had been fun. Had her idea not panned out, she had no clue what would have worked. She was lucky to know him well enough to play on his concerns. Had he not been so kind or caring, there would be no catching him what so ever. She understood why his ability was so valuable to the Empire.

They reached the lecture hall, both professors relaxed at the desk. Guardian Stein rose to his feet, accepting the trackers and noting them on a clipboard. "Good time the both of you. You'll get your marks in a few days."

They thanked them and wished them a happy break. The rest of the day was theirs to spend as they saw fit. She turned to Aelius, the pair walking in silence in the hall. "We have the rest of the day." She opened with. "Is there anything you want to do?" He thought about it a moment, a small smile crossing his lips before he shook his head. She arched a brow at him. "What?" She asked, full of curiosity.

"You wouldn't want to..." He trailed off, not divulging his idea.

She wasn't sure if he was purposely playing with her, or genuinely convinced his idea would be rejected. "Try me."

He stopped mid step. "Do you want to spar?" He asked.

She let out a laugh despite herself. "That's what you thought I'd say no to?"

He creased his brow in confusion. "What did you think I was going to ask?"

"Nothing." She chuckled. "Full sparring? Magic and all?" She asked with a mischievous grin.

He broke into a grin to match her own, heading towards the stairs. "Magic and all." He replied. "I want to see what you can do."

***

They had been lucky that the Mage's arena had been open for a session. With exams in full swing it was hit or miss if it was available for training. A quick check of the schedule outside revealed that it was open for hours. They stepped inside, Aurora ditching her cloak, and Aelius his winter jacket. She opened the gate to the arena, turning over her shoulder to him. "Against projections, or each other?" She asked.

"Projections." He answered simply, holding the gate open for her. "I want to work *with* you."

She felt her cheeks heat ever so slightly at the way he declared his preference. She turned away, moving forward to the centre of the arena. He was a gentleman, that was all. She pulled out the controlling Artefact, scrolling through the options. "Any preference?" She asked as he stepped in beside her.

"Surprise me."

She needed to get a hold of herself. She was getting dangerously close to developing a crush on him. She shook her head of the thought as she skimmed and selected at random. As she tucked the Artefact into her pocket, the ground shifted and shuddered around them. Sand built up underfoot as water rushed in around them. Aelius instinctively grabbed her hand, pulling her into his arms and ran. She wrapped her arms around his neck, amazed at the rate of speed that he ran. In mere moments, they reached the side of the arena, now a newly formed beach.

Salt water stretched out before them, a demonic creature, or several, undoubtedly lurking beneath the surface. Ocean water licked the bottom of her boots as small waves washed ashore. There were several demons that resided in the water. Krakens and sea serpents would have required the full arena submerged under water. That ruled them out. It left one option: sirens.

A sound rolled out amidst the waves. It was soft at first, building in beautiful melody. She gasped, reaching for her ears. She weaved a concentrated form of air, immediately blocking her ear canals. She worked her jaw at the sensation, as if it would pop the sudden pressure. The only sound she could hear was the beat of her own pulse.

She turned to Aelius, hoping she wasn't too late. He covered his ears, knowing immediately what creature lay in wait. She stood in front of him, waving for his attention. His face was strained, apparently fighting the growing sound of the call. She motioned for him to take his hands down. He shook his head, not understanding what she was planning. She raised her right hand, tapping at the golden ring wrapped around her middle finger: her Allspeak ring. Her mother had made it a habit to use sign language with her, especially in crowded places. It was particularly helpful in such a scenario.

Trust me she signed.

Aelius sighed, bringing his hands down. He would simply have to have faith. Aurora quickly brought her hands to his ears, forming the same intricate weave she had done on herself. He winced and worked his jaw, much like she had moments ago.

Now what? He signed.

We wait. She responded with a smirk.

Aelius studied her, not quite sure what she had in mind. He turned his attention back to the water. It wasn't long before three sirens popped their heads above the waves. Their hair floated on top of the water, each one a little different. A blonde, a brunette, and a red head watched with their dark inhuman eyes, the waves causing them to bob up and down ever so slightly. Their faces, were truly beautiful, stunningly so, as they calculated their next moves. The drawings and renditions in the texts did not do these three justice.

Two of the sirens finally dove beneath the surface, the brunette remaining. Slowly she made her way to the beach, her eyes never breaking from their concentration on Aelius. Moments later, the blonde and red head reappeared on a rock formation several feet from shore. As the pair settled themselves on the rock, their full forms could be seen. Silvery blue fish tails hung over the ledge, their upper bodies completely bare, save for a collection of shells and gems on strands of necklaces. Their mouths moved, song ringing out from their perfect ruby lips, but due to Aurora's quick action, they were safe from their call.

Aelius turned to her, the brunette having reached the shallows of the water. The siren sat herself up, waves lapping against her scaled hips. She flipped her long locks over her shoulder, making sure every inch of her was on display, joining the others in song.

What now? He signed.

Make her think she has you. She instructed. *Get close and use your blade. I will take the other two.*

He gave her a concerned look, but she had told him to trust her. He turned to the siren, melting his cold expression. Her crimson lips curved into a pleased grin as he stepped towards her. She leaned further into him, reaching a slender hand with long nails up to pull him in. She knew from her research that those nails were far more like talons, ready to gut him at just the right moment.

Aurora turned her attention to the other two, ready in the wings for their sister to bring in her victim. They would rush to her side, eager to drown him when the time was right. She held her hands at her side, ready to act the moment Aelius did. It would need to be a carefully timed attack - one second too early or too late would ruin the element of surprise.

Aelius leaned into the brunette, her hand wrapping around a fold in his shirt. She pulled him in, her face mere inches from his. His motion was quick. The siren's face went from pure lust to shocked agony. A blade he had tucked away in his belt found its way deep inside her ribcage. Her tail coiled up and flailed, water splashing everywhere as her black blue blood spilled out.

Aurora had been a beat behind, making sure to act as he did. Aquatic demons could not live without one simple element - water. She raised her hands, pulling the very water from their bodies. They barely had a second to register what had happened to their sister before their physical forms were stripped away. Dark mists of vapour trailed away from them, pooling far from the beach. Aurora guided it far from them, not daring to test the toxicity of siren mist. In mere seconds, mummified corpses fell atop the rock formation, crumbling into the water.

By the time he stood and turned to her, the simulation began to fade away. She turned to Aelius, flashing him a smile as she removed the weave of air in their ears, and conjuring a gust of air to dissipate the mist of siren around her. Something new formed through the bond - sheer amazement and awe.

Chapter 17

Winter break was quickly approaching, with just a couple of days before the semester's end. Aurora had the fortune of no exams that day other than watching the Guardians run their obstacle course. Just as the Guardians were tasked with watching their Defence exams, the Mages were tasked with supporting their course runs. It was thought to be morale boosting to watch each other perform at their peak.

"You okay, Mari?" She asked cautiously. She had noticed Mari was a little off that morning. There were normally morning training sessions, or at very least a run to warm up before classes. That morning, however, she had slept in to a reasonable hour.

She arched her back in a stretch. She heard a few cracks and pops as she twisted. "Ahhhh, it's fine." She responded as she moved into a series of stretches. "None of us know what they'll have for us. There's no sense in freaking out about it."

She had watched Mari and the others train on the obstacle courses before, but the exam was always more complicated. It would be an adaptive test of their ability to problem solve as well as physical prowess. Guardians needed to be at the peak of physical endurance and adaptability to protect their Mages. Injuries were not uncommon, but she hoped that her friends avoided them none the less.

She kept Mari company before they had to head down for the exam. Many lingered back, gathered in small clusters as they waited for the exams to start. Some of the Mages moaned on about not wanting to stand around and watch, but she appreciated the opportunity to see them in action. Maybe it was because she hadn't had to endure years of it, but to her, it was exciting.

She had bundled herself in her winter cloak, a pair of soft mittens, matching hat and scarf. Mari had made sure to mock her that morning, but she had reminded her that she didn't have a Guardian's heat. Mari, in comparison, had kept it to a form fitting jacket and thin leather gloves. Her knee high boots had thick treads to ensure she had grip in the snow, or whatever conditions the course had for her. An ear band kept her ears warm, but according to her, a hat and scarf would be a liability.

Their boots crunched in the snow as they headed towards the rear of the campus where the course awaited. She knew that the course itself would remain behind a glamor, to avoid anyone sneaking a peek. A few students had already arrived, clearly eager to start their exam. It wasn't long before most had gathered. Their professor marched up with the remainder of students. He was short compared to most Guardians she had seen, coming up to the shoulders of most of his students. His bald head was contrasted by his thick dusty grey beard that was styled into a harsh line. He had a permanent glower on his face, but was reportedly quite nice despite his countenance.

"Line up!" He barked out, clipboard of names in hand. The Guardians obediently got in line without a single word.

She wished Mari good luck as she got herself in order. She shuffled between Leila and Dae while the Mages rearranged themselves to watch things unfold.

The professor nodded in satisfaction and clicked an Artefact to collapse the glamor. With a shimmer the exam course was revealed. As her eyes ran along the course, her mouth gaped open.

"Welcome to the assault course." Their professor boomed. "You will start here and run through several obstacles. You will run through the entire course as quickly as possible. Accuracy is just as important as speed. You fall, you fail. You miss, you get docked. Don't screw it up."

One by one the Guardians ran through the course. There were a few close calls, but none had fallen so far. Some earned a disapproving shake of his head as the professor scribbled his notes on time and skill. Finally it was Aelius' turn.

She could feel his quiet-calm radiate through the bond. She knew he would be fine, but her heart raced as he approached the start point.

With a nod of his professor's head, Aelius was off. He scaled the rock wall with an impressive speed. He made each hold look effortless as he climbed twenty feet above the ground. He hoisted himself atop the wall and practically ran across the balance beam. Blasts of fire magic hurtled at his body, courtesy of professor Rossi's contribution, but he dodged each with ease. Her own pulse pounded away in her ears, but his face was completely stoic.

He kept a steady pace, even as he came to the end of the beam. It didn't seem to register to him to pause or take a beat. Pillars scattered the ground before him, barely large enough for someone's foot to land. He bounded from pillar to pillar with a cat like grace. She held her breath as he made the several feet leap from the final pillar to a platform. He landed with a crouch, immediately going down the pipe tunnel that led back down to the ground.

He crawled out and ran straight for the trip wire stretch. Watching his classmates go first would be no advantage, as the pattern changed from student to student. He easily evaded each trip wire until reaching the final stage. Daggers lay at the ready. Projection targets mimicking different creatures settled before him. One after another he released the daggers at the heart of the projections. She made the mistake of blinking while he worked. After what felt like only seconds, Aelius had completed his course. He dropped the remainder of daggers in his hand to the snowy ground as the completion buzzer rang out.

The entire group burst into applause. "Well done." His professor announced as he made his final notes. His eyes met hers for a brief moment, his face breaking out into a bright smile. She couldn't help but return it, cheering out for him among the others.

As the last student completed the course, the professor stepped in front of them. Professor Rossi left with a wave, eager to be done with it all.

"In first place, with top marks, we have Aelius Cirillo!" He bellowed. Applause broke out and Mari cheered loudly with her for him. He smiled with a hint of embarrassment and gave a small wave. "In a close second, we have Cael Torres" applause continued, but the professor did not pause. "And Victor Conti in third. Congrats to you all, and well done for first term. You will receive your final grades before you head home. Now off with you."

The students broke from formation into a babble of relief and chatter. "I'm *so* glad that's over!" Mari exclaimed, a wide grin spread across her face.

Aelius was close behind his sister, a reserved smile on his face. He had been quite proud of himself initially, but it seemed as if he didn't want to boast or brag after the results had been announced.

"Congrats on first place." She stated as he reached their group.

He smiled at her, a swell of pride radiating through the bond.

"I think we need some sort of victory drinks." Dae added as he pulled Mari into him. She giggled and wrapped her arms around his neck.

***

They had all decided on a round of drinks in the common room that night instead of venturing all the way out to Vilcas. The Guardians had been keen on a proper night out, but with the Defence exam looming over their heads the next morning, the Mages had protested.

One round turned into several before everyone finally headed to bed. Try as she might, sleep was not her friend that night. After waking again in the wee hours of the morning, she found herself staring at the ceiling yet again. With a sigh, she headed out to the common room for a tea. She wrapped a blanket around her shoulders as she shuffled quietly, hoping that a chamomile tea may just do the trick.

She rounded the corner in the dark, moonlight streaking through the windows being her only guide. She ran a hand along the wall, searching for the light switch. She flicked on a light in the kitchen, clutching at her heart in fear as Leila came into view. Her heart ached at the sudden thundering of terror, a cry escaping her lips.

"Good lord. Leila you scared me!" She exclaimed in an attempted hush. She was fully awake now. Any hope of sleep was long gone now.

Leila, however, wasn't herself. Aurora stepped closer with caution. Her eyes were glazed over, looking off in the distance somewhere. She didn't see Aurora in the slightest.

"Leila?" She called out warily.

"Nuh uh..." Leila muttered to herself, barely audible at all. It sounded as if she were disagreeing with herself over something.

"Leila I think you need to get back to bed." She advised gently.

"Can't...can't...can't..." She kept repeating to herself in a quiet loop. "More...more pressure. Needs more." She continued as she started walking towards the hall way.

She knew one of the worst things to do was wake a sleep walker, but there was no telling where she would go if left to her own devices. Aurora hurried after her, gently taking her by the shoulder. Her blanket fell to the floor in the process, but it didn't matter. She turned Leila around carefully and led her back towards the dorm hall. "Let's head back to your room, Leila." She explained gently.

She took her down the hall, thankful she remembered her room number. She lightly knocked on the door, knocking a second time after no answer. Her room mate, Joanna, answered begrudgingly. "Sorry." She whispered. "I found her out in the kitchen."

Joanna blinked a moment, realising Leila was indeed not herself. She grabbed her by the wrist and muttered a thanks as she pulled her friend inside. As the door locked, she felt resolved that she had done the right thing. She trudged back to the kitchen and scooped her blanket up from the floor. It was going to be a long night.

Chapter 18

It was defence exam day. Aurora sat on the edge of her bed, and stared at the floor. She knew that she had put the work in. She had a solid plan in place. It didn't stop the swirl and twirl of nerves in the pit of her stomach. Mari stepped out of the shower, fresh from her morning training session. Her classes were over for the term, but she insisted that the consistent training sessions were essential.

She rubbed her hair with a towel as she stepped into the closet. "You'll be fine." She shouted out to Aurora as she got herself dressed for the day. "You showed me the other day. You've got this."

She sighed and flopped back on the bed to stare at the ceiling. "I know..." She answered. "I just want to get it over with so I can stop feeling irrationally nervous."

Mari chuckled as she stepped out, ready to go. "You can't always logic your way out of emotions you know."

She flipped over to face Mari, propping herself up on her forearms. "I hate emotions sometimes..." She grumbled. "So stupid."

Mari laughed and pulled her up to her feet. "Come on," She insisted. "Half of it is probably being hungry. We'll get some breakfast in you and it'll be better."

She wasn't the only one who was on edge. Several of her Mage classmates were scattered through the Dining Hall, all with the same look of nerves and dread spread across their faces. It was Leila that made her the most concerned, however. She had hoped that after getting her back to bed last night, that she would have seemed better.

"I'm worried about Leila." She confessed. "I ran into her last night and she was sleep walking; kept talking to herself. I managed to get her back to her room, but I don't know..." They both stole a glance at her. It was then that Joanna stepped in behind Leila and placed a hand gingerly on her shoulder. It took her a moment to snap out of her thoughts and look up at her room mate. She gave her a forced smile.

"Looks like Jo's got it covered." Mari remarked as she took another spoon of oatmeal. "Leila's an over thinker. Just like someone else I know..." She trailed off, giving Aurora a loaded look.

"Fair enough." She sighed. "I'll mind my business."

***

Their exam was held in the Mage's arena. Professor Rossi stood before the arena gate. She held her clipboard firmly at her chest as she took in every one of her students and their Guardians. "You will display your technique twice today. The first demonstration will be a control display. Your second display will be an active display in reaction to a live projection. I want to see how your technique is supposed to be performed versus how you react under pressure. Any questions?" The class was silent as her cold eyes scanned the students. "Good. Guardians in the front row. You need to see what your Mages are capable of up close. You have five minutes before I start calling names."

Aurora exchanged glances with Mari. She gave her an assuring nod before turning back to Dae to encourage him as well. She took a deep breath and climbed the stairs a few rows to observe. She watched as the Guardians broke away to sit in the front row. Mari took a seat at the beginning of the aisle, wanting to be nearest to the gate it seemed. Aelius settled in beside her, turning to give her a small smile and a wave from his seat. She waved back, feeling all the little bit more relaxed knowing he was there.

"First up," Rossi's voice cut above the chatter. "Dae Choi."

Mari jumped to her feet and let out a loud cheer. Some of the other Guardians joined in with a light scattering of applause and support. Dae shook his head and chuckled to himself as he headed down into the arena.

The gate shut firmly behind him as he stepped towards the centre of the arena. He explained that his demonstration was a water based spring trap. He conjured what looked like a simple puddle of water several feet in front of him. Once something stepped into the puddle, it would trigger an automatic response to encase and drown the offender. Rossi nodded in approval as she took her notes and clicked the simulator. The terrain quickly changed to a forest clearing. Dae recreated his puddle trap, this time making it look like a small pond, and headed for cover in the trees. It wasn't long before a manticore stalked out of the trees into the clearing. It scanned the area and finally noticed the pool of water. It checked its surroundings before bending down to drink. The instant the creature's mouth touched the surface, the water sprung to life and encapsulated it.

It thrashed and riled with panic, but the bubble of water held strong. Dae stepped out from the tree line and maintained his weave. Paws swiped desperately, bat like wings beat with fury, but nothing could help it. Dae's conjure worked seamlessly and the water moved against the manticore's attempts, refusing to give any sway. Bubbles trailed from its mouth as it gasped for air. The manticore jerked slower and slower, finally dead and drowned from Dae's defence technique.

The water gave way, the body of the manticore dropping to the grassy clearing. Applause rang out, Mari of course being the loudest. Rossi clicked the simulator once more and the arena reset itself. Dae stepped out to Mari sweeping him into a giant hug. "Get back to your seat, Mr Choi." Rossi called out with annoyance. He hurried up the stairs and took a seat next to Aurora. "Great job." She whispered with a smile.

"Thanks." He whispered back, all of the stress faded from his face.

Rossi stood and called out her next student. "Leila Fadel."

She got to her feet slowly, but moved toward the gate. A few of the Mages gave a small cheer of encouragement, her nerves clearly written across her face. She flashed a nervous smile and proceeded to the arena centre. "I will be demonstrating an Earth trigger system." She began with a slight waver in her voice. "When something steps on the unsuspecting root, a poisoned spike defence is triggered to impale or wound."

Aurora creased her brow in concern. She ran her eyes along the line of the arena barrier. Something didn't look quite right. "You see it?" She whispered to Dae as she nudged him.

He leaned into her, keeping his eyes on the arena. "See what?"

"The shield. It doesn't...*look* right." She tried to explain.

He dismissed with a shrug. "I don't see it. It always goes up. It's fine."

She dropped it. She was likely looking for something to be wrong. What was important was focusing on the exams at hand. It wouldn't be fair for her to interrupt Leila.

Leila proceeded to conjure what indeed look like a simple series of roots onto the arena floor. She conjured a pebble and stepped back far enough to not worry about her own safety. She tossed the pebble at the series of roots, and within a heartbeat, a good dozen or more black spikes bolted up from the ground. They held for a moment before slowly retracting back into the ground. She could see a few beads of sweat forming along Leila's brow, but she had ultimately held it together. She smiled in relief. She knew how hard she had been working to do it well.

Rossi finished her notes and clicked the simulator. The same forest clearing Dae had just used settled around her. Aurora noticed a shift in Leila; her anxiety building. She seemed to tremble ever so slightly, her hands showing it the most. She took a deep breath, willing her hands to stop shaking. Approaching footsteps of a demonic creature could be heard from the opposite tree line. Her breath shuddered as she quickly tried to recreate her defence system. Her body trembled despite all attempts of calm breathing. Slowly, the roots reformed in the ground, the stomps of heavy footsteps approaching ever closer.

Thick hooves met the grassy clearing floor as a massive Minotaur stepped out from behind the trees. Leila had not had time to find cover and hide. The Minotaur leaned forward, arms arched out and bellowed at her. Leila screamed in terror, clamping her hands over her ears. They all knew it was preparing to charge. She had only moments before it would bolt full force at her with its long, pointed horns. She staggered backward, unable to tear her eyes from it. They all knew that the projections in the arena weren't real, but when you were right in the middle of it, it was hard to tell your brain it wasn't all very real. Several of the Guardians had even raised to their feet in concern, Mari and Aelius included.

The Minotaur scraped its hoof through the grass, kicking up large clumps of dirt. Once, twice, and then it leaned in for a charge. Leila turned with a cry and raised her hands above her. In one swift moment, she called up a wall of thick wood around her and triggered her spike technique early. The students took cover out of instinct despite the shield in place. Except...

A wet squelch sounded as a thick, black spike had lodged deep into Mari's chest. Right below her collarbone on her right side, the spike pierced her straight through. Blood dripped in slow, thick drops from the tip protruding several inches from her back. She stood in shock as she coughed. Fresh blood sputtered out of her mouth with each hack. Her knees gave way as she started to fall. It was then that everyone had finally processed what was happening.

Aurora was on her feet before she had a moment to think. She had no idea she could even move that fast. She didn't care who she tore through as she shoved other Guardians out of her way. Edwyn tried to grab her arm to pull her back, but she ripped it out of his grasp. The blood sputtering from Mari's mouth had already started to turn dark, nearly black in colour. A choking, wheezing sound started to come out from the back of her throat. It was then that the tremors started. Aelius held her tight, fighting the seizing motion, tears of rage and sorrow streaming down his cheeks.

"Mari!" She cried out, holding her head in her hands. Mari's eyes had rolled back into the back of her head and the tremors grew in intensity. One of her arms flung up in a sudden movement, hitting Aurora square in the nose. Her eyes stung with tears as she winced and grabbed her nose. Her glasses lay somewhere behind her as she heard the crunch of glass and metal on the concrete floor. None of it mattered. Mari was dying.

She wiped the tears from her eyes and grabbed a hold of her shoulders. Screams cried out from around her, but they were nothing but noise. She felt Edwyn's hands on her, trying to pull her back, but refused to leave Mari's side. Something started to bubble beneath the surface. Heat flooded her veins. It wasn't the heat of the Guardian bond, or the heat of anger. It was searing, burning sunshine; liquid, molten lava within her very being. It boiled within her, needing to be released.

Before she knew what she was doing, she grabbed a firm hold of the spike and pulled. She could hear Aelius curse at her and demand what she was doing. She could feel his panic and despair through the bond, but she shoved it down. It didn't matter. It was all just background noise. She dropped the spike with a clatter to the ground. Those behind her jumped back as if it would jump up like a live viper. She wiped her left hand on the side of her breaches and placed both hands over the oozing wound. Thick, black blood curdled out of the entry wound.

Mari continued to thrash in Aelius' arms as she hovered her hands above her. The warmth wanted its release. She closed her eyes and willed it out. Gold orbs pulsed out of her, directly into the wound. What started as a few at first, soon turned into a steady stream. The tap had been opened and had no intention of stopping. The relief was immanent. She sighed as the overwhelming sensation started to ebb. As she opened her eyes, she finally saw what she was doing.

Mari's body had grown still as her wound knitted together. Her chest was still caked in a sludge of black blood, but it had stopped oozing. Her ragged breathing regulated, and colour started to return to her golden skin. The golden orbs started to slow, no longer desperately seeking Mari's wound. With the last trickle of light ceasing, she finally turned her palms up to herself in disbelief. She slowly blinked and finally met her eyes with Aelius in front of her. His look of pure shock was the last thing she registered before she lost consciousness.

Chapter 19

It was only a matter of seconds before she regained her senses. Her head swam and throbbed in pain, but it didn't matter. She shook her head in an attempt to clear away what lingered. All that mattered was Mari.

She tried to sit up, but was held back. It was then that she realised that someone held her. She looked over her shoulder to see that Edwyn cradled her in his arms. She blinked up at him a few times, trying to make sense of what was going on. She pulled away from him and leaned forward to where Mari leaned into Aelius' arms.

"Mari?" She called out cautiously.

It was then that she saw a smile cross her lips. Relief flooded her. "Hey, Ari." She replied drowsily. She was alive. Whatever she had just done had worked.

Hot tears rolled down her cheeks as she burst out into relieved laughter. She knew that she likely looked like a mad woman, but she didn't care. Mari was alive. Edwyn carefully grabbed her by the shoulder. She could feel from his touch that he was concerned, but didn't want to force her. She turned to face him, finally taking in those that had surrounded them. Mages and Guardians alike lingered, all wondering the same thing - what just happened?

"You saw that, right?" She heard a pair of Mages whispering amidst themselves. They stared at her, glancing over at her glasses that lay broken several feet away.

Aurora cast her eyes down, knowing what they saw.

"Get both of them to the medical wing." Professor Rossi barked. *"Now!"*

She let out a small yelp as she felt Edwyn scoop her effortlessly into his arms. She instinctively wrapped her arms around his neck, despite knowing that he had a firm hold on her. Her head swirled with an array of emotions; rage, pain, and confusion. Never had Aelius bombarded her with so many things. She leaned her head into Edwyn's shoulder, not able to make sense of any of it. Everything became a sensory overload coupled with a piercing headache.

Aelius eased Mari to her feet and asked her quietly if she wanted help walking or to be lifted. She shooed off his offers of being carried, and simply slung an arm through his for added support. "You have her?" Aurora heard Aelius ask.

Edwyn nodded, holding her even tighter. Hurt and even what felt oddly close to jealousy flared through the bond.

***

The doctor had reviewed her over thrice by the time he finally decided he was satisfied with his findings. "It's what it looks like, Miss Thomas." He began. "It seems that you somehow have Solis lineage in you."

Her stomach dropped at his words. She knew what she had done and logically what it had to mean. The problem is how many questions it raised.

"Miss Cirillo has been given a clean bill of health." He added, seeing that his previous statement had started to settle. "If it weren't for what you did, she most definitely would have died today. You did well." He assured with a gentle pat on her shoulder.

She gave him a small smile of thanks as he left her curtained room. She waited a moment before sliding to her feet. Everything felt numb. Her entire life had been a series of lies. She shuffled through the hall to the medical wing lobby, ignoring the quiet comments and protests from the support nurses.

She finally snapped to at the sound of Mari's voice. She stood there before her, bright and energetic as ever. Her face lit up the moment she saw Aurora and rushed her with a fierce hug. She felt her feet lift from the floor as she squeezed harder and harder. Mari set her back down and grabbed her by her arms and leaned down ever so slightly to match her eye level. "I can't thank you enough, Ari."

She let out a small laugh in response. "You're alive, Mari. That's thanks enough for me."

She gasped as Aelius wrapped them both into an embrace. She could swear she heard a sniffle from him before he released them. "Thank you." He managed to finally get out.

"Me too." Dae echoed, his tone clearly drained from the entire experience. She hadn't even seen him past Aelius at first, but it was clear that he had been waiting the entire time for any news. She grabbed his hand and squeezed.

Mari took Aurora by the arm. "We're going back to our room and we're going to talk about all this. We are not dealing with anyone else."

She looked at Mari in surprise. "You should be with Dae, Mari." She argued.

She shook her head. "He's okay. I'll be with him later."

He nodded in agreement. "It's fine. I know she's okay."

With that, she let Mari take her back to their dorm. People openly gawked and whispered, but she ignored it. She had zero mental capacity to deal with it at the moment. It could be tomorrow's problem. The moment the door shut behind them, she knew she was able to fall apart. Mari held her as the shock set in and the shakes started to take her. Her teeth chattered as if intense cold had set into her bones. Mari rubbed her arms and held her tight. "It'll pass. Once it does I'll get tea or something stronger."

"S-s-strong-ng-ger." She stammered through chatters.

A few minutes after her shakes and trembles passed, Mari reached under her bed for a bottle of vodka. She searched a moment for a couple of clean glasses and settled on clean mugs before pouring. Aurora wrapped her hands around the mug and took the shot immediately, passing it back to wordlessly ask for another. Mari obliged and poured another.

"What are you feeling?" She asked as she took her own shot of vodka.

She sighed as she contemplated it. It wasn't a simple answer by any means. "A lot." She started, swallowing another shot before setting the mug to the side. "My mother lied to me. *A lot.*"

"You had no idea?" Mari asked as delicately as possible.

She shook her head. "Makes sense why she kept me hidden away and never let me go to school." She half muttered to herself. "I'll be back." She explained as she headed to the washroom.

She closed the door behind herself before splashing cold water on her face. She patted it dry and leaned her hands on the ledge of the countertop. Her reflection stared back at her with her real eye colour. She had gotten so used to the glasses that had no prescription. She had always wondered why her mother had insisted she wear them all the time when they didn't help her see any better. She had wondered why they turned her eyes a pretty green like her mother's instead of her piercing ice blue, just like... It made sense now.

She stepped back out into the room, seeing Mari speaking with someone at the door. She turned with a serious look on her face. "The Dean is asking for you."

***

She followed the Dean's assistant through the halls to the office. She had only ever seen her from behind the desk, but as she followed behind her, she noticed just how small and frail she was. She held herself with an important dignity, looking down on all of the students that bustled through the Academy, but she barely came up to Aurora's shoulder. She felt the warmth of the vodka spread through her body by the time they reached the office. She was thankful in that moment that she had stopped at two.

The assistant opened the door and returned to her seat behind the desk. She stepped in and let the doors fall closed behind her. Dean Reyes waited for her, leaning against the front edge of her desk. She uncrossed her legs and stood up to greet her. "Miss Thomas."

"Dean Reyes." She responded curtly, remaining where she stood. She crossed her arms beneath her chest and stared back at the Dean.

The Dean let out a small chuckle at the show of defiance and walked around to take her seat. She leaned her elbows on the desk and rested her chin in her hands. "What a morning..." She broke the tense silence with a smirk.

She sighed before finally taking a seat before the Dean. She had a feeling she might be here a while. "It was negligence." She stated a matter of factly. "None of this would have happened if the shields had been in place. They weren't right before her exam."

"They weren't...*right?*" The Dean pressed.

She fought the impulse to roll her eyes. "They weren't working properly. If you really looked you could see that it wasn't activated to keep the spectators safe. Is it not supposed to be automatically triggered?" She felt her anger rising.

"They are. What I am interested in is the fact that you can see it." She countered.

She paused. "Is that not...normal?"

The Dean rested her hands on the desk. "It's not. It's likely correlated with the rest of your hidden talents."

And there it was. She wondered how long it would take her to address it. "I didn't know." She responded defensively.

The Dean shook her hand dismissively. "I don't believe you did, and you're not being accused of anything, Miss Thomas. I believe your mother put many things in place to keep things concealed, even from yourself."

She chewed her bottom lip at the thought. It certainly seemed that way. All of the Artefacts, all of the lies and moving around. "Why?" She finally spoke out loud, almost too quietly to hear.

Dean Reyes sighed. "She probably wanted a happier life for you."

She looked up at the Dean, surprised that she had spoken the question out loud. "What do you mean?"

Reyes leaned forward. "Anyone with Spirit magic is a part of the Empire's lineage. Spirit magic is incredibly rare and even more valuable. I imagine your mother wanted to let you live a life outside of their influence."

She had a point. Part of her history class catch up had been details of the Imperial Family tree. Anyone born with the ability to conjure Spirit was kept close. She would have been forced to grow up in the castle under the tutelage and guidance of the Empire. "Do you know who my father is, then?"

She looked up at the Dean and saw her physically tense. She tried to hide it, but it looked like a shock surged down her spine. "Knowing the truth will not make your life any better, Aurora."

"That's not a no." She pointed out.

"You're right. It's all that I can say, however." She confessed with a sigh and a wince. For some reason it looked as if even that round about statement wore on her. She studied the Dean, wondering if there was any chance of gleaning anything else from her. Just as she opened her mouth to press more, the Dean cut her off. "Anyway, in lieu of this all, you will be granted access to the restricted section of the library."

"There's a restricted section?" She questioned. She had spent countless hours in the library. It had nearly become more of a home than her own dorm room, but she had yet to find any hint of a banned section.

The Dean gave a knowing smile. "It is not common knowledge for many reasons. Each Dean has the responsibility to move any texts that contain privileged or out of date material into a special section of the library. It is forbidden to dispose of any texts in our library, so this was the next best thing."

"But I don't understand why *I* am being given access. What does it have to do with me?"

"Your newly presented abilities are incredibly rare and unique. We do not have the authorised staff to help guide and teach you. I will be writing to the Empire to ask what we should do about you, but until then, I suggest you research and read up in the library." She gave her a look over the rim of her glasses, insisting she read between the lines as she slid an old iron wrought key. It was different from the key to her dorm room, much older and worn.

She nodded in response. "I will."

"Very good." She concluded as she rose to her feet. "The head librarian will show you where to find the glamoured door. If you think of anything else, you know where to find me." She guided a hand towards the door, implying that they were finished no matter what Aurora had to add.

She stood as well and thanked her for her time. It wasn't until she was on the other side of the thick doors that she realised that she had been completely distracted from her anger and talking points. She hit the back of her head on the door in frustration. So many of her questions were still unanswered. She looked down at the heavy key in her hand. Maybe the restricted section was the Dean's way of helping.

With a deep breath, she decided to head back to her dorm. There, she could figure things out. Or, at least have another shot. The clack of hurried heeled footsteps echoed in the hall. She turned to her left, wondering who strode down the hall with such purpose in their steps.

Chapter 20

Astraea had a fake smile plastered across her face as she marched towards the Dean's office. She hadn't had much interaction with the princess, but none of it had been pleasant. There was just something about her entire energy that didn't sit right with her.

"Aurora." She lilted in greeting.

"Astraea." She replied cautiously.

"Be a dear and follow me, would you?" She asked sweetly. She extended a manicured hand to her as if to join hands like friends and skip through the halls. She stared down at the hand she offered her. It didn't feel right.

"I'm alright, thanks." She stated simply, her arms crossed at her chest. She could hear the scoff of the Dean's assistant in the background. She knew that a majority of the staff idolised the princess. How dare she turn down such a perfect angel?

"I really must insist." Astraea pressed, doing her best not to grit her teeth in frustration. It was her eyes that gave her away. "We really must chat."

With a sigh, she decided to follow her. It would do no good arguing against such insistence. The look in her eyes told her that she would have this conversation whether she wanted it or not.

The pair walked in silence, Astraea guiding her to an empty tutoring room. It was the same as the ones she used in the secondary campus. Perfectly sized for a private discussion.

"Now," Astraea began, content that they had some privacy. "I want to know exactly what you've been playing at." The fake pleasantries were over. Her true expression showed.

"What are you talking about?" She asked, completely confused.

"You've clearly got Solis blood in you." She sneered. "I need to know which one of my cousins to tear apart. You're clearly someone's bastard that they were either oblivious to, or didn't cover up properly. Either way, it's someone's problem."

Her brow shot up in surprise. It was the first time hearing her speak this way. "I honestly have no idea, and I can't help you."

Astraea rolled her eyes and scoffed. "You're not stupid, Aurora. You can't seriously expect me to believe that you had no idea."

"I didn't." She insisted simply. "I'm only realising now how much my mother kept from me."

Astraea studied her for a time, trying to discern whether or not she was telling the truth. "Well whatever the truth is, don't expect any favours from me. I will *not* be helping you."

***

By the time she returned to the dorm, she could hear heightened voices. Her body tensed as she approached cautiously, but as she got closer, she was able to discern it was Leila who sobbed at their door. "I'm so sorry." She cried out.

Mari wrapped her arms around her and pat her on the shoulder. She locked eyes with Aurora as she inched closer. "It's okay, Leila." She assured.

"No one blames you." Aurora added.

Leila gasped, unaware that she had just arrived. She burst into a fresh flood of guilt ridden tears. "I never m-meant t-to..." She stammered.

Aurora wrapped her arms around her as well, the three of them now half standing in the doorway. "None of it was your fault. You were just doing your work. If the shield had been in place, none of this would have happened. Everything is okay."

She sniffled and hiccuped as she wiped away her tears. "If it wasn't for you, though...I-I just don't even want to think about it..." Her eyes welled up again at the mere idea of what may have happened.

She brushed some of the hair from Leila's eyes. She blinked up at her and gave her a strained smile. "Focusing on what may have been can drive anyone mad." She explained. "We're here to talk, but after today, we don't dwell on it." She gently held her face to make sure she truly heard her words. *"No one* here blames you. So don't go blaming yourself."

As the sun started to set outside their window, Leila finally agreed to head back to her own room. They had gone over it all, rather in circles, until she was talked out. She had calmed significantly, but it was clear that there was some lingering guilt within her heart. It would take time for her to let go of it.

"How did you get so calm and wise with your words?" Mari teased as they shut the door behind her.

Aurora laughed in response, as she took off her boots in favour for some slippers. "I'm always better at giving advice than following it. I can be super insightful for anyone other than myself. Super useful..." She admitted with a dose of sarcasm at the end.

Mari paused, looking as if she was debating her next words. With a sigh, she decided to just spit it out. "Did you know?"

Aurora sat on the edge of her bed and shook her head. "I wish I had. I wish she had trusted me enough to know."

"Maybe she thought she was protecting you?" She offered as an option.

She let out a wry laugh. "Oh I have no doubt that she thought she was protecting me. And I'd get it if I was five, but I'm almost twenty years old. Now I'm left here trying to pick up pieces and put them together."

"I'm pretty sure she figured she had more time." Mari pointed out.

"I know..." She replied, pulling her knees into her chest. "I'm just so *mad* at her, but also love her. I want to scream at her, but hug her. It's all just a lot. Simple would be nice..." She sighed.

"I think simple might be behind you, Ari."

She jumped as a sharp rap sounded on the door. Mari got up to answer, finding Aelius at the door, a stern look on his face. "Mom wants to talk. To *both* of you." He explained.

Mari stepped aside, letting him in. She locked the door behind him and walked to her beside table. "Drink?" She offered. He shook his head, taking a seat in one of the chairs by the fireplace.

"You talked to her already then?" Mari asked, settling herself on her bed.

"I didn't want her finding out from the Dean." He responded gruffly.

Mari sighed. "I know, you're right. Give it." She beckoned with her hand.

He arched a brow at her. "Use yours." He protested.

She stuck her tongue out at him as she rolled over to grab her own com out of the bedside table. She set her drink down and flipped the Artefact open. It quickly lit up as she made a quick selection to call her mother. It barely rang once before her mother picked up.

An image of their mother projected from the small Artefact. From where she sat, Aurora could see that Mari very much took after her mother. She was a beautiful woman in her late forties with the same thick curls, much longer than Mari's, however. "*Amaris Maria Cirillo.*" She called out in a lecturing tone. "What is happening at that school that my *only* daughter is getting skewered alive while watching an exam?!"

"It wasn't her fault." Mari argued, sitting up at the sound of hearing her full name. "Leila was just trying to run through her demonstration and got upset."

"Oh I'm not blaming the Mage!" Her mother explained. "It's the faculty's fault for not securing the arena. I'm going to skin Sophia alive if it's the last thing I—-"

"Alright, come on now dear." A low voice cut in. Mari's father appeared in the projection as well, attempting to soothe his enraged wife. He was an older version of Aelius with a short hair style and well trimmed beard. Streaks of grey dusted his temples and peppered his dark beard. "There will be a full report and we will speak with Soledad about it once the data is reviewed. The important thing is that our daughter is safe."

Mari's mother let out a sigh, her husband's words enough to settle her slightly. "I suppose..." She grumbled.

"It's all due to Aurora here." Mari added, getting up from her bed to sit down beside her.

Before she knew it, Mari got in right beside her, putting her on display for her parents. Her cheeks grew hot from embarrassment, not expecting to meet either one in that moment. "Oh...uhm...hi." She stammered, unsure of the appropriate greeting to use under the circumstances.

"This is her?!" Her mother exclaimed, seeming to grab her Artefact closer to examine.

"Yes, mom, this is Aurora." Mari chuckled. "If it wasn't for her, well..." She trailed off, not quite sure it was appropriate to make the dark joke that she had been considering.

Mari's mother's eyes welled with tears as she tried to keep herself from sniffling on camera. "Thank you, Aurora." She mustered. "You have *no* idea how much it means to us that you were able to Heal our daughter. I...I just..." Her emotions got the best for her as she choked up. She passed the Artefact to her husband for a moment while she attempted to collect herself.

"My wife and I are eternally grateful to you, Aurora." Mari's father picked up where his wife left off. "We would very much like to have you over sometime to thank you properly."

"You don't have to thank me, sir." She insisted, a little unsure of exactly how to address him. She had heard that he was an important official within the Empire, and didn't want to misspeak. "I honestly had no idea what I was doing. I just knew that I had to do something. Mari means...she means a lot to me and I couldn't just stand by.."

Mari looked over at her, tears glistening in her eyes as well. She wrapped an arm around her and pulled her into a half hug. She leaned her head against hers. "I love you both, and we're going to rest up I think. I promise to let you know if anything changes, but the doctor checked us both over thoroughly." She assured.

"I'll be keeping watch, dad." Aelius chimed in from his seat. She had almost forgotten he was there on account of how quiet he had been.

She saw their father nod in approval. "Good." He replied sternly. It seemed that Aelius had his father's nature. "I want to know immediately if anything changes."

"Love you!" Mari called out, blowing a kiss to them both before clicking the Artefact shut. She sighed, dropping it by her side on the bed. "Well you met my parents." She chuckled.

"They're nice." She smiled. It was clear that there was a lot of love in their family.

"They're a little crazy, but I love them." Mari admitted, shuffling over to her own bed. "Are you really staying over?" She asked with a slight sneer as she turned to her brother.

He gave her a challenging glare as he leaned back into his chair. "It's not up for discussion."

"You're taking my bed then." Aurora chimed in, surprising them both. Aelius flushed bright red, opening his mouth to protest. "I mean...no! I'll share with Mari. There's no way you're going to sleep in a chair like that. It can't be good for your back." She rambled, realising how her comment must have sounded.

"I'm not taking your bed." He explained as he stood to his feet. "The floor is fine. I'm going to grab a few things from my room and then I'll be back. No arguing." He added, pointing at his sister.

"Sorry about him." Mari apologised once he left. "Whenever he's upset, he gets even more protective."

She knew exactly what Mari meant. She could feel every bit of turmoil that bubbled beneath the surface. His face was calm, but she felt every shred of worry, hurt, and desire to fix things. She had felt how helpless he felt while Mari thrashed and sputtered. "I felt it, Mar." She explained. "I felt every bit of panic and worry he had for you in those moments. He loves you more than you know."

Mari bit her bottom lip, knowing that she was right. She ran her fingers through her hair. "I know. I drive him crazy, but he's a good brother. I'll go easy on him." She downed the last of her drink, setting the glass on her bedside table. "I'm going to see Dae for a second. I won't be long."

"I'll be here." She replied, giving her a hug to send her off. She could see the effects of the day start to settle in her eyes. She had been concerned when she insisted on staying with her instead of being with him.

With Mari gone, the room felt suddenly quiet and very empty. Everything had felt so chaotic and fast, that she had barely had a moment to sit and register everything. She sat herself in front of the empty fireplace, sparking a fire inside. She watched the flames dance and crackle, the warmth radiating on her face.

She heard a knock on the door, the bond confirming it was Aelius. She opened the door for him, an over night bag slung over his shoulder. He scanned the room, turning back to her with a questioning look. "She went to see Dae." She explained before he could ask.

He set his bag down on the floor by the chairs. "Can't say I blame her." He sighed, sitting on the arm of the chair.

She took a step to him, reaching out to hold his hand, but stopped herself. "Are you alright?" She asked.

He looked up at her, the pain in his eyes finally starting to show. "I..." She could feel it through the bond, even if he didn't say it aloud.

"It's okay if you're not." She explained, taking the seat beside him. "We don't have to talk about it if you don't wan—"

He finally met her eyes, the look he gave her cutting her off. "She almost died in my arms." He finally stated. "I was right with her and couldn't do *anything.*"

She grabbed his hand in hers. "You did everything you could."

He looked away, not wanting her to see the emotions that welled up. "It's my job to take care of things; to protect the people I care about. What sort of Guardian can't even protect his little sister?"

She grabbed him by the chin, turning him back to look at her. "There will always be things out of our hands." She assured him. She felt as if her heart were breaking at the pain he radiated through the bond. He always seemed so self assured and in control, but he was torn apart inside. "She will be okay. It can't all be on you."

The sound of a key turning in the door was enough to make Aelius jump to his feet. He turned away from her, wiping his eyes with the back of his hand. He stood, his arms crossed at his chest and seemingly fine by the time Mari stepped in. She herself looked as if she had been crying as well. "Dae says hi and thanks for letting him borrow me." She stated with a half laugh.

"You could have taken your time." She explained, knowing it was likely a hard time to be away from him.

Mari shook her head. "It's fine. I should probably turn in before it's too late. Besides, Aelius promised dad I'd be under observation. Don't want to get him in trouble." She teased.

Chapter 21

Aelius had kept to his word, sleeping on the floor. She had started to protest, but knew it would be a futile effort. Stubbornness ran strong in the Cirillo family. Aurora had finally managed to convince him to at least take a pillow and spare blanket, but there was no convincing him of sleeping anywhere else.

By the time Aurora woke, she noticed Aelius lounging with a book by the fireplace. He peered up at her, pressing a finger to his lips in a shushing motion. She checked the bed beside her, seeing Mari still asleep soundly. She slipped out of bed and took a seat beside him. "She okay? She never sleeps in." She whispered.

He nodded. "She sleeps in if she's sick or not well. I'm sure yesterday took a lot out of her."

"What are you reading?" She asked, surprised to see him with a book. He closed the text and turned it over to her. One of her mother's books on ancient Artefacts had been the subject of his attention. She looked back over to the bookcase behind her bed. "Sneaky." She responded with a smirk, realising that he would have had to step silently to select it from her side of the book case.

He did his suppress a grin, but failed to do so as he opened the book back up. "Maybe..."

"What time is it?" They heard Mari groan.

He shut the book and placed it on the side table. He fought the instinct to rush to her side and remained in his seat. "It's around eight. How are you feeling?" He asked.

"Like I spent an entire day training." She sighed. She sat up, her hair wild from tossing in her sleep. "And hungry."

He chuckled to himself. "Well hungry is good. Get dressed and we'll go get something to eat." He declared.

Mari agreed, heading immediately for the shower. Aurora tucked herself in the chair, waiting out of the way for her turn. It was then that she heard a chiming sound ring out. Aelius perked up, turning to the side table where he had placed her book. He opened his communicator, his mother displaying as soon as it lit up.

"How is she?" She asked, a hint of anxiousness in her voice.

"Morning, mom." He greeted her calmly. "She just woke up. She's tired and sore, but it's to be expected. She's in the shower and I'll be getting some food in her before we head home."

Her mother relaxed, letting out a small sigh. "She slept well?"

He nodded. "She tossed and turned a little, but nothing concerning."

"Thank you, sweetheart." She appreciated. "I'm glad you could keep an eye on her."

"Of course." He responded with a nod.

"What time do you think you'll be home?" She asked, wanting to be prepared.

He glanced over at the washroom, hearing the shower turn on. "I would wager around lunch time, but I'll let you know when we're looking to leave."

"Okay good. I'll have the guest room set up by the time you get here."

He creased his brow in confusion. "Guest room?" He asked.

"Of course! I can't expect Aurora to share with your sister."

She straightened at the sudden mention of her name. Aelius glanced at her a moment, before turning back to his mother. "No mom."

"What do you mean *no*?" She countered. "You're bringing her home with you, Aelius."

He paused a moment, choosing his words carefully with his mother. He stood to his feet and positioned himself by the window, giving Aurora a little bit of space. "She's not ready, mom. Don't push her." He stressed.

She blinked a moment, surprised that he was standing up for her without her having to say a single word. It wasn't that she didn't want to meet their parents, it was simply too soon.

"That sweet girl is going to be on her own over the holiday. How can you just say no and not bring her home with you?" His mother argued.

"If you're really so concerned about her being alone I can stay here and make sure she's taken care of." He retorted. There was a slight challenge to his tone, without being disrespectful.

She finally huffed in frustration. "I don't like it."

"I know, mom. But she needs time. We will make sure to bring her once she's ready."

"Alright then." She conceded. "I love you, and get home safe and sound."

"Love you too." He said before clicking the com shut. He turned back to her, and gave a sigh. "Sorry about all of that. She means well, but can be pushy."

She shook her head. "It's okay. I know she was just trying to make sure I'm taken care of as well. You didn't have to argue with her on my behalf though."

He gave her a small smile. "You aren't ready, and she needs to learn that no means no." He chuckled.

The door opened with Mari stepping out drying her hair with a towel. "Your turn, Ari." She stated as she headed into the closet.

***

"You're sure you don't want to come back with me?" Mari pressed as she slung her bag over her shoulder.

"Just as bad as mom..." Aelius muttered under his breath as he waited.

She stifled a chuckle, shooting him a look. "Thanks, Mar, but I am in no place to go home and do...family stuff. Some silence and solitude sounds perfect right now."

She sighed. "My parents are going to give me hell for not bringing you with me, you know. They're not the type take no for an answer."

She smiled. "Oh I know. Aelius already defended me on the com while you were in the shower. I just think I need books and sleep right now."

"Sounds boring." She stated with a scrunch of her nose. "Sometimes boring is good." She wrapped her in a tight farewell hug. "I'll see you soon."

Aelius hung back a moment, suddenly uncertain of how he should leave her. She looked up at him, equally unsure if she should hug him like Mari or simply wave him off. He chose for her, bringing her into a soft hug. "Have a good break, Aurora." He said gently, releasing her from his hold. He paused a moment, as if he was hesitating his next move. He reached into his bag, giving her the same pouch he had done before. She had come to learn there would be chocolate inside.

A soft smile formed on her face at the gesture. She had no idea why he would do it every so often, but it was sweet of him. "Thanks, Aelius."

He gave her a nod and turned off down the hall. She wasn't sure how she felt as she watched him leave. It was conceited of her to think that he felt anything more than friendship. Aelius was a good person, far better than most she had ever met. He was kind, thoughtful, and intensely protective. For her to presume that his actions had any romantic motive would just cause problems.

Aurora sat down in one of the chairs with a sigh, her first semester marks staring at her on the table. They had arrived when she was in the shower apparently, her name scrawled across the envelopes in an ornate font. There was no time like the present she decided, cracking the letters open one by one. Artefacts was a perfect one hundred, and History scoring a ninety. Her eyes continued down to Pact Formation - a fair eighty-five percent. She had hoped for better, but it was still a decent grade.

Defence 101, however, was blank. An asterisk was in place of the grade. She flipped the page over to see what notes there could possibly be.

In lieu of events during examinations, students will be exempt from the final exam. Students should report to Professor Rossi in the new year for their final grade.

She sighed and dropped the paper back onto the table. She wondered if her healing performance would have any sway on her final grade. It was definitely growth from the beginning of her year, if nothing else.

She ventured over to the washroom to brush the stale feeling from her mouth. She stared back at her reflection, uneasy at the eyes that stared back at her. She had gotten so accustomed to wearing her glasses, that it was second nature to see the soft green colour looking back opposed to her natural ice blue. She wondered if she would ever get used to not having them there anymore. She had been guilty of trying to push up the frames that no longer sat on the bridge of her nose far more often than she cared to admit.

She waited until mid day before finally leaving her dorm. She knew that she was capable of being around others, but she wanted to avoid it if at all possible. She grabbed a little something to eat and then headed straight for the library. Her eyes trailed the walls, wondering if there were possible clues to the location. Having been hidden for so many centuries, it was unlikely. She would just have to wait for the librarians to return after the break.

She nestled herself into the library, knowing there was no need to worry about what anyone else thought. As she settled herself in the silence, she realised that it was quite possible that she was the only one in the entire campus at the moment. There was no chance of any of the children being left unattended. It was mandatory for the minors to head back. There may have been one or two in the secondary campus, but as for the collegiate - there was not a sign of another soul. It was exactly what she needed.

***

The quiet had been peaceful for a time, but it became a little eerie in the night. She was surprised at just how accustomed she had become to having others around. It was the middle of the night when she woke with a start, the feeling of a fleeting nightmare making her heart race. On instinct, she turned to look for Mari, only to be reminded how very alone she was. She sat up, pulling her knees into her chest, suddenly regretting her choices. Maybe she should have gone home with Mari after all.

She found herself closing her eyes, focusing on the bond. She felt the soft hum of her connection to Aelius. She had felt the shift in the intensity of the bond as soon as he left the Academy. Their professors had warned them of the difference in connection based on distance. A permanent bond would be unaffected by distance, but temporary bonds didn't hold the same strength. There were limitations.

She lit a fire, the darkness of the room and deafening silence starting to creep in on her. Her heart regained a better rhythm as she watched the flames dance. She missed him. There was a calming presence to Aelius that she had become accustomed to. She wasn't sure just how, or when, but being separated from him for so long had started to feel uncomfortable. It must have been a side effect of the bonding.

She sat up with a start, wondering if it was her mind playing tricks on her, or if it was real. She checked again, certain this time. Aelius was back. She grabbed her watch from her bedside table, checking the time. What could be possibly be doing coming back in the wee hours of the morning, a solid week before the break ended?

She settled herself back in bed, concentrating on the bond. A wave of peace and comfort washed over her as she felt him enter the Academy grounds, getting closer and closer. Without realising, she drifted off to sleep.

***

She woke the next morning, sunlight streaking through a gap in the curtains. She grabbed for her watch, seeing it was well into the morning. She tested the bond, confirming that it hadn't been a dream last night - Aelius was back. She slipped out of bed, getting herself cleaned up before venturing out. Why had he come back so soon? Should she bother to track him down, or let him come to her? And when did she become just so preoccupied with him?

She splashed cold water on her face, feeling quite stupid first thing in the morning. It wasn't like her to get so twisted up about someone else's actions. It had to be the bond. She wouldn't be so hyper aware of him if it wasn't for the attachment they shared.

She stepped out into the common room, resolving herself to making some breakfast and playing coy. She wouldn't go chasing him down in search of answers. If he wanted her to know, he would find her and volunteer it. Besides, it wasn't as if she was owed that information. He had every right to make his own choices without checking in with her.

As she poured herself a fresh cup of French press coffee, he stepped into the common room. He was slick with beads of sweat from training, his cheeks flush from the cold. He took the sight of her in a moment before breaking into a smile. "Morning." He finally stated.

She set her mug down on the counter and smiled back. "Back so soon?" She asked, mirroring his expression.

He approached, taking a seat on a stool by the island counter. "That alright?" He asked in a teasing tone.

She fought to suppress a chuckle. "Fine by me." She replied, leaning her elbows on the counter, hovering her mug over her lips.

The following days passed by with a calm quietness. Aelius was simply there, never encroaching or forcing his way into things, but around. It was comforting to know that she wasn't alone. She could feel him training, feel him working away on things. She slept better than she had in days. It was peace.

Chapter 22

A new semester meant a new roster of classes. Pact Formation continued as a new class, but Magic had flipped to Offensive magic this term. The name of a new teacher, Professor Duncan, made her optimistic. She wasn't sure she could handle another semester with Professor Rossi at this point. The other two classes on her list were Herbology 101 and Mixology 101. They were undoubtedly sister courses that fed into one another based on their suggested reading.

The students trickled into Pact Formation, the same lecture hall as last semester. She took a seat in the centre near an already seated Dae and Leila. Thankfully, both looked refreshed and rested from the time away. Part of her had been worried about Leila, but she seemed back to her confident self.

"You have a good break, Aurora?" Leila asked warmly.

Aurora took a seat beside her and sat her book bag down. "It was quiet. It was amazing. How about you? You get to see your family?"

Leila nodded with a bright smile. It seemed that she was just as pleased that they could speak again as friends. "It was just what I needed. I had a good talk with my mom and she helped a lot. She arranged a talk with Dean Reyes even to make sure everything was...okay." She said cautiously.

"And everything is good?" Aurora asked.

Leila nodded. "It was like you said before the break - no one blamed me and it was a freak accident that the shields were down. I was worried that everyone would all agree it was all my fault, but it was good to hear they didn't."

Aurora gave Leila a small smile. "Good. You don't need that."

Her attention turned to the door as Aurora felt Aelius approach the lecture hall. His eyes landed on her immediately and gave her the smallest hint of a smile. She openly smiled in return and shifted her book bag to the floor. Without a word he climbed the stairs and took the seat where her bag had been. She turned to him, debating whether or not to say anything when both Professor Steins entered the class.

"Good morning and welcome back everyone." Guardian Stein announced.

"We hope everyone had a restful and relaxing break." Mage Stein continued. "We are looking forward to another eventful and productive semester with you all."

"We will continue our studies of your pact bonds this semester. Last semester was an introduction to you all. This term we will be focusing on the ability to hone in further, but also to be able to effect the bond itself." Guardian Stein explained.

"Both Mages and Guardians have their own abilities with the bond, as I am sure you have experienced and researched." Mage Stein added. "We will be covering unique aspects separately this semester. It is important for you to understand what you are able to do and manipulate."

She stole a quick glance at Aelius beside her. She wasn't sure how she felt about manipulating the bond. Having a better grasp on it, however, wasn't a bad idea. There were times when the swirl of emotions had become muddled - uncertain what was hers and what was his. It would be nice to have a break and gain some clarity.

Class felt longer that day as the Steins reviewed their overall syllabus and expectations. She checked her watch, knowing that there wouldn't be an awful lot of time between the subjects. Seeing the restlessness and boredom in their students, the Steins released them. Most of the Guardians were off at their inhuman speed out the door, not wanting to be late. She wished she had their advantage.

By the time they reached the classroom, most of the class had already arrived. She took a seat near the front alongside Dae, happy to have a friend to sit with. Their professor had been had already been in the room, if the items resting on the teaching desk ahead was any indication. She recognised Professor Duncan from her entrance exam the moment he stepped through the door. Students immediately hushed as the man in his late thirties with messy dark auburn hair and a trimmed beard to match strode his way to his desk. He stood in silence for a moment, trying to get a good measure of them all. "I've heard you've all had quite a year already." He commented. His voice had a slight lilt to it as he spoke. His accent was diluted, clearly a man who had been long from his home country.

"I don't care what you've been through and done so far this year. I'll judge you based on what you do here in this class."

She wondered if his comments were any hint at last term's exams or not. She had no doubt word of what happened had made it through all of the faculty by now. She had never personally spoken to him - her entrance exam being performance only. All she could do right now is hope he would be an improvement from Rossi.

They spent the class reviewing the first two chapters of their course text and listening to Professor Duncan review the subject matter. As he excused the class, he paused and added, "Miss Thomas. Come see me before you go."

She stopped a moment as she had been packing her book bag. "I'll catch up for lunch in a second." She explained to Dae. He gave her a quick nod in response and hurried on his way. He had no interest in awkwardly lingering in what could very well be a lecture.

She approached the desk, bag slung over her shoulder. Duncan watched as the others trickled out of class. When the remainder of students had left, he finally turned back to her. "I heard you made quite the waves last term." He remarked, his arms crossed at his chest as he leant his back against the chalk board wall.

"That's one way of putting it." She answered with a hint of a laugh.

"I also heard she had you doing single channels."

She clenched her jaw a moment. "Yes." She responded simply. "We were not allowed to do blends."

He rolled his eyes and sighed. "So stupid." He cursed. "I don't care how anyone wields in my class - just as long as they do it well. Singular, dual - I don't care. I don't have the time to be buggered over details. I care about the outcome, not the process. Alright?"

She blinked, taken aback by the aggravation in his tone despite it being supportive. "Yes sir." She answered in an unsure tone.

"Right." He stated, content that he had addressed the matter. "That's all. Wanted to make sure you knew you don't have hold yourself back here."

She smiled to herself. "Thank you, sir."

"Now get out of here." He dismissed with a wave of his hand.

She stifled a laugh at his demeanour and headed out of his class. He was absolutely rough around the edges, but there was a soft heart there.

The new semester's schedule took a moment to get used to, but the new routine was quickly under way within the first week. She hurried into Herbology as Pact Formation released, sitting in her usual spot beside Dae.

"Can anyone tell me what cicuta virosa does to a Mage?" Professor Li asked the class. He had a calm presence in his voice as he taught. It was the right balance between commanding yet engaging.

Paige shot up her hand quickly to answer. She was average in magic abilities, but seemed quite knowledgable in Herbology. "Cicuta virosa, commonly called water hemlock, disrupts the nervous system and the ability to access Magic." She answered.

"Very good." Professor Li replied. "What of Datura?"

The class was silent a moment, before Leila nervously raised her hand. Professor Li nodded.

"Datura is also known as moonflower. It causes hallucinations and intoxication."

"Correct." Professor Li stated. "Lastly, what of aconitum?"

Aurora rose her hand this time. She sensed a theme. "Aconitum, also known as Wolfsbane, is known to cause convulsions and disruptions to the flow of magic."

"Indeed, Miss Thomas." Professor Li acknowledged. "Now," He continued. "You may be wondering why I am asking about these three specifically. In the Middling realm, these are used in small doses for a variety of medicinal purposes. In high doses, they are fatal to Middlings. For you as Mages, however, they have a different effect. We will be researching these three plants over the week in tandem with your Mixology course as a combined study. Please turn to page thirty in your texts."

***

Mixology with Professor Singh picked up where Professor Li had left off. "I hear that Professor Li covered the trio today?" She asked the class. She was a small woman in stature, but possessed a vibrant energy. The class nodded in acknowledgment and she continued. "Very good. Now, can anyone tell me why we have an interest in these three plants together?"

Eli rose his hand. "They all have an effect on a Mage's magic supply."

"Precisely." Professor Singh stated. She called up a diagram on the board behind her. "When combined in the right balance, these three plants can cause a block on a Mage's magic supply."

The class grew tense at the mention. It was one thing to exhaust your own magic supplies, but to be drugged and cut off was terrifying.

"It honestly is something that isn't commonly used anymore, but the Academy requires that we go over it just in case. We will spend this week reviewing the chemical compounds and chemistry of what is commonly referred to as Witches Bane. I have a small dose here if anyone is brave enough to test a sample. Any volunteers?"

Silence filled the room. To volunteer would be madness. Aurora looked around at her classmates, not a single one daring to step forward. She raised her hand. Dae's eyes grew wide at the idea, shaking his head in hopes of dissuading her.

"Come on." Professor Singh beckoned.

She rose to her feet, doubt creeping in as she stepped towards the head of the class. Professor Singh held out a small vial with a dropper. From afar, the liquid inside looked like black ink, but as you got closer dark swirls of purple roiled inside. Professor Singh squeezed the top, pulling in several millilitres of the inky substance.

"This is a concentrated formula. Just a few drops will do. It will give you a sense of the flavour that you would want to watch out for. Let me know what you taste, and what you feel."

She indicated for Aurora to open her mouth. She took a breath before obeying, tilting her head back. She felt three drops hit her tongue before she closed her mouth and swallowed. It was disgustingly bitter and acidic all at once. Her throat burned as she swallowed, her stomach churning in burning nausea immediately.

She grimaced before explaining. "It's extremely bitter and acidic. I think I might—" She stopped before she could finish her sentence. She grabbed for Professor Singh's desk to steady herself. The professor was quick to grab a hold of her arm to help steady her. Her head swirled as numbness started to creep down her body into her limbs. Her knees started to give way, but the professor supported her. She called over for an extra hand, Dae rushing to her side to help guide her to her desk.

"What Miss Thomas is experiencing is the neuro effects of the Witches Bane. Her body is starting to go numb, and right about now, she should also be feeling a cut off from her magic supply."

Aurora nodded in confirmation, her words currently escaping her. She was amazed at what only three little droplets could do to her body. She held her head in her hands, begging the room to stop spinning.

"When brewed correctly, Witches Bane will hit in a staggered succession. First, as you can see here, you get the effects of Water Hemlock on her nervous system. Next, we should see if she starts to have any hallucinations from the moonflower."

A bang sounded at the door, that made the class jump. She looked up to see Aelius panting in the doorway, a look of panic on his face. She blinked a few times, trying to discern what was happening as he rushed to her side. "What happened?" He demanded.

Professor Singh was quickly at her desk. "I take it you are her Guardian?" She asked, placing a hand on his shoulder.

He refused to take his eyes off of Aurora. "I am. I asked *what happened?*" He stressed.

"She'll be alright." She assured in an almost dismissive tone. "She merely volunteered to test out a bit of Witches Bane. The effects should wear off in the next few hours."

She looked up at the professor, her eyes wide. She would be like this for *hours?*

"I will be taking her, professor. She is no state for class." Aelius interjected, sweeping her into his arms. There was no moment to object. Firmly in his arms the world seemed to spin a little less.

Professor Singh stammered in protest from behind her, but there was no arguing with him. He carried her out of class, a few trickles of laughter heard behind.

It wasn't until they were out in the hallway that he bothered to say anything. "Don't *ever* do anything that stupid again." He commanded.

She buried her face in his neck, her eyes closed to help stop the swirling in her head. "I won't." She responded sluggishly.

Chapter 23

She woke several hours later tucked into her own bed. She brought a hand to her head at the ache that pounded, confused at how she had gotten there. She blinked a moment, her memories coming back to her. Aelius had collected her from class, Mari meeting them out in the hallway. He had felt the drug hit her through the bond and rushed to her side. Mari had followed behind in concern and had let him into their room for her to sleep it off.

She slipped out of bed, feeling much more herself. She flexed her finger to test the feeling in her extremities. Nothing amiss. She turned to the fireplace and conjured a fire. Her magic connection had resumed. She let out a sigh of relief that things were back to normal. A growl in her stomach and a check of her watch told her it was time to eat.

She headed off to the Dining Hall, hoping to find either Mari or Aelius and thank them for looking after her. Never did she think volunteering with a professor would cause her such trouble.

As Aurora rounded the corner towards the common room, she found herself face to face with Leila.

"Hey" Leila greeted with a slight smile. She paused a moment, as if she debated continuing down the hall or carrying a conversation. "You mind if we talk?" She finally asked.

"Not at all." Aurora responded, uncertain of what seemed to be the matter. She followed Leila as she led her off to the side, out of the middle of the hall.

"I wanted to apologise." Leila explained, her hands fiddling as she worked through the words.

"Leila, it's—" Aurora started to protest.

Leila shook her head. "No, Aurora I need to. I didn't handle bonding day well and I held Aelius not bonding with me against *you*. It wasn't fair of me to do that."

Aurora gaped slightly in surprise. She was simply happy that they had been able to move forward since exams, She had never expected an apology or direct conversation about their awkward falling out. "Thanks, Leila. I hope you know that I had no idea he was going to volunteer, and I'm really sorry for any hurt I caused." She responded, grabbing one of her hands gently.

Leila startled ever so slightly at her touch, but it melted into a soft smile. "You didn't do anything wrong, Aurora. It was easier to be angry at you than at him. Or well...myself really." She confessed with a slight laugh at herself. "It was a stupid one sided crush. I thought that he *might* like me back, but then he bonded with you and...well. What's done is done."

"I really did think we were becoming friends before all of that." Aurora added.

Leila's smile grew. "Me too. Can we...start over maybe? Forget that I was stupid over a guy?"

Aurora mirrored her smile, pulling Leila into a hug. "I'd like that."

Leila chuckled, returning the hug. "For what it's worth, I *do* think you guys make a good couple." She added as she stepped back.

Her mouth dropped open in shock. "Leila, we're not—"

Leila let out a soft giggle. "It's okay, Aurora. I can handle you guys being together. I don't own him, and he has *never* smiled like that for anyone. Don't worry about it, I'll see you later, okay?" She patted her on the shoulder and headed back on her way to her dorm before she could say anything in protest.

Aurora touched her cheeks, feeling that they were hot to the touch. Did they really come off that way? Aelius was kind to a fault, a gentleman really. Were people reading into that kindness and filling in the blanks? She refused to let herself be carried away by other people's ideas. Until he said something himself, made some sort of move, there was no sense in thinking that they would ever be anything more.

She continued on her way to the Dining Hall, hoping to catch either one of the twins. She had to thank them for all they did. It had been stupid of her to blindly volunteer in class. It was clear that Professor Singh wasn't overly cautious with her students' well being.

The sound of books, papers and tin hitting the stone floors rang out in the hall. Aurora checked to see if anyone else hurried to help, but seeing no one bothering to check, she found her way over. She peaked her head around the corner to see Professor Andersen in a pile of mess. He looked up in a fluster, and flushed red upon seeing it was her. "Miss Thomas!" He exclaimed. He hurried to pick up his materials as she moved closer.

"Let me help you, Professor." She explained as she started picking up loose papers and books.

"Oh you really don't need to." He insisted as he rushed to gather things. "You shouldn't trouble yourself."

"I don't mind." She insisted with a smile.

He relaxed ever so slightly, but she could still tell there was a change in his demeanour towards her. She saw the same nervousness and excitement he had whenever he was around Astraea.

"Has your new term been going well, Professor?" She asked as she reached over for another text.

Andersen pushed up his glasses to the bridge of his nose. "I believe so, but it's hard to say so early. Not everyone is as enthusiastic about studying as you are, Miss Tho-or wait. Should it be Solis?" He realised with a sense of concern.

She fought the instinct to sigh. "Miss Thomas is perfect." She answered. She truthfully had no idea what she was supposed to go by now, but she was in no hurry to change anything.

He sighed in relief, clearly concerned of making a social blunder. "I certainly don't want to offend."

She gave him a small smile as she handed him her collection. "I don't think you possibly could, Professor Andersen."

He took the papers and books from her as they both stood to their feet. "Thank you very much, Miss Thomas. And if you ever need any help researching more about your...family tree, please let me know. I would be most happy to help."

"I appreciate the offer, and you would be the first person I ask." She explained as she bid him farewell.

She let out a sigh once he left. He very well had a point. There were things she didn't know, things she needed answered. The Dean had explained that there would be no specialised tutor for her. All she had was the restricted section. She reached into her book bag and wrapped her fingers around the old iron key. If she hurried, she would catch the last shift librarian before she headed out for the night. Speaking with Mari and Aelius could wait.

With a hurried step, she made it to the librarian's desk with minutes to spare. Ms Smithe, the head librarian, gave her a questioning look. "May I help you, Miss Thomas?" She asked as she came around from behind the desk.

She straightened and gave her a smile. "Yes please, Ms Smithe." She dug into her bag and pulled out her key. "I was wondering if you might be able to show me the way."

Ms Smithe checked around for possible spectators before giving her a quick nod. "Just a moment." She nipped back behind the desk and put up a sign that read "CLOSED" before returning to her side. "Follow me." She insisted, hurrying off to the back of the library.

She followed closely behind Ms Smithe as they walked the length of the grand room. As they approached the back wall, they climbed a winding staircase to the second level. She had been up top a few times before, but not many of her texts had led her up this way. Ms Smithe checked over her shoulder to make sure she was keeping up. With a nod of approval, she continued towards a back corner. A quick check around confirmed that there was no one watching. She beckoned for the key in Aurora's hand as they reached a blank space in the wall, barely two feet of space between some shelving. Ms Smithe ran her fingers along the wall, finding a tiny groove that was barely noticeable in the dim lighting. She placed the key inside, flat against the wall. The wall itself seemed to shudder and groan until a small door popped open from the gap.

"You're allowed to borrow whatever it is you need. You don't need to check anything with us. There is a ward on the door that keeps track." Ms Smithe explained as she waited outside the door. "Only you are allowed inside - no visitors. The door will lock behind you and you push to open from the inside. Any questions?"

She shook her head in response. Ms Smithe bid her farewell and happy reading. She watched as Ms Smithe left the way she came, slowly descending down the spiral staircase to the main floor. With a deep breath, she crossed the threshold into the restricted section.

As informed, the door shut behind her. The key pushed through the door and dropped into her hand and the edge of the door sealed as if it had never been there in the first place. The sudden silence was deafening. A faint glow of false magic light pulsed from the sconces on the walls. Her eyes adjusted to the dim light, as she took in the room - about the size of one of her classrooms at first glance. Several rows of shelves about seven feet tall filled the room. The shelves themselves weren't tightly packed and left quite a bit of room for additional works. The smell of old paper and ink washed over her, reminding her of her childhood. She wondered if any of the texts she had poured over while Artefact hunting was in here. She didn't imagine anything she researched previously would have any reason to be considered a banned text, but who knew what previous Deans deemed unfit.

She stepped forward, puffs of dust billowing out from underfoot. She let out a small cough and covered her mouth. She ran a finger along the shelves, checking for any indication of sectioning. She started at the front and worked her way back. It was slow work, scanning through hundreds of book spines, wondering whether or not any would be useful. Finally, after what felt like ages, one peeked her interest. *The Study and Analysis of Spirit Wielding by Gregori Ramos - A Modern Translation*

Her breath caught as she gingerly plucked the book from the shelf. The leather-bound book was beautifully crafted, but decades old. She cradled it in her arms as she shifted herself underneath one of the false lights. She opened the pages carefully with a creak.

The Study and Analysis of Spirit Wielding was an instrumental text originally written by Gregori Ramos, the first Emperor's advisor. The original texts have been translated from the original Latin for modern learning. Published 1813

She clutched the book to her chest. This was exactly what she had been looking for. The original in Latin would have been invaluable, but it was doubtful to find texts several centuries old in working order. This would have to do.

She headed back to the wall where the door had been and pushed gently. A faint glow appeared where the doorway would be. A quiet click sounded as the wall opened and fresh air found her lungs. With her text tucked safely under her arm, she headed back to her room.

***

Settled into her bed with optimal lighting, Aurora gingerly opened the pages. Older books were nothing new to her, but she still wanted to be careful. It took her a couple of hours before she found what she really wanted to know: capabilities.

Spirit magic is still under observation as we only have two generations of Solis' to study. At this time, it appears that Spirit magic presents as several different specialties. Unlike Elemental Magic, the abilities of a Spirit wielder do not appear to be universal. Elemental techniques can be trained and honed. In Spirit wielders, the specific abilities appear to be innate. More data will be necessary to determine whether or not this is a universal truth.

The four branches of Spirit abilities are as follows: Purification, Healing, Reading, and Foresight.

Purification: *The ability to fully eradicate a demonic creature. It is the only method, to date, to truly eliminate a demonic creature from existence.*

Healing: *The ability to cure or mend injuries or illness. Death is the only limit.*

Reading: *The ability to determine one's true intentions or thoughts.*

Foresight: *The ability to foresee events to come through dreams, or sometimes waking visions. Accuracy of visions and how far into the future have yet to be confirmed.*

The sound of Mari entering the room caused her to jump and slam the book shut.

"You okay, Ari?" She asked with a look of concern.

Aurora relaxed as her heartbeat slowed. "Finally went to the restricted section." She admitted as she held up the book in her hand.

Mari's eyes widened. She dropped her bag to the floor and sat on the bed across from her. "What is it?"

"It's an old textbook from the early nineteenth century." She began. "I think it used to be part of a course here at the

Academy. It's based on the original research of the first Emperor's advisor."

"Woah." She responded, leaning forward to take a look.

"I want to see if I can find anything else written by him, or research on his works." She added, as she pulled the book to her chest. Professor Andersen would likely know if anyone would.

"A good idea." Mari agreed. "Keep reading. I'll be out of your hair in a second. I just needed to grab something before I head over to Dae's tonight." She added with a smirk.

She readjusted, thankful that she wouldn't have to be a third wheel in her own room.

Abilities seem to play to the strengths of the wielder's character. For example - the First Emperor is a master of Purification. This was the first of the Spirit abilities to present in him. The Emperor has also been known to use some Healing abilities.

In contrast, his two eldest children have begun to present different abilities. , his eldest son, has presented a great fortitude in Reading abilities from a young age. His eldest daughter, Kaitlynn, has been experiencing more and more vivid premonitions. Her dreams and visions have provided invaluable information in the fight against demonic creatures. Research into a correlation between character and abilities will need to be conducted.

The last line struck her. If what Gregori theorised was true, what did that say about her?

Chapter 24

The darkness seemed endless that deep in the ocean. Sunlight would never penetrate that far. The only light this far down was cast from certain fish or man made. There was a deafening silence at these depths, an overwhelming sense of nothingness.

Despite the emptiness, there was something wrong. The sound of her own pulse pounded in her ears, steadily rising the longer she searched. The sound and sensation of movement in the water struck fear into her heart. She froze in place, not daring to move, not daring to call attention to herself. Slowly, orbs of light started to appear. One by one, like stars illuminating in the night, they began to show what lay before her.

Body after lifeless body floated in the water. One by one, they were illuminated by the orbs of light. Six bodies in grey scattered the scene like rag dolls in the abyss. Mages. Six full fledged Mages all dead. Her eyes scanned the area, looking for any sign of their Guardians. They were harder to discern in the darkness, but she finally spotted them. One was torn in half, straight through the torso. Another was missing a leg, another both arms. Blood swirled all around.

Silent screams escaped her lips, nothing but bubbles leaving her. She clamped her hands over her mouth, another swirl in the waters hitting her. Something was here. Whatever had done this was still there.

She turned, feeling movement behind her. She strained her eyes, torn between needing to know what caused such devastation, and also praying that it wouldn't find her. There was a short list of beings capable of such an attack. None of them were something anyone wanted to face.

Tentacles, endless in length, swam past her. She froze in place, knowing that whatever it was was gargantuan. A rumble rang out, a warning, or maybe even laughter. It circled her, the rushes of movement tossing her from where she hovered. She would be next in the hunt.

Aurora woke with a start, her heart thundering in her chest. Some nights, not every night, she had dreams. Sometimes they were nothing; sometimes they were intensely vivid. She rubbed the sleep from her eyes as she tried to recall the details. Her dream had been intensely vivid; as if she were truly there observing the aftermath of a brutal scene. There were very few creatures that could do damage like that. All of the details pointed to a Kraken, but they had been believed to be long extinct. Her dreams were getting creative it seemed.

She looked over to the bed beside her, long empty with Mari having already left for the morning for training. She checked her watch. It seemed as if Mari was taking longer than usual. She started to get ready, pausing a moment as she felt a wave of emotion hit her through the bond. Something was wrong. She hurried to get dressed, heading out to the common room. With no sign of Aelius or Mari in the common room, she continued on to the Dining Hall. Breakfast was still running for the next few minutes and was worth a wager.

She felt the shift in energy the instant she stepped through the door. The hall was mostly empty, save for a few students scattered around the tables. Her eyes quickly landed on a cluster of her friends. Mari, still in her training clothes, wrapped herself around Dae, his face buried in his hands. Her stomach dropped. Something was definitely wrong. She hurried over, Mari looking up to see her there.

"Dae got a call about Hana." She stated gravely.

Hana was Dae's older sister, a highly regarded water Mage. She had graduated three years previously and had quickly climbed the ranks of field Mages alongside her long term partner as her Guardian. Professors had been known to compare the siblings, but Dae never took it as an insult or negative thing. He had always aspired to be just like his sister, seeing her as a level of excellence as something to rise to. To get a call *about* his sister, not *from* his sister was in no way good news.

Aelius shared a look with his sister and she gave a nod. He rose to his feet and took Aurora aside. "His sister was stationed out near the Mariana's Trench." He explained. She had remembered Dae talking about her work out that way. It was his dream to get stationed there along side her, using his water techniques to defend Pacific Rim gate. "His parents called first thing this morning. They got word that she passed in a training accident."

Her brow creased in confusion. "That doesn't make any sense."

Aelius nodded in agreement. "I know, but that's what the report stated. In all honesty, what really happened is most likely classified. Hana wouldn't have gone out in a simple training accident."

Her attention shifted back to Dae, a mess being consoled by his closest friends. "What can we do?" She asked. There had to be something, anything they could do for him.

Aelius crossed his arms and sighed. "I'm not sure there is anything we *can* do for him." His heart ached with a mix of helplessness and frustration all in one. She loved being able to read him better and discern things through the bond better, but knowing what he truly felt beneath the surface at times was hard.

Her heart broke for her friend. She knew all too well the sorrow and uselessness of losing someone so senselessly. There would be no answers, no closure, no satisfaction of knowing that they were at peace or in a better place. There was only anger, pain, and confusion.

She walked past Aelius and put a hand on Dae's shoulder. "You're not alone." She stated. He looked up at her, his eyes red from crying, but dry. He looked as if he had spent his sorrow and had entered the stage of numbness. "Everything is going to be horrible for now. There's nothing any of us can do to change that, but we are here for whatever it is you need."

He gave her hand a squeeze as he listened. "I think..." He paused, his brain lagging a moment as he tried to form the words. "I think I just need to go be with my parents right now."

He stood to his feet, Mari with him for support. They walked off together, undoubtedly off to the Dean's office before he left the campus. She sat down at the table with a sigh as she rubbed her eyes.

"We're not going to talk about it?" Leila finally spoke up, breaking the tense silence.

Aelius shot her a warning glare. "No, Leila." He stressed. *"We're not."*

Leila glared up at him from across the table. "Your dad will know something about it. You *know* he'll be able to give them closure on what *really* happened."

"And you think he's going to break protocol, risk the safety of the Empire for that?" Aelius shot back.

Edwyn placed a hand on his best friend's shoulder, trying to ease his building frustration. "I think Leila just means that there must be something he can do. Something he can say that won't threaten whatever confidentiality is in place."

Aelius shook his head and sighed. "You have *no* idea what you're talking about..." He muttered as he rose to his feet and headed out.

Aurora watched Aelius storm off and shove the door in frustration. She could feel the frustration and anger that seethed within him. The door slammed against the wall with an echoing bang. She jumped in her seat at the sound. Tears welled in Leila's eyes.

"It's okay, Leila." Edwyn assured as he reached out a hand across the table. "He just needs to process it."

Leila sniffed, blinking back the tears, refusing to let them fall. "He's a stubborn jerk sometimes." She muttered.

Edwyn chuckled to himself. "Without a doubt." He agreed. He turned to Aurora, his stare lingering a moment before deciding his next words. "How are you holding up?"

Aurora blinked in surprise. All of this going on and he was checking on her? "I'm okay?" She stated, uncertain of what to make of his question.

Edwyn leaned forward a bit, resting his arms on the table. "I just meant with everything, with...you know." He explained poorly as he pointed to her eyes.

It was then that she realised what he really meant. He wasn't checking in about the news of Hana, but her own baggage. She bristled. She couldn't tell whether his change of subject was genuine concern, or gossipy. She studied him a moment, no idea what to make of him. They had become close as friends over the past few months, but something about his forwardness had started to feel uncomfortable. She couldn't quite place it. It wasn't as if he had done anything wrong. It just...didn't feel right.

"I'm okay." She responded simply, rising to her feet. "I think I'm going to go check on Aelius." She couldn't just let Aelius be off on his own, not when he was feeling that complex swirl of emotions.

She stepped out into the hall, testing the bond for his location. A quick check placed him out in the training arena. She felt his pulse race and his knuckles bruise. He was training off the frustration. She quickly grabbed her cloak and headed out to the grounds. By the time she caught sight of him, she saw that he was busy taking on three projections at once. Aurora stood there watching, not daring to interrupt him while he worked through things.

As he finished off the last projection, the arena shifted, settling back to a normal flooring. He panted, a few beads of sweat forming down his skin. She could feel that the training had done little to take the edge off. He turned to her, anger still in his eyes. As he registered her, his eyes softened, a flash of embarrassment flitting through the bond. He averted his eyes from her, unable to meet her gaze.

"They don't understand what you're trying to do." She stated, closing the gap between them. "They're caught up in the grief of it all. They're just thinking of how they can help Dae, not the bigger picture."

Aelius stared down at her, processing her words. She could feel a faint sense of relief and an ease of the anger. "I can't ask my dad to make exceptions. Once you open yourself open to that, it can be hard to stop. I can't ask him to blur the lines, even if it *is* for family."

She placed a hand on his arm. "It's not easy being the responsible one all the time."

His shoulders released, letting go of the last bit of tension he held. He leaned his head down, resting his forehead on the top of her head as she wrapped her arms around him, hugging him tight.

***

A cloud hung over the Academy as news of Hana and her team filtered through. A total of twelve died that day. It seemed as if everyone were tied to one of the team members in some way or another.

Aelius kept his usual strong face on, but she could feel every pang of hurt that rang through the bond. He had been close to Hana, though not as close as Mari had been. Their families had been so intertwined that it was natural for him to be so affected.

Classes went on as usual, but the mood was heavy. No one spoke much outside of lessons. She checked the bond every so often, not wanting to directly bother him, but wanting to confirm he was alright. Before she knew it, night had fallen. Her stomach rumbled, hours passed when she should have had dinner. The library had a way of masking the hour - undoubtedly due to the lack of windows.

She sighed, arching her back with a sigh and a stretch. She returned some of the books to a cart by the librarian's desk, and slipped one into her bag before heading for the common room. The Dining Hall would be closed at this hour. As she rounded the corner into the common room, she caught sight of Aelius in the kitchen. He glanced up at her, a streak of what looked like flour dusting his hair. He immediately straightened, pushing something behind his back on the counter behind him.

"You alright?" She asked suspiciously, stepping closer.

He checked around, confirming that they were alone before taking the plate from behind him. A small cake, vanilla with white cream and strawberries sat on the counter. She glanced up at him, Aelius looking at her reaction, not what he had made. "It's not much, but it *is* your birthday..." He explained in a half mumble. Her mouth dropped open ever so slightly, bringing a hand up to cover it. In the midst of everything she had completely forgotten about it. Her brow creased a moment, wondering how he possibly knew. Her confusion must have read not only on her face, but the bond. "You mentioned your birthday in our first card game, remember?"

She looked back up at him, surprised he had actually remembered that. It had been so long ago and in passing. "But..."

He scratched the back of his neck, stepping back a touch. "Sorry, I just thought..."

"Sorry?" She gaped. "What do you have to be sorry about?"

He looked back to her, a touch of embarrassment radiated through. "Just with everything going on I thought it would be nice. A...well a distraction. Sorry if it overstepped."

A sad smile crossed her face, her head tilted to the side ever so slightly. "Not at all. It's sweet." She responded fondly. "Will you share it with me?" She asked, laying her hand over his.

Chapter 25

She woke the next morning groaning at the crick in her neck from falling asleep in a weird position. She stretched her arms over her head and arched her back. Without Mari, she knew she had slept in. She cursed as she checked the time on her watch. She had stayed up far later than she intended, talking about birthdays past and how they celebrated with Aelius. It had been nice to talk about her mom with him and how they had always cooked together. It had been a nice distraction.

She slung her bag over her shoulder and plaited her hair as she hurried to class. There was no time to waste spending it in front of the mirror, her shower rushed that morning. She quickly swiped a muffin off of the common room counter and stuffed it into her book bag. She knew Aelius would give her a lecture about eating properly if he caught her, but she simply didn't have the time.

She paused in the hall as she saw Professor Andersen head towards his own class. She broke into a run, hoping to catch him before he stepped away. "Professor!" She called out.

He jumped at the sound of her voice, nearly dropping his papers again. "Miss Thomas." He remarked once he steadied himself. "Is everything alright?"

She collected her breath. "Yes, I just wanted to catch you while I saw you." She confessed. "I was wondering if you knew of any works by Gregori Ramos?"

He furrowed his brow in a mixture of concentration and confusion. "You mean the Emperor's Advisor?"

"Yes sir." She nodded.

"I can't say that I can, but let me see what I can find." He admitted. "They would be quite old, but I will see what I can come up with."

She gave him a smile. "Thank you, Professor. I'd greatly appreciate it."

They bid each other farewell as he turned into his class and she ran off to her own. She would ask the librarians and maybe even the Dean as well, but she knew that Andersen was most likely her best bet.

By the time she made it into Pact 102, she knew she was late. Professor Stein gave her a disapproving look as she tapped her wrist. "Punctuality, Miss Thomas." She lectured as Aurora took her seat.

"Yes, Professor. I'm sorry." She apologised as she shrunk down beside Leila and Joanna. She was glad that she had finally had the chance to clear things up with Leila. She knew that she hadn't done anything wrong, but it was still considered a social faux pas in the Mage community.

"As I was saying," Professor Stein continued. "We will be practicing the ability to block the bond today. There will be times where it is important for you to block the ability for your Guardian to feel your side of the bond. Whether it is a simple manner of privacy and separation, or a legitimate safety concern, it is an important skill to learn. It is a unique ability of Mages. Guardians are not able to visualise and block the bond like we are. Open your texts to chapter five and we will go over the process." She instructed.

It took a great deal of visualisation and concentration, but eventually there was progress. The texts as well as Professor Stein reviewed different methods to make it work. Some envisioned a wall, some a drawbridge, but each Mage needed to figure what made sense for themselves.

"Be aware that you will still be able to feel your Guardian even though you place a block up." Professor Stein explained as the students practiced creating their blocks. "You will be able to feel the moment your block is successful. Your Guardians are aware of what you are practicing today, but the sudden sensation will still be alarming to them."

She closed her eyes in concentration. She tried a few of the ideas that had been suggested. None of them felt correct. The swell of power and feeling from Aelius had definitely been increasing as she got closer to him. Being able to block him might be a good idea to preserve their friendship. Things had started to become confusing. Blocking him from her emotions might be able to maintain things better.

She paused, trying to envision what the bond with Aelius was like. Some described it as a raging river. Others considered it like lightning. To her, Aelius felt like a steady pulsing life line. He was constant, steady and true. There was no flares or surges to him. He simply felt like he was a piece of her.

She breathed, trying to figure out how to create a block from a living piece of her. Envisioning a damn did nothing. She tried building a wall of bricks, only for it to come crumbling down. She breathed a sigh of frustration, being told to keep at it. "It can be difficult when the bond is strong." Mage Stein explained, a hint of a smirk on her lips. She flushed at the insinuation. Apparently it wasn't just Leila that thought things were more than they were.

She closed her eyes again. If he was a piece of her, maybe she needed to bind it shut. She tried picturing a long piece of cloth, tying it off like one would a bleeding limb. She made some progress for a moment, but the knot broke apart almost instantly. She sighed, a bead of sweat starting to form at her temple. She took a deep breath, trying again. This time she visualised sewing the bond closed. She closed off the stitch and sliced it away.

She opened her eyes, wary of trusting that it held. A wave of panic and concern flooded her. She laughed out loud as she realised she had done it.

"I imagine he's not too pleased, is he?" Joanna asked, having successfully blocked Cael several minutes earlier.

She rubbed the side of her temple, a small headache forming at the strain. "Not at all."

"Same here." She explained. "It's probably a comfort knowing we're okay."

She sighed and leaned back in her seat. "It's nice to have a little privacy though."

Leila gave her a questioning look. "What's it like being bonded to Aelius?" She could tell there was a slight twinge of pain at the question. It was something she must have wondered plenty of times before.

"It's..." She paused wondering just how to word it. "I feel safe with him. It's nice knowing that he is there and I can rely on him. I want to be that for him too. I want to be a Mage worthy of being bonded to him, you know?"

There was a hint of sadness in her eyes, but she put a smile on her face regardless. It seemed like she really did want to be friends, even if she thought Aurora was some sort of competition. "That sounds really nice."

"If you have successfully managed to create a block against your Guardian, I suggest you test your limits." Mage Stein announced to the class. "Release the block and try again, or even see how long you can keep it in place. This is a test of mental fortitude and strength. This will much easier to some. Do not get discouraged."

"Yeah they're not going to like that..." Leila sighed, the strain of blocking starting to show on her face.

"Ah, they'll manage." Joanna teased.

By the time class wrapped, several of her classmates looked exhausted. She felt the strain herself as she finally released the hold. She snipped away at the visualisation of the stitches, a flood of relief washing over her. She grabbed her book bag and headed for the door. Aelius stood waiting for her, arms crossed at his chest.

She swallowed at the look on his face. Frustration simmered through the bond, his face matching his emotions for once.

"Good training?" She asked as she approached, completely ignoring the reason for his displeasure.

"I don't like it." He stated simply.

"You don't say." She teased.

He glared down at her, doing his best to suppress a chuckle at her. "I really don't."

"It's an assignment. I'm sure you'll have one similar soon. I'll get a taste of my own medicine." She assured as they headed down the hall for some lunch.

He shook his head, matching her pace. "Guardians don't practice that. We...have our ways of blocking the bond, but we're not supposed to block ourselves from our Mages."

She paused, her brows creasing in confusion. "What do you mean?"

"Guardians are supposed to be at the beck and call of their Mages. Mages are...well understood to be the ones in control." He explained as best as he could.

She realised just how out of touch she was on the Mage-Guardian dynamics. "I guess there's a lot more I wasn't aware of than I thought..." She admitted.

Aelius peered down at her, placing a hand on top of her head. "It's alright. You're smart. You're learning."

***

After a week, Mari and Dae finally returned to the Academy. It was after morning classes as they broke for lunch that she ran into the pair in the main hall. Dae looked as if he had not managed to get much food or sleep during his time away. Aurora eyed him warily as he headed back to his room.

"Is he okay?" She asked once he was out of earshot.

Mari sighed. Dark circles had formed beneath her eyes as well. "He's taking it hard, but he will be with time. I'm just glad I was able to be with him."

Aurora laid a hand on her shoulder. "What about you? I know Hana meant a lot to you as well."

Mari gave a sad smile in response. "She was like a big sister to me. I annoyed her and followed her around. She would tease me and call me the little sister she never wanted." She explained with a chuckle.

"I'm sorry, Mar. I wish I could have met her. She sounded like a wonderful person."

After a moment Mari finally shook her head as if to shake the negative emotions out of her head. "Never mind all that. What about you? I'm gone a week and I'm hearing all sorts of talk that you're dating my brother?"

Her jaw dropped open at the accusation. "What?!" She exclaimed, her voice hitting a squeaky tone that she didn't quite realise she could make.

Mari laughed and slung an arm around her shoulder. "I would take that as a no then?"

"Mari I am *not* dating Aelius, I swear. And if I was, *which I am not*, you would be hearing it from me, not someone else." She defended herself in a semi state of panic. "What is *wrong* with people?" She groaned.

Mari let out another laugh, the second louder than the first. "Oh, Ari…" She sighed as she lead her towards their dorm. "People are really bored here. They love nothing more than to gossip."

As they approached their room, a small parcel wrapped in brown paper and twine laid against their door. Mari bent over to pick it up and turned it over. A small piece of paper was tucked into the twine. She slipped the paper out and read the messy scrawl. "Hope this is what you're looking for." She read aloud. She looked to Aurora and gave her a quizzical look. "You expecting anything?"

Aurora took the parcel in hand. "Not especially." She answered trying to rack her brain. "Oh! It must be from Professor Andersen. I asked him about other works by Gregori Ramos." Mari gave her a look that indicated that she had no idea what she was talking about. "The guy that wrote the original book from the restricted section."

"Ohhhh." Mari responded as she opened up their door. She tossed her bag that was slung over her shoulder over to her side of the bed. "I think I'll check this after classes. I have to head over to Herbology soon." She explained as she set the parcel down on her night stand. She paused, checking Mari over. "Do you need anything? I can head to the library tonight if you need a little quiet."

Mari turned to her and gave her a small smile. "That'd actually be really nice." She sighed. "I just need to sleep."

Aurora gave her a nod and filled her book bag with her things. She paused a moment before swiping the parcel into the bag as well. The library would be just fine for examining whatever Andersen had left for her.

Chapter 26

urora settled in her usual back corner of the library. She used to circulate in different spots, but this spot had become hers. Something about it just felt like home. Gingerly, she pulled at the twine that wrapped the parcel. The brown parchment fell away to reveal a simple, black leather-bound book. *Diurnalis* was imprinted on the front in gold - Latin for journal.

She cautiously cracked the cover open. The pages were definitely several centuries old. Scrawled in ink on the first page was the name she had hoped for: Gregori Ramos. She closed the cover and rose to her feet, heading straight to the librarian's desk. With pages this old, there was no way she wanted to risk damage with the oil from her fingers. There were likely protection charms put in place, but she didn't want to risk any damage, not with something this valuable. She was back within minutes, a pair of thin white gloves in hand. She gingerly put them on, reopening the book.

It took her a moment, but the words came to her. So many of the old texts she would read for her Artefact research had been in Latin. Her mother had always insisted on knowing the language for herself. Many of the Artefact researchers used modern devices to help them translate, but Emily had never trusted them. She was thankful for her mother's stubbornness now.

She read through the entries one by one. Gregori had recorded from the start of the Empire's creation. Many entries were about the formation of government, and some battle details. Finally, she got to the information she had hoped for.

March 26 1475

I have been tasked with observing the eldest children - hoping to learn more about their innate gifts.

Caleb shows the ability to determine ones character and read basic thoughts. I have my doubts about the strength of his ability. I believe he is downplaying the extent of his talent.

Kaitlynn shows the ability to predict events through dreams and the occasional waking vision. She has already foreseen the outcomes of several crucial battles and has saved countless lives with her predictions. At first, she was only able to see a day or so in advance. Currently, she has made predictions as far as a fortnight ahead. We will continue to observe her talents.

April 10 1475

I cannot understand it. Just yesterday General Landon was absolute. He refused to join the cause at the southern gate, publicly declaring he would not march his men to death. Yet, this morning, in the round table, he volunteered. He was not himself. His eyes were glazed over like a fog. I spoke with the palace doctor to examine the General afterwards, but he found nothing. I fear he may have been poisoned. When I brought it up with the Emperor, he insisted that the General must have finally realised the error of his ways. I am not so sure.

May 9 1475

I have decided to test Kaitlynn's abilities with something non human. Her abilities have presented well with humans, but I wonder if they work on creatures. How I would love to test her against a demonic creature, but I fear there is no way to do that safely.

My daughter's cat will be an excellent candidate. It is a terribly stubborn creature that not even I can predict. I want to see if she can predict its decisions.

I may test to see whether Caleb can detect the cat's intentions or thoughts as well. Maybe his abilities are beyond humans.

May 26 1475

I had made plans to bring Chestnut, my daughter's cat, to observations this week. Kaitlynn approached me between meetings today. She begged me to leave the cat at home. She refused to elaborate on the matter, but it appears that she has seen something related to the cat. Even her nanny seems concerned. It appears that Kaitlynn has been having more nightmares of late.

I am unsure of how to proceed.

June 2 1475

I am convinced that Caleb is downplaying his abilities. He is a highly intelligent young man, but he is not a strong actor. His facial tells give him away, which is to be understood for a child his age. I want to research him further, but I am growing concerned of his character.

I broached the subject with the Emperor, but he only took it as praise of his genius son. He will not listen to any concerns regarding Caleb. I need to find a way to get through to him.

June 10 1475

Caleb is a cruel child. I cannot tell if this is how he has always been, or if he has been warped over the years by his Reading ability. I can see now that there is none of his father's kindness in him. Stories had always circulated from his rotation of nannies and governesses, but many dismissed the tales as rumours. I am not so sure anymore.

Kaitlynn excused herself from study as soon as she saw Chestnut in the cage. She claimed to be ill, but I saw the sorrow and disappointment on her face as she left the room. I should have heeded her warning.

The Emperor needs to understand that his child is disturbed. What Caleb did to that poor cat is beyond words.

June 15 1475

There is a fifth ability. Compulsion.

The entries simply stopped. She flipped the pages through, hopeful that maybe one of the empty pages beyond it held something. There was nothing. Just six simple words.

What had happened to Gregori? She knew from her lessons that Caleb had succeeded the throne about a decade later. Clearly he had not been able to warn the Emperor of his concerns. What really worried her, however, was the so called fifth ability. If it was what she thought it was, things were so much worse than she thought.

***

Her tutoring sessions had picked up, giving her plenty of clients to take on. Working was a welcome distraction from overthinking about what her abilities could mean, and what she might discover about herself as she went on. Her original trio sat before her for an essay review session.

"This essay is all about choosing a Middling fairy tale or lore that has ties to an actual Artefact. You need to write about how they relate, differences, and the basic functionality of the Artefact. Have any of you chosen one yet?"

Jessica raised her hand, slowly becoming more comfortable and confident during their sessions. "I've chosen to write about what Middlings call a Magic Mirror."

"Excellent choice. What can you tell me about them?" She asked, creating a bullet point list on the black board behind her.

She picked up her notes, reviewing them as she made her points out loud. "Middlings refer to a Magic Mirror in fairy tales like Snow White. It advises an evil magic queen and speaks back to her. This would be an example of early communicator style devices."

"Well done." Aurora complimented. "Make sure that you address specific points and see if you can break down how the ancient communicators differ from the modern ones. Graciela?"

Graciela straightened, collecting her own notes. "I was looking at doing either magic brooms or a magic carpet." She explained.

"Those are both good options. What's holding you back on making the decision?" Aurora asked.

Graciela sighed. "Well brooms seem to be the more obvious choice. They are pretty much a staple of Middling magic culture from what I understand. I just don't know if it's too obvious."

"Fair enough. I wouldn't over think it. Don't worry about it being a common choice. Just make sure your details and your points are strong. Do your research, and make sure you have a solid understanding of the lore and the mechanics." She advised. "What about you, Jensen?"

Jensen leaned back in his chair, closing his notes shut. "I'm going to do a wizard's bag. So many stories have magic bags that can hold anything. They're just portal devices. You create a portal in the bottom of a bag, closet, drawer, etc. and then attach it to a larger storage space. I've got it covered." He stated arrogantly.

"I would make sure you explain it from an Artefact perspective and less from a portal aspect. If you focus on the portal mechanics and less on what makes it an Artefact, Jung *might* disqualify it. She's particular." She cautioned.

The cocky look on Jensen's face faded as he realised her point. He sat up and added the important notes to his book.

Aurora stretched with a yawn as she left her class. She had found a good stride with most of her students. She enjoyed the one on one sessions, but something about the group sessions was so much more stimulating. She headed back to the collegiate side, knowing that it wouldn't be long before faculty locked the doors for the night.

As she passed through the halls, she heard more and more murmurs and excitement about the upcoming Equinox. She sighed, nearly forgetting about it all. Gifting for the Equinox was unlike others. To give a gift during the Equinox meant that it was someone you cherished and loved. You didn't give something to just anyone - it meant something.

"You're back!" Mari exclaimed as she unlocked the door.

Aurora laughed, setting down her bag on one of the chairs by the fireplace. "Missed you too." She jested.

"I wanted to ask a favour." She admitted, sitting down on the edge of her bed.

"What's up?" She asked, taking off her boots.

"Well, the Equinox is coming up, and I really don't know what to get Dae." She confessed. "I've been racking my brain and honestly everything I think of just doesn't seem good enough. Not...boyfriend gift material. Will you come with me on the weekend?" She pleaded.

Aurora chuckled. "Of course. I don't know if I'll be any use, but I'll do my best."

"Thanks, Ari." Mari gleamed. She paused a moment, wondering if she should ask. "What about you?"

Aurora stopped, her second boot half on. "What *about* me?" She repeated back.

"Well...you know..." Mari started.

She arched a brow at her.

Mari sighed, deciding she needed to be more direct. "Are you shopping for anyone?"

She averted her eyes, not sure if she could look at her at the moment. "Who would I possibly get anything for, Mar?" She asked, avoiding an answer.

"Look," Mari stated. "He's my brother so it's a bit weird and...well a little gross, but I think you would be good together."

Aurora turned to her in shock, her other boot dropping to the floor. "Mari, I told you it's not like that."

Mari chuckled. "Look, he's not saying anything, you're not saying anything, but we all see the way you two look at each other. One of you needs to make a move already."

Aurora looked away, her face bright crimson. People had been saying it a lot lately, but she didn't want to rely on their thoughts. Aelius was the only one who's opinion on the whole thing mattered. He had never made a move. He had never blatantly flirted with her. There had been moments that hinted at it, but nothing overly obvious. Everyone might be right that he liked her in that way, but he needed to be the one to confirm that.

"Don't worry." Mari assured her, seeing that she had made her embarrassed. "I'll get it out of him."

Aurora flopped back onto her bed letting out a groan of frustration. She had never been so timid or shy about any guy before. She had flirted and even briefly dated before back in the Middling realm, but it was never anything serious or lasting. She knew better than to form lasting attachments when they moved so often. This was different. This was an investment. If she gave herself into admitting feelings for him, it was not just some guy. This was someone who had become her friend, someone who made her feel safe and cared for. He was the brother of her best friend. "If I liked him," She started, sitting back up to face Mari. "—and I'm *not* saying that I do, it is so much more than dating *some guy*. He's your brother, Mar. He is either close friends or related to everyone I have gotten close to here. If I fall for him and he doesn't reciprocate, I've made things awkward. Or say we date and then something horrible happens. Who do you think everyone is going to take the side of and who do you think is going to be cast aside?" She explained, very much aware that she was bordering on rambling.

Mari arched a brow at her. "And you don't think I know all of those feelings?" She asked. "Do you not remember Dae and I? We've been best friends since we were kids. Our families have been close since before we were born. I know those feelings all too well." She lectured.

Aurora sighed, realising if anyone would understand it, it would Mari. "I just don't know if I can take that risk, Mar. I wouldn't want to risk losing your friendship."

Mari laughed, grabbing her into a tight hug. "Oh you know that if *anything* ever happened I'm keeping you right? You're stuck with me, Ari."

Aurora let out a tight breath she had held. She eased into the hug, wrapping her arms around her friend. Her friendship was still new to her. Risking something like that terrified her. "Well...I might have an idea for an Equinox gift then..."

Chapter 27

Vilcas was bustling with students and local alike. With the Equinox right around the corner, shops were busier than usual. They headed straight for the textile district, Mari having recommended a certain shop for her idea.

A bell rang out overhead as they stepped into the shop. The shop was close to Mari's favourite where she had picked up her several outfits earlier in the year. This one, however, specialised in men's wear. A young man, only several years older than them, stepped out from the back where he was hard at work on a piece. He wore a simple apron over his brown pleated pants and a cream coloured shirt. He removed the sewing needle from his mouth, pinning it in one of the pockets on the front of his apron.

"Miss Cirillo." He greeted with a nod.

"Hey Reggie!" She exclaimed. "My friend here is looking for something. You still have Aelius' measurements on file?" She asked, running her fingers over the fabric of some jackets on display.

Reggie scratched the back of his head, leaning to peak at something in the back. "Yeah I'm sure what we have down should be the same. Measured him at the beginning of the year. Hasn't changed has he?"

"No." Aurora answered, a slight shake of her head.

"Alright we should be good then." Reggie explained, grabbing a note pad from the sales counter and a pencil from behind his ear. "What can I do for you?"

"Mari said that you sometimes do custom orders." Aurora began, reaching into her bag. She pulled out a notebook, sketches of her idea inside. "Would you be able to make something like this in black?"

He peered over at her sketch, chewing on his bottom lip as he considered it. "I made something similar if you want to take a look?" He offered.

Aurora nodded, putting her notebook away. He turned to the back, looking for what he had in mind. He came back a moment later, a brown men's leather jacket on a coat hanger. He was right that it was fairly similar, but not quite what she had in mind. "Would it be possible to shorten it to his at the hips like the sketch? I was thinking it would be in more of a Middling fashion, if you know what I mean."

Reggie nodded in agreement. "I can do that. Will take a little tweaking of the pattern, but nothing drastic. I can have it done."

"Would it be possible to get it for next weekend? I was hoping for it to be an Equinox present." She asked cautiously.

Reggie sighed, considering the work that needed to go into the piece and his current workload. "I mean..."

"I would pay extra for a rush order, of course." She offered, knowing that it likely would mean some late hours for him.

He perked up at the offer, the mention of an extra charge swaying him to accepting. "I think we can make an arrangement."

They left the shop, her wallet a little lighter than she had hoped, but happy that she had found something. She knew she was taking a risk having something made for him, but part of her really wanted to do something for him. He wouldn't be eligible to wear blacks for another two years, but if she had it made in the Middling fashion, it could be something he could wear on his adventures. Something about him suited a well crafted leather jacket.

They headed further into town, on the mission for something for Dae. Aurora reached into her bag, pulling out one of the chocolates Aelius had given her. Every few weeks like clockwork he would bring her a little pouch of them. She offered one to Mari as they walked to the next store, hoping to find something for Dae.

"Want one?" Aurora asked.

Mari took one in hand popping it into her mouth. "I didn't know you liked that brand of chocolate." Mari commented. "They're hard to get around here."

Aurora tilted her head, examining the pouch they came in. "I had no idea. Aelius just...gives them to me every so often. Never says anything, just gives it to me."

Mari stopped a moment. "How often exactly?"

Aurora paused as well, considering the timing. "I don't know...once a month or so I think?"

Mari snickered to herself, covering her mouth with her hand as she made the connection. "Oh mom will be so proud..."

Aurora blinked, trying to figure out what Mari had realised. "What?" She asked, catching back up to her.

"He's giving you chocolate during your time of the month, Ari." Mari stated, trying not to laugh at the realisation.

Aurora's eyes grew wide, part mortified, part in awe. "Are you serious?" She exclaimed. She thought about it. Now that she looked at it, the timing lined up. She rubbed her hand over her face, embarrassed that she hadn't made the connection earlier. He must have felt everything through the bond to make the gesture. "Oh god..." She muttered to herself.

Mari chuckled to herself as she slung an arm over her shoulder. "Come on, let's head in." She explained, leading her into one of the shops.

Mari had browsed a few stores, but nothing seemed quite right. "Why are men so hard to shop for?" Mari groaned.

Aurora chuckled in response as she ran her fingers along the fabric of scarves on display. "No idea." She admitted. The only men she had been around growing up were fellow workers on the dig sites. Her mother had never dated, and neither had she for that matter - not seriously at least.

Mari inspected a series of dress shirts on a rack, each nearly identical to the last. "I'm pretty sure it's because they just buy themselves whatever it is they want. And if they *don't* buy it for themselves, it's because it's too expensive."

"Probably." She agreed. She considered herself lucky that she had come up with an idea for Aelius. Maybe it was the fact that they weren't in a relationship that took some pressure off of the whole process.

Mari sighed in frustration. "I give up." She declared. "I need coffee for my brain to work."

She chuckled as she followed. They turned down a few streets before they made their way to the most popular bakery in town. The bakery was alive and bustling with customers. Dozens of ornate pastries and cakes sat behind a lit glass case. The aroma of freshly baked bread and espresso hit her nose, making her mouth water. The walls were lined with a simple pale yellow wallpaper and some framed pictures. There were photos of the first owners, other generations of bakers, and even a beautiful painting of the Royal Academy.

Most seats were taken, but thankfully they were able to grab one in the back. She nibbled on one of the cookies Mari grabbed to go with their coffee, her mind mulling over options. "What about a reserve Artefact?" She asked out loud.

Mari paused, about to dip her cookie in her drink. "That's actually a really good idea." She admitted.

She smiled. "I remember he mentioned them before. He is pretty good about managing his magic, but having a reserve on hand never hurts."

"Thanks, Ari!" She exclaimed, quick to finish her drink. "You ready to go?"

She laughed as she hurried to drink her coffee without scalding her tongue. She could always eat and walk.

They went back to the other side of town, closer to the path back to the Academy. There, there were several Artefact shops. Her favourite specialised in antiques, but for the moment, they went to one that carried modern pieces. There were several sections, neatly arranged depending on needs. There was a shelf of communicators with several varieties quite similar to what Mari and Aelius owned. She would have to consider getting one of her own before long. It wouldn't hurt to be able to stay in touch with friends over the break.

Over by the cash was a glass case filled with various magic reserve Artefacts. They ranged in a variety of styles, but generally looked like small glass vials. When empty, as they currently were, they looked quite ordinary, but once a Mage took the time to fill them, they looked as if they were filled with a living glowing liquid. The magic itself was not a tangible fluid, but when the Artefact was prepped, it gave the appearance of it. Mari looked over the selection, finally settling on one with iron metal work around the vial. Most Mages wore it around the neck, but others had been known to store it on a chain at the waist much like a pocket watch. Dae could decide later.

Pleased with her selection, she turned to Aurora. "Anything else you want to do before we head back?"

"A book shop would be good, actually." She thought out loud.

"I think there's one around here." Mari explained. "I'll cash out and take you."

It had been a while since she had been in a book shop. The familiar comfort smell of books new and old hit her the moment she stepped inside. There was nothing quite like it. The shop owner was an older woman with glasses perched at the tip of her nose. She greeted them with a wave and turned back to the stack of books in front of her. Even Mari settled in, scanning the titles of several books on nutrition.

She toured the shelves, examining the different sections of the shop. She didn't have a specific book in mind, but it never hurt to see what was out there. She smiled, examining a section of fiction novels. She grabbed one, a romance novel set in the Middling realm. A quick scan of the back told her it was about a Guardian who travelled to the Middling realm undercover, falling in love with a helpless Middling woman. Aurora refrained from chuckling to herself, wondering if the author had ever even met a

Middling. She had plenty of school texts to consume her time, but it never hurt to have something for fun.

The shop owner rang her up, handing her the novel in a simple paper bag with a thanks. The bell on the door chimed behind her, announcing another customer. She smiled as she saw Professor Andersen walk in from the chill. He gave her a smile and nod as he made eye contact.

"How are you, Miss Thomas?" He greeted.

"Quite well, and you, professor?" She replied.

"Oh just stopping in to see if my order arrived. I asked Ms Gerwin here if she could order me in a text I was missing." He explained, waving to the shop owner behind her.

"Well I hope she has it for you." She responded as she started towards the door. "Oh! I forgot to thank you for the journal." She added.

He turned to her, his brow knit in confusion. "I'm sorry, the wha—" He was cut off by a trio of primary students rushing in through the door and pushing past. One of the chaperones chased behind, winded from their liveliness not far behind.

"Sorry." She breathed as she rushed to keep up with the children.

Professor Andersen fixed his glasses, his eyes fixed on the young woman who had apologised. "Not a problem, Julia." He assured as he followed her.

Aurora fought a chuckle as she continued out the door. It seemed as if it would be futile to continue their conversation. Mari waited for her outside the door, eager to get back. "All set?" She asked.

She lifted her bag in response. "All set. Let's get back."

By the time they got back to the gate, the sun had started to set, lighting the sky in a burnt orange hue. Many of the students had started to trickle their way back to the academy, but the town would surely still be busy with Equinox prep.

By the time they entered the main hall, Aelius was waiting, leaned against one of the main pillars. He pretended to look unbothered, but she could feel the hint of curiosity that swirled through the bond. "Busy day of shopping?" He asked.

"Have you been waiting for us to get back here like a puppy?" Mari teased, shifting one of the several bags she had.

He stood up, flustered by her puppy comment. "I wasn't waiting..." He grumbled.

Aurora suppressed a giggle as they headed further in. "It was a productive day." She answered.

He leaned over, attempting to peer at the bag she held. "You get anything special?" He asked.

Aurora glanced up at him, clutching the bag to her chest. "Just a book." She answered, almost defensively.

"Why so curious, Aelius?" Mari chimed in. "Wondering if you're getting something?"

He turned away to clear his throat, trying to avoid anyone seeing the shade of pink his cheeks flushed. "Of course not." He answered. "Just making conversation..."

Chapter 28

With the excitement of the holiday upon them, classes released early that Friday. No one seemed in the mood to focus properly - students and professors alike. Aurora found herself suddenly quite nervous about her plan. The jacket had been delivered by the shop the night previous, matching her vision perfectly. It was simple and classic in design, perfect for adventures across the Middling realm.

She had already taken the first step of having it made. Aurora took a deep breath. If he somehow got upset or felt awkward about the gift, she could simply blame the cultural difference of not having grown up around the Equinox. She hoped it wouldn't come down to it, but she needed the back up plan to have the resolve to do it.

Mari packed a bag across from her, adding last items for the weekend back home. "Are you *sure* I can't bring you home with me?" She pleaded.

Aurora sat herself on the bed beside the simple gift box. "It feels like this is a really big deal of a holiday, Mar." She began. "I feel like it would be a lot of pressure."

Mari sighed, knowing she was right. "You know my mom very well may kill me for not dragging you along. I already got enough shit from her during winter break."

Aurora let out a soft chuckle. "I know, and I'm sorry for the headache. I just...I'll come during the summer." She decided out loud. "I promise."

Mari squinted her eyes, examining the validity of the statement, before zipping up her bag. "Alright then. I'll take it."

Aurora stood to her feet, wrapping Mari in a hug. "Thank for understanding, Mar. I'll be ready soon."

Mari returned the hug, gripping her tight. "I know it's not easy. You're stronger than I would be."

She gave her a disbelieving look as she released her from the hug. "I seriously doubt that. You're a real life Amazon, Mar."

She broke out into a bright grin. "Why thank you." She preened.

"This is for you." She explained, pulling out a small box from her pocket.

Mari grabbed her into another tight hug. "Ari!" She exclaimed. "You didn't have to!"

She laughed, returning the hug. "Of course I did. You're my best friend."

Mari released her, tears glistening her eyes. "Mine too." She agreed, getting a hold of herself. "I left yours by the fireplace."

A knock at the door stole their attention. Her stomach fluttered, feeling Aelius through the bond. She bit her bottom lip, knowing that the moment was upon her.

"Brother." Mari greeted with a pretend glare as she opened the door.

Aelius stood in the hall, a bag slung over his shoulder. He peered over his sister's shoulder, not bothering to give her his attention. His eyes locked with Aurora's, the nerves in her stomach reflected through the bond.

"I'll get out of your way then. Meet you out there." Mari announced, knowing that he was unlikely to respond. She snuck around him, heading to main hall.

"All set for the trip home?" Aurora asked, tucking a strand of hair behind her ear.

He paused, seeming as if he wanted to step inside. His eyes darted behind her, seeing the box on her bed. "Just about." He stated.

She looked up at him, feeling her pulse quicken. "I..."

"Come home with me." He blurted out, taking a step towards her. The look on his face told her that he was just about as surprised as her by his statement. "I mean...*Please.* Please come with us."

She stared up at him, very much wanting to accept, but knowing she couldn't handle it. Not yet. She grabbed his hand, the heat of him positively radiating against her skin. "In the summer." She answered. "Not yet. I just...can't. Not yet."

He let out a small sigh, knowing she was right. He could feel her tension and apprehension through the bond, just as she felt his heart race in pace with her own. "Summer it is then."

Aelius turned to his bag, hesitating a moment before opening it. He pulled out a gift, pausing as if he was debating with himself to make the move. He handed it to her, a nervous smile on his face. "I...I got you something." He explained.

She looked up him, a bright smile forming on her face as she took the gift in hand. Relief flooded her, some her own, the rest his. She set it down on the table by the fireplace, grabbing the box that laid on her bed. "I got you something too." She admitted sheepishly.

He did his best to keep his face neutral, but couldn't help the smile that formed. He looked as if he wanted to tear it open in that moment, but restrained himself. "Thank you." He stated sincerely.

Aurora stared up at him, both feeling the swell that grew between them. She desperately wanted to know what he was thinking. She knew that sharing gifts like this had so much more weight to it then other occasions. He brought a hand up to her face, gently dragging his fingers into her hair. He leaned in, Aurora closing her eyes in anticipation. She felt his heart thundering just as fast as her own.

"Aelius! You coming?" A voice called down the hall.

Aelius stopped, leaning back to look down the hall and let out a sigh. He turned back to her, frustration at the moment being interrupted. Before she knew what had happened, Aelius pulled her into a tight hug, his hand caressing the back of her head. She had sworn he was about to kiss her in that moment. She inhaled, taking in his scent, doing her best to not radiate frustration. He released her, staring back down at her. He leaned in, pressing a tender kiss on her forehead. "I'll see you soon. We'll talk when I get back." He promised, turning to head home.

She waited until he was down the hall before closing the door. She let out a sigh, leaning against the door. His actions and feelings through the bond all pointed towards romantic feelings. If they had had just a moment longer, maybe, just maybe...

She shook her head, knowing it would do no good to dwell on it all weekend. If she started to ruminate and scour over every detail now, she would be at it all weekend. It would maddening.

She reached into her bed side table, picking out the romance novel that she had purchased last week. Diving into someone else's love life would be a perfect distraction. She got herself settled, ready to immerse herself in what was hopefully something wonderful.

***

Aurora had managed to devour most of the book before her stomach growled at her to eat something. She put the book down, looking up to see the sun had already started to set. A glance at her watch told her that it had been several hours already. She sighed, stretching her arms over head and releasing a crack in her neck before starting her way to the common room.

The emptiness of the halls reminded her of her winter break. It had been nice to be alone for a time, but after a while it had become uncomfortable. She was glad it was just for the weekend. She put together a plate of meats and cheeses, and grabbed herself some bread. She didn't have the energy or desire to make a proper meal.

She polished it off quickly, making sure to wash her plate. There was no sense in leaving a mess for later. She headed back to her room, remembering presents awaited her. She had been so caught up in the moment with Aelius that she had completely forgotten to open what they have given her.

She sat down at the fireplace, pausing at what she saw. Three gifts sat on the table, neatly arranged waiting for her. She checked the tags on the gifts, noting one from Mari and two from Aelius. She could have sworn he had only given her one, but she could have been wrong. She grabbed Mari's first, opening the neatly wrapped paper gingerly. Inside was a book on nutrition for women during training. She chuckled to herself, thankful for the research. She knew that Mari had been talking about customising a plan for her since they had been practicing more often, but this would provide a good base as well.

She put the book off to the side, turning to the pair of gifts from Aelius. She cocked her head to the side, noting the difference in wrapping paper. She picked up the larger of the two first, running a finger under the paper. A box the length of her fore arm opened to reveal a pair of sleek daggers. Her brow shot up in surprise at the gift. She picked up one in her hand, turning it over and examining the craftsmanship. It was surprisingly light in her hand, the curved blade glinting in the light. Sigils had been delicately carved into the sides she noticed. *I will strike my target true.*

She placed the dagger back in the box, setting it to the side.

It rattled and clinked as she picked it up, making her wonder what could possibly make such a sound. Inside, was a tin of loose leaf tea and a small box of biscuits. She cracked open the tin, inhaling the scent. She coughed, noting the overpowering aroma of peppermint and other herbs she couldn't quite place. She closed the lid, figuring that a tea by the fire and a book sounded like a perfect addition to the evening.

She brought the tea with her to the common room, putting a kettle on to warm. She stopped the water before it boiled, not wanting to burn the leaves. There was no label on the tea, so it would be a gamble on the temperature.

She brought the teapot and a mug on a tray back to her room, seeing no sense in going back and forth. She set it down on the table, conjuring a fire as she walked to the closet to grab a blanket to cocoon herself in. She poured herself a cup, blowing on the steam that furled around before taking her first sip. She grimaced at the taste, a note of bitterness hitting the back of her tongue. She debated a dollop of honey as she took another sip. The flavour grew on her, but it wouldn't have been her first choice. It was still incredibly thoughtful of him.

She nibbled on the cookies, finishing off her first mug of tea. She let out a yawn, pouring a second cup. She was surprised that she was tired this early, but it *had* been a long day. She rubbed at her eyes, arching her back in a stretch. She was nearly done the book now. Just a few more chapters and she would reach the end. She took another sip of tea, the warmth of the fire, and the coziness of her blanket making it a losing fight against sleep.

She knew he was close, but couldn't lay eyes on him. She could feel his presence, hear the cadence of his footsteps, but couldn't seem to find him. She turned, finally catching sight of him several steps out of reach. She quickened her pace, reaching out to him. In a wisp he was gone. She called out to the bond, seeing him off to her right. She reached again and again, each time losing him just as she was about to make contact.

Her heart raced, wondering why he couldn't stay in place. She needed him. For what, she wasn't quite sure. She simply knew she needed him. She tried to focus, tried to make sense of her surroundings, but was met with pain. She winced, grabbing at her head as she fell to her knees. It didn't make any sense. She breathed, trying to calm herself, to ease the searing pain that pressed against her skull.

She opened her eyes as she felt a touch on her arms. Aelius was there, holding her gently. He tried to speak to her, but he made no sound. She furrowed her brow in confusion, opening her mouth to speak. Her own voice was gone. She reached to her throat, wondering what was happening.

Aelius continued to shout at her, desperate to get her attention. She tried to focus, watching the shape of his mouth. "Wake up." She finally heard. It was faint, like the sound was coming from under water, but it was there. She stared, almost as if she weren't quite certain.

"WAKE UP!"

Chapter 29

Her eyes sprang open, her heart thundering in her chest at the dread of her dream. She blinked a few times, confused by the sensation in her head. Her head swirled with a sense of vertigo that made no sense at all. She creased her brow in confusion as she blinked and tried to make sense of the things. She tried to sit up from her slouched nap position, but immediately realised her body was heavy and numb. Nothing answered to her command, hoping that she would even have a twitch of a few fingers.

It was then that she noticed him in the dark. Dressed entirely in a dark grey stood a man she couldn't quite put her finger on. His face looked familiar in a way, but not enough to know for certain. A quick flash of shock crossed his face before his expression shifted into delight. In his hands he held the pair of daggers that Aelius had gifted her, admiring their beauty in the firelight.

The man turned to her, leaning into her with a wide grin spread across his face. "Well hello, sweetheart." He greeted in an uncomfortably friendly tone. He was mere inches away from her face, her body refusing to move away even a millimetre.

He chuckled to himself at her attempted struggle. He stood back up and tucked away the daggers he had been contemplating. "I see the tea worked well." He commented as he idly ran a finger along the handle of her tea pot. Her eyes darted to it, the familiar bitterness hitting her. Witches Bane.

"When brewed correctly, Witches Bane will hit in a staggered succession." She blinked her eyes, not believing the blurry shape of Professor Singh in front of her. Her voice echoed through the room in an unnatural way. *"First, as you can see here, you get the effects of Water Hemlock on her nervous system. Next, we should see if she starts to have any hallucinations from the moonflower..."*

"Now," He continued with a pretend sigh. "What *are* we to do with you?" She forced herself to focus on him, trying her best to take in every detail. He was fairly young, probably only a few years older than her. His hair was a sandy brown, swept back neatly. His soft brown eyes made him appear kind and approachable. He looked rather ordinary - not quite handsome enough to be striking, but in no way ugly or overly remarkable. He was perfect for blending in.

She tried again, in vain, to move. It felt as if she was trying to fight against a current, her body slow and heavy. A bead of sweat formed and trickled its way down the back of her neck. Her eyes tracked his as he squatted in front of her. "You know, I was going to make things look like a suicide, but I think that we can have a lot more fun than that, don't you? Such a shame to let things go to waste."

He reached over, selecting one of the blades that Aelius had taken the time to choose for her. He unsheathed the blade, taking a moment to truly admire the detailing involved. "A beautiful blade." He chuckled to himself. "Let's see how sharp it is, shall we?"

He started at her collarbone, tracing along the centre out towards her shoulder joint. Her body was numb, but she still felt a bit of tug and pull as the blade was dragged along her skin. The heat of blood pooling and running down felt almost as if it were happening to someone else.

He looked into her eyes as he scored her skin. He watched her intently, his face falling into disappointment at her lack of pain. He sighed, examining the blade, now wet with a hint of her blood. "Well that's no fun." He groaned. "That tea really numbs you, doesn't it?"

She stared back at him, doing her best to look as unfazed as possible. Her body may have been useless, but her panic was all too real. She would have loved to retort snarkily, but even moving her mouth was futile.

He set the blade down a moment, pulling her closer by the seat of her chair. He kicked her legs apart with his boot, pausing as he examined her position. He rose to his feet, arranging her body so she was seated properly, almost as if he was setting up a game of pretend with a doll. "There." He stated, happy with his work. "Let's test just how effective this stuff really is."

Aurora's heart pounded in her chest as she watched him select one of the blades from his belt. They were smaller in size, looking more like throwing knives, made for speed and accuracy. With a simple flick, almost too quick to see, one of the blades lodged into her shoulder, pinning her against the chair. A grunt escaped her lips, the feeling of the blade lodging deep into her flesh..

"Hmm." He remarked, examining her expression. "Interesting. Very interesting..." He leaned back, reaching behind his back for a larger blade.

She felt her stomach churn as she watched him turn the blade in his hands. He leaned in, pushing aside her skirts. He placed the blade into the top of her thigh, dragging it along the surface. She winced, the feeling of the cut burned. Her intruder's eyes lit up at the reaction. He pressed harder, a whimper escaping her lips. Tears started to roll down her cheeks as she felt a bit of the numbness fade from her face.

He pulled the blade back, wiping her blood off on her shirt. His eyes remained fixed on hers, not wanting to miss a single reaction she might have. He pressed the tip into her other thigh, taking the time to replicate the same marks on the other side. She grit her teeth, forcing herself not to give him a single sound. He delighted in her reactions. She wouldn't give him the satisfaction.

His face moulded into a grimace as he pressed harder into the second cut. "It's no fun if you don't play." He insisted, leaning some weight into it.

She finally lost her hold on her control and let out a cry. He broke out into a wide grin, appreciating the moment. "There. Isn't that so much better?"

The stranger pulled back, wiping the blade off on her skirt this time. The sound of the blade scraping against the fabric of her uniform sent a chill down her spine. She glared at him, panting as the pain seared through her body. Sweat started to bead down her back, her heart thundering in her chest. As much as things had started to hurt, she took it as a good sign. It meant that the Witches Bane was starting to wear off, even if it was just a little bit.

She tested her magic source, desperate to take hold of even the smallest shred, but it was like scraping her hands against slick glass. She could feel it right there, but just couldn't quite grasp it. Her head swirled as the pain in her shoulder throbbed. He shifted his stance, ready to grab another one of his blades. She knew it would be now or never. In one last attempt to clamp down, she finally grabbed a hold of a sliver of magic. It wasn't enough to conjure something, but it was enough to draw on something existing. Her eyes darted to the fire she had conjured earlier, her saving grace. With every ounce of strength she could muster, she pulled at the fire in the fireplace, slamming it into her attacker's back. He cried out in shock as he instinctively swatted at the flames.

He slammed into her chair as he attempted to snuff out the flames that coated his back. She fell to the floor with a thud, knocking some of the air from her lungs. The blade in her shoulder pushed deeper, the hilt hitting the floor during her fall. She cried out, unable to muster the strength to do anything about it.

It was his boots that she saw first. He stood before her, finally having taken care of her little trick. Wooden vines sprouted up around her, the rough edges cutting into her skin as they took hold of her. They coiled around her wrists and ankles, even winding around her rib cage. They pulled her up, settling her at his eye level. The stranger seethed, panting from his encounter with the flames. The vines tightened, matching his growing frustration. He stepped closer, his face mere inches from hers. "Nice try." He chuckled, vines climbing their way around her neck.

She let out a choking sound as they tightened around her throat. "It gets so boring sometimes." He explained, taking her in. "It's always 'make it look an accident', or 'make it look like a heart attack'. There's no fun or artistry to it anymore."

Tears formed on the edge of her eyes. She willed her body to fight, trying to pull against the hold he had on her. He laughed at her attempt, clamping them down harder. "See, I'm torn." He began, pacing before her. "We're having so much fun, aren't we? But...this *has* gotten messier then it was supposed to be." He turned back to her, staring into her eyes.

He sighed, running his hand through his hair. Her blood stuck to it, making strands clump together in a sticky mess. "You really shouldn't have woken up, sweetheart." He explained, clearly unhappy with having to wrap up his idea of fun.

He raised a hand, clamping his fist shut. Any room she had had to breathe before was gone. The woody vines cut into her, scraping against her skin. Blood trailed down the vines, falling in large drops onto the carpet below. Her eyes darkened around the edges, details starting to grow dim and blurry.

Tears of frustration and anger welled in her eyes. She should have listened. She should have gone home with Mari and Aelius. Had she just listened to them, none of this would have happened. She wished that she could feel the bond, but the tea must have dulled any last connection she had to him. He was simply too far away to reach one final time.

She willed her body, any part, to move, to fight. Heat and rage simmered through her. She desperately tried to clutch onto any shred of magic she could. She didn't care what element it was, she could make do with anything. A burning sensation built within her, growing into a blaze. It felt familiar, but didn't make sense in the least. Her rage bubbled within her, hot tears rolling down her cheeks as she fought against heavy lids. She looked up, a small smile forming on her face at a final hallucination - exactly what she wished she could see. Her eyes rolled back and her head dropped, finally losing consciousness.

Chapter 30

Aelius appeared just in time to see her head fall forward. He appeared silently, not daring to move too suddenly. There was no telling what he would find when he entered. Before him stood an assassin, clothed head to toe in a dark grey. A Mage.

He stepped forward, ready to strike, but something made him freeze. Golden light emanating from Aurora lit up the room. The assassin seemed equally shocked, taking a step back. It was then that Aelius knew he had to act. With one swift motion, he stepped forward, grabbing a hold of one of the many blades at the assassin's belt and the side of the assassin's head. Aelius quickly stepped to the side, pulling him away from Aurora as he drug the blade clean across the assassin's throat. Blood sprayed out as the assassin let out a sputtering choking sound, his hands clawing away at Aelius' hold on him.

Before he could drop the assassin to the floor, a blinding beam of golden light shot out from Aurora. He covered his eyes instinctively, the body dropping to the floor with a thud. The light faded almost as quickly as it had appeared. Coming to his senses, Aelius rushed to her side, ripping away the vines at her throat with one quick tug. His heart lifted as he heard her take a raspy breath of air. He moved on to the others until she dropped limply into his arms.

He held her tight, his own breath ragged and unsteady. Adrenaline coursed through his veins, his earlier kill not nearly enough to satiate his boiling rage. Someone had wanted her dead, and not gently. They had dared to torture her, to play with her. A single death was not enough to quell what burned inside him.

He rose to his feet, cradling her in his arms. It then that he realised what that beam of light had been. A hole bore through the wall, the edges still smouldering where a beam of Purification had blasted out of her. He would have stopped to examine and truly appreciate the power that had just shot out of his Mage, but now was not the time. Her link through the bond was weak and fading. She needed medical attention. *Now.*

He teleported them both to the Academy gate. There was no teleporting through it - a protection against intruders. He stepped through the gate, walking at a quick pace as to not jostle her with a run. He knew she was injured, but not to what extent. He couldn't risk making her injuries worse. The moment he stepped through the gate he teleported them again. He was home.

The sound of ceramic shattering on the tile echoed through his home. It had been late, the wee hours of the morning, but Cora, his mother had been up anyway. A cup of tea shattered on the kitchen floor at the sight of her eldest coated in blood. She rushed to his side, a million questions in her head. "What happened?" She finally demanded.

Aelius walked over to the nearby dining room table, gingerly placing Aurora down. Aurora's face winced at being placed down, but her eyes remained closed. He could feel her through the bond - the ill effects of Witches Bane rampant through her veins. "An assassin." He finally managed, barely registering his mother's concerns.

Footsteps pounded in the nearby hall, Mari rounding the corner with a look of confusion and concern on her face. "What the fu—" She froze in place, taking in the bloody scene in front of her. "ARI!" She rushed to the table, Aelius putting an arm out to stop her from touching her.

"Don't touch her." He hissed, the feral need to protect her taking over.

Cora approached cautiously, laying a hand on her son's shoulder. "We're here to help, honey." She said gently. "You have to let us."

Aelius turned to Cora, sadness touching his eyes as he realised she was right. His father stepped in the room, his face a cold calmness as he took in the room. "Start explaining." He ordered sternly.

Cora made quick work of bringing over medical supplies as Aelius explained what had happened. She cut away at what remained of Aurora's blouse, knowing she needed to address the dagger first and foremost. Mari placed her hands on Aurora's shoulders as Cora pulled. Aelius winced at the sensation, fighting the urge to rush to her side. Mari immediately put cloth and pressure on the wound, blood pouring out from both sides. "I'll hold this. Pass me the—"

Aurora woke, a cry escaping her lips. Her eyes snapped open, registering an unfamiliar room, and someone pinning her body down. She tried to fight, thrashing and swinging against everyone. "Ari, it's okay!" Mari tried explaining.

Aurora didn't hear her. There was only panic. She was still weak from the tea, but they were all concerned of hurting her by restraining her. Aelius stepped in, gently holding the side of her head. "Aurora." He called out to her calmly. Her breath was quick and panicked, as her eyes met his. She couldn't be certain of what was real and what was the tea. He stroked the side of her head, keeping her head calm so she could focus on him. She stopped thrashing, her heart still racing. Her breathing started to slow, becoming a more even tempo.

He smiled down at her, loosening his hold on her. "It's okay." He assured her. She gave him a soft, almost drunken smile as her eyes fell back and closed again.

Cora paused a moment, making sure she was truly asleep before administering a pain reliever. With surgical speed, she sewed up both sides of the wound. Aelius stepped back while his mother worked stitching wounds and bandaging her up. His father, Elias, was at his side with a glass of scotch in hand. Aelius accepted it, taking a long sip. Elias put a hand on his son's shoulder, partaking in his own.

"I'm going to make sure the guest room is in order." Mari explained once they had finished their patch work. Cora worked at wiping away blood that had started to crust over her pale skin.

"I'll set up on the floor." Aelius stated, not taking his eyes off Aurora.

"You need to sleep. I can take watch." Mari offered.

He shook his head. "You're alright. I'm not leaving her."

***

Aurora opened her eyes, her head searing with a splitting headache. She winced as she sat up, the room spinning for a moment. She blinked, unsure of where she was. The room was modest in size with light blue grey walls. She winced as she moved, the memories of last night starting to hit her. She looked down, a fresh night gown on her. One that she didn't own. She pulled back at the neck of the night gown, a set of bandages wrapped around her shoulder. She pushed aside the blanket exposing bandages wrapped around both of her thighs.

Something stirred beneath her. She tensed as she leaned over the side, seeing Aelius under a thin blanket on the floor. He sat up, his eyes red from lack of sleep. "You're awake." He stated, his voice low and gravely in the morning.

She clutched the blanket around her, suddenly mortified at the idea of him seeing her like this. "You…"

He was quick to her side, seated beside her. He hesitated a moment, unsure if he should touch her. She looked up at him, tears welled in her eyes. He grabbed her into a gentle hug, her face buried in his shoulder. He caressed the back of her head. "It's okay. You're safe."

She pulled back, wiping away the tears from her eyes. "Where are we?" She asked. Her throat felt as if it was on fire. It felt like someone had taken a grater to the inside of it and poured vinegar down it for good measure. Her voice was barely a whisper, raspy and ragged in sound.

"I brought you home." He stated. "It was all I could think of."

"Thank you." She said, a sad smile on her face.

A light knock sounded at the door. "Can I come in?" Mari asked cautiously.

Mari opened the door at their offer, a tray in hand. "I heard voices and thought you might want a little something." She explained. She brought the tray over, setting it on the bed. Tea, just the way Aurora liked it and a plate of scones and jam sat on it. "How are you feeling?" She asked as Aurora took the cup.

"Awful." She admitted with a hint of a laugh. "I probably look worse."

Mari winced, trying to keep a straight face. Her expression confirmed what she figured. She knew she likely looked like death warmed over. "Everything will be better with a good shower and some rest." Mari assured her.

Aurora took a sip of her tea, realising what Mari was wearing. She wore a simple dress in pure white. Silver flowers embroidered the bodice, lantern sleeves billowing down to her elbows. "The Equinox..." She remarked, setting her tea back down on the tray. "I—"

Mari put a hand on her forearm, insisting she relax. "I love you, but shut up. Before you try to say something stupid like you were interrupting or something."

Aurora eased, a feeling of guilt still in the pit of her stomach. She looked over at Aelius, averting her eyes as soon as his gaze met hers.

"Aelius get out." Mari ordered sternly. He opened his mouth to protest, but she refused to let him get a word in. "I'm going to check her dressings. Go get something to eat and see mom and dad. I've got her."

He glared at his sister, wanting to argue, but knew she was right. He stood with a huff, following her command.

Mari watched him leave, waiting until the door was firmly shut before turning her attention back to Aurora. "Can I check?" She asked, careful not to rush her.

She nodded, looking off to the side as Mari gingerly peeled back the bandages. She couldn't bring herself to look just yet.

Mari let out a sigh of relief, happy with what she found. "That spirit salve really does wonders." She explained, readjusting her night gown. "We can get you into the shower and I can change the dressings after."

She looked at Mari, knowing she was likely a mess. She nodded, following her out of the room. She held her hand, following slowly down the hall to a washroom at the end. Mari handed her towels, urging her to help herself to whatever she needed.

She placed the towel on the counter, terrified of checking her reflection. Slowly, she lifted her eyes, knowing she needed to do it sooner or later. Tears stung her eyes as her heart clenched in her chest. She knew that she would look terrible, but not like this. Her eyes were completely red, the vessels in her eyes having burst. Her hair was crusted with blood, matting in streaks of disheveled locks. She peeled away the bandages that wrapped around her throat, her shoulder, her wrists...

A sob rang out of her throat as she took it all in. Memories came to her in flashes, in broken pieces that didn't make sense. A knock rapped at the door. "Aurora. Are you okay?" Aelius asked. She could feel his worry through the bond, knowing that nothing was okay with her.

She sniffed back her sobs, wiping away the tears that streaked down her face. "I'm okay." She assured him in a staggered voice. "I'll be okay. Sorry."

She heard him sigh outside the door. "Don't be sorry. I'll be here on the other side. It's okay."

Showering was slow and painful work. Mari had been right that the spirit infused salve had done incredible work. Without it, the wounds would still be raw and bloody. The stitches in her thighs looked almost healed, the stitches already starting to fall out. The wound in her shoulder, however, would still need much more time to heal. She was lucky that it had missed her joint and connective tissue. Things could have been far worse.

It felt better to be clean. It was a small thing, but it made her feel that little bit more human. A memory had struck her as the water from the shower sprayed across her face. A flash of the assassin on the carpet in a pool of blood crossed her mind. Her heart raced at the image, her hand bracing against the wall of the shower as she tried to settle herself. It was hard to tell what was real and what had been the Witches Bane.

Aurora opened the door, towel wrapped around her. She peaked her head out, knowing that Aelius would still be waiting for her. "Uhm..." She started, unsure if she truly felt comfortable running down the hall in just a towel. "Can you get Mari for me, please?" She asked.

He turned to her, quickly realising that all she would be wearing was a towel. He cleared his throat. "Be right back."

He barely took a step before Mari rounded the corner with clothing and first aid kit in hand. "I've got it." She assured Aelius, pushing past him.

Mari set the clothes and kit down on the counter, washing her hands before she got to work examining the wounds. She was cautious and gentle, quite certain that everything was still tender.

"Where did you learn to do all of this?" Aurora asked, cutting the tense silence.

Mari applied a new layer of salve before wrapping fresh bandages over each injury. "Mom taught me. Guardians learn basic first aid, but mom never thought it was good enough. She wanted to make sure we knew how to take care of things when they got *really* bad. You can't always get to the hospital quick enough." She winced as Mari got to work on her shoulder. "Sorry." She apologised.

Aurora shook her head ever so slightly. It was all she could manage. "It's alright. Thank you."

Mari paused, unsure of her words for a moment. "It's the least I could do, Ari. I'm just glad I can help."

Aurora leaned her forehead against Mari's. "I can still say thank you." She chuckled.

Chapter 31

Once she was bandaged and dressed, they stepped out of the washroom. Aelius had remained in the hallway. He straightened himself as he saw her, no longer leaning agains the wall. He scanned her, noticing her hair unbrushed and wet. "Do you want a hand?" He asked, as he took a strand in hand.

Aurora averted her eyes, knowing just how how bad they looked. "I couldn't really brush it with my shoulder..." She explained, trailing off in embarrassment.

"That's not what I asked. Do you want help?" He repeated gently.

She stared at the floor and nodded. "Thank you."

"Everything's in her room." Mari explained taking the remaining medical supplies back to her mother.

Aelius took her hand in his, gently pulling back to the guest room. He sat her down on the bed, grabbing a brush from atop the dresser drawer. He sat down behind her on the bed, gingerly brushing out her hair. She was surprised he was capable of being so gentle, taking care of her with ease.

Her surprise must have registered through the bond as he worked. "I used to take care of Mari when we were little. She could never take care of her own hair. It used to be much longer when we were kids." He explained as he started sectioning her hair. His fingers made quick work of a French braid.

He placed a hand on her good shoulder once he was finished. She turned to face him. She was still uneasy about her appearance, but she couldn't help it. He gingerly brought a hand to her cheek. "He never should be able to lay a finger on you." He confessed.

She leaned into his touch, closing her eyes. "You saved me." She replied. She could feel the guilt that radiated through the bond. She knew that there was nothing she could say that would ease the feeling, no matter how non sensical it was. "If it weren't for you, he would have succeeded. Thank you, Aelius."

His eyes rimmed with tears as she spoke. He pulled her into him, taking care to be careful with her. Just as she didn't want him to see her this way, he would rather she saw him only in his strength.

A knock sounded at the door. "We're in the family room when you're ready." Cora announced through the door. "We need to discuss some things."

Aelius released his hold on her, despite very much wanting to remain. "We go when you're ready." He explained simply.

"It's okay." She stated, standing to her feet. She extended a hand to him with a small smile. "Let's go."

They were seated in the family room by the time they got there. Elias and Cora sat together with Mari in a chair to the side. A loveseat remained empty for Aelius and Aurora to sit down on. He helped her sit before joining her, making sure he didn't sit too close. "We got a hold of Dean Reyes." Cora explained once they had settled. "She is aware of what happened and they are taking care of it."

"What...*did* happen?" Aurora cautious hesitantly.

Cora exchanged a glance with Elias. He gave a nod to his wife. "It looks like someone hired an assassin to eliminate you." Elias explained, a business like tone to his voice. "It's not certain who or why at this time, but the Guard will investigate."

Her brow shot up in surprise. To have the Royal Guard investigate meant it was taken incredibly seriously. "Are you sure?" She asked.

"Something like this is not to be taken lightly." Elias stressed. "The Academy is supposed to be a safe place for the students to learn and train. We need to get to the bottom of this for your sake, but also for the sake of all of the students attending."

She gave a small smile. "Thank you, sir."

His expression softened, a smile forming on his face. "No thanks needed. And...Elias, *please*. Sir is so formal."

A small smile formed on her face. She was thankful for everything. For their care, for their concern, for their investigation. They didn't need to do any of it, yet here they were, rallying around her. She blinked rapidly, trying to keep back the tears that stung her eyes. Aelius grabbed her hand, squeezing tight.

"The medical wing will be up and running come lunch time." Cora added. "They'll be there to do a thorough check and make sure everything is healing properly."

"Thank you." Aurora responded, doing her best to keep the warble out of her voice.

Cora saw right through her, giving her a sad smile. "Is there anything else we can do to help, sweetheart?"

Aurora shook her head. "You've done more than enough. I'm just so sorry to interrupt everything, an—"

"You didn't interrupt anything." Cora cut her off, a hint of sternness in her tone. "Aelius did the right thing in bringing you here. We are incredibly proud of him and immensely thankful that he was able to take care of you. I want you to get the idea that you have done *anything* wrong out of your head now."

She felt a swell of surprise and pride through the bond. She could feel his guilt and worry all this time. She was glad it was starting to ebb away. "I will."

***

By the time they were set to head back to the Academy, both Mari and Aelius were full fuss over her. The pair argued over which one would assist her, but ultimately Aelius won playing the Guardian card. Mari grumbled, but left it to him. He stared down at her, giving her a small smile before slipping a hand around the small of her waist. He pulled her into him, her hands bracing against his chest as he teleported them to the portal. It wasn't long before they were in front of the Academy gates. Mari appeared beside them, just a heartbeat behind.

Aurora looped her arm through the crook of his elbow as they walked through the main gate. She was fine to walk on her own, but it was stiff and painful work. He took his time, making sure she didn't move too quickly. The moment they were through, he pulled her back into him, teleporting directly outside of the medical wing. It was an odd sensation, almost like free falling. She wasn't sure if she would ever get used to it.

A young nurse jumped at the sudden appearance of her and the Cirillo twins. She clutched at her heart, as she tried to gather herself. The nurse called over her shoulder, announcing their arrival to the doctor. In moments, Aurora was whisked off behind a curtain, fussed over by several nurses and the doctor. She could feel the worry and irritation Aelius held as he paced nearby.

Blood draws and scans confirmed that Cora had done a fantastic job of patching her up. Her shoulder would need additional attention, but considering the hour and the materials on hand, Aurora was in very good condition. The nurses led her out, several vials of medication and tonics in hand. Aelius stepped in the moment she was released, taking the container of medication out of the nurse's arms. Before the nurse could object, he shot her a warning look. She shut her mouth, not daring to get in the way of a protective Guardian. "Just make sure she takes them as directed." The nurse advised. He nodded, giving Aurora his arm.

Mari waited in the lobby, her arms crossed at her chest as she paced. She looked up as soon as she registered them, a feigned smile on her face. "Dean wants to see you." She explained.

Aelius glanced down at her, a small nod between them, as they slowly made their way down the hall to the Dean's office. Every so often Aelius would stop, giving her a moment to catch her breath. He looked as if he wanted to keep teleporting her, but he knew she would argue against it. They took their time, eventually reaching the Dean's doors. Her assistant was already seated behind her desk, a look of pity on her face as she took in Aurora's appearance. The assistant gave them a small nod, giving permission to go through. With a light push, Aelius opened the door to the office, revealing the Dean reviewing a stack of papers at her desk.

"Come come." Reyes urged. She beckoned them with a hand, shutting the doors with a gust of wind as they stepped in. Aelius guided Aurora to a seat, making sure she was settled before sitting at her side.

"Now then," Dean Reyes began. "You've had quite the night it seems."

Aurora was used to the Dean's dismissive or joking manner about things, but she felt Aelius tense at the tone Reyes took. He clenched his jaw, maintaining a professional attitude. Aurora laid a hand on his, hoping he would calm. "I did. I'm not even fully sure what happened to be honest." She confessed.

"It's alright, Miss Thomas." The Dean assured her. "Cora and Doctor Jensen gave me most of the details. Sanitation stopped by this morning and filled me in on their findings as well."

Her stomach dropped. From the fragmented memories she had, she knew it would have been a most unpleasant start to the morning. "I'm so sorry." She managed.

Dean Reyes scoffed. "None of that." She insisted. "You did well, Miss Thomas."

She looked up in surprise. "Thank you?"

"There aren't many that could hold off a trained assassin, especially after taking a hefty dose of Witches Bane." Reyes explained. "Where did you get it anyway?"

Aurora's attention flitted to Aelius for a moment before returning to the Dean. "It was in a gift addressed to me from Aelius"

She could feel a swirl of emotions through the bond. Shock, anger, confusion... "Aurora I would never—"

She placed a hand on his arm. "I know. You'd never do *anything* to hurt me. It was obviously planted by that man somehow."

Aelius' shoulders relaxed as he sat back in his chair. She swore a small smirk crossed the Dean's face for a brief moment as she turned her attention back to her. "Miss Thomas is correct, Mr Cirillo. No one would ever think that you had a hand in it. What we need to do is get to the bottom of this. As you know, I've spoken with Elias about all of this, and I assure you that we will be investigating with the utmost of care."

Aurora nodded, happy that everyone seemed to be on the same page. "I was wondering. What am I to do about my room?" She asked hesitantly. She wasn't sure how one got that much blood out of the carpet.

"Your things have already been moved. You and Miss Cirillo have already been moved to room one thirty five."

Reyes explained as she slid a new key across the desk. "Miss Cirillo should have her key by now."

"Thank you." Aurora acknowledged, taking the key in hand. "If there's nothing else, I think I'd like to go back to my room now." She explained wearily.

The Dean rose to her feet, Aurora and Aelius following suit. "I hope that you let me know if there is anything you need, Miss Thomas." Reyes commented as they all moved towards the door. "I will make sure you are informed of anything we find."

She thanked the Dean again and let the grand doors close behind them. She let out a sigh, her body and mind still exhausted. She wondered if there would ever be enough sleep for her to feel normal again.

"Let's go." Aelius urged, offering his arm to her. She looked up at him, quite certain that he would never let her out of his sight again.

***

It felt as if everyone's eyes were on her as Aurora sat in class. Though she was on the mend, there were still obvious hints of the assault. Her eyes were still more red than white, and the bruising around her throat and wrists were still quite visible. She was thankful, at least, for the length and layers of her uniform to hide the worst of things. If she hadn't been so tired of it all, she would have found it amusing to hear all of the different versions of what had happened. She had heard everything from the assassin being sent because of her mother's old gambling debts to her being a runaway gang member that needed to be eliminated. None of it made very much sense.

Professor Singh was late to class that morning, entering in a rush. Singh apologised to the class as she settled her papers on her desk. As Aurora looked up, their eyes met, tension settling in her stomach. The look on Singh's face didn't sit quite right with her. It looked like an odd mix of excitement and curiosity.

Aurora was unfortunately correct as Professor Singh called out for her at the end of class. She paused and gave Dae a glance and a nod. He had agreed to be part of an annoying protection trio with Mari and Aelius. One would always be at her side whether she liked it or not. Dae, at least, was the most reasonable. He thankfully gave her far more space than the Cirillos.

Professor Singh waited a moment for the other students to file out before turning to her with a smile that she had a hard time containing. "I am so sorry to hear what happened, Miss Thomas." She stated, trying to force her expression and tone to be solemn instead of brimming with curiosity.

"Thank you." Aurora replied, doing her best to hide her irritation. "I'm quite alright, but thank you for the concern. If that is all—"

"No actually!" She exclaimed, trying to keep it cool. "I wanted to know if I could discuss your experience with you."

She tensed, hoping to avoid another questioning. "I really don't think—"

"Oh please!" She pleaded, cutting her off yet again. She clasped her hands around Aurora's. "To have first hand account of a dosage like that, and so fresh, is rare. There are texts and records, but to speak with you and ask directly would be instrumental."

She bit the inside of her cheek as she debated her position. The entire exchange put her on edge, but she did have to agree with Professor Singh in part. Witches Bane had become such a rare mixture. She had done her own reading on the mixture, and the last round of test subjects had been in the late nineteenth century. It had been reported in use in rare occasions, but it had become such a risky substance, that no one voluntarily studied it.

"What would you like to know?" She asked with a sigh.

***

Professor Singh had proceeded to question her for a good thirty or so minutes before a knock rapped on the door. She jumped at the sound and checked her wrist watch. "My word, look at the time!" She exclaimed. "I'm sorry to have kept you so long, Miss Thomas."

She gave her a polite smile as she stood to her feet. "I imagine it's my Guardian here to collect me." She responded with a fake laugh.

She pushed open the door to confirm her guess. Aelius gave her a questioning look as she stepped up to him. "What took you so long?"

"Professor Singh wanted to know all about the effects of Witches Bane from personal experience."

His jaw clenched. "She can go down to the library like everyone else." He grumbled.

She let out a soft laugh as she placed a hand on his chest. "Let's go get some dinner."

Chapter 32

As Aurora approached her door later that week, she paused. A note had been taped to her door - her name ornately scrawled across the envelope. She pocketed her key, breaking open the seal. It was a request from Professor Jung, asking to see her. She checked her watch for the time, wondering if it may be too late. She headed upstairs, taking a gamble on whether or not Jung would still be in. She knocked on the door despite it being ajar.

"Come in." Professor Jung called out.

She pushed the door open gently and stepped inside. Classes had wrapped for the weekend, most students were eager to leave right away. Professor Jung looked up from her marking, a soft smile crossed her lips before turning back to her work. "Sit down while I finish this." She directed.

Aurora took a seat in one of the front row desks, peeking a glance at the stack of papers on the desk. It was only a moment before Professor Jung set down her pen and folded her hands together. "Now then," She started. "How are you, Miss Thomas?"

She straightened at finally being addressed. "I'm alright thank you. And you?"

"I'm quite alright." Jung answered politely. She tilted her head ever so slightly, studying Aurora. "I'm sure you're wondering why I called you here."

Her stomach flipped at her words. She knew that she had done nothing wrong, but the air her professor held felt almost ominous. Jung was known for being a serious woman, but there was something different about her tonight.

Jung leaned to the side, reaching inside her desk drawer. She carefully placed the necklace she had shown her on her first day, the one that looked eerily similar to her own. "I asked you before about this necklace. Do you know why?"

Aurora subconsciously brought a hand to the spot on her chest where her lost necklace had always hung. She never had found it. "I had one that looked just like it." She answered, an unsure air to her tone.

Jung let out a small sigh as she picked it up. "This was a prototype created by your mother back when we were students."

Her eyebrows shot up in surprise. She had always known her mother to be examining Artefacts, but never creating them. Artefact creation required a great deal of engineering knowledge swirled in with the magical.

"It's intended purpose was to suppress or conceal magical talents. Your mother had been inspired by magic reserve Artefacts. She had always wondered if a Mage could fill a vial, could they somehow conceal an element of magic as well." She leaned toward Aurora, pointing a manicured nail to a tiny blue gem inlaid with the intricate silver work. "The gemstone determines which element it is supposed to suppress. This one was constructed to contain water magic. Our Dean at the time would hear none of it, and ordered the project shut down. Mages were not Engineers, after all. He demanded that your mother focus on her future."

She took the necklace in hand and ran over the bends and twists in the silver. Her mother had not only secrets, but hidden talents as well.

"I asked you if you knew of it since you were her daughter. I wondered if she maybe continued her development work."

Aurora looked back up to the professor. "You think *my* necklace was made to suppress Spirit?"

Jung nodded. "Your friend Mr Lewis brought me this recently." She stated as she pulled out a second necklace - the very one she had been missing.

A hint of a gasp escaped her lips as Aurora reached for it without thinking. She held the two side by side, truly comparing them. It was undeniable that the work was done by the same designer. Where Jung's necklace had a blue gemstone, hers was made with a pearly moonstone. Her own had been made with yellow gold opposed the silver of Jung's, but the similarity of the design was undeniable. She clutched the necklace tight in hand, the edges of the pendant pressed hard into her palm. She slowly returned Jung's necklace as she tucked her own into her bag. What had Edwyn been doing with it, and why hadn't he returned it to her? She had lost it months ago. What made him turn it in now?

"Did mum make my glasses as well?" She asked, knowing that questions of Edwyn would need to wait.

Jung pondered a moment. "I'm not sure. At first glance, they looked fairly similar to medical spectacles, but it appears that they had been modified. I have heard of theories of visual modification Artefacts through the centuries, but haven't seen a confirmed example. I wager she either made them herself, or modified an existing pair to suit your needs."

Her fists clenched in her lap, her nails pressed into her palm. Her mother had gone to great lengths to hide things from not only the world, but herself as well. Why? Why was it so important that she didn't know herself? "You knew my mother." She stated simply. "How?"

Jung's face grew serious. "We were friends as girls. We were in the same year together at the Academy many years ago. We were actually room mates at the collegiate level." She explained, a soft fondness creeping across her expression as she spoke.

"You would have known of any boyfriends then." She pressed. Her growing anger made her bolder. She wasn't sure if she liked it or not.

Jung tensed. She knew what Aurora was getting at. "I can't be certain who your father is."

Her eyes narrowed at the avoidance. "But you know who it *might* be."

The pair stared at one another in a tense silence. Part of her regretted pushing the matter. Jung had shown her nothing but kindness and faith. She risked losing her confidence. "I have a lot of marking left to do, Miss Thomas. I must excuse myself for the evening." She remarked, laying a hand on the hefty pile of papers.

There would be no further discussion. It was clear that she knew something, presumed something, but refused to speak on it. She would need another route. "Of course, Professor. Thank you for your time, and returning this to me. I appreciate it." She excused herself politely. She gripped the strap of her book bag, slung over her shoulder, as she stepped out.

She kept the tears at bay until she closed the door behind her. Tears of anger, betrayal, and sorrow streaked down her face. She tapped the back of her head against the wall, angry at her mother and herself. Every answer sparked new questions. She wiped the hot tears from her face with the back of her hand. It would take time, but she would get the answers she wanted.

Movement caught her attention from the corner of her eye. Aelius came running and slowed to a light jog as he approached her. He had undoubtedly felt the swell of emotion from her and come running. He had agreed to give her space during waking hours, but she couldn't fault him for being protective. She gave him a soft smile as he brought a hand to her cheek.

"Why were you crying?" He asked, holding her gently by the side of her arms.

"I just...I just feel like I keep finding out more and more that my mom hid from me, and I don't understand why." She confessed, her voice breaking.

He pulled her into a hug, making sure to be gentle with her injuries. "What happened?"

She calmed her breathing, hating how weak she felt around him. Something about him made her unable to lie, unable to keep pressed down and locked away. Something about him just brought everything to the surface, out in and open. She hated it. "Not here..." She explained, regaining a hold of herself.

Chapter 33

She didn't want to have this talk out in the middle of the hallway, not where anyone would overhear. She grabbed his hand without thinking, leading him along to her room. The new room was just like her previous one, minus the bloodstains on the carpet and the hole in the wall. She still felt a little uneasy, however. There was still a feeling she couldn't quite shake.

She opened the door, the room dark and empty. He followed her silently, waiting for whatever it was she had to say. He took her lead, sitting down in the chairs by the fireplace, waiting patiently for whatever it was that was bothering her so much.

She sat forward with a sigh. "Professor Jung left a note for me - that she wanted to talk. I thought it might be about the tutoring session I missed because of well..." She trailed off for a moment, not wanting to fully address the incident. "She ended up talking about my mother."

He leaned forward, resting his forearms on his knees.

"She told me how she knew my mom back at the Academy. That they were even room mates at one point." She paused, unsure of exactly how to put the next part into words.

He put a hand on her knee, causing her to look up at him. Damn him and his ability to coax things out of her.

"You remember that necklace I lost?" He nodded. She pulled it out of her pocket, dangling it between them. The gold caught the light as it swung ever so slightly. "She told me it was something my mother had made. That she had made a prototype when she was a student."

His brow creased in confusion. "How did Jung get it?"

Aurora let out a soft laugh, sliding it back into her pocket. "Apparently Edwyn had it. He turned it into her and she said she wanted to make sure I had it back. I have no idea why I am only getting it back now."

"That makes no sense..." He spoke aloud, not understanding what the two had to do with one another.

She slipped it back into her pocket, leaning back in her chair. "My thoughts exactly." She sighed. She waited a moment, unsure if she should say more. She knew they were close friends. The last thing she wanted to do was to cause issue between them. It was her problem, not his. "I'll have a talk with him about it. It's fine."

Aelius was tense, uncertain of his words. She looked over at him, recognising the uneasy feeling that pulsed through the bond. "You should ask him about the dig site in Cayman Islands while you're at it."

She stared back at him, trying to get a read of his emotions. "What are you talking about?"

He sighed, averting his eyes a moment before explaining himself. "Edwyn's parents are Artefact archaeologists as well, Aurora. You should ask him about the Cayman Islands."

"But what does that have to do with—"

He took her hand in his, his face quite serious. "It's not my place to talk about it. I don't have all the details. It's his place to talk about it with you, not mine."

She stared back at him, knowing that whatever it was was serious. She wracked her brain, trying to figure out just what Edwyn could possibly have to tell her. If his parents were Artefact archaeologists, there was a possibility that they would have worked with them before. "What was his last name again? It starts with…"

"Lewis." Aelius answered simply.

She sighed, trying to recall any Lewis'. She was fairly certain she had read publishings by them, but she had no memories of meeting them. She definitely didn't recall Edwyn. She would have remembered meeting another child her age. "Do you know where he might be?" She asked.

***

They stood in the hallway before his door, Aelius waiting for her to be ready. He could feel her hesitation through the bond, waiting patiently for her go-ahead. She finally turned to him, knowing that she couldn't stand there forever. Running through the questions in her mind wouldn't do her any good.

Aelius turned the key in his door, opening it to reveal a room nearly identical to her own. Edwyn looked up from his bed, consumed by his studies. His eyes darted between the pair, a slight squint in his eyes as he tried to read the scenario. He put his book to the side, standing to his feet. "Should I…go?" He asked uncertainly.

Aurora's eyes widened at the insinuation. "No, I—"

"She's here to talk about the Cayman Islands, Edwyn." Aelius answered for her.

Edwyn straightened, his attention back on Aurora. He sighed after a moment, sitting back on the edge of his bed.

"Yeah I figured that might come up." He commented. "Take a seat."

She listened, stepping further into the room to take a seat in one of the chairs. She crossed one leg over the other, her hands in her lap as she waited an explanation. Aelius placed his hand gently on her shoulder, causing her to look up at him. "You want me to stay, or to give you a moment?" He asked quietly.

She glanced back to Edwyn, trying to get a read on him. "I'm fine with him staying if you are."

Edwyn looked up at Aelius and gave him a nod. It was then that he took a seat beside her, not opting for his own bed.

"So what has he told you?" Edwyn asked, trying to get an idea of where to begin.

She glanced over at Aelius, who sat silently. "Just that I need to ask you about the Cayman Islands. He said it was your place to tell me, not his."

Edwyn nodded to himself, knowing his friend well. "Well...I'm going to presume you really don't remember anything, do you?"

Her brow creased in confusion. "What do you mean?"

He pursed his lips a moment, seeming to expect the answer, but also not pleased about it. "The summer I was eight years old, I was with my parents on a dig site in the Cayman Islands. They normally took jobs during the school year, not wanting to work while I was home. They made an exception this time. There was a specific researcher that they wanted to work with. Your mom."

Her stomach churned at yet another secret. Her eyes darted to Aelius for a moment, his hand laying on top of hers.

"You and I became fast friends. Best friends even. I had never met anyone like you, Rore." Edwyn continued, a sadness in his eyes as he recalled the memories.

She felt her jaw clench at the nickname. "Only my mom calls—called me that." She stressed, not pleased that he referred to her that way.

He looked up at her with a slight pain in his eyes, but gave her a small smile. "Sorry. I didn't realise that would..." He sighed. "Sorry."

She gave him a small nod. "It's okay." She replied, needing to get to the bottom of things.

"My parents and your mom worked all day. It meant we were left to our own devices. Exploring stuff. You showing me different ways you could weave magic. It was fun." He let out a soft laugh to himself as he recalled the memories. "There was...well one day we decided we wanted to see what they were working on. There was a cavern that lead into a chamber that they were trying to unlock. There was a pretty significant gap across, but I insisted we could make it. We almost did, but we ended up falling. I took the brunt of the fall, breaking my collarbone."

Aurora stared at him as he paused. Edwyn looked back at her, trying to read her expression to see if anything might happen to come back to her.

"When I came to, I saw you Healing me. Your glasses were broken and it was the first time I saw your real eye colour. I knew right away what it meant, but you had no idea. Our parents heard the commotion and came running. My parents didn't see or notice anything, but your mom knew. I could tell from the way she looked at us."

Aurora chewed her bottom lip as she concentrated, "Why don't I remember any of this?" She asked, desperately trying to recall anything about the island. There was nothing but a growing headache.

"Tell me this," Edwyn began, leaning forward. "do you have gaps in your memories sometimes? Things you can't really recall. Headaches that form when you try to?"

She squinted her eyes at him slightly, wary about how accurate he was. "Maybe..." She replied uneasily.

"That's how it was for me for a while. There were pockets of that trip that were fuzzy. Like the memory was just out of my peripherals when I tried to remember it. I'm pretty sure your mom wiped both of our memories. You obviously more so."

She felt a swell of nausea build in the back of her throat. How could her mother wipe entire weeks of memories from her? Was it *that* important to wipe away who she was? What she could do? Aurora rose to her feet, her head starting to spin and her pulse racing. "I've got to go..." She managed to get out before rushing to the door.

She felt both Guardians stand to their feet, but it was Aelius that followed her. She knew he would follow no matter what she said. Part of her wanted to scream for him to leave her alone, but the other part knew she needed him.

Her pulse pounded in her ears, her chest getting tighter and tighter. She tried to force herself to breathe and not hyperventilate, but she was losing the battle. She made it as far as the women's dorm hall before she staggered. She didn't have the chance to fall before Aelius had her in his arms. He steadied her, bringing her tight against his chest. Her entire body shook as she sobbed.

Mari perked up as she reached their room. Her face instantly fell as she saw the look on Aurora's face - red and splotchy from crying. "What did you do to her?!" She demanded, rushing to her side.

"He didn't do anything." She defended before Aelius could get a word in. She could feel him tense behind her at the accusation.

"What happened?" Mari asked soothingly, gently taking her away from Aelius' side.

She looked up at Mari, exhausted emotionally and physically. "I think I just need a shower and to go to bed." She stated, turning to the washroom in a zombie like state.

Aelius waited a moment, watching her leave before turning to his sister. "I told her about Edwyn." He explained, his arms crossed at his chest.

"What about Edwyn?" Mari asked, unaware of what he was talking about.

"He knew Aurora when they were kids. It looks like her mother wiped quite a few memories over the years." He explained, his own heart aching from the pangs of betrayal Aurora felt.

Mari looked over to the washroom. "Daaaamn..." She muttered. "I've got it." She assured her brother.

He gave her a nod. "Anything happens, you let me know."

"Will do."

Chapter 34

She ran her hand along the wall as guidance. The rough rock walls scraped against her fingertips as she worked her way through the cavern without much light. Faint orbs of firelight floated before her, giving off a warm glow and harsh shadows. She stepped slowly and cautiously, the fire orbs eventually turning around a bend.

As she rounded the bend a cavern opened up. Fire orbs split apart from one another, growing in number to better light the open space. As the light spread, it revealed Emily.

She felt tears well in her eyes as she rushed forward to wrap her arms fiercely around her mother. "Mum!" She squeaked out.

Her mother's arms found their way around her as a laugh rang out. "Rore," she responded as she stroked the back of her head affectionately.

Aurora pushed back from the hug, remembering the anger, the betrayal she felt. She wanted to be utterly disgusted with her, but at the same time, she was still her mother. She was here. "How are you here? Where are we?" She finally managed, her tone harsher then she would have normally used.

Her mother smiled softly at her, ignoring the hurt in her voice. She brushed a strand of hair from her daughter's face behind her ear. "Sweetie, you know where we are."

Aurora looked around the cavern, trying to understand the space. There were no identifying marks that she could tell, and she couldn't recall it from any of their excursions. She looked back to where her mother had stood, but she wasn't there. Her breath stilled as she whipped her head around for any sight of her. She let out the breath as she located her mother behind her, near the entrance she had just come through. "I don't know." She responded in an unsure tone. An uneasy feeling starting to grow in the pit of her stomach.

Within a blink, her mother was back at her side, an affectionate smile on her face. "Just think." Emily insisted.

Aurora stepped backward slowly, her eyes fixated on Emily. "This doesn't make sense." She muttered to herself.

The fire orbs started to spin around the room, shadows dancing on the walls. Faster and faster they spun, drawing in closer around Emily. "You need to pay attention, Rore." Emily called out to her. "You can't listen to her."

Her brow creased in confusion. "Listen to who?" She called out, stepping closer to her mother. The fire orbs spun faster, creating a barrier between them. "Who, mum?"

Her only response was a sad smile before the fire orbs extinguished, casting the cavern into darkness.

Aurora woke with a jolt, her heart thundering in her chest. Tears of pain stung her eyes as she was met with a searing pain in her head. She brought a hand to her head and rubbed her eyes and the bridge of her nose.

Mari was at her side in an instant, a gentle hand on her arm. "Are you okay, Ari?" She asked, clearly worried.

She focused her eyes, the pain ebbing away as she fully woke. "Yeah, sorry, Mar." She assured, giving her a fake smile. "Just a bad dream."

Mari studied her, not buying the act. She sat down on the edge of her bed. It wasn't like her to skip morning training. Aelius must have told her what had happened. "I'll be okay, Mar." She repeated a little more earnestly this time. "It's just...a lot."

Mari pulled her into a hug, her warmth sinking in. "If you want to talk about any of it, I'm here whenever you want. Or we can hit something." She offered, releasing her from the embrace.

"Hitting is good." She joked.

Mari let out a laugh, happy to see her attempting some humour. "Let's find something to beat up then."

***

By the time she had run through a series of obstacles and targets with Mari, her body screamed at her in pain. She felt weak from last night's panic attack, her heart still feeling quite raw from the ordeal. Taking her anger out physically helped, though. She wanted to desperately to be able to question her mother - ask her why all the lies and deception were so necessary.

She lay on her back, her eyes closed as she caught her breath. "Hydrate." She heard Mari command. She cracked an eye lid open, seeing Mari holding out a water bottle for her. She propped herself up, grabbing it from her. "Never seen a Mage do that well on one of our courses." She complimented as Aurora drank.

"Yeah they don't have her fire." Aelius commented from behind. She nearly jumped at the sound of his voice, not expecting him. She sat up properly, taking another swig of her water.

"Your turn?" She asked, knowing he would finish the course in mere seconds compared to her.

He sat down across from her. "Came to check on you. Glad to see you training." He explained with a warm smile.

"And I'll take my leave..." Mari chimed in, giving them a wave.

Aurora opened her mouth to speak, but it was no use. Mari had already put quite a bit of space between them.

"Feeling better?" He asked, genuinely checking up on her.

She rose to her feet. "The pair of you certainly like to worry about me, you know." She teased.

"It's my job to worry about you." He countered, a hint of a smile on his lips.

"As my Guardian, you mean?" She teased, looking up at him.

He stared down at her, the gears seeming to work in his head. He looked as if he wanted to say more, to declare something else. She felt a hand on her cheek as he leaned in, her eyes closing.

"Whooo, Aelius!" A pair of Guardians cheered out from behind them. She felt him tense, just millimetres from her lips at the sudden cry.

He whipped over his shoulder, something between a curse and a snarl escaping his lips before he grabbed her tight. He had teleported her before, but it was still new and unsettling. She held on to him as they landed, the sudden movement staggering her slightly.

It was when she looked up that she saw that they were in a dorm room - hers. He leaned a forearm against the wall behind her, frustration written across his face and simmering through the bond. She held onto the edge of his shirt as she looked up at him. "No more interruptions?" She asked.

A mischievous grin spread slowly across his face before he leaned back into her. "No more interruptions." He agreed, his lips on hers as he finished his words.

It was as he kissed her that she truly realised how much she had been craving his touch. She had been dreaming of just what it would feel like - taste like. She pulled him further into her, needing more. He slid his hands around her waist, lifting her up against the wall. Her legs wrapped around him as he cupped her from beneath.

He pulled back from their kiss for a moment, both of them a little breathless from the sudden embrace. He looked as if he wanted to say something more, but changed his mind as he turned away from the wall. She tightened the hold her legs had on him as he slid a hand under her back. He leaned her down slowly, gently. He placed her on her bed, taking in the sight of her in a moment before leaning in over her.

Aurora wrapped her arms around his neck, savouring every moment. The smell of him was intoxicating. There were times where he added a hint of cologne, but it was natural scent of him that drove her crazy. Never had she felt anything like him. She knew part of it had to be the bond - feeling his emotions and desire entangled in her own, but the intensity of it was incomparable.

He pulled back from their kiss, looking into her eyes. He bit his bottom lip, debating with himself on taking things further or not.

She could feel the inner debate through the bond. She sat up slightly, reaching for the edge of his shirt with a tug.

"Kiss me." She breathed, wanting to be every bit of a bad influence on him.

He groaned, unable to fight against her. He rushed into another kiss, deeper and hungrier this time. "You're evil." He chuckled as he moved his kisses along her jaw to her neck.

He leaned on his forearm, brushing hair from her face as he stared into her eyes. "We need to stop." He confessed, almost pained at stating so.

She arched a brow at him. "And why's that?" She asked.

Aelius took in a deep breath, almost wavering in his resolve. "Because I won't be able to stop soon." He groaned.

"And that's a bad thing?" She asked with a smirk.

"Yes?" He stated, debating his own thoughts. "Yes, it is." He resolved out loud. "You deserve to be taken on dates. To be spoiled. You deserve planned moments, not us just rushing in."

She stared up at him, surprised to hear him say such things. She brushed a stray lock of hair from his eyes, tucking it behind his ear. He closed his eyes, leaning into her touch. She leaned into him, planting a soft kiss on his lips as her response. She wanted more - so desperately wanted more, but his way sounded sweet.

"You're special to me, Aurora. I don't want you regretting anything or feeling like you were rushed." He explained.

"You're a romantic." She chuckled, smiling at him. "I never would have thought it when we first met." She teased.

He rolled onto his side, laying beside her. "For you, I am."

Her heart weakened at the comment. When had he become so smooth with his words?

Chapter 35

Aurora woke that morning, sun streaming through a break in the curtains. She looked to the side, seeing a fully clothed Aelius still soundly asleep. Nothing had happened that night - he had stayed true to his declaration that she deserved more than spur of the moment. Instead, they had spent the night talking, laughing, and stealing the occasional kiss. As she watched him sleep, it was painfully clear just how beautiful he was.

As she rubbed the sleep from her eyes, a glint of gold caught her attention. Placed ever so carefully on her nightstand a small golden box glimmered in the sunlight. She snatched it up, turning it over in her hands. At a distance, it seemed to be a plain gold box, small enough to fit in the palm of her hand. At a closer look, fine etchings could be seen engraved into the box. A series of sigils ran around the perimeter, each one acting as an entry key to a password. Her breath held as she gingerly input the only code that came to mind: her mother's. Each sigil lit up with a faint glow as she touched them until a distinct crack: the lid popped open. Carefully, she grabbed a hold of the lid edge, pulling it open fully.

The box appeared empty at first, but a faint yellow glow began to grow and pulse inside. The Artefact in her hand would contain whatever memories and memorabilia the owner wished to store, showing up as a projection once fully activated. She remembered seeing her mother keep a box just like this one, but never recalled seeing it function. She had always lectured her mother about keeping different passwords for her devices, but in this moment she was thankful for her lack of originality.

It was then that she heard him stir, finally waking up. He gave her a sleepy smile, brushing his hair from his face. "Morning." He stated, his voice deepest when he freshly woke.

"Morning." She greeted, returning his smile.

He sat up, noticing what she held in her hand. "What's that?" He asked.

She glanced down at the activating Artefact in hand, raising it up for him to see better. "I think it was my mom's." She explained, still not fully certain of it herself.

He shuffled in closer to her, pulling her into him to examine it together. She leaned into his chest, her nerves calming ever so slightly being enveloped by his arms.

After what felt like ages, images started to project out of the box. A smile spread across her face as she recognised photos of her mother and herself. She turned to Aelius, explaining what they saw. "My mom and I were at a dig in Peru when I was ten, and I must have spent weeks trying to convince her how well I'd take care of one of the alpacas. How we could spin all the wool and make all the sweaters we wanted."

Additional images started to pass through. They appeared to be working backwards in time, the images getting older and older. Some had images of her with others, undoubtedly other Artefact hunters or researchers. She placed a finger on the projections as they loaded, pausing them to take them in better. She had never seen some of them; images of her as a little girl and toddler.

Baby pictures of her started to project and she couldn't help but smile. Most images were of her, but the occasional photo with her mother in them made her heart ache in a bittersweet sort of way. She closed her eyes a moment to keep the tears that welled up at bay. She felt Aelius tighten his hold on her, but let her have a moment. She desperately wished she could hear her mother narrate the story behind each image, to tell her what she was doing at that moment, or what milestone she had just reached.

An image of her as a tiny baby swaddled in a hand made blanket appeared, undoubtedly reaching the end of the images stored. She moved to shut the box, but another image popped up that halted her movement. She recognised the clothing in the image: a Royal Academy uniform.

She pulled the box in close to her, not wanting to miss a single detail. The image before her was of her mother, undoubtedly around her age, and what looked like a much younger professor Jung. She held a finger over the image, pausing it in partial disbelief. The smile on her mother's face was bright and full of life. The tears that she had been holding back finally spilled over.

She released the image, letting more play out. A life, a rich and happy one, played out before her. Images of strangers in the familiar navy blues passed by, obviously close friends of hers. One friend, however, stood out among the rest. A young man with silver hair appeared in more and more of the images. His piercing ice blue eyes were all too familiar. Images of the Imperial Family were included in many of the history texts she had spent so many hours reviewing earlier this year. She knew the Emperor, Castor Solis, had been a student the same time as her mother purely based on ages, but to see him included in her collection of cherished images was something else entirely.

She felt her pulse quicken as images continued to pass, more and more featuring Castor. Part of her wanted to shut the box and ignore the growing feeling in the pit of her stomach, but the need to know superseded it. The images stopped, the last one looking to be Emily on her first day of collegiate levels. She stood in her collegiate uniform standing in front of the main castle. It was like looking in the mirror. Her hair was cut shorter and her eyes were emerald green, but she was absolutely her mother's daughter.

She chewed her bottom lip, wanting more. Seeing the images her mother chose to save and cherish in secret gave her a half truth. The images were a suggestion, but not confirmation. It was entirely possible that it was someone else. Nothing in the images suggested anything beyond friendship or acquaintances at the very least.

"That was…" Aelius mumbled, trailing off as he realised what he was about to say out loud.

"Yeah…" She sighed. She was wondering if she was crazy to think it, but for him to start to say it out loud meant it definitely looked that way.

As her mind raced, a faint beep sounded from the box and a glow pulsed. It regained her attention and she pressed a flickering sigil on the side. Wondering what could possibly come next, she watched as a series of letters projected out of the box. Nausea swelled in her stomach, but she knew she had to check. She selected one of the collections.

June 20 2000

C,

I can't believe that we're almost Collegiate students. After this summer, we'll be in the final stretch before we graduate and become full fledged adults. It's wild.

Sometimes I dream of running off and starting my own shop. I'm sure there's an engineer somewhere that would take me under his wing and teach me what the books won't. I hate that my father won't let me take summer classes at Discovery. I wish he understood.

You're the only one I can talk to about my work. No one else gets why I want to pursue engineering. Everyone goes on about my talent being wasted on tinkering, that I need to be out in the field protecting the realms. I get that, but why can't they understand I can do both? If I can do my "tinkering" I can use it to help others in ways besides fighting demons.

Artefacts just make sense. I'm sure I can do something incredible if I was just allowed to do it. Right now I have to hide things, do it in secret. The last time my father found my tools, he destroyed them.

I dream of us working together. I dream of being in the palace with you, working day in and day out on improving the wards, on refining shard weapons. That's where I'm meant to be. Not in combat. You see that. You see me.

Counting the days til graduation,
-Em

June 22 2000

Em,

You have no idea how much I dream of our work together. With you by my side, we will finally fix what is wrong with the Empire. You have no idea how much is rotten from within, Em. It all needs to go.

I dream of our days together as well. You'll be head of the Artefact unit, crafting each and every advancement for the Empire. I have every faith in your vision. I know that with you crafting our tech, that we will become unstoppable. No demon will stand a chance with you in charge.

Did you have a chance to review the schematics I sent you? What did you think of them? I was thinking it might be the way to go. It's an early concept, but I was thinking with your help we could really make it something. Let me know what you think.

Write to me this summer. A summer without seeing you every day is insufferable. Maybe I can come with an excuse to have you summer at the palace. Do you think your father would mind?

Missing you already,
-C

June 25 2000

C,

I like it. It needs work. A lot of work. But I like the idea. If we could successfully gather the power between them, it would really make a difference. It is risky to pool magic, but I think that with enough research and proper testing it can be done.

I like the sound of you being in charge. You're the only one who seems to see my dream. I want to make yours come true too, you know. I think that us working together would really make a difference. I want the world you want.

And I think you and I both know that anything with an Empirical stationary would be enough to make my father swoon. He would likely pack me up and ship me off to you himself. I'm certain we could find one excuse or another. A summer without you would be unbearable.

Summon me any time you wish,
-Em

July 16 2000

Em,

I'm sure your father has received word by now, but I wanted to write to you myself. In a fortnight, the Thomas family will be hosted privately at the Palace. The fact that I have to wait even that long is killing me, but I can finally have a count down to when I can see you again.

I have a list. A list of every nook and cranny of the Palace that I want to show you. Every hide away of mine, every meaningful moment, every spot that can be just ours.

Is it possible to speed up time? Can we look into that?

Counting the days,
-C

July 18 2000

C,

I have never heard such a noise uttered from a man as I did when my father received the notice. I thought for a moment that he might actually faint. I am quite sure I could shave my head and he wouldn't notice, he is that elated.

Of course, he isn't has delighted as I am. It has only been weeks, but it feels like forever. I will absolutely be looking into the time adjuster for you, on one condition: we also find a way to slow time once I am with you again. Only way it will be worthwhile.

Looking forward to every secret hide away,
-Em

August 6 2000

Em,

I'm writing this as you set off in hopes of distracting myself and also stopping myself from keeping you here. It was not enough time with you. I don't imagine there ever will be enough time with you. I could spend a lifetime with you and it would never be enough. I have no idea how you do it, but you make me crave you, need you.

I need to find a way to have you summer here next year. A summer program at the Palace that you mystically end up awarded might be a good way to ensure I have you to myself. I'll have to work on it. I can't bare to spend another summer apart.

Is it autumn yet?
-C

August 8 2000

C,

A summer trapped in the Palace sounds phenomenal. I'm sure that between the two of us we can come up with something.

In nearly a month we'll be back at the Academy, and things will be right again. We won't need to worry about parents or advisors breathing down our necks. We can actually see one another each and every day again, and I cannot wait.

Where are we on the time accelerator?
-Em

August 18 2000

Em,

I'm sorry for the delay. The amount of meetings they have me booked in now is insane. I swear, there are some days where I barely have a moment to breathe. You'd think they were prepping me to take the throne tomorrow.

The new school year is so close I can practically taste it. I cannot wait to see you in the collegiate uniform. I know I'll miss the secondary on you, but I can't stop thinking about what you will look like in the collegiate. How can I focus in a meeting when I get to see you again in mere days?

Soon,
-C

Sept 15 2000

C,

I hate that I had to pair with Karlson today. You have to know that him kissing me repulsed me. It killed me to watch you bond with Gemma. I know it has to be that way, but it still hurts. It's not your fault, just as much as it's not mine, but I still hate it. I can't wait until we learn how to shut off the bond. It's wrong that it's him and not you.

Maybe one day...
-Em

Sept 16 2000

Em,

Being paired with anyone but you is torture. It took everything in me not to deck him there and then. It's your feelings I want shouting through the bond, not hers. It's your thoughts I can want to be woken by. I know how I feel about you, but to feel what you feel directly is something I can't stop imagining. It's agony knowing that someone else is bonded to you in a way I can never be.

Chapter 36

With her stomach a pit of dread, she snapped the Artefact shut. There was nothing to doubt now. Her mother had been very much involved with Castor Solis, Emperor of the realms. More lies. More complications.

She felt Aelius' hand on her chin, snapping her back into reality from the downward spiral. "It'll be okay." He assured her.

She gave him a strained smile. She knew he meant well. He was a wonderful comfort and support, but this was beyond an embrace and supportive words. This would require actions, many questions, and certainly a lot of careful navigation.

The sound of a key in the door made her sit up fully, Mari opening the door before either of them could move. Mari's mouth gaped open as her overnight bag came to the floor with a thud. "Y...you..." She stammered.

"We're dating." Aelius stated dryly, putting an arm around Aurora's shoulder.

Mari finally regained her senses, kicking her bag into the room and letting the door slam shut. She rushed to the foot of Aurora's bed, landing with a bounce. "Finally!" She exclaimed, a giggle escaping her lips. "Took you long enough!" She chided her brother.

He let out a soft chuckle. "Didn't it take you...eighteen years to date Dae?"

She scrunched her face into a playful sneer and punched him in the shoulder. "Ha, ha. Screw you."

He laughed as he let her hit him. "I should get back to my room and shower." He explained, slipping his arm away from her, but stopping to grasp her hand. "I'll see you tonight." He added, giving her hand a light squeeze before heading out.

It wasn't until he had left that Mari turned back to her, an excited look on her face. "What *happened*?" She asked. "I mean...I don't want to *know* know, but what happened?"

Aurora laughed, relieved that Mari was happy about it all. Mari had assured her earlier that it was fine with her, but when things actually came to it, she was legitimately excited. Aurora had been terrified for it to damage their friendship.

"It just...sort of happened." She explained, trying to recount it in a way that wouldn't gross her out as his sister. "We were talking about things and he kissed me."

Mari grabbed her hands in hers. "I'm happy it's you." She beamed. "Seriously. He can be a stubborn ass, but his heart is far too kind and sweet for his own good. He needs a good person that won't take advantage of that. I can't think of anyone better for him than you."

She blushed at the heartfelt complement. She knew it was genuine and not just her being nice. "I...thanks, Mar. I really hope so."

It was then that the glint of her mother's Artefact caught Mari's eye. She picked it up, creasing her brow as she studied it. "What's this?"

"Ah...well..."

***

A simple demonstration of Aelius kissing her in the hallway was all it took to shift her entire class' perception of her. The pair were often seen together, being friends and bonded, but being in an actual romantic relationship came with so much more. He now greeted her with a soft kiss, he would take a hold of her hand to walk with her, and he openly smiled. It seemed that his constant smile was the most shocking to their peers.

The energy in Offence class that morning had shifted. Some of her classmates seemed to have a joke that they refused to share, whereas some seemed rather disappointed by her. Leila greeted her that morning with a slightly sad smile, but was friendly none the less. "Morning, Ari."

"Morning." She replied, suddenly very aware of the eyes on her.

"I hear congratulations are in order." Leila half whispered, leaning in.

Aurora flushed slightly, uncertain how to bring it up. "Thanks." She responded somewhat awkwardly. "Everyone seems oddly interested in it though. It's a little..."

"Weird?" Leila added.

"Yeah, weird. You'd think I'd be used to whispers and gossip by now." She laughed at herself slightly. "Feels different when it's about a personal choice I made instead stuff I can't control. If that makes *any* sense what so ever."

Dae clapped a hand on her shoulder as he approached his seat. "Took him a while, didn't it?" He chuckled, taking the seat beside her.

"Have you and Mari been discussing this?" She laughed.

"Oh yeah, we had a bet going." He smirked, pulling out his books. "Thanks, by the way. Mari was convinced you'd have to make the move. She had no faith in our boy."

"Poor Aelius..." She defended with a hint of a laugh.

***

Aelius was waiting for her by the time classes wrapped up for the day. His face broke out into a bright smile as soon as his eyes landed on her. The excitement and joy he exuded through the bond was nearly enough to physically stagger her. It was impossible to keep being swept away by him. She bounded up to him, wrapping her arms around his neck as she stood on the balls of her feet. He slipped his hands around her waist, a low chuckle escaping him.

"How was your day?" She asked.

He leaned into her, pressing a tender kiss on her lips. "Better now." He answered.

She did her best to suppress a smile, but lost. "I have lessons tonight, but do you want to have dinner afterwards?" She asked, slipping her hand into his.

He walked beside her, heading towards the staircase. "Sounds good to me. I wanted to ask about your schedule over the weekend. Do you have any sessions? Any plans?"

She glanced over at him, an eager look on his face. "I have a session booked Friday at seventeen hundred hours. After that, I am completely free."

His smiled brightened. "Room for your boyfriend then?" He asked, kissing the back of her hand. His lips felt impossibly hot against her skin. He always felt as if he had a borderline fever, but it was simply his natural body temperature.

"All the room for my boyfriend." She replied, finding herself grinning at speaking the word boyfriend aloud. It felt cheesy, almost juvenile, but it also left her feeling positively giddy. She had never had a *boyfriend*. She had never had a proper relationship. Her life before never gave her an opportunity to put down roots or form any lasting relationships. Everything was new to her with him.

"Good." He responded, following her lead towards her dorm. She had supplies to grab before her sessions, and Aelius seemed entirely intent on walking her all the way, not wanting to lose a moment if he could help it.

"Any particular plan in mind?" She asked, switching out her personal school books for her tutoring books.

He leaned against the wall as he watched her prepare, his arms crossed at his chest. "And ruin the surprise?" He asked. "I think not."

She grinned at the mention of a surprise. She wondered just what he would have in store for her. She stared up at him, dying to press him for details, but resolving herself to letting him have his mystery. "Just let me know what I should wear then..." She countered, leading the way to the secondary campus.

"I'll let you know." He assured her, taking her hand in his again.

She gave him a brief kiss goodbye as she passed through the doors to the secondary campus. Many of the students had opted to change into their summer dress, the heavy jackets and layers from when she first started having been shed. She quickly slipped into her tutor room, Jessica already waiting for her as she poured over her notes.

She turned up to Aurora as she entered the room, a bright smile on her face. "Hey, Aurora." She greeted. She had definitely opened up and become less timid through the year. She still seemed a little uncertain around her peers, but with her, she had relaxed.

"How are you feeling about your exam prep?" Aurora asked, setting her bag down at her desk.

Jessica sighed, closing her notebook. "Pretty good...I think." She responded.

Aurora tilted her head to the side, hands on her hips. "You'll do fine. You have a good grasp on everything. Your biggest hurdle is second guessing yourself. Once you get over that, you'll be just fine."

Jessica nodded, knowing what she said was true. She was her own worst enemy. "You're right." She agreed as the others made their way in.

***

The weekend had arrived, and the curiosity of what Aelius had in store for her had become maddening. She fiddled with her hair in the mirror, ready a good fifteen minutes before he was set to arrive. She appreciated that he was always punctual. She had learned that some of her classmates were very much on the tardy side. Things would come up and there was always the possibility for delays, but the respect for someone else's time was such a simple thing that went a long way.

He had instructed her to wear layers to the date. Still uncertain of what he had in store, Aurora opted for a light linen dress. She tied the belt tight around her waist, the skirts falling down around her knees. The sweetheart neckline followed into two simple straps over her shoulders, her arms covered with nearly transparent white billowing sleeves that cut off at her elbow. It was light and airy, perfect for the warm late spring days that were upon them. A shawl lay on her bed in case the night took a chill, but she doubted she would need it. Not with the heat Aelius radiated.

A knock rapped on the door, her pulse quickening at the anticipation. She opened the door, his face lighting up at the mere sight of her. She felt her cheeks flush at his reaction. He wore a simple outfit - a light dress shirt, navy vest and breeches with brown boots that came up just past his ankles. His hair had been pulled back save for a single strand that refused to stay put near his temple.

"Ready to go?" He asked, extending his hand to her, a disarming smile across his lips.

"One second." She told him, turning to her bed to grab her shawl. She slung it over her elbow, making sure she had her key before joining him in the hall. Wherever they were going, she was all in.

๖

Chapter 37

As she joined him in the hall, Aurora noticed a wicker woven basket clutched in his other hand. A blanket roll sat on top between the lid and the handle. Her eyes moved from it to him, a brow arched wondering where he was possibly taking her.

Sensing her brewing question he tsked at her. "You've waited this long. You can wait a moment longer."

She fought the laugh that wanted to escape for him calling her out. "Fine." She conceded, wrapping her arms in the crook of his elbow. "Lead the way."

He could have easily teleported her to wherever they were going, but he wanted to take advantage of every moment with her. The evening air was warm on her skin, as they stepped out the main doors. The sun was starting to lower in the sky, a few hours of daylight left before an undoubtedly beautiful sunset was upon them.

Other students seemed to be out and about, fully enjoying the beautiful turn of weather. The temperature had been somewhat unpredictable as of late, but they had been fortunate. They made it all the way to the main gate, walking through, chills and all. It was when they stepped out of the way, making sure not to block the path of others that he turned to her. "Nearly there." He assured her.

He guided her off to one of the nearby woods between the Academy and Vilcas. A small worn path led them through a thicket of trees that parted into a perfect little clearing. A small stream trickled nearby - wildflowers collecting around the fringe of the clearing. Aelius stopped, setting down the basket. He grabbed the blanket, unfurling it in one swift motion and set it onto the ground. "After you." He insisted, motioning for her to take a seat while he set up the rest of their date.

She listened, getting herself settled while she watched him pull item after item out of the basket. First was a set of stemless wine glasses and a bottle of red wine. He set it beside her as he continued to pull out plates, cutlery, cloth napkins and containers of food. Finally satisfied, he took a seat beside her. "Wine or water?" He asked, not wanting to presume.

She picked up the bottle of wine, handing it to him. "Wine, if you're joining me." She explained with a smile.

He mirrored her smile, grabbing the bottle from her hand, his fingers lingering on hers for a moment before taking it. He opened it with a pop, pouring them each a glass before corking it again. He held up his glass to hers with a gentle clink for a cheers.

"What made you pick this spot?" She asked, her first sip of wine going down smoothly.

He tilted his head to the side, as he took his time enjoying the sight of her. "I came across this spot when I was younger. I always thought it was serene - perfect for a moment away from everything, but not too far." He explained, taking a sip of wine.

"It can be a lot being around everyone else at the Academy all the time." She agreed.

He gave her a small smile as he sat up, turning to the containers. "I brought...well a little bit of everything." He began, showing her each. He grabbed one of the plates and handed it to her. She grabbed a little of each, taking some meats, cheeses, and fruit. Once she was set, he sliced her off a piece of fresh bread, placing it on her plate. She gave him a soft laugh as he finally grabbed some for himself.

"Can't say I've ever done a picnic." She explained between bites. "You do this for all the girls?" She asked teasingly.

Aelius tensed, his mouth agape ever so slightly. "No, I—"

"I was kidding!" She interrupted, realising what she meant as a joke must have hit a nerve. "I'm sorry." She stated, letting out a sigh. "I just...well you're *you* and having past girlfriends is a given."

He studied her eyes a moment before letting out a soft chuckle. "A given, eh?" He asked, his tension easing away. "Yeah, dating at the Academy is...not conducive to someone like me."

She stared at him a moment, truly at a loss for what he meant by that. "Someone like you?" She finally asked.

He picked her glass up, handing it to her as he settled back in to explain. "People here tend to get bored pretty easily. And when that happens, they start playing games. I have no interest in all of that. If I'm going to be with someone, I want it to be genuine. Honest."

She felt the heat of his gaze as he explained himself. "Did something happen?" She asked, feeling like there was something more.

He averted his eyes for a moment. "I'm sure you've met Karina." He started, not enjoying the topic of conversation. "I dated her back in Secondary. I thought she was a good person, someone who actually cared about me. She ended up just wanting to add me to some...bet. Some sort of list she has going with some of the other girls. When I found out about it and how she had been treating Amaris behind my back...well it wasn't pretty."

She could feel a dull twinge of betrayal he felt while discussing it. "I'm sorry." She responded, not fully certain what one was supposed to say to something like that.

He shrugged. "It was a while ago. Just...makes things different is all. Unfortunately a lot of the girls here are quite similar, and it's not something I'm interested in. I just figured I wouldn't find someone worth while until after I graduate."

"And now?" She asked.

He brought a hand to her cheek, brushing a strand of hair away. "I found myself an exception."

A bright smile crept across her face at his words. She leaned into him, laying a gentle kiss on his lips. He slid his fingers into her hair, returning and deepening the kiss ever so slightly. His touch was intoxicating, addicting. She had never felt such an electric response to the mere touch of someone's skin.

He flashed her a mischievous smile, leaning back as he popped a grape in his mouth.

She squinted her eyes at him with a smirk as she took a sip of wine. He very well knew that he was teasing her. She would need to get him back at some point or another. "Well, it's not like I have a whole lot of experience either." She stated, leaning back slightly.

He arched a brow at her in disbelief. "You are far too beautiful and intelligent to go unnoticed."

She fought a smile, her cheeks flushing a tint of pink. "I have had a few dates, been with...well two guys, but I've never had a *boyfriend*." She confessed as she stared into her wine glass. It was easier than seeing the look in his eyes. "I was just never around long enough to be something more."

He brought his hand under her chin, propping her gaze up to him. "Why are you embarrassed by that?" He asked, feeling what she did through the bond.

"Well..." she muttered, unsure how to answer it. There was no logical reason for it, but it was the worry, the concern that it would change how he saw her. That his feelings for her would shift once he learned more about her.

"We all have our past experiences." He assured her. "Each one of them makes us who we are. They shape the choices we make. I happen to rather enjoy who you are."

She laughed, feeling the worry that had built dissolve away. She knew was right. Honesty is what he stressed he needed. She leaned into him, kissing him as her answer.

He brought a hand to her hair, running his fingers through it, truly taking her in. "You are so beautiful."

She smiled at him, still in a state of disbelief that someone as perfect as him would consider her so. "You're crazy." She disagreed with a smirk.

He shook his head. "I'm not. You're the most beautiful woman to me. Inside and out."

Something welled up within her, almost as if she was about to cry. It felt vulnerable and raw, completely taking her by surprise. She wasn't quite sure how to take such compliments, such heartfelt honesty. She knew that he meant it. That he truly believed it.

"Are you okay?" He asked, sensing her swirl of complex emotions.

She nodded. "Just not used to...*this.*" She did her best to explain.

He gently brought her into him, kissing her gingerly on the forehead. "Me neither." He agreed. "But there's no rush on anything. We take everything at whatever pace we want."

She tensed ever so slightly, surprised at what he was getting at. "Well, I didn't mean—"

He smiled at her, stroking her hair. "We have all the time in the world, Aurora." He explained, placing a soft kiss on her forehead. "I want you to be fully comfortable with everything before all of that."

She looked back at him, suddenly cursing her emotional response. She knew he had a point. She leaned her forehead against his. "No fair..." She mumbled.

He let out a rumble of a laugh, giving her a sweet kiss, before rolling her off of him. "Not fair at all." He chuckled. "But it will be worth it."

Chapter 38

Spring was fully under way, with summer not far behind. Aurora was finally happy not to play the weather guessing game, wondering if she would need a cloak or lighter layers any time they ventured over to the Mage training facility.

Professor Duncan was waiting for them, his boots resting on the ledge of the seats before him in the spectator seats. He was leaned back quite lazily, his arms crossed at his chest as he noted who filed in. As the last of the stragglers entered, he swung his feet off the ledge and stood up. "Alright, you lot." He bellowed. "Line up and we'll get on with it."

The students looked to one another as they started to shuffle into a line. The doors to the arena swung open. "We're going to do a bit of target practice." Duncan explained from the seats. "I don't care which element you use, just do it well. Hit each target as quickly as you can and get out. Got it?" Murmurs and nods broke out among the students. "Right. Off you go."

Eli had lined up first and stepped into the arena cautiously. Going first was always a risk, especially with a wild card for a professor like Duncan. A forest scene activated around him, a small stream running through a thicket of trees in varied sizes and shapes. Once settled, card like targets appeared through the scene. They were simple in shape, a rough outline of a human, painted in bright yellow with targeted spots and rings through the outline. On further study, each ring indicated a level of points. A scoreboard appeared overhead, a zero displayed.

A series of beeps rang out through the arena, a countdown as numbers descended from five, four, three, two...

The targets came alive, moving about the forest. Eli sprang into a run, firing off streams of air at each target. Points tallied up on the board overhead as each was hit. Eli was focused on speed over accuracy, but was quickly wrapped within five minutes. A buzzer rang out as the last target was hit, his numbers ceased to change. Cheers broke out for him as he stepped out of the arena and it reset for the next challenger.

Aurora checked the line up and tapped Dae on the shoulder. "Trade spots?" She asked in a whisper.

He peered around and nodded as he stepped behind her. "You alright?"

"Remember what we went over with combining the water and air together?" She asked. He nodded in response, remembering their first combined training session last week. It had been a welcome distraction from grief for him. "This is perfect practice for it. Watch my weaves as I go and try it."

As each student went, a leader board appeared overhead as well. Each student was ranked in order of score points and speed. She shook her hands out in preparation as her turn approached. She was determined to be on top.

The arena reset as she stepped inside, the buzzer countdown rang out. Five, four, three, two...

She raised her hands in a firing position; two fingers out, two curled in and her thumb up. She conjured beads of water encapsulated by air magic and fired them off at rapid speed. The air magic shifted the beads with pinpoint accuracy, hitting the hundred point on each target. One by one they toppled, some even cracked in half with the intensity of the hits. It took only two minutes before the completion buzzer rang out: the fastest time out of any.

Silence met her as she stepped out of the arena before a delayed applause broke out initiated by Dae. She looked up over her shoulder to check the leader board. First by far. A proud smile broke out on her face as she heard Duncan call out, "For any of you wondering, that's how it's done!"

***

"You should have seen it, Mar!" Dae exclaimed over dinner that night. He had been recounting their target assignment to the group with great fervour. "I did a pretty good job of it, but no one came close to her accuracy and speed."

She pushed at her dinner, slightly uncomfortable with the compliments, but also enjoying the fact that it was praise over rumours. "Dae is under selling himself. He did really well with blending the weaves. He's learning really well."

Mari arched an eyebrow at her as she pointed her fork in her direction. "Take the compliment, Ari. Living well and acing things is the best way to shut certain people up."

She laughed at herself and resumed her meal. "Alllriiight..."

"Miss Thomas?" She heard from behind. She turned, seeing Professor Andersen with a small smile on his face.

She swallowed her mouthful before standing to her feet. "Evening, Professor." She greeted.

"Oh no need to stand!" He insisted, feeling somewhat awkward at her rising to greet him. "I just came to pass along a request from Professor Jung."

"Is everything okay?" She asked with a slight tilt of her head.

"Oh nothing is the matter." He assured with a dismissive wave of his hands. "She just asked me to let you know she wanted to speak with you. She mentioned something about the secondary practice exams."

"Thank you, professor." She replied with a smile. "I'll finish up here and head straight up. Thank you for letting me know."

"You're most welcome, Miss Thomas." He responded with a slight bow of his head. She stifled a laugh as he did so. He had really become so formal around her after her Solis revelation. She didn't have the heart to correct him on it.

She took her seat again once he turned to leave. "Looks like I'll catch up with you guys later." She explained, turning back to her meal.

"Hope she doesn't keep you too late." Mari pouted.

"Who knows." She shrugged.

***

Aurora was quick to finish the rest of her meal and gather her things. She had hoped to relax that evening, but something told her she wouldn't have much of a chance for it anymore.

She had no doubt her students had done well. They had all prepped, keeping her quite busy the last few weeks. She wondered if all the results had been marked yet. Maybe she wanted help grading. It was hard to tell with her sometimes. She reached the classroom, the door slightly ajar. She knocked, pausing for the answer.

"Come in." Professor Jung called out.

She stepped inside, closing the door behind her. Professor Jung gave her a warm smile from her desk and beckoned her inside. She took a seat across the desk, sliding her book bag over the back of the chair. "You did a wonderful job with the secondary students." She commended. A small smile crossed her lips as she felt a swell of pride. "They all spoke highly of you, and thank you for all of your hard work with them. I am just finishing up the test exam results, and they have all done splendidly. If you're interested, I am quite sure we will have the position open next year for you as well."

"That would be wonderful, Professor. Thank you very much." She replied, aware of just how helpful the extra funds had been.

Professor Jung eyed her a moment, resting her chin on interlaced hands. "Everything is going well, otherwise?" She asked.

She blinked a moment, surprised at the personal question. They had spoken before of her mother, but her demeanour always made personal matters seem a little closed off.

"Well..." She managed, debating whether or not to address her mother's Artefact.

Jung arched a brow at her, giving her the space to continue. "Yes?"

She stared back at Jung, finally choosing direct honesty. "A few weeks ago someone left an Artefact in my room."

Her brow creased in concern. "What sort of Artefact?" She asked.

"It was my mother's. It was not in her belongings after she passed. Someone had to have taken it, and for some reason placed it in my room." She explained.

Jung kept her face neutral, but she could tell from a flicker in her eyes that it effected her. "And why would they do that?"

"I'm not fully sure." She sighed. "I just know that it had... it had images and letters from my father on it."

Jung leaned back, her hands resting on the desk before her. "You're certain?" She asked cautiously. Aurora nodded. She sighed, mulling over her words before finally stating "I think you need to speak with the Dean."

"What does Dean Reyes have to do with anything?" She asked.

"Your father was the one who appointed Dean Reyes. They have an...accord." She explained. "Your family is not an ordinary matter. I am certain it is quite complicated, and it's something you need help with. Dean Reyes will be a good first step."

Anger started to build within her. Professor Jung had known all this time and refused to tell her. She had stated before she had a suspicion, but to outright know who she referenced and link the Dean to him.

Her nails dug into her palm as she fought speaking her mind. She was torn - part of her wanted so badly to unload her anger and frustration on her, but she also knew that she would be damaging one of the few positive relationships she had with the professors here. Angry tears started to sting her eyes as she did her best to blink them back. "I'll make sure to do that." She finally managed to reply curtly.

She rose to her feet, grabbing her bag from the back of the chair. "If you'll excuse me."

It wasn't until she closed the door behind her that the angry tears fell hot on her cheeks. She tapped the back of her head against the wall, appreciating the emptiness of the halls. Why were all of the adults around her incapable of being straight forward? Did no one trust her to be able to make a decision, keep a secret, or know her own mind? She was far from a small child - she had a right to know certain things.

She wanted to scream in frustration, but it would do no good at the moment. She needed to compose herself. Having a tantrum would make her look even more like the child they all thought she was. She wiped the tears from her cheeks and took a deep breath. At the very least, she had found out her next step - speaking with the Dean. She had been just as vague and avoidant as the others, but maybe with her recent proof, she could finally get something more from her.

She paused a moment, feeling Aelius moving quickly through the bond. Within a moment, she saw him run up the stairs. A sad sort of smile crept across her face as he rushed to her side. "What's wrong?" He asked, gingerly touching the side of her arm.

She pressed into him, wrapping her arms around his back. She took a deep inhale of him, the very smell of him enough to help calm her. "It's nothing..." She dismissed, her heart rate starting to slow.

He leaned his chin on the top of her head as he held her tight. "You know I can tell when you're lying." He commented with a hint of a chuckle in his voice.

She laughed, burying her face deeper into him. "I know..."

Chapter 39

Exam week had quickly snuck up on them. Her tutoring sessions and personal studying consumed much of her time. Where most of her peers had become apprehensive and anxious for the upcoming exams, she welcomed it.

Aurora stepped into her first exam located in the Academy's greenhouse. The exam would be a hybrid evaluation between both Herbology and Mixology. Professors Li and Singh had come to an agreement that combining the exams would be the best way to test their abilities. Many of the students were nervous about a practical exam over theory, but she had to agree that it was a great way to put their knowledge to use.

The greenhouse was filled to the brim with various plants. Professor Li had gone over many of them in person, but several she recognised from sketches in their texts only. She hoped her studying would be enough to win her a good grade. "Good morning, everyone." Professor Li greeted, Professor Singh right beside. "We will be conducting your dual examination this morning. In a moment, we will be announcing a tonic we want you to craft. You will have two hours to collect, prepare, and mix the tonic for review."

"You will be graded on your knowledge, technique, and effectiveness of the tonic." Professor Singh elaborated. "We will grade you separately, but remember that mistakes in one area will effect the other."

Leila gulped nervously beside her, but Aurora gave her a pat on the shoulder of assurance.

"You will collect your samples from here and prepare your materials in the lab next door." Professor Li added. "Any questions?"

The class murmured, but no one raised a hand.

"Very well." Professor Singh stated. "We will be asking you to prepare a Protection Tonic. You have two hours starting...now."

The students jumped to it. Some knew exactly what to grab, whereas others hesitated, unsure of where to start. It was easy to tell who was confident in their work, and who was watching carefully to see what the others gathered. Aurora knew exactly what to go for.

Protection tonics weren't a single formula sort of brew. There were many variations of ingredients one could use, but specific blends had far more effective properties than others. They were commonly used before entering battle with demonic creatures centuries ago. It was believed that taking one would help ward off possession, dark magic, and maybe even stave off death.

She grabbed a basket for collecting her materials. She went for the flowers first, grabbing echinacea, white heather, and chrysanthemum. A few gave her a side long glance at the quantity she took. She had a plan. She made her way over to the herbs section taking clippings of mint, basil, and a clove of garlic hanging overhead. She could feel Leila's eyes on her, trailing close behind and grabbing everything she did. Her last stop was a cabinet near the doors filled with jars of spices and minerals. She grabbed an empty glass jar off of a desk and poured black salt and peppercorns in it before heading off to the lab.

She knew her mixture would be vile to the taste, but in the end the potency would be effective. A simple tea of the flowers wouldn't be so bad, but with everything else combined, it would be enough to make one sick. She started to lay out her ingredients out on the bench. She rolled out the herbs and pounded them, bringing out the oils before starting to process them. She took her time, creating a potent tea with the flowers and grinding her spices into a fine powder. All of her processing, simmering and reducing resulted in ten vials worth of the tonic. She poured and corked five, the remaining tonic remaining in her pot.

She stared at the remaining tonic, wondering if she was crazy for what she intended to do. She looked up at the others working away, most students finished by now. She let out a long breath and shook out her hands. If she was going to do it, it would have to be now.

The notes from what happened on the Equinox conclusively pointing to one cause of death: Purification. In theory, she should be able to call it forth again. If she could somehow manage to add a small portion of Purification into the tonic, it would guarantee her a perfect score. She had made sure to double the batch just in case she was unable to, or somehow managed to shatter her vials in the process. She wanted to make sure she had something to present.

With ten minutes remaining, she grabbed the pot of tonic and moved to the corner of the lab. If things went sideways, she wanted space between her and the others. She took a deep breath, hands hovered over the pot. She could feel others look over in curiosity, but she tuned them out. She tried to recall how it felt last time. Her memories were still fragmented, but she knew now that the heat and burning that had built within her as she was dying was the Purification trying to break free. She could feel her heart race at the memory, the panic and desperation resurgent within her. She closed her eyes and focused the energy to her hands. Elemental Magic was a draw from outside, whereas Spirit felt like it resonated within. She hadn't had much time or drive to practice her Spirit. Part of it was that she didn't have a teacher, another being that she almost didn't trust herself to practice. The only times it seemed to come to her was in desperation. She wanted to see if she could conjure it rather than it driving her.

She felt the heat build in her hands, her palms growing hot. She risked opening her eyes, seeing a building glow from her palms. She turned her palms upward, the light wavering and flickering as she studied them. The heat in her palms ebbed and flowed in intensity with the light. She steadied her breathing as she turned her palms down, just above the pot on the corner desk. She did her best to focus the power in her palms, releasing just a sliver of it. She winced as a drop fell from her palms, hitting the liquid below with a hiss and sizzle. The tonic below immediately boiled, steam hitting her hands. She whipped her hands away, not wanting to suffer steam burns.

She shook her hands at her side as she leaned forward to examine her work. The tonic had settled into a simmering heat, a few bubbles still rising as the temperature settled. She broke into a smile and a slight laugh at the sight. She checked her palms, the heat and glow having dissipated. She grabbed the handle of the pot and poured the contents into her remaining vials with just minutes to spare.

Students had gathered nearby to watch her work, but as she turned to return to her lab bench, they stepped back as if she held a live viper. The vials in her hand swirled with the faintest golden glow of Spirit, the smile on her face just as bright.

Professor Li stood with his back firmly against the wall, his arms crossed at his chest. He eyed the tonics she laid out with the utmost suspicion and distrust, his face tight and his eyes wide. Professor Singh, on the other hand, was positively fascinated. She held one of the vials up close to her face, allowing the light from the windows to peer through the swirls of golden light. She chuckled with delight watching the light move and flow as if it truly were alive. "Incredible." She breathed.

"We will test it later." Professor Li stated from where he stood.

"We need to test it *now*." Professor Singh argued, finally tearing her attention from the vial. "This is *incredible*!" She exclaimed.

Professor Li scanned the room, taking the other students into account. He finally stepped closer to Singh, risking the proximity. "It's not safe to test around the students." He explained in a hushed tone.

Astraea stepped in, a serious look on her face. "I agree with Professor Li." She added in the same hushed tone. "Aurora has *not* been trained in Spirit, and we have no idea what the side effects of this would be."

Professor Singh considered it a moment before turning to the students that were equally as curious. "We test hers last. Anyone who wants to leave while I test it will be welcome to." She announced to the class, turning back to Li. "Happy?"

He made a non committal grumble in response and Astraea simply let out a sigh. She flashed a quick glare at Aurora before stepping back, her back pressed against the wall. Professor Li headed to a locked cabinet, several restricted substances locked away inside. The particular item in question was dehydrated demon.

Professor Li slid thick rubber gloves on before handling the jar filled with an inky black powder. He locked the cabinet behind him, cautiously approaching Professor Singh and the submissions. A small sample of dehydrated demon powder would be placed in a bowl. If the tonic was successful, a fizzing chemical reaction would occur. The more intense the reaction, the more effective the tonic. It was the safest way to test, as they weren't about to bring a live demon to the Academy.

One by one the submissions were tested. Some were lack lustre, barely causing a reaction. Others fizzed drastically, some even almost violently. Finally, it came time to test Aurora's. The class seemed to debate whether or not it would be safe to observe.

"Anyone who wants to leave, should do so now." Professor Singh declared as she prepped the final sample.

A few students wavered on leaving, but ultimately decided to hang back near Astraea and Professor Li instead.

Aurora stepped in beside Professor Singh, wanting to see her work first hand. Professor Singh gave her a bright smile as she readied the sample. It looked like there was a hint of madness to it, but Aurora decided to label it as excitement. Her breath held as Professor Singh poured in a small trickle of the tonic.

With a flash and crack, the bowl in front of them exploded. Aurora called a wall of air around herself and Professor Singh on instinct as she shielded her face. She could hear shouts and cries around her despite a slight ringing in her ears.

"I *told* you!" He shouted in frustration at Professor Singh. He checked on students, making sure none were harmed by the reaction.

She turned to Professor Singh, making sure she had protected her. "That was *amazing*!" She cackled.

She felt a firm grip on her upper arm and turned around in surprise. Astraea had a firm hold of her, a glare on her face. She pulled her off to the side, not caring who saw. "Do you see what I mean?" She cried. "You could have killed someone! You can't just mess around with Spirit like a child."

She blinked in surprise. She never thought she would agree with her. She turned and looked around the room, really seeing the aftermath of her experiment. The bowl they had tested her sample in had been blown apart, shrapnel strewn across the room. The smell of thick, dark smoke lingered in the room, a hint of pepper stinging her eyes. Part of her was impressed by the sheer force, but there was also the regret of damage done.

"I'm sorry." She confessed. "I didn't think—"

"Clearly!" Astraea cut her off. "*Think* before you use what you have." She spat, storming off out of the classroom.

***

Word had gotten around quickly to the Guardians, several hurried over to the lab to check on their Mages. They must have felt the sudden swell of panic and excitement through the bonds and come running. Edwyn and Mari were quick to Leila and Dae's sides, eager to confirm that they were safe. Guilt churned her stomach as she considered just how much damage she could have done to her friends.

Aelius skid in the hallway as he rounded the corner to the room. "I heard there was a commotion in the exam." He stated, worriedly checking her over. She couldn't bear to meet his eyes.

"It was me." She admitted, almost completely monotone.

He stopped, his brow creased in confusion. "What do you *mean* it was you?"

She sighed, finally meeting his stare. "I infused some Purification into a Protection Tonic."

His eyes grew wide as his mouth dropped open in surprise. "You were able to do that?" He gaped.

She wasn't quite sure what to feel. Pride at being able to do what she set out to do? A bit of shame for it being so volatile? "Well, I just thought..."

He put a hand on the side of her face. "The fact that you were able to do that with no training what so ever is incredible. Just...*please*, next time be a little more careful?" He pleaded.

Aurora looked up at him, studying his stare. She knew he was right. She was definitely in need of some guidance, but it was pretty amazing what she was able to do completely on her own. Reading about Spirit magic really wasn't enough to conjure the Magic safely. She couldn't rely on near death experiences to guide her magic either. "I promise." She assured him, leaning into his touch.

He pulled her into a hug, burying her face in his chest. The smell of him overpowered her, bringing her added peace.

They headed back to her room, her mind racing with the details of what had just happened. She knew that with Aelius by her side they would figure it all out. There was no need for him to over speak things or figure it all out for her. His support was plenty.

"I'll come check on you after my exam." He explained as he laid a gentle kiss on the top of her head. She nodded in response, unlocking her door and letting it close with a click.

She leaned against the door and let out a heavy sigh, finally alone to process what had just happened. She had been so excited, so pleased with herself that she had *actually* been able to do what she sought out to do. She had been able to freely call the Spirit forth, rather than relying on animal instinct. But Professor Li had also been right. She could have done serious damage, even kill someone had she not acted quickly after that blast.

Who was she to think that she could just blindly go along experimenting with magic she had no idea how to control? Did she really think that she could just read some books and some research notes and start practicing a brand new form of Magic with no repercussions?

She took a deep breath, banishing the thoughts of a downward spiral. It would do no good to ruminate in that what ifs. What she needed was a safe space to experiment without worrying about harming others. Maybe this summer she could find somewhere secluded enough for her to work and train. She nodded to herself, resolved to make it work. If the Empire wouldn't help her, she would help herself.

Chapter 40

Exams had wrapped. It felt surreal for an entire year to be finished. A single year had turned everything she knew about herself upside down. Prior to all of this, she thought that she had a fairly good grasp on who she was and where she came from. She wished her mother had trusted her, had had faith in her being mature enough to handle it. She still had so many unanswered questions.

She stood in the hall in half a daze. Her peers were alive with relief and excitement to be finished with the year. Aurora, however, was left with undesirable paths to take. Aelius waited for her, resting on the edge of one of the fountains outside the Mage training facility. After last semester's debacle, Guardians were not allowed to spectate examinations. The barrier had been fixed, but the Dean had stated that she refused to take any chances.

He lit up at the very sight of her, her own excitement bubbling to the surface as well. She broke into a run, jumping into his open arms. He pretended to stagger a moment as they both laughed. "Good exam?" He asked, setting her back to the ground.

She settled herself beside him on the fountain ledge. "I think so. It's nice that Duncan lets me dual weave. Makes it easier."

A swell of pride surged through the bond at her words. She had started to realise it was all for her. He loved hearing her speak about about working things out and being a stronger Mage. He deserved the best Mage out there - a partner to equal his skills. "You're incredible." He stated, leaning in for a gentle kiss.

"But not terrifying yet?" She giggled, tucking a stray strand of hair behind his ear.

He tried to suppress a smirk at her comment. "You might have to demonstrate for me. It's been a while since I've seen you fight."

"Oh really?" She asked, leaning in to kiss him.

"I think so." He teased back. "Good thing we have all summer for you to show me."

She leaned back, staring at him. He truly meant it - looking forward to enjoying her all summer. She had been so focused on trying to find a way to train and better herself in Spirit magic, and here he was having planning a summer together. Maybe both were possible. "All summer?" She asked playfully.

He pulled her back into him. "If you'll have me." He replied, leaving it up to her. Every ounce of her wanted to melt into him - give in to him. Being swept up in him would be the perfect way to avoid everything she needed to do - everything that should have been taking her focus. It would be so easy, so satisfying to just fill her heart and mind with him.

A soft smile met her lips as she gave him a gentle kiss. "You're the perfect distraction, you know." She finally responded.

He arched a brow at her, unsure of what she meant. "Distraction from what? Your exams are done. What else is there?"

She let out a sigh, knowing that there was only so much procrastination she could do. "More like what I have been putting off." She admitted.

His playful demeanour settled into his usual serious mask. "What do you need?"

She stared up into his eyes. He was so good to her - so supportive. "Remember the other night when I was upset?" He nodded. "Professor Jung confirmed she knew all along that my father is...well...*you know*. She told me I should speak with Dean Reyes. That they have an *accord* and she would be the best person to speak with about moving forward."

Aelius took her hand in his, knowing just how difficult everything had been for her. "Then we go over and talk to her. Best to do it now before the year's out."

She knew he was right. There were mere days before the semester was over. Once the campus emptied it would just make tracking answers down more difficult. She gave his hand a gentle squeeze. "Let's go."

***

Most students at this point had finished their exams. All that was left was to receive marks and dissolve the pact bonds for the year. Most of the halls were empty - students choosing to enjoy the beautiful weather on campus or in town.

The hall to the Dean's office was empty, save for her assistant being her desk. She glanced up, eyeing the pair of them with an unreadable expression.

"Is the Dean available?" Aurora asked, her stomach fluttered with nerves.

The assistant peered down at the schedule on her desk. "She has a fifteen minute window." She answered dryly, a slight tilt of her head suggesting Aurora knock.

Aurora thanked her, rapping her knuckles on the door.

"Come in!" The Dean's voice called out.

With a heavy push, she opened the doors and stepped into the office, dimly light for the time of day. Aelius was right at her side, a welcome sense of calm. The Dean waited for her behind the desk, an odd look in her eyes. Aurora stepped closer, getting a better look at the woman before her. There was a glossed over look in her eyes, almost as if there was a faint fog to them. Her expression was overly happy and her movements ever so floaty. "Sit down, sit down!" She directed excitedly.

The pair took their seats before her desk, Aurora refusing to break eye contact with Reyes. The Dean had always seemed a little quirky, a little unconventional, but this was odd even for her. "Are you alright, Dean Reyes?" She asked warily.

The plastered smile never wavered. "Of course!" She confirmed. "The year is almost at an end and the summer awaits. What isn't there to look forward to?"

"Right..." She responded, her eyes scanning the room for any sign of anyone else in the room. There was no sign of any one else, but there was a feeling she couldn't quite shake. "I wanted to talk to you about my parents." She admitted.

The topic sparked no reaction. "And how may I help with that?" She asked.

Aurora chose her words carefully, the suspicion of some sort of interference growing. "You knew my mother, correct?"

"I did." She agreed with a nod.

"And you knew my father?" She pressed.

The Dean paused a moment, as if the question was processing and lagging in her brain. "We talked about this, Miss Thomas." She finally managed, the eerie happiness in her tone and expression slipping for a moment.

"You said my life wouldn't improve by knowing." She recalled. "I am at a point where I am *pretty* certain I know who it is, but I need help confirming it. I can't think of anyone else I can go to to help me."

The mask had found its way back on her face. "What makes you think I can help you?"

"I think you know my father quite well and speak with him rather frequently." She implied.

"There are quite a few people I meet with on a regular basis, Miss Thomas. I'm not quite sure what you—"

"Castor Solis, Dean Reyes." She cut off. "I am quite certain that Castor Solis is my father." Saying the words aloud made her want to vomit, but it had to be said.

The Dean's face fell from the happy mask to pure neutrality. She sat up perfectly rigid and silent, the only movement to be seen was the slight twitch of her right hand. Aurora stared at her in confusion, waiting for something, anything to happen or be said. After what felt like several minutes, the Dean seemed to reset and smile at her once more. "I can't wait to hear all about your adventures this summer, Miss Thomas. You really must write." She stated with a chilling smile as she stood to her feet.

Aurora blinked in confusion, completely confused as to what just happened. "I'm sorry, but—"

"You really must write and keep in touch." The Dean repeated as if she had become a broken record.

She stood to her feet, an uneasy feeling growing. Her eyes scanned the room again wondering if someone may be lurking within the shadows. Her eyes flitted to Aelius, a wary tension across his face as well as he maintained a close distance to her. The Dean ushered them towards the door, an agitated insistence to their pace. Aurora turned back to her again, hoping there might be something she could get through. She opened her mouth to speak, but the Dean pulled the doors open with a pull of Air Magic.

"So wonderful to see you, both." The Dean declared, shaking Aurora's hand. The feeling of a cool piece of metal pressed against the palm of her hand.

The Dean moved to return to her office, but stopped in her tracks. She held for a beat, frozen in place like she had been just moments earlier. She finally turned back to Aurora, a serious look on her face. She grabbed Aurora into a tight hug before she could react. "I've given you everything I can." She whispered into her ear. Her voice sounded tired and strained. "Use it."

With that, the Dean let her go and returned to her office. The doors closing quickly behind her with a second pull of Air.

They waited in uncertain silence a moment before Aelius gingerly took her by the arm. They walked down the hall a moment before he finally spoke. "Something wasn't right."

She looked up at him, knowing exactly what he meant. "You saw her eyes, didn't you?"

He pulled her into him, teleporting them back to his room. She clutched to him, getting a little more used to the sensation, but it still made her unsteady.

"A little warning would be nice." She chuckled, stepping back a moment.

His eyes scanned the room before he relaxed his shoulders. "Sorry." He replied, placing a gentle kiss on her forehead. "I just figured what you were about to say was best not overheard."

She looked up at him, surprised at just how right he was. He was far more perceptive than most gave him credit for. "You're right." She sighed, making herself comfortable in one of the chairs. "You should sit..."

He took a seat across from her, resting his forearms on his knees.

"I'm...Well I'm not sure just how much you know about Spirit magic considering your father's work." She began.

Aelius sat back a moment, considering her words. "I am pretty sure things are kept the way that they want it. My father is careful to not break any disclosures."

She nodded. "So...you aren't aware of Compulsion?"

His eyes squinted at her words. "Compulsion?" He asked with an air of uncertainty.

She let out a small breath of relief. She knew that Mari and Aelius had a different level of access and knowledge then most of the students due to their family status, but she was thankful that he was ignorant in this. That he wasn't keeping secrets from her. "I have been doing some reading. I think the look in the Dean's eyes and the way she was speaking was due to Compulsion."

He listened intently, making sure to take in what she said. "And it has to do with Spirit?" He asked.

She nodded. "I believe it's a form of Spirit magic that the Solis' don't disclose. I have been reading about it in a journal written by the first Emperor's advisor. He seemed to believe that it was a form of magic used to control others."

She could feel the tension spike through the bond. He refused to let it show on his face, but she knew it was there. "It would explain things." He finally stated.

"But why?" She spoke aloud to herself as she rubbed her temple.

She felt Aelius take her hand in his, giving a gentle squeeze. "We'll figure it out. We can talk to my dad and see if there is anything he recommends."

She looked up at him with a start. For him to ask his father to intervene was no small ask. "I *can't* ask that of you." She objected, knowing how much that meant.

"You can." He assured her. "He can point us in the right direction without breaking protocol. He cares about you as well, Aurora."

A pang of guilt still sat in her heart. She knew it was likely a grey area to ask for help from his father. They had all told her they wanted to help her and owed her for what she did for Mari, but they had already helped her after her attack. They didn't owe her anything after that. It was too much to ask for more.

He felt her swirl of emotions, bringing a hand to her cheek. "Nothing is too much for you." He insisted.

She felt tears start to sting her eyes. She sniffed and did her best to blink them away. "It is." She argued, looking away - unable to meet his gaze. "There's no reason—"

"I love you." He countered.

Her breath held, her attention snapped to him.

Aelius knelt before her, taking her hands in his. "Nothing is too much for you, because I love you. I will move heaven and earth to make sure you have whatever it is you need." He took her hand, placing it over his heart. "I'm yours. All of me. You deserve more than I can ever give, but I will spend my life trying to come close."

There were no words - nothing that she could say that would compare to what he had just confessed. She leaned into him, slipping her arms around his neck and kissed him.

Aelius returned her kiss, holding her tight. She felt the weight lifted from his confession, his sheer joy of her kiss, as it flooded her through the bond. It was almost overwhelming, taking her to the edge of what she could withstand. They had been told that the temporary bonds were but a fraction of the bond that a full fledged Mage and Guardian were paired with. She wondered how she would ever be able to survive him if this was just a portion of him.

He pulled back from her, leaving her slightly breathless. He let out a soft chuckle as he stroked a strand of hair from her eyes. "You don't have to—"

"I love you too." She cut him off. She knew that she hadn't said it aloud, but she did. She hadn't considered admitting it to him, not any time soon, but with him declaring it first, there was no sense in holding back any longer.

Aelius broke into a bright smile, sheer joy flooding the bond. His emotions burned bright - far more than she had ever expected when she had first gotten to know him. He had seemed so reserved, so proper. What she felt, what he showed her very much proved otherwise.

"All of me is yours." She explained, sliding his hand over her heart. Despite the layers of her uniform, she could feel the heat his palm radiated as her heart raced. "And I will spend every day striving to be the partner worthy of fighting at your side." She added, placing another kiss on his lips.

Chapter 41

Aurora woke with a start, bolting upright in bed. Her heart thundered in her chest at the pounding on at the door. Aelius was already on his feet, a dagger in hand. He took a breath, relaxing a fraction that it had just been the door and not something more. He dropped the dagger back on his bedside table before answering the door.

He cracked the door a sliver to speak to whoever had startled them awake. Aurora slid her knees into her chest, straining to hear what they said. The quiet murmurs were far too faint for her to discern, but the tension eased through the bond. Whatever it was, wasn't too serious. He shut the door, turning back to her with a neutral look on his face.

"What is it?" She asked.

He walked back to bed, slipping back in beside her. "That was the Royal Guard. There are orders to stay put until further notice."

"They woke us up at this hour to tell us that? Why?" She pressed. A glance at her watch told her it was well before six.

He pulled her into his arms. "I'm not sure." He explained as he snuggled into her, his face deep in her tousled curls. "It can wait."

She let out a soft chuckle, wrapping her arms around him. He was right. Whatever it was could wait. Curled up in bed with him, basking in the glow of last night was far better than anything else.

They had about fifteen minutes of rest before a chiming sound rang out. Aelius let out a grown, instantly knowing what it was. He rolled over, reaching over to his side table. He turned himself away from her as he opened up his communicator. "What?" He grumbled.

"What do you mean *what?*" She heard Mari chastise him. "The whole campus is on lock down."

"I know, Amaris." He retorted. "The Guard stopped by about fifteen minutes ago. If that's it, then—"

"I spoke with dad." She interrupted him. He sat up, suddenly much more alert. His gaze flitted to Aurora for a moment before he finally got out of bed, repositioning himself to the window sill.

Aurora slipped herself out of bed, heading towards the closet. It wouldn't be much, but the other room would give him a semblance of privacy. She paused, only a moment to grab her jacket from the floor, remembering yesterday's events.

It wasn't long before she shut the door behind her that she could hear Mari's muffled voice speaking with Aelius. She knew he wouldn't ever mind her overhearing what they said, but it seemed somewhat private. She would rather keep out of it unless he expressly said otherwise. She sat herself on the floor of the closet, making herself comfortable. She slid her hands into the pocket of her jacket, her fingers closing around whatever Reyes had given her yesterday.

The small brass Artefact was barely the size of her palm and cool to the touch. She turned it over in her hands, wondering if there was any indication of an opening. As she ran her thumb along the side, a small crack sounded. A faint glow worked from within, quickly projecting a series of exchanged letters. It was then that she realised it was a modernised version of a memory box, much more compact than her mother's.

She passed through the letters, wondering what the Dean could have possibly wanted her to have.

April 26 2007

Soledad,

There was an understanding to your appointment, that I am quite certain you recall. There are always going to be things we do not wish to do. Innovation is not without trials and sacrifice.

You are behind on your quota. The others have complied. I do not understand why you are having such difficulty. If you cannot find a way to help us meet our numbers, we will have to start taking matters in our own hands.

You have a week.

Get it sorted.
-Eldritch

She stopped a moment, trying to make sense of the names. She knew that Dean Reyes' first name was Soledad due to letters and paperwork that included it from time to time. That was simple enough. It still raised the question: who was Eldritch? She wracked her brain trying to recall anyone by that name, but couldn't. She turned back to the letters.

April 30 2007

Dear Eldritch,

I assure you that I recall the understanding you refer to. I also happen to remember the oaths I took to protect and guide the students. I simply cannot fathom that this is the only option we have. There have to be other options that we can take. Have we really run out of felons already? What happened to using them?

I refuse to take any part in this. Ask other things of me, but not this.

Find another way.
-Soledad

May 1 2007

Soledad,

I think you mistake me. You act as if you have an option here. This is a direct order from the Emperor. We both know what happens when people fail to meet his demands. The longer you resist, the less time you have to meet your quota. I personally don't care whether or not you comply, you just happened to be the first candidate on his list. The choice is yours.

Two days,
Eldritch

May 3 2007

Eldritch,

Clara Petrov, Timothy Hearst, Min Wu, Anna Schluyer. They will meet your needs.

Call off your men,
Soledad

Four names. Who were they, and what needs did they have to meet? She went to access more, when she heard a rap at the door. With a jump she snapped the Artefact closed. Aelius gave her a confused look, seeing her curled up on the floor of his closet. "What are you doing?" He chuckled as he offered her his hand.

She took his offer, standing to her feet. "I was just—." Before she could fully answer, a cry rang out in the hall. They shared a look, before Aelius rushed to the door. Aelius leaned out, checking whatever was going on. Aurora hung back a moment, knowing whatever it was, it wasn't good. Aelius finally turned back to her, a solemn look on his face.

"It's the Dean." He explained quietly. "Her assistant found her in her office..."

Aurora gave him a look, hoping that she wasn't misunderstanding. Another wail from the hall coupled with the look in his eyes told her she wasn't.

A chill ran down her spine which quickly turned to nausea. She ran for the washroom, knowing that she was moments away from upending everything. She made it just in time, emptying all she had and heaving a few extra times for good measure. She rinsed her mouth out wishing very much for a toothbrush at that moment. Aelius knocked at the open door as she substituted a helping of toothpaste on her finger.

She looked up at Aelius in the reflection, her eyes rimming with tears. "You okay?" He asked cautiously.

She spit out the toothpaste and rinsed. "No." She admitted, setting it down. "We just saw her last night. It doesn't make sense."

He closed the gap between them, hugging her gently from behind. "I'll speak with my father about last night.

They need to know about her behaviour and the
Compulsion."

Her eyes darted towards the closet where she had
tucked the Artefact away. "I need to show you something."
She responded, heading to the closet to show him. She
pulled him over to his bed so they could sit while she ran
through it. "It's a series of letters between Dean Reyes and
someone called Eldritch." She explained, flipping through
until she reached where she had left off. "He keeps asking
her for names, but I'm not sure yet what it's all for."

He nodded, listening as she started pouring over the
additional letters.

January 5 2008

Soledad,

*The latest yield was not as potent as we could have hoped. Are
you certain that you have been providing adequate specimens?
Oslac's specifications were very clear on the details. We will need
another list before the end of the month.*

*If this latest batch doesn't work out, then we will need to
readdress things.*

Sooner rather than later,
-Eldritch

January 8 2008

Eldritch,

*I assure you that I triple checked the numbers myself. I have
been making sure each and every one of the graduates meet his
specs. I am doing my part. Perhaps his calculations are off.*

Eliza Chapman, Jessie Moore, Adam Black, Samantha Smyth.
-Soledad

She reread the last letter in the Dean's own hand. Graduates. The names she was giving were graduates. Most of them looked to be female - most likely Mages. It didn't sound like they were being screened for interviews. The threats and guilt made it seem far more ominous.

January 12 2008

Soledad,

I assure you that Oslac's calculations are not the problem. It has been brought to light that maybe the problem is the age of the specimens. We want to see what younger Magic does. Next quarter we want current students. We will give you time to think it over. Four students by next quarter.

-Eldritch

January 15 2008

Eldritch,

You cannot be serious about current students? How are we going to be able to excuse it with current students? Field Mages can be covered up in training accidents and combat. The Academy is prided on its safety. How are we going to explain away four students in one quarter?

-Soledad

January 23 2008

Soledad,

You don't need to worry about how things will look. It will not come back on the Academy in any way. We have begun work on articles about the increase of Mage burn out in schools these days. It's really such a shame how many of our best and brightest are spending themselves before they can be an asset to our Empire.

Anything can be spun and worked away. Don't worry about any of that. It is your job to provide us with names and numbers. We expect four names by the end of the quarter.

-Eldritch

She audibly gasped, covering her mouth with her hand. "They're not burning out." She finally managed, dropping the Artefact to the bed. "They're sapping the magic from them."

Aelius picked up the Artefact, scanning the documents for himself. His face was stern, his emotions simmering into a building anger beneath the surface.

"Why would she give this to me, of all people?" She thought aloud. "It's not like I have access to anything or can publish this."

Aelius clicked the Artefact shut and placed it between them. "You have access to me." He stated.

"What do you mean?" She asked.

"I think I know who Eldritch is."

Chapter 42

Aurora sat up straighter at his words. It made sense. Aelius and Mari had access to far more people within the Empire than most students would due to their parents. "Who—"

Her question was cut off by the sound of a key in the door. Aelius jumped to his feet to be met with Edwyn making his way in the room. "Sorry." He immediately apologised, raising his hands defensively. "Madelynn kicked me out after, well...she wasn't in the mood for company after the news."

Aurora slid out of bed, making sure to take the Artefact in hand before standing. "It's okay I was just heading out anyway."

"You don't have to leave on my account!" He objected, not intending to ruin their moment.

She gave Edwyn a small smile, continuing to grab her things. "It's okay, honestly. I should get going to check on Mari, anyway." She turned to Aelius, raising on her tip toes to give him a small kiss on the cheek. "We'll talk later. Love you."

Aelius grabbed her hand gently before she left, pulling her in for a proper kiss. "I love you." He responded, nearly making her change her mind.

Edwyn's eyes grew wide and his mouth gaped open at witnessing the sudden exchange. Aurora could hear his reaction as the door closed behind her. She stifled a chuckle at his enthusiasm for his friend. It was a welcome moment in contrast of the sudden cloud that hung over the Academy.

It seemed as if the news spread quickly, most students out of their rooms now. Some openly sobbed and consoled one another, whereas others seemed almost agitated by the entire thing. She slipped past cloisters of students, making her way back to her room.

She opened the door, seeing Mari and Dae together by the fireplace. Mari looked up at her, a hint of red at the edge of her eyes. Aurora quickly dropped her things by the door and rushed to her side. "Mar, you okay?"

Mari gave her a small smile. "I'm fine, just..." She sighed, leaning her head back. "I never expected Soledad to...well I guess you never do, right?"

Dae rubbed her on the shoulder. "I'm sorry, baby."

Mari leaned into him, resting her head on his shoulder. "We would have her over at ours sometimes. My parents weren't super close with her, but we'd have her over for some of the parties. She was always nice to us. Funny."

Aurora knelt before her, taking her hands in hers. "I'm sorry, Mar. She was a special lady."

Mari paused a moment, sitting up as she made a realisation. "Where were you?" She asked, giving her a quizzical look.

Her cheeks flushed crimson as she stammered a moment, uncertain of how to exactly answer that to his sister of all people.

Her brow shot up in realisation. "Oh!"

"Sorry I should have said something, or left a note, or..."

Mari waved a hand at her dismissively. "It's fine." She chuckled, happy for the distraction.

***

The entire Academy felt as if it were turned upside down as staff and students prepared for a grand funeral a week after her death. It was announced that a state funeral would be prepared for Dean Reyes despite the dishonour surrounding her death. Such events were normally reserved for members of the Imperial Family, but Dean Reyes was considered an elite member of the Empire; an exception to the rule had been made. There had been many debates among students whether or not her actions called for such an honour, but ultimately it was the Emperor's decision.

Aurora stood in her room, notice in hand. Select students had been chosen to attend the service and not be in the public crowd. Students who were the top in their class, such as herself were included on the list. Students with high ranking parents, like Mari and Aelius, were also invited. She put the notice on her bed and checked her reflection in the mirror. Normally only professional Guardians were permitted to wear black, however funerals were the exception. She had been at a loss of how to dress, but Mari had helped with a visit to the shops in Vilcas. There had been no energy or drive to be selective, but Mari had insisted on making sure she was dressed appropriately.

She straightened the cuff of her bolero at her wrist. Mari had chosen a modest dress for her; fitted through the bodice and flared to the floor. The lace bolero was overlaid, making it appropriate for the church service, but light enough to combat the building summer heat. The finishing touch had been a black fascinator pinned in place of her hair in a simple low bun. She had never understood the allure of hats, but she was aware that formal events called for them in the Empire. Mari knocked at the door, wearing a dress not unlike her own. Her hat had a few feathers arranged at the back opposed to her fascinator; pinned in place on top of her delicately styled curls. It was odd to see her so feminine and put together, but she managed to look beautiful both ways.

"You ready?" She asked with a tilt of her head.

"Let's go." She answered, turning off the lights and heading out the door.

The service was to be a full day affair. A processional of Guardians were to the march the coffin from the Academy through the streets of Vilcas, to the portal that would end at the doors of the Imperial church. Commoners and previous students would line the streets; only the elite and lucky few would be permitted entry to the service. Rumours circulated that the Emperor himself would deliver the eulogy. Many believed it to be madness, but some argued that since he had been the one to appoint her to the position, that it made sense.

Aurora walked arm in arm with Mari as they headed to the main gate. Aelius had offered to take her, but Mari had argued that she wanted Aurora to head over with her. It had been a short argument, but in the end Mari won, Aelius resolving himself to head over with some of the other Guardians.

The processional would start in just under an hour and everyone needed to be ready at the church ahead of time. The school, normally a sea of navy and purple was stark black. The tailors in Vilcas had been busy keeping up with the surge in orders, some students having to resort to old pieces from back home. She was thankful for Mari's sway with shops in town.

Most students had begun to gather along the grounds, getting in place for the upcoming processional. For them, it would be as close to the service as they would get. The handful of invited students trickled their way down to the gate. Carriages waited for them to usher them through town to the portal. Aurora and Mari found themselves across from a pair of third years. The pair were labelled as this years most promising new recruits. She had had the opportunity to meet them in passing, but never really had a chance to speak with either one. It seemed wrong to make small talk now. A simple nod and polite smile would suffice.

They eventually passed through the town, more and more people starting to gather in preparation. Some had managed to get together suitable blacks, where some did their best to pass off dark browns as "close enough". It wasn't long before the carriage stopped just short of the large portal set up for the service. A grand oval swirled like a pool of silver not quite ever settling in place. An uneasy reflection pooled back as she got closer, almost making her nauseous. She had never had the chance to study portals, but the idea of it fascinated her.

She turned to Mari, hesitant to touch it without her. She had been through a portal before to get from the Middling Realm to the Academy, but this felt different. This portal would lead her uncomfortably close to the palace. Mari grabbed her hand and squeezed it reassuringly. She raised a hand to the mirrored liquid and pushed through first.

Aurora waited a breath before following. It would be fine with Mari by her side.

An added flush of heat hit her as soon as she stepped through the portal. The Imperial Palace was located farther south than the Academy, and was definitely warmer in climate. Intense sun beat down from the clear sky, the black of her dress drawing the heat to it. She was suddenly thankful for Mari's choice of lace.

Before them stood the Imperial Cathedral. The Palace itself was about a kilometre away, but the church alone was breathtaking. The architecture alone would be worth weeks of study and admiration. Pure white stone was the basis for the monument, intricate details only a taste of what lay within. She followed Mari, climbing the stairs one by one; unable to take her eyes from the craftsmanship. Not watching where she stepped, she stumbled forward. Mari let out a soft chuckle as she reached to catch her arm. "Watch where you're going." Mari teased in a whisper.

"It's stunning." She breathed.

"Never been inside." Mari explained, her arms crossed at her chest as she looked up at the building. "Dad's been here enough with work, but he never took me in. Said he didn't trust me around the art."

"And I stand by it." A gruff voice commented from behind.

The girls whipped around to see Elias standing several steps beneath them. He was dressed in a military set of blacks, the only hint of colour being dozens of medals pinned to his chest. A soul blade hung at his hip, his hand resting against the pommel. His eyes appeared stern and discerning, but he soon broke into a bright smile as his eyes met his daughter's.

"Dad!" Mari exclaimed, rushing down the steps to jump into his arms.

Elias broke out into a rumble of a laugh, his arms wrapping around his daughter. "Good to see you, sweetheart." He replied as he hugged her tight. "Even if it's under these circumstances."

Mari let out a small laugh as he set her down. "Aelius should be behind us shortly."

He gave a disapproving huff in response, his arms crossed at his chest. "He shouldn't be away from your side." He commented to Aurora, her brow shooting up at the remark.

"It's not his fault." Mari chimed in. "I told him I'd be taking Aurora for myself. He gets her enough."

Elias paused a moment before letting out a rumble of a laugh. At first glance, Mari's father looked to be a hardened stern man, but it was evident that he had a soft spot for family. Mari had told stories of how it seemed like her father was two separate men at times: the stern captain who took no excuses, and the adoring family man that would go to the ends of the earth to bring his loved ones joy. What was that like to have? "Fair enough." He stated. "Now then. You girls got here in good time. I have to head back to ready the processional, but I will be back. Happy I ran into you both before I was off."

"Love you, dad." Mari said as she got another hug before he left. He was gone in a blink, using his teleportation to whisk away to the portal. There was no sense in wasting time with a gift like that.

"So..." Mari turned to her. "Walk around the grounds, or head inside?"

Chapter 43

The cathedral rendered her speechless. She had never followed The Church of the Empire, but she had learned enough of the basics from History class. The Church of the Empire elevated the Imperial Family as messengers of God, blessed with the gift of Spirit. She stood in the entrance in awe, hoping that her lack of knowledge and inner workings wouldn't fail her today.

The smell of frankincense hit her immediately as they walked through. There were other notes of incense swirled in, but it was hard to discern them from others. She couldn't put a finger on it, but there was something to it that made her feel ever so slightly at ease. White and black marble lay underfoot, their footsteps echoed against the walls and high ceilings as they stepped. Light poured through the intricately designed windows at the back of the building, not leaving a single corner of darkness. Pew after pew lined each side, leaving room for hundreds of parishioners. It was evident that this church was most definitely for the affluent and elite; not the every day man. Stunning statues and paintings lined the walls, ranging from saints to an ornate sculpture of the first Emperor himself.

She stopped before a striking carving of the first Emperor. A caption at the base of the sculpture explained that it was a depiction of receiving the gift of Spirit from God. He stood, arms up to the heavens with head cast back, welcoming the newfound power. The artist had taken great lengths to design the look of pure adoration and gratitude on his face. Whoever had arranged the works, had made sure to place the Emperor in a spot where natural light would pour and cascade down as if one were watching God bestow Spirit.

"First time?" Mari asked in a whisper, leaning in to her ear.

Aurora let out a small laugh in response, still unable to take her eyes off of the sculpture. "Yeah my mother wasn't much for church."

"We go a fair amount." Mari explained as they continued down towards the pulpit, studying each piece. She opened her mouth to continue, but was cut off by the sound of footsteps from behind. Members of the church started to prepare and set up for the service. Mari grabbed the inside of her arm gently and pulled her away. "Looks like we better head outside."

Fresh air filled her nose as soon as they stepped outside. She closed her eyes and inhaled, letting it fill her lungs. "There you are." She heard Aelius call out.

She opened her eyes to see him standing several steps below them, much like his father had done just moments earlier. Aelius lacked his father's blade and decorative medallions, but the look was eerily similar.

"We were just killing time inside while we waited for others." Mari retorted with a roll of her eyes.

"Really?" He asked, clearly unimpressed with her choice of phrasing.

"You know what I mean. Lighten up." She sighed, pushing on his shoulder as she came down and passed him.

Aurora shook her head slightly as she let out a small chuckle. She followed, stopping a couple of steps ahead of him. It was rare to be on eye level with him. She leaned forward, planting a soft kiss on his lips. "I'm glad you're here safe."

He smiled at her, tucking a stray strand of hair behind her ear. "Me too. It's better when I'm by your side."

She did her best to stifle a smile at his words, but failed miserably. More and more attendees began to arrive, many appearing to be incredibly important. She made sure to remain close to Aelius and Mari, a slight worry of being separated growing within her. He slid his hand in hers, undoubtedly feeling the flutter through the bond.

It wasn't long before they found Cora in the crowd. Her light brown hair was pulled into a low bun with a feathered hat pinned on top. She wore a fitted black bodice with a high low pleated skirt beneath. Black breaches and knee high boots were underneath giving off a more modern style than either of the girls. Her face lit up the instant she spotted her children, arms open wide to pull them into an embrace.

She caught Aurora into the hug as she stood between the twins. Their mother was undoubtedly a Guardian as well as she squeezed them as if a shred of ease might result in their escape. She was just slightly shorter than Mari, coming up to her eyebrows in height as she released them from her hug. "My babies." She cooed, bringing a hand underneath Mari's chin.

"Mooooom." Mari protested, her eyes scanning for people over hearing.

Her mother chuckled in response. "What? You're my babies. I don't care how tall you get!"

Mari's cheeks flushed a slight shade of pink in embarrassment, whereas Aelius smiled fondly. Aurora herself couldn't help but smile at the aggressive affection she had for her children. It reminded her of her own mother.

"And Aurora!" She exclaimed, just realising she had forgotten to address her. She pulled her into her own hug, the air forced out of her lungs by the sudden embrace. "It's been too long since our last call."

She patted her arms on her back before being released. "I'm sorry, I got so caught up with exams and everything." She had been pulled onto family calls more and more, Cora insisting on speaking with her for several minutes on her own even. It had felt a little out of place at first, but over time she had grown more comfortable with things.

"Oh of *course* school comes first! We'll have all sorts of time over the summer, anyway." She concluded rather dismissively as she scanned their surroundings. "Come along." She ordered, slipping an arm around her. "They're starting to get us settled in. It won't be long before things are ready. You come stand with us, dear."

"But..." She started to protest.

"Nonsense." She insisted, not wanting to hear a word of it. "You're with us."

She awkwardly followed Cora, feeling awfully like an orphaned chick trailing after a mother hen. It was clear that Mari's parents were people of high social standing the way others nodded and even bowed as they passed by. They walked past rows of pews, finally stopping only a few rows from the front. The only ones allowed ahead were reserved for the lower ranking Imperial Family members. The Emperor and his immediate family would be seated in special pews to the side.

She swallowed, feeling as if every eye were on her. She was suddenly thankful for Mari's choice of headwear. The fascinator allowed her a little more shielding of her eye colour. Maybe, just maybe, it would allow her to pass off as anyone else.

Rows of attendees rose to their feet. The Imperial Family had entered. There were only two occasions where a member of the Imperial Family would wear anything but white: school blues; or a funeral. They nearly blended in with the sea of black, but several of them still managed to hold an air of superiority in their demeanour. It was those with lower titles that came first; likely Barons and Baronesses all the way to Grand Dukes and Duchesses. Their fashions got progressively finer in quality as they stepped forward and took their seats in the pews before them. It was then that she saw him. Astraea, a haunting beauty in black, had her arm wrapped around Victor's as he rigidly escorted her down the aisle. She attempted to keep a mask of demure mourning, but she could see the faint smirk at the corner of her lips. Victor, however, had a glaze over his eyes that she had unfortunately started to recognise.

She barely had a moment to worry about Victor before she realised who was not far behind: the Emperor. Her breath held as she watched him glide past; completely unaware of her presence. The moment he sat himself in place, she felt she could finally breathe. She had managed to remain under his radar. She prayed that it remained that way.

Everyone remained on their feet as the bishop finally entered. It was only when he approached the pulpit and gave the order that everyone took their seats. The bishop was older, and unfortunately had a way of droning on that lost her attention almost immediately. It wasn't entirely his fault, however. She found herself staring at Victor, wondering why he would possibly be Compelled. She had heard that they were unofficially betrothed since childhood, but his demeanour and actions certainly did not read as someone in love with the Princess. With the recent events of Soledad and her Compulsion, she felt her stomach churn at what he could possibly be enduring. She chewed on her bottom lip in thought, rising to her feet as she felt a nudge on her arm from Mari.

Prayer after prayer, hymn after hymn took place, yet she knew none of it. She followed along as best as she could, making sure to take Mari's lead. After what felt like hours, the bishop stepped down to allow for a eulogy given by none other than the Emperor himself. She froze in place, terrified that if she moved an inch, he would hone in on her.

He stepped forward, clearing his throat as he placed the cue cards prepared for him on the pulpit. "Soledad Reyes was a remarkable woman who fought tirelessly for the Empire. As many of you well know, the appointment of Soledad as Dean was my first official act as Emperor. There were those who did not see what I saw. They did not agree with appointing someone so young in such an important role. I knew Soledad from my days as a student at the Academy, and I knew first hand the type of woman she was. I saw the dedication, determination, and passion for the protection of the realms. I saw a woman who would let nothing stand in her way to do what it took. It is with a heavy heart that we lay such a woman to rest. We pray that the Lord take you in his light, Soledad."

Another prayer followed before the Emperor stepped down and returned to her seat. He had scanned the audience as he spoke, but she had remained lucky. With a final blessing, the bishop concluded the service, releasing them. Everyone rose to their feet yet again, the bishop leaving first, followed by the Emperor and his family.

It was as he left that his eyes met hers. It was the briefest of moments, but she swore he looked at her. His eyes squinted ever so slightly before turning away, continuing down the aisle. She froze herself in place, refusing to let her knees buckle. There was a chance she had imagined it, a chance that he had looked at either of the twins beside her.

As the last of the Imperial Family stepped out of the side boxes, the remaining people filtered out. She followed closely behind Aelius, terrified of being separated and on her own. He squeezed her hand, wordlessly assuring her that he would never let it happen. Outside of the Cirillo clan, there was not a single soul she felt she could trust here. Mari patted her on the shoulder to assure her. Aurora gave a small nod in thanks as she shuffled along the slow moving line out of the church.

"I thought you only had two children, Elias." A man's voice commented from behind.

Mari's father turned to the sound of the voice, his stance just a little straighter as he did so. Aurora turned as well, wondering who would illicit such a response.

A wiry man with forehead creases and streaks of grey through his fine hair stood behind with the faintest hint of a smirk across his face. The cut of his clothing marked him as an elite, as did the arrogant way he held himself.

"Eldritch." Elias remarked with a slight nod of his head.

Her breath held as she did her best to avoid openly staring at the man. Her eyes flitted to Aelius, wondering if her thoughts were correct. A small nod was all the answer she needed. He had explained earlier that he had a good guess of who the Eldritch from the letters had been - the Emperor's advisor.

"Just the two." Cora answered, putting a protective hand on her upper arm. "Aurora, here, is our daughter's best friend, and our son's Mage. She was invited as one of the top students at the Academy and we thought it best to keep everyone together."

Eldritch turned his attention to her openly. He arched a brow at her as he scanned her. Face to face with him, she felt her blood pound within her veins. "She has an uncanny resemblance to a woman I used to know..."

"Eldritch!" A voice cried out over the crowd before Aurora could bother to comment. The voice was like nails on a chalk board to her ears. Her hand waved over head, beckoning his attention.

"Excuse me." Eldritch stated with a slight nod of his head before sneaking off to his summons. He moved in a hurry, dodging and sneaking between others with a serpent like ease. He broke the space between others and the wide berth given to the Emperor and his family. Eldritch bent into a sweeping bow to Astraea and the Emperor. They were too far to make out their words, but Astraea flitted her eyes up to meet her own. She touched her father's arm, leaning in to whisper in his ear. It was then that he finally turned his attention to his daughter.

"We need to go" She stressed, gripping Aelius' hand tight.

Mari looked between the two, uncertain what was going on. "Is everythi—"

It was then that his eyes met her own. Across the bustling crowd, the Emperor stared at her as if she were the only soul present.

Chapter 44

Mari leaned into Cora to give some sort of excuse as Aelius started to lead them out of the crowd. They turned and twisted, slipping between one after another, uttering pardon me and excuse me as necessary. The crowd eventually thinned as they got closer to the portal. Relief started to pulse through her, nearly away from them all.

She slowed her pace, not wanting to stand out and call attention to herself as they finally broke free of the masses. Mari fell in beside them, no longer a step behind, only to be met with a pair of Royal Guards. They stood out against the sea of black - military uniforms in black with panels of white and gold accents. Their expressions were stoney and unreadable. She paused a step before attempting to step back into the crowd, but was met with another pair right behind.

"With us, Miss Thomas." One ordered.

A quick look at Aelius was all she needed to know. There would be no sense in arguing or fighting it. She turned to the one who had made the order and gave a nod. They separated her from the twins, whisking her off to the side of the church and through a private door. They led her through corridor after corridor until they arrived at a small room with a small table and set of chairs. She was instructed to sit and wait. The door slammed shut behind them and footsteps thundered away. She remained in her seat, scanning the room for any sign of an escape. The walls were plain, not a single window or trace of other doors. They had chosen this room for a reason. Her mind raced at what was to become of her. It was clear that Astraea had said something to her father. Had he any idea of who she was, who she *really* was to him? All of the possible scenarios filtered through her mind before finally she heard a set of approaching footsteps. She fought the urge to stand to her feet, and remained seated, doing her best to project a look of calm.

The door handle turned and the door creaked open to reveal Eldritch. He had a smug look on his face that was itching to be punched. He shut the door, taking his time as finally selected the seat opposite of her. Her pulse pounded in her ears as she watched him.

"It appears that we have a problem, Miss Thomas." Eldritch interrupted. "I am not sure if you are aware of who I am, but I am the personal advisor to the Emperor himself. I am here to...discuss matters."

"I gathered." She explained, doing her best to remain civil and keep the venom out of her tone. "What matters?"

"It has come to the attention of the Empire that there may be some complex lineage involved here."

"I thought that my abilities were brought to the attention of the Empire after what happened in my exams. I was given accommodations and everything." She countered.

Eldritch sat back in his seat, his hands folded on top of the table before him. "It was, but your *specific* paternity seems to be a whole other matter. It is one thing when your lineage was one of the Barons or Dukes. This suspected paternity is a whole other level of complexity."

"You mean the fact that Cas—"

"You do *not* get to speak his name freely." Elritch spat, the first real show of emotion he had expressed. She was taken aback for a moment, surprised at the intensity of his response. He realised his mask had slipped a moment, and corrected himself. "We both know what the likelihood of your paternity is. That is a problem."

She leaned back in her seat, crossing her arms beneath her chest. "I did not cause the problem."

Eldritch gave a soft chuckle. "I am fully aware, Miss Thomas. It is, however, your responsibility in how you handle this situation."

"Don't go talking about it, essentially?" She asked.

"Correct." He agreed. "I'm glad to see we are on the same page here."

"What else?" She asked.

"We will need to confirm your paternity before anything else moves forward. This, unfortunately takes time to arrange." He explained.

Her brow creased in confusion. "What's to arrange? I'll give you a saliva swab now and be done with it."

A small smirk crossed his face as he let out a soft chuckle. "I do believe you're mistaken, Miss Thomas. We cannot allow some Middling means of confirming something as important as offspring of the Emperor himself. That is simply not how things are done. We have our own process back at the Palace. You'll be called upon when things are ready."

The way he spoke in a round about way, not confirming a single detail to her, did nothing to soothe her nerves. If a simple DNA test wouldn't suffice, what could they possibly have to prepare to confirm her paternity? "Is there anything else?" She finally spoke up.

"Well," he continued. "There are two things in fact. Firstly, we cannot have you sharing details of your... suspicions freely. Is there anyone you have shared this information with?"

She stared back at him, mulling over her options. She could lie. She could tell him that no one knew, but it could very well cause issues down the road. She had to bet on the Cirillos having enough influence to remain safe. "Aelius and Amaris Cirillo know. That's it."

He squinted his eyes at her, processing the details. "Not ideal, but manageable." He finally sighed. "They know protocol due to their father. Keep it that way."

"Fine." She stated curtly. "And the second?"

"It appears that you have been experimenting with magic beyond your control." It seemed that even the news of her exam had gotten back to them. "Until we provide you with a tutor, that is to cease."

She clenched her jaw, fighting the urge to tell him to go screw himself. "And when would that be?"

"I can't guarantee anything." He avoided the answer.

"It's not safe or wise for me to wield things blindly. I had every intention of practicing alone. Safely." She insisted. She refused to be helpless, to only ever be able to use it in a panicked state.

He scoffed at her, adjusting himself in his seat. "You seem to act as if any of this is up for negotiation, Miss Thomas."

"I'll be fine." She replied with a sneer.

He arched a brow at her, his smirk gone from his face. "Yes, but will your friends?"

Her stomach dropped at the threat against the others. "They have nothing to do with any of this."

"And I would very much like to keep it that way." He responded, checking for invisible dirt beneath his nails. "I don't especially enjoy having to dole out punishment, but I am not above it, Miss Thomas."

She clenched her fists, her nails digging into her palm. "We both know that's a lie." She stated through gritted teeth. "You seem very much like the type of man who enjoys dishing out punishment as he sees fit."

He studied her a moment, trying to size up if there was anything she might know. "Keep in line, Miss Thomas, and you'll never have to find out." He ordered. "Your friends' wellbeing is contingent on your behaviour."

She glared, but bit her tongue. Her palms itched with heat, begging to be released. She had come to realise it was the draw to use Purification. She released her clenched fists and shook them at her side. Part of her very much wanted to release it here and now, but provocation was the last thing she needed to do. There was one of her, and who knows how many Royal Guards outside. She was in no position to start swinging.

"Very good." Eldritch commented, seemingly satisfied with her obedience. He rose to his feet and tugged at the cuff of his jacket. "I believe we have covered everything here. Unless you have any questions for me?"

She placed her hands back on the table top, the burning finally starting to subside. "When can I expect to know about this test?"

His eyes flitted up, looking as if he were trying to recall and calculate. "Optimistically before the end of summer, but realistically? We are likely looking well into your second year."

Months. It could be months of her waiting for whatever it was they needed to do. "I guess I have no other option."

He chuckled, seemingly surprised by her comment. "Indeed." He agreed. "You would do best to lay low, Miss Thomas." He started for the door, giving two quick and one long raps. The door was opened by one of the stationed guards. The door shut firmly behind them as she remained seated. She listened to their heavy footsteps leave the hall before finally managing to stand to her feet. She repeated the same knock Eldritch had given, the door creaking open. "I would like to leave now, please." She informed.

The sun had begun to set by the time she was released. The sky had turned a hint of orange blending into a striking pink as she finally left the corridor. Mari and Aelius remained standing outside, not several feet from the door. Her eyes darted to the Guards that held her back before rushing to Aelius' arms. "Did they touch you?" He asked, his voice tight as he scanned her over. He would have known had they done any physical damage to her, but she knew he would have felt all of her emotions. She could sense just how much worry and rage coursed through him. He knew he had to allow them to take her, but he had hated every second of it.

"I'm fine." She insisted, burying herself into his chest.

Mari stepped away for a moment, letting them have some space. They were the only remaining people, save for the lingering Guards that were scattered through the grounds.

She pulled out of his embrace, feeling more grounded. She slipped her hand into his, pulling him towards the portal.

"Are you sure you're okay, Ari?" Mari asked cautiously as she fell in beside them.

She gave her a soft smile. "I am. It was a telling off more than anything." She glanced around, making sure the Guards were far enough away. Guardian hearing was inhuman. There was no assurance that they would have any privacy even at this distance.

It wasn't until they were on the other side of the portal that she had any comfort in disclosing more. "Neither of you can say anything about Castor." She finally continued, safe from eavesdroppers.

"It's confirmed then?" Aelius finally asked, walking as slowly as she wanted. The carriages were long gone and they would need to walk the length of the town.

She shook her head. "There is some sort of test they need to arrange. Could be months. Only then will they confirm it openly."

"Well," Mari chimed in. "looks like we just need to have a fantastic summer to distract you then."

She couldn't fight the smile that Mari radiated. It was hard to stay serious for too long around her. "Your mom insists I'm spending it with you." She chuckled.

Aelius let out a small groan. "I'm sorry." He apologised, knowing just how insistent she could be.

She leaned her head on his arm. "It's fine. It's sweet. Better that then her hating me and not wanting me anywhere near you."

"She very well might love her more than you, Aelius." Mari teased, slipping her arm in the crook of Aurora's elbow. "We're keeping her if you mess this up, you know."

"Thanks..." He responded dryly.

Chapter 45

With the funeral concluded, things could finally move forward again. Classes, exam marks, and Unbonding had all been put on hold until things had taken place.

She stepped out, her uniform perfectly in place as she headed to Pact Formation 102. Aelius had assured her the Unbonding would change nothing, that they would get through it together, but dread still settled in the pit of her stomach. Everyone seemed to be on edge that morning, knowing what awaited them. The Steins had a long day ahead of Unbonding each and every student. First years were first in line, followed by Second and Third years.

"Today will be hard." Guardian Stein announced before the class. There was a definite air of dread and sullenness through the room. "Breaking a Bond is excruciating business, even with the trial bonds. Professor Singh has prepared vials of tonic to help numb the after effects, but general malaise, physical aches, and depression can be expected."

"We urge any students who have prolonged symptoms to get in touch with their doctor during the break. It is an expected side effect of the year long bond, and we want to make sure that you look after yourselves." Mage Stein added.

"Just what we need…" She muttered, barely audible to Mari beside her.

Mari let out a quiet chuckle in response, but she knew that Mari was on edge just like she was. She had had enough to deal with these past several weeks without worrying about how hard this Unbonding would be on her.

"We will call you down by Mage. We advise you take the tonic right before the Unbonding." Guardian Stein advised.

The circle on the stage was quite similar to the one they had made earlier in the year. She scanned the circle while they waited for the professors to get ready for their long day. She eyed several runes that were different; dedicated for breaking the bond that had been put in place. Mage Stein pulled out a Spirit stone, glittering with golden light, whereas Guardian Stein pulled out a list of names.

"Liam Sullivan." Guardian Stein called out.

She watched as Liam rose to his feet, his partner Eli giving him a reassuring squeeze of his hand before he started down. Lily, his Guardian, was close behind, an uncommon look of worry on her face. She was normally airy and lively, but even Lily seemed to be effected about the worry of what lay ahead. Both grabbed one of the small purple vials and gave a clink of a cheers before downing the tonic. Liam kept his face in check while Lily openly grimaced at the taste as they settled into place.

The circle lit up once everyone was in place. Where the glow of the pact formation had been a pristine white, the Unbonding glow was a faint red. The difference struck her, wondering what it could possibly mean. It wasn't long before Lily let out a cry of pain. Unbonding seemed to be quick work; no need of contact or a kiss to seal. The circle dulled once more, having done its work. Liam did his best to keep his expression in check, but even he staggered a little as he reached out to offer Lily support. She wiped a tear before grabbing him into a hug. Their bond had been platonic, both of their partners being bonded to one another in place, but their friendship had been strengthened during their bond.

The pair made their way back to their seats slowly, their partners taking them into hugs. The class had been tense before, but it was only sharpened now.

"Dae-Hyun Choi." Guardian Stein called out.

Dae stood to his feet, a look of dread on his face. Mari stood beside him, hand intertwined with his. "We'll be fine." She assured him with a bright smile. It was absolutely an act, but it was a welcome one.

The pair took their time down the stairs, each grabbing a tonic. Once in place, they both downed their portion.

The circle lit a glow in red once more, fading away after mere moments. Mari winced, doing her best to keep a brave face on. Dae kept his in place, save for the tears that fell. He instantly reached out for Mari, both holding each other in a tight hug despite the class watching. No one said a word.

The pair eventually made their way back up to their seats beside Aurora. Her breath held, wondering what she could possibly say to help. "You okay, Mar?" She whispered.

Mari turned to her, a false smile plastered on her face with eyes glassy from tears. "I'm fine." She lied.

She wrapped her arms around her friend. "Drinks when this is done." She assured.

"Aurora Thomas." Guardian Stein called out.

Her stomach dropped as she let her hold of Mari go. Aelius rose to his feet first, extending his hand to her just as he had on Bonding day. A bittersweet smile formed on her face at the memory - seemingly forever ago now. She placed her hand in his, descending the steps together.

Aelius paused a moment as they reached the table filled with tonics. He grabbed one, offering it to her first. She took it in hand, waiting for her him grab one as well. With one quick swallow, she felt the liquid trail down her throat. It was a unique blend of burning and numbness that seeped through her. She shuddered as the after taste hit the back of her tongue.

She followed Aelius as he stepped up onto the stage, stationing himself across from her. She looked up into his eyes, not ready to be broken apart from him. She knew that their love was not tied to the bond. It was built on the foundation of their friendship. It was bolstered and strengthened by the bond, surely, but it was not the cause of it. Testing that theory still made her uneasy.

As the circle lit, she was thankful for the numbing effects of the tonic. A searing pain coursed through her veins, somewhat dulled by whatever she had consumed. Without it, it would have surely been agonising. The burning filled her to the brim, erasing every trace of the bond that had been within her. She cried out as the sensation of liquid fire filled every pore. She steadied herself as the circle's light finally faded away. The sudden absence was hollowing. She had been blocked before, but it had never felt empty or devastatingly isolating like this. She absentmindedly clutched at her heart as she looked up at Aelius. Her eyes burned with tears that fell hot on her cheeks.

Aelius swept her into his arms without a word. Her feet lifted from the floor as he carried her away. She didn't care what anyone else thought. All she wanted was him - to feel him again.

One by one the other students went through their Unbonding. Not a single one went without the tonic. Seeing how peers reacted even when dulled was enough to ensure help was taken.

"Please make sure to take care of yourselves over the next few days." Mage Stein implored. "Seeking help and support is not weak. Anyone who had bonded before will understand what you are experiencing."

The class broke out in a sullen sludge, many undoubtedly heading for a distraction from the pain. She followed Aelius in a haze, not fully hearing what anyone else had to say. Without realising, she kept trying to reach out, to touch him through the bond, and met with nothingness. She hadn't realised just how often she reached out for him until he wasn't there.

***

It hadn't taken long to pack up her things. She walked away with considerably more than what she had entered with, but it was still manageable. Uniforms would be left behind, new ones in their place for second year, but the handful of books, Empirical fashions, and other small items would be coming with her.

For the first time in what felt like forever, she got dressed in her old clothes. She felt nearly naked in the tank top and jean shorts compared to what she had gotten accustomed to wearing during her first year at the Academy. Mari stepped out of the washroom, tugging at her shorts. She had managed to find a pair that fit, also borrowing a t-shirt. The shoes were the only thing that seemed out of place; her own running shoes no where near sharing size. "Why is everything so short?" She asked, nervously trying to pull them lower.

She let out a small laugh. "I mean...you *are* taller than me, so it looks shorter on you. But, this is nothing. You should see what a lot of the girls our age *actually* wear. This is considered modest."

Mari's face paled a moment. "This is fine." She stated. She was in no way a prude, but layers and length were something you got used to with Empirical fashion.

She jumped at a sharp rap at the door. Mari answered, Dae standing before her. His mouth dropped open at the sight of her. He had seen every inch of her, but this was something entirely different. "Mari, you..."

"God, get in!" She exclaimed, pulling him into their room.

He staggered as he caught his footing from the sharp pull. He took her in fully and chuckled to himself. "Babe, you look *amazing*." He confessed.

Mari flushed as she grabbed at the hem of her shorts. "I dunno..." She admitted. "It's awfully short."

"You make it look fantastic." He admired as he wrapped his arms around her waist.

Aurora stifled a chuckle as she turned to her belongings for a moment. Everything was set. All she had to do now was leave. Her heart was heavy at the prospect. Getting distance from everything was exactly what she needed, but it also meant leaving what had started to feel like home behind. They would be back before long, but it felt odd.

"We'll stay in touch, I promise." Mari assured Dae. "Once we get settled, we'll make sure to have you join us."

Dae peered over Mari's shoulder. "Are you *sure* it's okay, Ari?" He asked hesitantly.

She nodded. "Of course it is. You know you're my friend too, right?"

Dae chuckled, easing a little at her reaction. "I know, but I just..."

She smiled at his consideration. "Aelius will join us too. We'll have our time, just us girls. All good." She assured him.

"I can't wait to see it all." Mari sighed. "An adventure every day."

Aurora let out a soft laugh as she slung her bag over her shoulder. "You really have never been, have you?" She asked. "It's really not that mystical."

Mari grabbed her own bags, handing one of the smaller ones to Dae. "It's different and new. That's mystical enough for me."

"Fair enough." She responded. "It'll be a lot of newness for me and all. A lot of the places on your list are spots I've never been."

With bags and suitcases in tow, the group made their way out towards the main hall. "We'll figure it out." Mari grinned. She had seemed to quickly get over her discomfort in the new clothes, distracted by daydreams of all the places they would see.

She looked ahead, ignoring any of the stares and funny looks they got as they crossed the grounds. She knew just how out of place the pair of them were, but she had given up on paying the reactions any mind.

As they rounded the corner into the main hall, Aelius stood waiting for her, his leather jacket from the Equinox slung over his arm. A bright grin broke across her face as she rushed up to him. "I tried to wear it for you, but it's too hot right now." He admitted a tad disappointed.

She laughed. "It's definitely not a summer jacket." She agreed. There would be plenty of cool enough evenings that would warrant it. She couldn't wait to tour the Middling Realm with him. She slung her arm in the crook of his elbow, following the others to the main gate.

They stepped through the gate, nearing the main portal outside the border. She left her bags to the side for a moment, stepping away with Aelius to say her goodbyes.

"It's just two weeks." She assured him, seeing the pang of sadness in his eyes.

"I know." He sighed. "I hate not being able to feel you through the bond anymore. I can't check on you."

A soft laugh escaped her lips as she slipped her arms around his neck. "I'll see you soon." She reminded him, placing a soft kiss on his lips.

He leaned his forehead against hers. "I love you."

"I love you too."

He kissed her again, gripping her tight, before he let her go. She would miss him - terribly. She already ached for him, debating whether she had made the right choice in not letting him come immediately. She knew it would be good to have a moment away - to have time just her and Mari. Absence making the heart grow fonder and all that.

She took in the view of the Academy, really quite breathtaking from the outside. The surrounding forests were in full form, the scent of floral blooms dancing on the wind.

She caught herself humming to herself that same tune that seemed to crawl its way into her ear from time to time.

Come away with me
And you all will see
A world beyond what you have known

Come away with me
Far beyond the sea
And forget all that you've been shown

For I see your dreams
And I know your heart
Give your all to me
So we never have to part

"You ready?" Mari called out. She snapped out of her little day dream and turned to her best friend.

"Let's go." She replied, grabbing her by the hand. It wouldn't be long before they were back. But for now, the distraction of adventure awaited.